The Darkness and the Thunder

1915: The Great War Series

STEWART BINNS

PENGUIN BOOKS

PENGUIN BOOKS

UK | USA | Canada | Ireland | Australia
India | New Zealand | South Africa

Penguin Books is part of the Penguin Random House group of companies
whose addresses can be found at global.penguinrandomhouse.com.

First published 2015
001

Copyright © Stewart Binns, 2015

The moral right of the author has been asserted

Set in 12.5/14.75 pt Garamond MT Std
Typeset by Jouve (UK), Milton Keynes
Printed in Great Britain by Clays Ltd, St Ives plc

A CIP catalogue record for this book is available from the British Library

ISBN: 978–1–405–91628–8

www.greenpenguin.co.uk

The Darkness and the Thunder

1915: The Great War Series

Stewart Binns began his professional life as an academic. He then pursued several adventures, including being a schoolteacher, specializing in history, and a stint as a soldier, before becoming an award-winning documentary-maker and, latterly, an author. His television credits include the 'In Colour' genre of historical documentaries, notably the BAFTA and Grierson winner *Britain at War in Colour* and the Peabody winner *The Second World War in Colour*.

He also launched *Trans World Sport* in 1987, *Futbol Mundial* in 1993, the International Olympic Committee Olympic Games *Camera of Record* in 1994 and the Olympic Television Archive Bureau in 1996. He produced FIFA's official history of football in 1989, *The People's Game*, the All England Club's official history of Wimbledon, *Wimbledon: A History of the Championships*, in 2001 and, in 2004, Tiger Woods' authorized biography, *Tiger*.

Currently chief executive and co-founder, with his wife, Lucy, of the independent production and distribution company Big Ape Media International, Stewart has in recent years continued to specialize in historical documentaries, including two series about the life of Winston Churchill, histories of the Korean War and of Indo-China, major studies of modern Japan and India and *Sport under Threat*, a documentary about terrorist threats at major sporting events.

His previous novels, *Conquest, Crusade, Anarchy* and *Lionheart* (The Making of England quartet), and *The Shadow of War*, the first of his Great War series, were published to great acclaim.

His home is in Somerset, where he lives with his wife and twin boys, Charlie and Jack.

To all those who endured the Great War

Author's Note

The Darkness and the Thunder is a work of fiction. Although largely based on real events, and while many of the characters are borrowed from history, names, characters, places and incidents are either the product of the author's imagination or used entirely fictitiously.

Some of the characters speak in their local vernacular, especially the old Pennine dialect of North-east Lancashire. Largely gone now, it was still spoken into the 1960s, and I remember well its unique colour and warmth. It was an unusual combination of Old English and the nineteenth-century 'Mee-maw' – the exaggerated, mouthed reinforcements of speech used to overcome the noise of the looms in the cotton mills made famous by comic actors such as Hylda Baker and Les Dawson.

The meanings of various East Lancs dialect expressions, as well as examples of Cockney rhyming slang and background facts about military terms, Victorian and Edwardian mores and various historical references, are explained in the Glossary at the back of the book.

Contents

PART FOUR: APRIL
A Gasping Death

PART FIVE: MAY
A Hideous Spectacle

PART SIX: JUNE

Heat, Dust and Diarrhoea

PART SEVEN: JULY

Flammenwerfer

Introduction: 1915

For all the combatants and civilians held in the terrifying grip of the Great War, any hope of a quick and decisive victory has been extinguished long before the icy chill of winter 1914 set in. Almost a million dead, the vast majority of them French and German, had seen to that. Britain has lost over 30,000 of her finest sons, experienced veterans of Britain's elite professional army, in the slaughter of the British Expeditionary Force. Back home, the news has been met first with incredulity, then with a growing feeling of dread.

By the beginning of 1915, the Napoleonic dash at the Front of the early days of the war has been replaced by the grinding horror of trench warfare. Optimism, elan and innocence have been supplanted by futility, lethargy and cruelty.

Now, winter's terrors are diminishing yet further the already enfeebled morale of the troops in their waterlogged pits and rat-infested warrens, reducing them to an even more pitiful state than in the aftermath of the dreadful battles of the autumn. As the men try to survive the squalor, the generals search in desperation for solutions to end the impasse.

The Western Front is a forbidding streak of barbed wire, shell-holes and trenches running from the North Sea to the Alps. Of its 402 miles, the noble Belgian Army holds the northern 22 miles and the indomitable French Army guards 360 miles to the south. In between, the scant remnants of the glorious British Expeditionary Force is the bulwark of just 20 miles, but it is a vital sector that protects the northern flank of Paris and one that will soon expand.

This is the continuing story of five communities of Britain's people, their circumstances very different but all of them part of the enormous tragedy that is unfolding. They and their homeland are being changed for ever by the catastrophic events of the Great War. The gruesome statistics of the death and suffering of 1914 are only the beginning. Slaughter on an even greater scale is yet to come.

PART ONE: JANUARY

In Winter's Chilling Grip

Friday 1 January

Locre, West Flanders, Belgium

The chilling hand of winter has grasped the hearts of the warriors of the Great War; her icy touch has put their martial passions into hibernation. There are still sporadic outbursts of fighting: persistent sniping, frequent skirmishes and long-range bombardments. Death is still commonplace, not only from combat but also from disease. However, the mass slaughter of the previous year has abated. Men who are cold and wet, hungry and exhausted, do not fight well.

If the ugly world of the trenches of the 400 miles of the Western Front is not quite the hell of the battles of the autumn of 1914, it is a purgatory where men are trapped in a torment of deprivation and anxiety. The deprivation has many guises: the hardship of an appalling diet, the stinging pain of trench foot, the death rattle of bronchitis, the indignity of insanitary conditions. But the greatest burden in this limbo of the winter of 1914–15 is a gnawing anxiety, an ever-deepening foreboding born of a certainty. It is an inevitability acknowledged by everyone on the battlefield: the hell of autumn's battles will soon return.

There is but one respite from the slow torture of the trenches: the heaven that is the billets located just behind the Front. Often not much better than squalid by civilized standards, they are nevertheless usually dry, sometimes warm and mainly well stocked with rations. Most importantly, they are relatively safe from the terrors of combat. For most battalions at the Front, five or six days in trenches are being alternated with an equal amount of time in billets.

Fourth Battalion Royal Fusiliers has been billeted at Locre, West Flanders, since Boxing Day. As billets go in this merciless war, the Hospice of St Antoine, its nuns long departed and the building now in the hands of the British Expeditionary Force, is almost a home from home. Despite the fact that it has been heavily shelled and lacks much of its roof, the sappers have made it waterproof. There is sufficient fuel from the nearby woods to keep its many fires going and in its cellars is a decent supply of rations. For men relieved of duties in the dismal trenches just a few miles away, a warm, dry refuge and a full belly are the stuff of dreams.

Locre itself is little more than a few houses straddling the crossroads of the routes between Ypres to the north-east and Bailleul to the south-west, and from Poperinghe due north and Armentières to the south-east. Ypres, the crux of the British defensive position in Flanders, is less than eight miles away and the French border is less than two miles distant in the opposite direction.

Not quite as flat but just as drab as other parts of the region, the landscape is featureless and monotonous. The small, red-brick cottages, their inhabitants long since gone to safer locations to the west, are faintly reminiscent of the more uninspiring parts of rural England – or at least they would be without the ravages of five months of war. The local church, L'Église St Pierre, still stands but is badly damaged. Its roofless nave provides space for the tents of a British Army field hospital, while its vestry has become a makeshift serjeants' mess for the Fusiliers.

The year 1915 is just thirty minutes old, and the sounds of revelry and celebration spill from the boarded-up windows and open door of the large, hexagonal room. Despite the biting cold, there are many serjeants standing outside in the night's ice-cold air, drinking, smoking and laughing. As they do at their home barracks at Albany on the Isle of Wight, the Royal Fusiliers, Londoners and proud of it, share the mess with their fellow Fusiliers, 1st Battalion Northumberlands and 1st Battalion Royal Scots. They make for strange bedfellows, having few folk memories in common and hailing from very distant corners of Britain. Nevertheless, each is known for its remarkable endurance on the battlefield and its notorious irascibility when at rest.

Inside St Pierre's spacious and once-grand vestry, Royal Fusilier Colour Serjeants Maurice Tait and Harry Woodruff have avoided all attempts to get them to join in the less-than-tuneful renderings of soldiers' favourite songs. However, they do smile at the latest popular ditty, sung with gusto by their fellow NCOs:

> *Do your balls hang low?*
> *Do they dangle to and fro?*
> *Can you tie them in a knot?*
> *Can you tie them in a bow?*
> *Do they itch when it's hot?*
> *Do you rest them in a pot?*

Do you get them in a tangle?
Do you catch them in a mangle?
Do they swing in stormy weather?
Do they tickle with a feather?

Do they rattle when you walk?
Do they jingle when you talk?

Can you sling them on your shoulder
Like a lousy fucking soldier?
Do your balls hang low?

'Well, 'Arry, another year's gawn, and wot a fuckin' year it was!'

Harry pauses and looks at his life-long friend and comrade in many battles. He is brooding again. 'New Year's Day, Mo? So wot's the point in makin' a fuss? It's just another day to die.'

Maurice has been getting used to Harry's increasingly sombre moods but, even so, is shaken by his morose comment.

''Arry, you miserable bugger, we ain't gonna cop it on New Year's Day!'

'Don't be too sure, mate. We got relieved on Boxing Day by the Worcesters; wot's the bettin' we go up the line tonight to give the country boys a cosy New Year's night in billets?'

Army veterans of almost twenty years' standing, Maurice and Harry are part of a breed that is becoming rarer by the day. The non-commissioned officers of the British Expeditionary Force have paid a brutal price in the first months of the war. As the two men glance

8

around the room, they see only a few faces they recognize from the Fusilier barracks at Albany, and none from India or the Boer War, where they both served with distinction.

'Thank fuck it's quiet this winter, Mo. My nerves was shot before Christmas.'

'Too right! One minute you was as miserable as sin, couldn't get a peep outta yer; the next you was shoutin' and ollerin' abaht killin' every Fritz in sight.'

'It's the bloody shellin', mate. I can stand most things, but not knowin' where the next one's comin' from drives me doolally.'

'Listen, 'Arry, if yer name's on it, that's it. No point frettin' abaht it.'

'You've got bottle, Mo. Dunno 'ow you keep an even keel when everyone's droppin' like flies. One of the Geordie boys was tellin' me that out of their twenty-eight serjeants wot came over in August, only six are still 'ere.'

'Same with us, ain't it?'

'Right . . . and we're two of 'em. So wot's the odds on us surviving another year in this khazi?'

''Arry, leave it be. Now you're makin' *me* windy!'

'So yer should be, mate! D'yer know how many of them Worcester farmer boys have been pinged by Fritz snipers since they relieved us?'

'Go on, surprise me.'

'No, guess, yer pillock!'

'Eight.'

'Seventeen! Fuckin' seventeen, Mo! Plugged through the eye, through the back of the head, between the eyes;

those Hun snipers are fuckin' Dead-eye Dicks, I'm tellin' yer!'

Maurice tries to appear blasé to calm Harry's bile. 'Should 'ave kept their heads down, shouldn't they? If yer keep yer nut dahn, Fritz can't put a fuckin' slug in it, can he?' Not wanting Harry to dwell any more on the stark arithmetic of the war, he changes the subject. 'Wonder wot those Fritz boys are up to wot we played football against on Christmas Day?'

'Pissed off and freezin' their knackers off like us, I should like t'think. But they was good lads, wasn't they?'

'Not bad for Huns!'

Maurice and Harry are friends from early childhood from Leyton, East London, and typical of their breed. They excel at the things men admire: soldiering, drinking, womanizing, cricket and football; they are streetwise, hard as nails; you would want to fight with them rather than against them. They fought together at Ladysmith and Mafeking in South Africa during the Boer War, and in India, putting down insurgent rebellions.

Within the ranks of the BEF in Flanders, they are already legendary: they are exemplary 'soldiers' soldiers' and can survive in the most challenging of circumstances. Loyal to King and country and their fellow Fusiliers, they fight fàir, but dirty if they have to; they demand discipline and respect and get it, from their men and their superiors. They have both been awarded the Distinguished Conduct Medal for their bravery at Merris during the Battle for Ypres in early November and have been promoted to Colour Serjeant, Maurice in C Company and Harry in B.

'I'm orf to bed, Mo,' grunts Harry.

'Sure? The New Year is less than an hour old.'

'I'm getting some proper kip in a decent bunk. I still fancy we'll be back in our trench tomorra night.'

As Harry makes his way from the serjeants' mess to his bunk nearby, a single shot rings out and echoes around what is left of St Pierre's ancient walls. He rushes towards the source of the sound: a dark corner in a side chapel off the nave.

'Careful, 'Arry. You na'er know wot yer goin' to run into these days. 'Ere – take your rifle.' Maurice throws Harry his Lee-Enfield and points his own into the shadows. 'Definitely not one of ours, mate.'

'I know, but it can't be a Fritz in 'ere, can it?'

Other NCOs appear behind Harry and Maurice, one of them with a Tilley lamp, which illuminates the sickening scene before them.

'Fuck me, 'e's only a kid!' Maurice turns away, shaking his head.

Harry takes charge. 'Go and fetch the adjutant. Tell him that another poor sod from the backstreets of nowhere has blown his fuckin' brains out.'

Avoiding the blood, bone and cerebral matter that is splattered everywhere, Maurice prises a pistol from the dead man's hand.

'It's a Mauser. Must have got it off of a dead Fritz officer.'

''Ope he shot the twat first,' is Harry's caustic response. 'Anyone know him?'

A serjeant from the Northumberlands answers. 'I do. He's one of mine; young Arthur Robson from Hexham. He's only been here a month. A good sort, but scared shitless most of the time.'

'Best thing, then; he ain't scared any more, is he? Some-one go an' get somethin' to cover that mess. It's makin' me want to puke.'

One of the older serjeants takes offence at Harry's bluntness. 'Show some respect, Woodruff.'

'For wot? Don't give me none o' that bollocks. This is a total shit'ole, an' that lad's better off out of it.'

Harry, closely pursued by Maurice, pushes past the throng of NCOs standing over the body.

'Leave 'im be, you lot; go an' get yer 'eads down. Two-bob says we'll be in the trenches tomorrow.'

Harry's gloomy prediction proves accurate. At reveille the next morning the battalion adjutant, Captain George O'Donel, announces that the 4th Royal Fusiliers are to relieve the Worcesters at the Front. They are to be in position by early afternoon.

'Told yer!'

'Go on, then: you was right.'

But Harry takes no pleasure in that. 'It's fuckin' rainin' again,' he mutters. 'I 'ate this bastard war. We're not even fighting Fritz any more. It's us against lice, mud and shite!'

'You forgot the freezin'-cold water and the rats.'

'Good point – and we're losin' the battle against all of 'em.'

'When's the last time we had a proper ruck and row with Fritz?'

'The last big one was old McMahon's Charge of the Looney Brigade at Hooge in November.' It had been at Hooge that Harry had got a bar to his DCM, for routing almost single-handedly a posse of German Guards

Grenadiers in hand-to-hand fighting. Not for nothing is he nicknamed The Leyton Lash.

'Don't know abaht you, but I'd rather be sluggin' it out wiv the Hun than rottin' in them fuckin' trenches.'

'Can't argue wiv that, 'Arry. But yer know wot? Like it or not, ours is not to wonder why . . .'

'Yeah, yeah; I know the score. Bollocks to it!'

British Army Field Hospital, Provost Lace Mill, Poperinghe, West Flanders, Belgium

The British Expeditionary Force field hospital in the old lace mill at Poperinghe is only six miles north of the Royal Fusiliers' billet at Locre and less than eight miles west of the vital British defensive fulcrum that is Ypres. The town is known as 'Pop', and the Provost Mill Hospital is known to everyone as 'Pop-Hop'. It is one of the most important receiving points for injured men from the Front.

Pop is also one of the most favoured places for soldiers seeking rest and relaxation from the trenches. It is the centre of the Belgian hop-growing region and a mecca for girls whose living is made by relieving men of the contents of their army pay packets in return for evacuating the fruits of their loins. The beer is excellent and cheap, while the girls, if not necessarily exceptional, are, except for those pitching to well-heeled officers, priced to match the modest pay of serving soldiers. In this bizarre war, men go to Pop to forget what they have done or seen, to fornicate without forming bonds or displaying emotion,

13

or to drink themselves into a stupor in which their fears and traumas are temporarily extinguished.

But too many men do not choose to go to this small, otherwise unremarkable little town. They are transported there on stretchers and in ambulances. They are taken there to recover from terrible injuries – or, they are taken there to die. The impromptu mortuaries, too many to count, are always full. As soon as one batch of bodies is taken out into Flanders' fertile fields for burial, another consignment of corpses arrives to takes its place.

Pop-Hop is full to bursting: men lie in corridors, lofts and outbuildings, as well as in the overcrowded wards. They have suffered injury from bullets, shrapnel, hand grenades and bayonets. Artillery fire is the biggest killer, accounting for more than half the injuries. Severe injuries usually result in death.

Chloroform is in short supply, and there is only one mobile X-ray machine for the entire BEF. Many operations and amputations have to be undertaken without anaesthetic of any kind. To the horror of the War Office and the senior staff of the Royal Army Medical Corps, field reports for the last five months of 1914 reveal that men with gunshot wounds to the leg have only a one-in-five chance of survival.

The situation is even worse for those with abdominal injuries. The same reports suggest that field surgeons are having to make ever more distressing choices about life and death. Knowing that a severe abdominal wound might take three hours to repair, as opposed to one hour for a wound to the head or a limb, doctors are putting to one side, usually with fatal consequences, one man with a stomach wound in order to save three with wounds to their limbs.

Adding to the wounds caused by the warriors and weapons of war, there are also myriad diseases and ailments created by adverse weather, poor diet, overcrowding and insanitary conditions. There are outbreaks of typhoid and bronchial illnesses of all kinds, and pneumonia is commonplace. There is also a new phenomenon called trench fever which causes headaches, shivering and muscular pain. It can last several days but tends to recur, taking men away from the Front for weeks at a time. It is thought to be spread by lice, which infest almost everyone at the Front and those in many of the support areas. The 'greyback', as the men have christened it, a common louse, seems to be everywhere, and no amount of washing or fumigating can prevent it coming back fitter and stronger than before. Rats thrive in the trenches.

Frostbite, to fingers, toes and noses, is common too. For the Scottish regiments, still emotionally wedded to their beloved kilts, it is a plague that extends to their knees and sometimes even further beneath their threadbare tartans. And if the nibble of frost's teeth were not unbearable enough, there is the threat of gangrene and amputation of fingers, toes or even whole limbs.

All sorts of remedies have been tried to prevent frostbite, including pouring hot rum into men's boots, but none to any avail. Rum has also been used as a treatment for another new malady, trench foot, with equally negative results. Recently, the more enlightened medical staff have come to realize that both frostbite and trench foot are caused by neglect. Changing socks and keeping boots dry, coupled with the application of iodine to trench-foot infections, are improving the situation significantly, as is a newly issued procedure from the Royal Army Medical Corps to use whale oil in men's boots.

Shrewdly, and usually with the support of their officers, some men, if they can find them locally, have taken to wearing gumboots. So successful has been the practice that the War Office has commissioned the North British Rubber Company to manufacture the boots in their thousands. Its mills in Edinburgh are running day and night to produce them in lorryloads.

Sadly, there are also less tangible maladies which are equally debilitating and distressing for everyone in Flanders. The less than generous call the sufferers malingerers or cowards; many have been sent home, some court-martialled and a few executed by firing squad. The more considerate suggest that the afflicted have had an 'attack of nerves', especially if the symptoms are presented by an officer. In common parlance, the men call it the 'colly-wobbles'; its mark is the 'thousand-yard stare'.

Gradually, the medics are calling it shell shock, as it is often brought on by heavy and relentless artillery bombardments. Whatever the name, the effect is devastating, typified by incessant shaking, bouts of incoherence, uncontrollable diarrhoea and unremitting anxiety and fear. There is little understanding of how to treat the condition, other than to send the sufferers home, where, for many, the condition worsens.

It is almost ten minutes before 1 a.m. on New Year's Day, and the staff of Pop-Hop are trying to bring to a close the patients' New Year celebrations so that they and their charges can get some much-needed rest. Many of the day staff have joined those on night duty to see in the New Year, and they have to be back on the wards at seven in the morning.

'Come on, Bron, let's get to bed.'

Bronwyn Thomas is enjoying herself. She is young and full of vitality, a nursing auxiliary with Queen Alexandra's Imperial Military Nursing Service. 'But Margaret,' she says, 'the men are having such a good time with their QUIMS! And so am I.'

The abbreviated form of their name, QAIMNS, is all too readily modified by the men, who call their nurses QUIMS. It is a crude name that amuses them, but less so most of the nurses, especially their formidable Australian matron-in-chief, Emma McCarthy.

'I know, but only some of them are enjoying themselves. The rest are very sick, especially the ones upstairs on Ward 3.'

'Just a bit longer, please.'

'No! Bed, now! That's an order, Nursing Auxiliary Thomas.'

'Spoilsport – just because *you*'re not enjoying yourself. You know something? You're turning into an old spinster!'

Sister Margaret Killingbeck is stunned by this acid response from one of her team. Margaret, still only twenty-four, is one of Pop-Hop's most senior and experienced nurses and Bronwyn's professional mentor. 'That's really unkind, Bron. I'm tired; you'll be tired in the morning, and the men need you to be fresh and alert.'

Bronwyn sees the hurt in Margaret's eyes and relents.

'Sorry, that wasn't nice of me. But I'm feeling good again, Margaret.'

Margaret has noticed this. Bronwyn, on the edge of hopelessness when they first met, seems to have overcome the traumas of her past and become again the spirited, eye-catching girl Margaret had been told about before they met. She smiles warmly at the younger woman and Bronwyn responds with a beguiling smile of her own.

'You're right: we should call it a night. Will you make me some cocoa when we get back?'

'Of course I will – as long as you stop calling me a spinster!'

'Promise.'

When the two of them get back to their nurses' quarters, just yards from the hospital, they light the fire and enjoy the cocoa they are so fond of. Fry's and Cadbury's, their favourites, are hard to come by, but there is a plentiful supply of Dutch and Belgian brands in Flanders, where *chocolat chaud* is so popular. Their latest discovery, Droste from Haarlem, is their new favourite, especially as its advertising extols the recuperative virtues of the cocoa with the image of an angelic girl wearing a nurse's uniform. Margaret has christened the girl 'Bron the Pan'. Whenever they buy a new tin Margaret draws over the image of the tray bearing a cup of cocoa the nurse is carrying and replaces it with a sketch of a bed-pan, a necessity at Pop-Hop, and something Bronwyn carries backwards and forwards dozens of times a day.

Because of the ever-increasing demand for beds for nurses, the two women now share a room. It makes for a very cramped living space but it suits their close friendship and is helping Bronwyn on her journey back to normality.

Cradling her mug as if it is the only source of warmth in the world, Bronwyn takes a deep breath. She is still tipsy from the evening's jollities; Margaret much less so. 'Margaret . . .' starts Bronwyn. She pauses, nervously.

Margaret tries to smile, but she can guess what Bronwyn is going to tell her and is anxious. 'Don't be shy, Bron. You know you can tell me anything.'

'Well, how can I put this? I'm beginning to feel . . . you know.'

'Yes. I think I do know . . .'

Margaret had found Bronwyn in a dockside pub in Tiger Bay, Cardiff, where she was servicing sailors and anyone else with coins in their pocket at two bob a time. Within weeks of leaving her home town, Presteigne, in Radnorshire, she had been drinking gin by the bottle, was addicted to Papine, a powerful morphine opiate, had served countless men and had contracted gonorrhoea. Only Margaret's intervention had saved the once-innocent country girl from an ignominious end.

Now, it seems that Bronwyn's interest in sex has revived, a thought simultaneously exciting and worrying for her mentor. Would she lose her friend's intimacy to a man?

'Is there anyone in particular who's taken your eye?' she asks.

She looks at Bronwyn and smiles wistfully as she thinks what has happened to them both in just a few months. She has told Bronwyn her own dark secret and has found a sort of contentment in her close proximity to the younger woman. She can indulge her longings for her, but nothing sexual has passed between them, so Margaret is free of guilt. But this contentment is now under threat.

Bronwyn responds teasingly. 'Well, at the moment, anyone in trousers – and especially those in bed without them!'

Margaret cannot help but laugh out loud at Bronwyn's earthy candour. 'Oh, Bron,' she says, 'I envy you your "normal" feelings. I feel the same way about you as you do about men, with or without their trousers . . .'

They both begin to laugh now and fall into one another's arms in fits of giggles, until tiredness overcomes them and they fall asleep.

In one of those quirks of wartime coincidence, as the two women sleep, the corridors of Pop-Hop are patrolled by Bronwyn's elder brother, Hywel. His journey to Flanders has also been far from conventional.

His younger brothers, Geraint and Morgan, had joined the Royal Welch Fusiliers, leaving him alone to deal with a declining hill farm on the Welsh borders. Bronwyn had brought disgrace on the family by having a lurid affair with Philip Davies, a man old enough to be her father, and a successful auctioneer, antiques dealer and highly prominent figure in the community of Presteigne. He had become a captain in the 1st Battalion Royal Welch Fusiliers and it was his death at the end of August 1914, in the aftermath of the Battle of Le Cateau, that had led Margaret to the farm, and Hywel, in search of Bronwyn.

Margaret's visit had a strange effect on Hywel. Her talk

of the horrors of the war and Philip Davies's slow and painful death offered him a place to suffer that was even darker than the hell of Pentry Cottage. He grabbed the opportunity to worsen his self-pitying torment, closed up Pentry Cottage, let the farm to a neighbour and within days was at the Royal Welch Fusiliers' High Town Barracks in Wrexham to join his brothers.

Hywel's beat of Pop-Hop's corridors is interrupted by the gentle voice of one of the senior medical officers: 'Colour, you should be in bed!'

'I know, sir. I'm just doing a quick round to make sure all is well.'

'That's very thoughtful of you, but you really should get some rest. You won't heal without it . . . Oh, and Happy New Year.'

'And to you, sir. Let's hope 1915 is a better year than the last one.'

'Indeed.'

Both men share the same hope but know in their heart of hearts that there will be little respite, at least not any time soon.

Surgeon Captain Noel Chavasse has been a godsend for Hywel.

On 8 November, at Zwarteleen, only three miles from Ypres, 1st Battalion Royal Welch Fusiliers attacked the German trenches across open ground and without artillery cover. The three Thomas brothers had been reunited and, being judged strong as oxen, as fit as fiddles and having exemplary training records, were chosen as part of an emergency detachment of reservists to be sent to France to get 1st and 2nd Battalions up to full strength. In particular, Hywel was identified as a marksman of exceptional ability, as good a shot as the regiment had ever seen.

Of the 109 young Welsh reservists who began the attack, only seventeen returned. Geraint and Morgan were not among them; their whereabouts became a mystery, as for so many men who were lost in the mists of battle in the closing months of 1914.

Hywel was spared the frontal attack and survived the day, having been positioned as a sniper on a Zwarteleen barn. He was exhilarated by the experience of sniping in defence of his comrades and found in it a purpose amidst the wretched mess of his life. But he, too, soon paid a price.

A German sniper found his position and smashed his right hand with a bullet that passed straight through his palm. Thinking his newly found gift with a rifle had been destroyed the day he had discovered it, and fearful that he may never see his brothers again, he prepared to end his life with his own rifle. Then destiny played a kindlier card. The remnants of his battalion stumbled across him on their way back to the British trenches and helped him back to safety.

Hywel had thought his career as a sniper was over, but for once the fates conspired in his favour, and doubly so. The bullet had shattered his right hand, but his left is dominant, and after much persuasion Captain Chavasse agreed not to send him home, as was standard practice for such a severe wound. Not only that, Chavasse ordered a reinforced glove to be made by the Desoutter Brothers in London, specialists in artificial limbs, so that Hywel could attempt to return to sniping duties.

As Hywel walks towards a former cupboard into which he has managed to squeeze a bed for himself, Captain Chavasse goes with him. 'How is the training going?' he asks.

'Well, thank you, sir. The hand is still sore, but the glove works a treat and is rock solid. In a funny way, it's even steadier than when I had full use of my hand.'

Hywel's glove is a very clever piece of improvisation. It is an extra-large officer's black cavalry glove, reinforced by sewn-in, bendable copper rods that allow him to position his disabled middle fingers so that they hold the barrel of his rifle securely. Fortunately, Chavasse's expert surgery has given Hywel full feeling in his thumb, index and little finger.

'Go easy on that hand,' says Captain Chevasse. 'It will take time.'

'I will, sir, don't worry. The next time I raise my rifle in earnest I will have a bead on the Hun who shot my CO, Lieutenant Orme, in the back. He won't get it in the back from me. He'll get one of my green spots right down the barrel of his sight, through his eyeball and, if you'll excuse my French, sir, clean out the back of his fuckin' head!'

Chavasse smiles warmly. 'Well, Colour, all the more reason for you to get some rest!'

At the beginning of 1915 the BEF occupies a newly extended, continuous line of trenches from the Canal d'Aire at La Bassée, just north of Lens, to the Yser Canal between Ypres and Diksmuide, a distance a little less than 40 miles. To the north, the Belgian Army holds the ground to the Channel, while the French hold the line all the way to the Swiss border.

Not surprisingly, now that the winter stalemate has produced a static war, coincidences and chance meetings are commonplace in the British sector of the Great War, especially in the BEF's major rear-support towns like Pop and Armentières. So it was when the Royal Welch Fusiliers marched through Pop's Grande Place at the end of October, sporting their white hackles and singing 'Sosban fach'. It was then that Bronwyn saw her three brothers for the first time since she had left Pentry Farm in disgrace at the end of August. Two of them – Geraint and her twin, Morgan – are now lost to her, missing, presumed killed, at Zwarteleen. She had encountered Hywel on Pop's wards shortly after the battle. He had initially disowned her, but they were soon reconciled. War creates many wounds, but it can also heal them, often making a bond even stronger than it was before.

The war also brought Margaret Killingbeck and Hamish Stewart-Murray together. They became close after sharing the emotional confession of Bronwyn's lover, Philip Davies, on his deathbed. Hamish, something of an aristocratic rogue, pursued Margaret avidly, unaware of her sexual preferences. Margaret, encouraged by Bronwyn, eventually relented. Flattered by the attentions of the handsome heir to the noblest dukedom in Scotland and hoping that she might finally find pleasure in a 'normal' sexual encounter, she gave in to his advances.

Hamish was satisfied with his conquest of the redoubtable English nurse, who looked so compelling in her scarlet-and-grey uniform. It cost him an expensive dinner and the finest bottle of claret to be found in Pop, but it was worth it. His conquests always are; he thrives on them. However, for some time to come, there will be no more, as he is now languishing in a German prisoner-of-war camp, having been captured at Givenchy on 20 December.

For Margaret, the encounter had not been as satisfying. Although it was not unpleasant, the frisson she hoped to find with a man did not materialize, leaving her with the guilt she has felt throughout her adult life about her 'abnormal' appetites, and now, especially, her longings for Bronwyn.

Blair Atholl Castle, Perthshire

New Year's Eve of 1915 at Blair Atholl Castle has been even more desolate than were its Christmas celebrations. Several tragedies have struck Scotland's most prestigious aristocratic family, leaving a pall over the entire household, estate and local community.

John James 'Iain' Stewart-Murray, the widowed 7th Duke of Atholl, Chief of the Murray Clan and Commander-in-Chief of the Atholl Highlanders, Europe's only surviving private army, is the most titled man in Scotland. But, thanks to the terrors of the Great War, he is now seeking solace in the arms of his mistress, Mrs Maud Grant, at her small cottage on the Blair Atholl estate. He was drunk during dinner and comatose long before the clock chimed the arrival of the new year. His family is scattered and grieving, his world, created by centuries of privilege, has been turned upside down.

Of his three sons, his middle boy, Lord George, known

as 'Geordie', has been missing since his regiment, the Black Watch, was in action at the Battle of the Aisne in September. The 'baby' of the family, Lord James, 'Hamish', was captured just before Christmas and is now incarcerated, fifteen men to a dormitory, with hundreds of Russian, French and Belgian prisoners in a disused oil factory in Germany. He spends his time refining his French and learning Russian. In return, he teaches English and, to a few far more intrepid souls, his first language, Scots Gaelic.

Only his eldest boy and heir, Lord John George, 'Bardie', is in Britain. But he and his wife, Lady Katharine, Kitty, left for Blagdon Hall, Northumberland, the home of their friend, Matthew, Viscount Ridley, on the 30th. From Blagdon, Bardie commands his regiment, the Scottish Horse, which, to his great frustration, is not at the Front but undertaking coastal defence duties in the north-east.

However, Kitty is in her element. After overseeing the knitting of 15,000 hose tops to warm the cold knees and thighs of the kilted men of the Scottish regiments, she has been asked by Dame Katherine Furse, the formidable founder of the Voluntary Aid Detachment, to join its committee to help improve the provision of nurses for the war. This means she makes frequent trips to London, where she can enjoy herself at some distance from her less than happy, childless marriage to Bardie, whose amorous pursuit of other women, and at least two resultant illegitimate offspring, are a source of great distress to her.

Of the 7th Duke's three daughters, all older than his trio of sons, only Lady Helen lives at Blair, where, in the absence of her long-deceased mother, she acts as châtelaine. Her older sister, Lady Dorothea, Dertha, is in England with her husband, Colonel Harry Ruggles-Brise, where he is recovering from a severe shrapnel wound he received at the Battle of Ypres while in command of 20th Brigade, 7th Division, of the BEF. Evelyn, the youngest daughter, is living with her companion in a small cottage in Spa, Belgium, to where she has escaped from the fighting around her home in Malines. Evelyn is yet another source of family distress, having been 'sent away' as a child as 'emotionally unstable' after repeated clashes with her mother. The old Duke thought it was for the best and hardly ever talks about her, but his draconian decision has eaten into his conscience ever since.

Lady Helen is the only Stewart-Murray at Blair for New Year. With a mere skeleton staff on duty, she has had dinner alone and is now asleep by the fire. But her slumber, uncomfortable as it is in Blair's cavernous and ornate drawing room with its huge fire almost extinguished, is disturbed by the handsome ormolu clock chiming 1 a.m. on the mantelpiece of sculptor Thomas Carter's masterpiece in Sicilian marble.

As is typical of the season and Blair's location in the Highlands of Perthshire, it is a bitterly cold night. In an appropriately subdued fashion, given the family's wretched circumstances, the few staff who are on duty offered her their New Year greetings an hour ago and went off to enjoy a more lively celebration below stairs.

Unlike the Blair celebrations of decades' standing, this New Year has not been piped in by a Highlander on the battlements, there were no fireworks lighting up the black night, no frolicking in the snow fortified by hot toddies and bacon sandwiches and certainly no early-hours cavorting in the countless bedrooms, where the sleeping arrangements are usually organized by the host to maximize the temptations of the flesh.

Helen's snoozing has led her to tip down her dress the dregs of her glass of Benedictine, her favourite postprandial nip. As she hastily wipes away the spillage with her handkerchief, she hears the sound she has been awaiting for several hours, the approaching footsteps of two men rattling along the highly polished oak floorboards of the second-floor corridor. One pair she is certain belongs to Jamie Forsyth, Blair's sagacious butler, who has had to remain on duty to greet the guest Helen has been waiting for all evening. From the rapid timbre of the second pair of shoes, she immediately recognizes the orderly gait of her friend and lover, Edinburgh businessman and sculptor David Tod.

Small, dapper, with a neatly trimmed, eleven-a-side moustache, he has dashed from Edinburgh in a mad rush. Thankfully, there were almost no other vehicles on the road to delay him. To her obvious discomfort in front of Forsyth, Tod embraces Helen warmly.

'You're four hours late!'

'So sorry, H, but my bloody car wouldn't start, and getting a mechanic out on Hogmanay is not easy.'

'But you did, I take it?'

'After a while, and in exchange for an exorbitant amount of silver – cash in hand, of course!'

Helen warms a little. 'Well, you'd better have a drink. Forsyth, send someone to get the fire going and bring Mr Tod a malt – a Speyside, please.'

Forsyth nods his head deferentially in the time-honoured way. 'Very well, Lady Helen. May I bring you another Benedictine?'

'Yes, Forsyth. Thank you.' The butler makes to leave and then stops himself. 'May I ask, have you heard from His Grace?'

'I'm afraid not. I did get a note the other day from Mrs Grant. He's still a little unwell, but on the mend, she says.'

'That is good news indeed. The staff all wish him a speedy recovery.'

'Very kind of you all.' David hands Helen a fistful of salt. 'See, I'm your first-footer, and here's for good fortune in 1915.'

'Thank you, but aren't you supposed to be tall and dark?'

'Hmm, you can't have everything, H.'

After Dougie Cameron, first footman, has turned the drawing-room hearth into an inferno and Forsyth has brought David a very large tulip (a style of whisky glass much preferred by the Stewart-Murrays) of Glenlivet and Helen another Benedictine, the two of them are alone. David toasts his hostess.

'Happy New Year, darling. I hope 1915 is a better year for you than 1914.'

Helen takes a large swig of her drink. She suddenly looks tearful. 'Oh, David, I do hope so, but I fear it may be even worse. Geordie is never coming home, Hamish will not be home until the war is over and Bardie hasn't even gone to fight yet. God knows what fate awaits him on a cavalry charger!'

'Don't fret, H. I don't think the cavalry are making madcap charges any more.'

'Don't be such a clever arse! So many men are not coming home. I don't know a single family which hasn't lost someone: from the house, the estate, the village, all my friends. Poor darling Evelyn is living in a cottage in the woods in the middle of nowhere, which could be under Hun control at any time. Papa is in such a bad way I doubt he will recover. I can't bear it!'

As Helen ends the list of the Stewart-Murray family woes, her eyes flood with tears. She goes to an occasional table, where, perceptively, Forsyth has left the bottle of Benedictine, and fills her glass with another large measure of the amber liqueur.

David has been hoping that he can usher in the New Year with a passionate tryst with Helen, a habit of which she has become increasingly enamoured.

'Let's go to bed, H, and lose ourselves in simple pleasures.'

Helen smiles. 'What a sweet thought, David. Perhaps in the morning, darling. Not tonight, there is too much sadness in my heart.'

David peers into his tulip of malt, sniffs its pungent aroma and takes a deep breath. He has decided to ask a question he has been wanting to ask for a very long time. He is suddenly taken by the moment but, despite being a man of some substance and of mature years, he is anxious. He gathers himself: 'H, will you marry me?'

'Good heavens, this is very sudden, David.'

'I know, but this is the first day of a new year. We're in

the middle of a catastrophic war that is changing everything. When it's over, the world will be a different place. What better time could there be?'

Helen's eyes swell with even more tears. 'Oh, David, Papa will be furious!'

'I know – I'm a common merchant! You should be marrying a baronet, at worst, but preferably a peer of the Scottish realm.'

Helen smiles a little and delicately wipes away her tears with the ends of her index fingers. 'An English peer would probably pass muster, but he would have to be at least an earl!'

David laughs. 'Well, I'm not an earl, but I could afford to lend some filthy lucre to an impoverished one, and I could sculpt one in clay, resplendent in his robes and ermine finery!'

'So you can – two gifts I so admire you for. You've earned the money Papa resents you having, whereas we've never had to earn our money and, of the six of us, not one has the talent you have.'

'You know, you're beginning to sound like a socialist!'

'Hardly, but I do believe that credit should be given where credit's due.'

'So, leaving the interesting subject of equality and justice to one side for a moment, what's your answer?'

'To what?'

'Don't tease, H!'

Helen's face breaks into a broad grin. 'Yes, you bloody fool! I'm so happy. But let's keep it to ourselves for now. Papa needs to recover from the loss of Geordie and get used to the fact that Hamish isn't coming home for the foreseeable future. But when the time comes, you'll have to go to him to ask for my hand.'

'I know. That's a prospect that fills me with total dread. But, as for the timing: agreed. Come on, let's take our glasses upstairs and see in the New Year properly.'

Helen smiles mischievously. 'David, when will you understand? This is Blair; I'll ring for Dougie to bring up our drinks . . . and the bottles, just in case we're in need of a bit of sustenance. Shall we have a hearty breakfast in our room – say, at nine?'

'Let's say ten. Don't want to rush things.'

David thrusts his arms around Helen's waist. 'So, have you changed your mind about consummating our engagement?'

'Well, as I've just agreed to marry you, I can hardly deny you your conjugal rights.'

Keighley Green Working Men's Club, Burnley, Lancashire

John-Tommy Crabtree, a volunteer in the newly formed D Company (Burnley) 11th Battalion East Lancashire Regiment, the 'Accrington Pals', is Keighley Green's former steward. But, as it is New Year's Eve and the club is packed, he has discarded the Melton blue uniform of Lord Kitchener's New Army and donned his old barmskin apron for a bit of moonlighting to supplement the King's shilling.

John-Tommy is a local legend, as fearsome a sight

with his shillelagh in his fist to deal with troublemakers as he once was in the Lancashire League with a brand-new cherry in his hand to skittle out opposing batsmen. He twice won the League Championship with Burnley Cricket Club, in 1906 and 1907, before going to Oldham in the Central Lancashire League as the club's professional.

On one memorable occasion at the end of the 1907 season he took six wickets for two runs against Church, Burnley's fierce rivals from Oswaldtwistle, to secure the title. It was a memorable feat, enshrined on a silver clasp around the match ball, which sits in pride of place behind Keighley Green's highly polished mahogany bar. John-Tommy played with and against the great English cricketing legend Sidney Barnes. He once ran him out, took his wicket on more than one occasion and on an unforgettable August day in 1904 scored forty runs, including two sixes, off his prodigious bowling. 'The day our John-Tommy hit S. F. Barnes fo' six o-er t'football stand' is still talked about at Turf Moor, the home of Burnley's famous cricket and football teams.

'C'mon, you lot. 'Ave rung t'bell; sup up an' get tha'sens 'ome. It's one in t'mornin.'

There is only a token response from the drunken revellers. So John-Tommy's huge shillelagh, Ireland's ancient weapon of war, given to him by Gerry Cooney, his father-in-law from Armagh, crashes on to the bar with a mighty thump. Over the years the shillelagh has made a deep impression in the same spot on the russet-red bar, the only indent in an otherwise glass-like, pristine surface. The members call it 'John-Tommy's fettlin' oyel.'

'That's t'last warnin'. Next time, a'll fettle sum'un's heed wi' it!'

It has been a big night, and the lant trough in the yard, which is the club's urinal, is so full that the local tanner, who uses its contents to soften his leather, has been asked to come to empty it as soon as possible. As John-Tommy frequently says to his more lubricated customers, 'If yon lant wer' full o' sixpenny bits tha'd pissed away, tha wouldn't sup s'much!'

New Year's Day 1915 has fallen on a Friday, so it is going to be a long weekend of drinking, especially as clubs like Keighley Green have avoided the strictures on pub licensing hours imposed by the government's draconian Defence of the Realm Act. But there will not be another delivery of ale until Monday, and John-Tommy is worried that he might run out. He knows he will be able to buy more from Burnley's plethora of ale houses and small breweries, but he will have to pay over the odds and then give it twenty-four hours to settle on its stillage. Anyway, that is a problem for the morning. D Company has been stood down for the long holiday, and he does not have to open the club until eleven.

He makes his way over to a group in the corner and bellows at them: 'On yer way, you buggers, get down t'road. 'As t'not got 'omes t'go t'!' He then lowers his voice. 'Get th'sels back in ten minutes and I'll stand thee a round.'

John-Tommy is forty-two, an age which meant he had to have a special dispensation to enlist in the army, but the group at the table are much younger. They are all friends and all proudly sporting their Pals' blue uniforms.

Tommy Broxup and Mad-Mick Kenny are both in their mid-twenties. Tommy was a weaver until he joined up, Mick a collier before he enlisted. Theirs is an unusual friendship in a town where the rivalry between the pit and the mill is fierce. Tommy is there with his wife, Mary, a weaver with strong views and a combustible temperament. Mick's wife, Cath, also a weaver and a woman with forthright opinions, is also there. In fact, it was the two women's radical politics that brought Mick and Tommy together. Cath is subdued, still recovering from the tragedy of the miscarriage of her baby just two days before Christmas.

Mary and Cath offer a rare sight in the club. Young women are not usually seen drinking, and certainly not without the requisite Lancashire shawl. But their presence is tolerated for two reasons. First, few men would challenge them: they are strong trade unionists, vehement supporters of the suffragettes and more than capable of belittling anyone who takes them on. Second, even fewer would dare cross Mick and Tommy, who are both cock o' t'midden in their local areas, celebrated street-fighters and highly proficient with both fists and clogs.

With the two married couples is a pair of seventeen-year-old former schoolfriends, Vincent 'Vinny' Sagar and Nathaniel 'Twaites' Haythornthwaite. They have become friends with the older men through Vinny's prowess at both football and cricket. In fact, so exceptional is Vinny's skill at football, he came close to being taken on as a professional at Turf Moor, the home of Burnley Football Club, the Clarets, FA Cup-holders and the most powerful team in the land.

When the six friends return to the club to enjoy John-Tommy's offer of an after-hours drink, the rowdy hubhub generated by a mass of drunken men has evaporated. The only other people there, apart from the pot-men and bar staff, are half a dozen bobbies from Keighley Green Police Station, the club's next-door neighbour. John-Tommy always offers a few gratis beers to the men of the local constabulary; a wise move given that he often stretches his opening hours beyond the club's permitted licence. Not only that: should a brawl break out, which occurs regularly, it is helpful to have the local constabulary on hand to add their arsenal of truncheons to John-Tommy's illustrious shillelagh.

As they lift their jugs of ale, the policemen pay their respects to Tommy and Mick. 'Respect' is the appropriate word. Although the two men's reputation is as 'feightin' lads', they have rarely been at odds with the large, heavily moustachioed keepers of local law and order.

'Ata alreet, Tommy, lad?'

'Aye, grand, thanks, Serjeant; an' thee?'

'Mustn't moither, lad; an' thee, Mick, how's tha doin'?'

'Alreet, Serjeant Shuttleworth, thank ye.'

Glasses are held up all round as polite smiles and New Year's greetings are exchanged.

One of the policemen, an outsider from Manchester, disrupts the well-mannered atmosphere. 'So, Mary. Still stirrin' things in t'mills?'

Mary fixes him with a steely glare. 'Well, lad; if I am, it's nowt to do wi' thee!'

There are bristles of displeasure around both Mary's table and that of the bobbies. John-Tommy intervenes with the kind of gravitas only a local cricketing legend can wield.

'Hey, think on, both on yer. It's New Year's Day, thu's lads at t'Front gettin' their fuckin' knackers blown off fer us. So think on; I'll 'ave no blatherin' in 'ere.'

He shouts to one of his bar staff. 'Our Stan, fetch another tray o' Massey's; lads 'ere a' parched like smoked kippers! An' fetch a Mackeson's an' ruby port fer Mary and a ginger ale fer Cath.'

Serjeant Shuttleworth nods at John-Tommy, appreciative of his wise intervention. He also scowls at the officer who tried to provoke Mary, making his displeasure very obvious. Several trays of drinks follow over the next hour, after which the bobbies go home to their beds, leaving Kitchener's recruits alone. Mick Kenny, his grieving wife, Cath, asleep in Mary Broxup's lap, is drunk and brooding. He has not been himself since the miscarriage.

'Yer know wot, I can't be doin' wi' another week, let alone a month, troopin' up an' down t'moors like toy soldiers. I joined up to feight fuckin' Germans.'

Tommy Broxup echoes Mick's ire. 'Aye, we've finally got rifles, but we've not a clue how to fire t'buggers. We get bayonet practice every day, but no firing practice.'

Vinny perks up, suddenly roused from a stupor induced by multiple pints of Massey's. 'That's cos there's no bullets fer us! Whatever they're mekin' is goin' t'lads at t'Front.'

As he always does, Twaites agrees with Vinny, nodding his head and repeating verbatim what he said.

Although tens of thousands of men from around Britain have answered the call to join Lord Kitchener's Pals' battalions, their training has been tedious and their uniforms and equipment slow in arriving. The initial enthusiasm for a war to save the civilized world from evil which swept the country in the autumn has begun to wane. This change in mood has spiralled yet further downwards as the scale of the casualties has become clear and as injured army regulars have come home with unnerving stories about the atrocious conditions in which they have been fighting.

Just before Christmas, D Company heard that it would go to an army training camp in Caernarvon with the rest of the Accrington Pals in early February. The news meant that their training became more serious, but there was no indication of how long they would be in camp, nor did it suggest that they would be on the front line in the foreseeable future.

John-Tommy tries to lift Mick's spirits. 'Mick, lad; it's like laikin' at cricket.'

'What is, John-Tommy?'

'Trainin' to be soldier.'

'I don't laik at cricket. I'm from Irish stock, wi don't tek t'cricket.'

'Aye, but yer know 'ow it's played.'

'Aye.'

'Well, then. It starts slow, teks a long time, an' tha' needs to be patient wi' it.'

Not convinced by the older man's analogy, Mick smiles politely and takes a final swig from his beer mug. 'I'm off 'ome, lads; ave to get Cath to her bed, she's been fair wore out since she lost our wee lad.'

With Mick and Cath gone home and Vinny and

Twaites staggering arm-in-arm through the club's door, Mary Broxup turns to John-Tommy. 'Ata stoppin' 'ere t'neet?'

'Aye, lass, tha's a bed in t'loft.'

'An' wheer's Mrs Crabtree?'

'In Wynotham Street, up Colne Road. We rent it off t'mill where Mary works t'four-loom.'

'She's called Mary?'

'Aye, Mary Cooney; Tyneside Irish. Her father, Gerry, was from Armagh. He went to t'Tyne fer work. He wer a riveter.'

'Yer got childer?'

'Aye, our Jack, he's four; an' Eileen, born last September.'

'Can I ask thee a personal question?'

'Go on, lass.'

'Tha's John-Tommy Crabtree, local hero, earnin' a bob or two 'ere; you're wed, got childer; why 'ave yer joined up wi' these daft buggers?'

'Na'then, our Mary; answer's plain as day: Wot's goin' on in Belgium's not reet. Nowt in Britain is reet, but if wi feight fer wot's reet in Belgium, we'll be able to feight fer wot's reet at 'ome.'

'Oh, John-Tommy, that's as good an answer about this bloody war as 'ave heard. But, ata reet abaht wot it'll mean fer Britain when it's o'er? I do 'ope so, I really do.'

'So do I, lass.'

John-Tommy gives Mary a big hug. 'Get your Tommy 'ome to bed; he's pie-eyed!'

'Tha's reet, 'e is. Sithee, then. An' thanks fer t'beers an' lookin' after t'lads; tha's a good lad, John-Tommy.'

Admiralty House, Whitehall, London

Winston Leonard Spencer-Churchill, Britain's First Lord of the Admiralty, spent most of Christmas Night 1914 and well into the early hours of Boxing Day poring over his charts of the Eastern Mediterranean. He has done so, hour upon hour, every day since. It is now two hours into 1915's bleak and cold New Year's Day and he is back at his desk, searching for a solution to the stalemate in the war against Germany.

He can still hear in the distance the remnants of the noisy revellers who have seen in the New Year in Trafalgar Square. His own celebration was a modest family celebration, a brief respite from his toils. His wife, Clemmie, his brother, Jack, and Jack's wife, Goonie, together with close friends the brilliant young lawyer and politician F. E. Smith and his wife, Margaret, joined him for a supper as good as the Admiralty's chef could muster. It had ended about an hour ago when the three women went to bed. The children, seven in all, in bed shortly after supper, are asleep in their bunks in the Admiralty's attic.

Jack and FE, both sipping cognac, are trying to persuade Winston, who also has a snifter of brandy close by, to leave his desk and call it a day. But he is not really listening. He simply repeats a forlorn sentiment both men have heard many times before.

'I cannot rest until we have an answer. Kitchener is gnawing at the war in France like a dog with a bone. The man's a born soldier and a good general, but he's as flummoxed as everyone else about what to do for the best. The

PM is desperate; he says everyone has an opinion but no one can make a compelling case. There seems to be no solution to the stalemate; only more and more sacrifice. Our men are wallowing in the mire of the trenches and I'm in front of a roaring fire, quaffing Hine's finest brandy. I can't bear it.'

FE, from Birkenhead and a modest middle-class background, and who has used his extraordinary intellect and commanding oratory to propel himself to the centre of British life, is a man Winston admires more than any other. Said to have the sharpest tongue in England, many of the things he has said have already passed into legend, especially those emanating from his eloquence in court and his cut and thrust with the judges. Famously, as a young silk, he so infuriated a judge that the judge snapped at him, 'You are extremely offensive, young man!' To which FE replied, 'As a matter of fact we both are; the only difference being that I am trying to be, and you can't help it.'

Concerned for Winston, believing that he is driving himself too hard, FE tries to reassure his old friend: 'Winston, you didn't put our men in the trenches, the Kaiser did.'

'I know, but I want to get them out of their morass and end their suffering. I want them marching to glory in Berlin, then I want them home.'

'Don't we all? But you can't do it on your own.'

'No, not yet, FE, but when I'm Minister of War I can . . . and will!'

Jack smiles at his brother's single-minded fortitude, a marvel he has witnessed for as long as he can remember.

He and FE have to be on a boat back to France tomorrow evening, and he knows that if any man can think of a way to prevent him and others repeating the daunting journey for years to come, it is his brother. Jack is on the staff of Sir John French, Commander-in-Chief of the British Expeditionary Force. Abjuring his lucrative work as a barrister, FE is filling the mundane role of Recording Officer of the Indian Corps attached to the BEF, a job that involves writing glowing accounts of their bravery for the British press.

Knowing how best to tempt him away from his maps, he looks at Winston mischievously. 'I'm going to make you an offer that would entice the most obdurate of men,' he says.

'Not another wager, FE. You know you always lose them!'

'No, it's a more sensual lure. New Year's Day will dawn in a few hours. It's going to be fresh and crisp. Put your maps away for a day. We'll all go to Hampton Court. Jack says he's going to brave the icy Thames for a New Year dip. I'll buy lunch at the Mitre: rib of beef, pink, and a first-growth claret. They have a very good '97 Haut-Brion. Clemmie says you won't come, but I insist. If you refuse, I'll tell Asquith that you're working too hard and losing your mind.'

'You wouldn't dare!'

'Wouldn't I?'

'I suppose you might. My dear fellow, you are a card! A very thoughtful offer; a good lunch by the river is very tempting, nearly as tantalizing as watching Jack make an arse of himself in a bathing costume! But I must stay here.

Asquith is at Walmer Castle, reading papers both Lloyd George and I have sent to him about opening a new campaign. I expect a response any day.'

Realizing that his proposal has made little impact on Winston and that one of his friend's less endearing qualities is pig-headedness in the extreme, FE relents. 'How bad is the situation?' he asks.

'Well, you two don't need me to tell you how grim it is at the Front. God help us, but at least it is no worse than a stalemate. It is in the east where we have our greatest crisis. All our reports suggest that the Russians are on their knees. If they capitulate, the Kaiser can hurl all his eastern divisions on to us in the west. If that happens, it will take time, but I wager that there will be no French celebration of Bastille Day in Paris this July. There will be field-grey uniforms marching along the Champs-Élysées, not the blue and red of the little poilu, and the tricolor flying over the Arc de Triomphe will be the black, white and red of the German empire.'

FE pours another large Hine into his even larger brandy balloon. Jack refuses the same, but Winston nods for one. FE sits down heavily, draws deeply on his cigar and follows it with a mouthful of cognac. 'Damn fine Hine, this!' He realizes he still cannot get Winston to focus on anything other than his maps. 'What will be the timing in the east?'

'Winter is providing a respite of sorts, but with the thaw will come a huge German offensive. The Russians can fight and are reasonably well equipped, but their leadership is bone-headed and their transport and logistics are calamitous.'

Winston at last stands up and takes a sip of his brandy. He does not savour it; he does not even realize he is imbibing it: he is too preoccupied. He starts to pace. 'On Wednesday, the head of our military mission to the Tsar's army was told by Grand Duke Nicholas that the Turks are rampaging through the Russian defences in the Caucasus. That makes the case much stronger for an attack against the Turks in the south.'

'The Dardanelles?'

'Yes, but I still prefer an attack to outflank the Kaiser in north Germany and join with the Russians. However, Lloyd George prefers the south, utilizing anti-German and anti-Turk sentiment.'

'So, is the scheme flawed?'

'Not necessarily, but it needs to be a joint navy and army undertaking, and Kitchener says he can't – although I think it's more "won't" than "can't" – spare any men from France. Without infantry, I have serious doubts.'

Jack's smile of admiration has turned into a furrowed look of concern. 'Winston, take a breather. It will do you good . . . *and* our cause: you will think clearer for a day off today.'

'That sounds like a reproach, Jack.'

'Not at all. We will have you back here for dinner, then you can catch up on the day for a couple of hours before getting an early night. You are mortal, like the rest of us. Or at least I think you are.'

'Tosh! It's the mortality of the boys at the Front that is of much greater concern than mine. I'll rest when they can. Now, bugger off to bed, the pair of you.'

The two men know when they are beaten. With

Winston wearing his current mantle as Britain's warrior-in-chief, neither brotherly love nor the acumen of the cleverest advocate in the realm can prevail.

Almost three hours later, with FE and Jack sleeping off more than enough brandy, Winston climbs the Admiralty's grand staircase to bed. It is midwinter, so dawn is some way off, but if it were high summer the sun would be well up and the cock would have crowed long ago. He asks the marine on duty for a 6 a.m. call, before slipping into bed next to Clemmie. He has woken her up.

'Darling, it's turned four in the morning. You're flogging yourself to death,' she says.

'Hardly, Cat. There'll be plenty of time for sleep when I'm in my dotage.'

'At this rate, you won't reach old age. When have you asked for a call?'

'Not for a while.'

'That means six, doesn't it?'

'That's a question of national security, darling. You may not be privy to the answer.'

'Don't be infuriating! Please go and sleep upstairs. I don't want to be woken again by some ham-fisted marine knocking on the door. And don't wake the children.'

'Darling, may I not go in and give them a kiss?'

'Of course, but do it quietly.'

Winston slips out of the bed and walks to the door.

Clemmie whispers after him, 'Pug . . . I have a madman for a husband . . . but I love you.'

'I love you, too, Cat . . . and I have a saint for a wife.'

*

Breakfast at the Admiralty the next morning is a light-hearted affair. Winston, perhaps feeling guilty about his obstinacy in declining lunch and despite having had almost no sleep, is in good humour and is keeping the children amused. When one of them teases him about his noticeable lisp, he repeats for them the phrase he used to recite as a child to help him overcome it: 'The Spanish ships I cannot see for they are not in sight.' But, as he does so, he greatly exaggerates his lisp, to the huge enjoyment of everyone.

He then tells them the stories of great battles of the past: Blenheim, Waterloo, Trafalgar, and Omdurman, in which he himself took part. He holds the children in the palm of his hand, a master of detail and a vivid storyteller.

At ten thirty the family members are ready to depart for their lunch in Richmond. As they rush down into the Admiralty courtyard Winston is approached by a signals officer who pulls him to one side.

'Bad news, I'm afraid, sir. The *Formidable* has gone down off Portland Bill – German torpedoes.'

He hands Winston a telegram. It reads: 'Hit at 02:20 hours and again as she sank. Went down just before 05:00 hours. Skipper, Captain Noel Loxley, and more than half the complement, 750 men, have gone with her.'

Winston beckons to FE and Jack. 'Do you mind if I rush back inside? Don't mention it to the girls – it will spoil their day – but we've lost a battleship, *Formidable*, and most of the crew. Bloody submarines! They're a curse.'

Jack sees the weariness in his brother's eyes. 'Would you prefer it if we didn't go? We could go to St James's

Park and feed the ducks and come back and keep you company for lunch.'

'No, that would spoil the day for the children. The river would be much better. There will be lots of entertainment to amuse the little ones, quite apart from you in your long johns.'

Winston tries to smile at the thought of his brother in a swimming costume, but it does not come; he's unable to disguise his devastation at the news about *Formidable*. He turns to look up Whitehall to see Lord Nelson on his column. 'War was so different in his day and, indeed, in mine, which was only a dozen or so years ago.'

The young political firebrand, revered and reviled in equal measure by his peers, who cares so deeply about his country and its fighting men, squeezes his eyes to fight back the tears. 'At Omdurman, we charged with our sabres gleaming in the sun against dervishes armed with spears. Now we fight with 15-inch Howitzers, Maxim machine guns, aeroplanes that drop death from the heavens and submarines that lurk in the deep ready to maim a 20,000-ton Dreadnought with a single torpedo. Fighting men have become no more than machine-minders for obscene instruments of death.' He pauses, staring into the distance. 'Where will it end – with yet more terrible ways of killing one another?!'

For once, FE is silent, overwhelmed by his friend's premonitions. Jack turns away, not knowing what to say. But his brother, suddenly composed, strides back towards the Admiralty. He has refound his resolution; there is a blaze in him once more, and he is murmuring to himself eagerly.

'Depth bombs! I need that report commissioned by Jellicoe!'

The two men, bemused, look at Winston as he walks away, muttering, 'The answer to submarines: depth bombs, that's what we need.'

Both FE and Jack are relieved that Winston's moments of despair have passed, rather than, as they often do, spiralling into a deeper melancholy. They know that he thinks of the British Navy as his kith and kin, as a vast family he adores. He has lost a lot of close relatives today. A fine welcome to his New Year!

Saturday 9 January

Towneley Hall, Burnley, Lancashire

Towneley Hall is something of an anomaly, sitting as it does, in all its medieval splendour, almost in the middle of Burnley, surrounded by the grit and grime of the town's innumerable cotton mills and its forest of belching chimneys. The hall has been home to the most eminent local family, the Towneleys, for over five hundred years. The family was celebrated for its military pedigree and staunch Roman Catholicism, but its wealth diminished significantly during the nineteenth century and the hall had to be sold, and has been owned by Burnley Borough Council since the turn of the century.

Most of the house and its 400 acres are now open to the public. For the thousands who live in endless, monotonous rows of back-to-back terraced hovels only a stone's throw away, Towneley's opulent rooms, fine furnishings and immaculate gardens are a source of fascination, illustrating for them a perfect picture of how the gentry live. They gawp in wonder at its colourful tapestries, fine furniture and gleaming armour as they stride along its oak-panelled Long Gallery, and are awestruck by its enormous Elizabethan kitchen. Many of them have relatives who were in service to the Towneleys and who have told them about the lives made possible by privilege and wealth.

As are people throughout Britain, the good folk of Burnley are in sombre mood. The short, dark days of a typical British winter create a half-light of gloomy shadows. Everything is drained of colour. The millstone grit of endless rows of identical houses and the cobbles, setts and flagstones of indistinguishable streets reflect through the constant drizzle, the leaden pall of smoke and low cloud from above. Everything appears to be either gull grey or shit brown.

But Burnley's hardy community is used to the melancholy of winter. It is the shadow of war that is having a far greater impact on people's demeanour. The casualty figures have stunned everyone, as has the realization that the stalemate at the Front could last for months, even years. Even more disconcerting for many is knowing that Lord Kitchener's new volunteer army is still in its early days of training and being equipped and that, when it is ready, it will be counted in millions, not thousands. It is not difficult to calculate the appalling arithmetic of what an army on that scale could mean in terms of future casualties.

Mary Broxup and Cath Kenny are walking around Towneley's impressive ornamental pond, admiring its soaring fountain. Their menfolk are at Turf Moor, where their volunteers' blue uniforms will gain them admission at half-price. It is FA Cup day, the first round of the 1915 competition, and Burnley, current holders of the famous trophy, are at home to Huddersfield Town, a club only six years old and from the Football League's Second Division. The game should be a formality for Burnley and, from the frequent roars the two women can hear from the ground, less than a mile away, that seems to be what is happening.

'That sounds like another! I'll wager our Tommy's owd socks that t'bonny lad Bert Freeman's scored it.'

'That's nowt much of a bet, Mary – Bert ollus scores! An', besides, who'd want thi' Tommy's owd toe-rags?'

After they giggle, Cath, suddenly serious, changes the subject. 'Tha knows I wrote to Henry Hyndman?'

'Aye, a'do.'

'Well, ave 'ad a letter back fra' 'im.'

''Ave yer now? Fancies thee, owd Henry.'

'Does 'e 'eck? I thought 'e fancied thee.'

'Don't be a barmcake. 'E's a good lad, a proper gent.'

'That doesn't stop 'im 'ankerin' after thee. Any road, I wrote to 'im at Christmas when we 'eard abaht lads goin' t'camp at Caernarvon. A told 'im, am not stoppin' i' Burnley if they're buggerin' off t'war.'

'Still want t'drive ambulances?'

'Aye, a'do, or summat to help t'lads at t'Front. Been thinkin' on it e'er since a lost me little lad afore Christmas.'

'So wot does Henry reckon?'

'He sez th's a crisis comin'. Not enough shells, guns, ammunition an' everythin'; an' not enough men t'mek 'em. He reckons women a'll be needed in t'thousands to do war work, an' that plans are already bein' med. He thinks it's goin' to be reet important fer us lasses an', harken t'this bit: he thinks we'll get vote at t'end on it.'

'Does he? That's all very well, but wot abaht t'unions, they'll not stand fer women doin' men's work.'

'He sez they'll 'ave t'; an' that Lloyd George has done a deal wi' 'em.'

Mary is still sceptical. 'But I don't want t'work in a bloody factory; a can do that 'ere!'

'Neither do I. I want to go t'France an' do summat proper.'

''As t'talked to Mick abaht it?'

'Aye.'

'An'?'

''E's not moithered. 'E sez a can suit me'sen.'

'So, wot next?'

'If wi go t'London, Henry sez he'll introduce us t'a Katherine Furse, a toff lass who runs summat called t'Voluntary Aid Detachment. He sez they're all proper well-to-do ladies o' leisure, women of means, who mek t'own way, buy t'own uniforms an' stuff. But Henry wants ordinary lasses like us involved.'

'Why?'

'So we can be sen to be doin' our bit as well.'

'But if they're all well off, how do'st wi manage? We've not got two ha'pennies t'rub together.'

'Henry sez t'Socialist Party will sub us.'

'Is that reet?'

'Aye.'

'How much?'

'Enough to get us t'France, buy us uniforms an' ten bob a week on top o' t'twelve bob wi get fra' Kitchener.'

'That's not a bad do! So how do wi get t'London?'

'Henry will send us t'brass fer train ticket.'

'Will 'e now? An' wot does 'e want in return, a bit o'er brush?'

'Mary, 'e's not like that! Besides, 'e must be seventy-odd.'

'Age doesn't stop a lad gettin' his knob out fer a bit o'

peggin'. Owd Bobby Leveret down our backstreet wer still wavin' his little willie at any lass who walked by well into his eighties. They reckon that when they laid him out in t'funeral parlour, 'e still 'ad an 'ard-on!'

'Don't be daft, yer silly bugger. Anyway, Henry's alreet. So, do'st want to do this drivin' malarkey or wot?'

Mary smiles. 'If thee is, am wi' thi, lass; but not until t'lads go t'Caernarvon.'

'Reet, then wi'v got abaht a month t'learn 'ow to drive. Ad best show an ankle to that lad at Trafalgar Mill who sed 'e'd teach us 'ow t'drive 'is lorry.'

'Aye, reckon tha'd better. But if a catch 'im sniffin' at my ankle, I'll lamp 'im.'

Cath and Mary make their way to the Wellington Hotel, the nearest pub to Turf Moor, where they have agreed to meet the four men in their lives: their husbands, Mick and Tommy, and their two young friends and fellow volunteers, the inseparable Vinny and Twaites.

In an acknowledgment of the hard times, Burnley Football Club has lowered its admission prices, but the stringencies of the Great War are severe and the crowd, a trifling 14,000, is significantly down compared to the previous season's average. Nevertheless, as the two women walk up Todmorden Road towards their destination, they swim against a tide of men clattering their clog irons along the cobbles. Sporting their flat caps, cotton mufflers and heavy moustaches, they look identical.

As they gave up wearing their Lancashire shawls long ago, Cath and Mary are conspicuous. On the whole, only 'posh' lasses and tarts walk the streets without a shawl, so they have to ignore the leers, whistles and obscene gestures of the waves of men washing past them. But they are keen to know the result. Cath's voice is strong enough to be heard above the din.

''Ow did t'lads laik?'

'Alreet lass' is one friendly reply; a less pleasant one is ''Ow dost thee laik, lass, a'bet tha's got a tidy game o' cock-tuggin' tha'sen!'

Eventually, someone shouts the score: 'Three–one: Bert Freeman, Bob Kelly an' Len Thorpe. We're off t'Crystal Palace agin. I 'ope owd King George 'as bin polishin' t'trophy!'

Cath smiles wryly. 'So, Mary, tha wer' reet abaht Bonny Bert, but tha' can keep Tommy's owd socks!'

When Cath and Mary squeeze themselves through the throng at the Wellington Hotel they find that their uniformed quartet of men sitting at their usual table by the fireplace have almost finished their first pint of Massey's.

Twaites grabs one of the pot-lads to order more drinks, but his gesture represents only a momentary interruption in a heated debate about the game. Tommy is the most animated.

'Sixpence fer that! That's three pints o' ale. Huddersfield laiked like amateurs. We shudda 'ad three brace o' goals. Our Vinny wudda got t'hat-trick.'

Vinny raises his jug in a salute. 'I would tha'!'

Ten minutes later, with the noise in the Wellington becoming deafening, Cath's patience in waiting for a break in the conversation has been exhausted. She cuts in: 'Mary an' me are goin' t'France t'drive ambulances.'

She speaks without raising her voice. No one hears her.

Mary repeats the information. 'Aye, Cath an' me are goin' t'war. We'll probably be theer a'fore thee buggers!'

There is still no response from the men. Cath tries again to provoke a reaction: 'Oh, an' Mary's runnin' away wi' a black chap!'

Tommy smiles. ''E can 'ave 'er!'

Mary responds with the flat of her hand, giving Tommy a firm clip around his ear which projects his cap on to the next table. There are cheers from all who see the blow.

'Did thee 'ear wot a said abaht goin' t'France?'

'Aye; ave 'eard it afore.'

'So?'

'Do as tha' must; tha' will any road.'

Cath gives Mick a dig in the ribs. 'An' thee, yer big lummox. What do'st thee reckon?'

'Suit tha'sen; like Mary, tha'll do as tha' pleases.'

'Is that all tha's got to say?'

Tommy relents, and Mick smiles mischievously. 'Sorry, our lass, wer only teasin'. Wot you're doin' is reet bold; not many lasses round 'ere would dream o' doin' it. We're proud o' both o' thee.'

Mary grins broadly. 'Reet, then buy us both a bloody drink!'

Walmer Castle, Kent

Walmer Castle is one of Prime Minister Herbert Asquith's favourite weekend retreats. The castle on the Kent coast just north of Dover, once a huge defensive fortress built by Henry VIII, is now a spacious home crammed with gilded portraits and memorabilia celebrating British history.

Asquith's host is William Lygon, 7th Earl Beauchamp, the new Lord Warden of the Cinque Ports. Walmer is the warden's official residence. Beauchamp and his wife, Lettice, are excellent hosts. They have six young children, so, with the addition of the many children of their guests, Walmer at weekends is a lively and noisy place, its long corridors and many rooms ideal for games of hide and seek and other children's amusements.

Asquith is at Walmer with his wife, Margot, and youngest son, twelve-year-old Anthony, known to his family as Puffin. Other guests include the Home Secretary, Reginald McKenna, his wife, Pamela, and their two young boys, Michael and David. Margot, Asquith's second wife, who much prefers London's more 'intellectual' circles, loathes Walmer. She thinks it cold and draughty, and that too much politics is discussed there, at the cost of more 'important' conversation.

The seating plan for dinner is a conundrum for the host and hostess. McKenna, a Cambridge mathematician by training and renowned for his meticulous attention to detail, has clashed several times with Winston in Cabinet. Winston thinks McKenna pedantic and unimaginative, while McKenna reciprocates with an overt repugnance for his younger colleague's 'dangerous belligerence'.

To everyone's relief, the two are kept apart at opposite ends of the table. Winston is seated next to Margot Asquith. After an hour or more of trivialities, Margot grasps Winston's arm, smirks impishly and lowers her voice: 'Winston, I hear on the bush telegraph that our host frequents various seedy West End premises for the sole purpose of cavorting with young men.'

'Good heavens, madam, are you suggesting that Beauchamp is a homosexualist? Bloody hell, the man's got six children!'

'Piffle! That's got nothing to do with it. Homosexuals are not infertile, and most have wives and families. Apparently, his moniker at Eton, 'Little Willie', was not a reference to his Christian name or the size of his male appendage but to his penchant for the little willies of the school fags.'

'Really, Margot, you should take care. What you're accusing him of is against the law of the land.'

'Well, if you'll forgive the pun, he's made his bed . . . !'

Margot, realizing that Winston is not titillated by her gossip about Willie Beauchamp, changes tack. She has heard that Winston has ambitions to be made Viceroy of India.

'I hear you crave Charles Hardinge's vice-regal cape when he retires?'

'Hardly "crave", Margot, but I did have a fancy for it a few years ago, especially after serving on the North-west Frontier in '97, but not any more.'

'Not enough elixir in India's well to quench your warrior's thirst?'

'Well, there is no shortage of adventure for a fighting man on India's borders, but it is as nothing compared to the contest here.'

'I suppose you're right. Most viceroys end up pickling themselves in gin and going gaga in the heat.'

'Quite, Margot.'

Winston leans towards Margot to share a confidence, knowing full well it will be in the Prime Minister's ear before the morning: 'It is the thrill of it here and now that intoxicates me. What we are doing in this great endeavour in Europe will be spoken of for a thousand generations. I could not be anywhere but at the heart of this glorious, delicious war!'

Margot is taken aback by Winston's bravado; just the effect he had hoped for.

'Isn't "delicious" an incongruous word for a war?'

'Yes, but I think you know what I mean. Perhaps I should be more careful in my choice of words, but I was put on this earth to lead, and leaders must relish the fray.'

Margot seems content with what she has wheedled out of Winston and purrs inwardly.

Later that night, as they get ready for bed, Clemmie warns Winston about Margot: 'You should be careful what you say to her. She keeps a diary and has an acerbic tongue. Also, you can't be sure that her version of conversations gets back to Asquith with any accuracy.'

'I know, but isn't it perverse: Venetia Stanley keeps a diary as well? So poor Old Block is having his life recorded in every detail by his wife *and* his mistress! It's very disconcerting in the War Council. He spends half his time scribbling notes to Venetia. I thought at first that he was keeping minutes, but Eddie Grey told me that he's putting down his private thoughts and sometimes reporting every word we say. I'm sure they're all going straight into her bloody diary.'

'Isn't that a huge security risk?'

'You're damned right it is!'

After breakfast the next morning Winston has a private conversation with Asquith. Notoriously unable to grasp the nettle of difficult decisions, the Prime Minister has been equivocating for weeks about the various options for a new front against Germany. Winston still favours a new theatre in the north, with the seizure of the German island of Borkum being his preferred choice, followed by an invasion of the Schleswig-Holstein mainland with the support of the Russians. However, there is strong support, especially from Lloyd George, for an operation in the south, against Germany's allies, the Turks, a plan which Winston thinks is not without merits.

'Prime Minister, a good dinner last night, was it not?'

'Indeed, very good. I imagine Margot was probing you about Beauchamp?'

Winston looks away awkwardly. 'Yes, she was a little. She thinks he's a bit of an old fruit.'

'She's right, but he covers up well.'

'Really, I had no idea. I can only think of what the old King used to say when another sodomite came to light: "I thought men like that shot themselves!"'

Asquith smiles. 'If that were true, Winston, there would be piles of dead men littering the streets of St James's from Piccadilly to Pall Mall. Now to more pressing matters. What am I to do about a new front? I've read your report about the northern theatre several times. It's compelling in the main, but I hear that there are some wise heads in your own Admiralty War Group who think it, to quote them, "preposterous", and that you are – forgive me for repeating their words – "ignorant and impulsive".'

Winston is annoyed, but not surprised, that the views of dissenters in his ranks have reached the ear of the Prime Minister. 'That will be Bertie Richmond, my Assistant Director of Ops. He thinks I'm quite mad, and apparently is so vindictive about me that he says openly that I ought to be hanged for treason.'

'A little harsh, I feel! Why don't you fire him?'

'That would be foolhardy. It's always good to have sceptics around to curb one's rashness, even if they are a damned nuisance. Besides, he's clever in a fiendish sort of way and knows which end of a ship is which, not an attribute with which everyone at the Admiralty is blessed.'

'That's unusually generous of you, dear boy.'

'I'm not quite as blinkered as some suggest, and I'm not always right.' Winston grins and playfully cocks his head to one side. 'But I'm rarely wrong. In fact, come to think of it, I can't recall the last time . . .'

'You know, Winston, being Prime Minister can be very dismal, surrounded as I am by some very grey men, which is why I prefer the company of women – but you're never dull, far from it. God bless you.'

'Thank you, Prime Minister.'

'Please call me Henry when we're alone, I prefer it to Herbert, which is too reminiscent of my plebeian Yorkshire roots, and certainly to Squiffy, which I know is my nickname among my enemies.'

Winston looks down at the floor, startled that Asquith knows about his derogatory nickname, a reference to his heavy drinking.

'Surprised? It's one of the many drawbacks of being PM. The security reports I read from Scotland Yard often include direct references to me. Some are much worse than that!'

As if to make a point, Asquith goes over to a table at the side of the room. There, under the stern glare of a huge portrait of a self-righteous Duke of Wellington, sits a tray of crystal decanters and matching tumblers.

'It's eleven, Winston; a loosener before lunch?'

'Thank you. A watery malt will do very well.'

'So, what's it to be? North or south? I've got you for Borkum; Lloyd George wants Salonika or Dalmatia with the Greeks; John French is talking about how we could go in with the Montenegrins and that he could spare a division to stiffen them – not that Kitchener would stand for it; Kitchener himself favours Gallipoli through the Dardanelles, but only with your navy, not his army; while a few others, including your good friend F. E. Smith, have talked about Smyrna or Ephesus. What are we to do? You can't all be right.'

'As you say, my firm preference is for Borkum in the north. Landings in the Balkans, in Palestine or an attack through Syria all have merits, but I don't believe we can force the Dardanelles without men from France, men that Kitchener won't release.'

'What do your admirals think about the Dardanelles?'

'Well, you know what Richmond thinks – that I'm a blithering idiot – but I'm waiting for a response from Vice-admiral Carden, in command of the Eastern Med.'

'What about Fisher and Wilson?'

'In favour, in the main, but Jacky Fisher grows more and more unpredictable by the day.'

'When do you expect to hear from Carden?'

'He's sent an initial reply, which suggests it's possible by ship alone, but asked for more time. I think we'll have his full report within forty-eight hours.'

'Very well. Let's make a final decision in War Council as soon as we've absorbed Carden's report.' Asquith raises his glass. 'Is he a good man?'

'Not bad. Getting on a bit.'

'Aren't we all? To his health and his wisdom. We can't have another year like the last one.'

'Hear, hear, Henry, and, if I may, a toast to the boys at the Front. God bless them.'

'Indeed, I would do anything to bring them home.'

'We will get them home . . . and with the gleam of a glorious victory in their eye.'

'I hope so, Winston, I hope so.'

Saturday 16 January

Kemmel, West Flanders, Belgium

'What's the time, Mo?'

'Quarter to five.'

'Nearly pitch bloody black an' it ain't fuckin' tea-time yet! Can't wait fer them longer days. I 'ate winta.'

Harry Woodruff and Maurice Tait have met for a cigarette at an agreed rendezvous point in the trench between their two companies. After four days in yet another new billet at Westoutre, 4th Battalion Royal Fusiliers has just arrived back in the trenches at Kemmel, six miles south-west of Ypres, where it has relieved 2nd Battalion South Lancs and 1st Battalion Honourable Artillery Company. Fourth Fusiliers is positioned on the extreme right of the 9th Infantry Brigade, itself the right flank of the BEF's 3rd Division, part of General Horace Smith-Dorrien's II Corps of the BEF.

Kemmel, its indistinct little red-brick houses and modest arable farms inconspicuously drab, is yet another West Flanders village that has lain dormant for centuries but which is now on the battle-line of the greatest war in history.

Not for the first time in the past few days dusk has brought a flurry of large flakes of wet snow. The thick blanket that is forming, which seems to muffle all sounds, will soon transform the landscape from one of dim silhouettes to one of sharp, pencil-grey outlines.

'Snow! That's all we need.'

'Stop bloody whinin', 'Arry. I came up to 'ave a fag wiv yer and all you do is moan abaht the weather.'

'Well, it's enough to send yer doolally tap.'

Maurice changes the subject. Harry has always been a moaner, but this war, now into its sixth month, has made him much worse. 'Wot do yer make of the new colonel – Campbell? S'pose he's a Jock?'

'Dunno. Seems all right, only seen 'im once. He'd only been 'ere a couple of days when he inspected my company. He woz climbin' down into the trench when he tripped over 'is own plates o' meat an' sprained 'is bleedin' ankle! I 'ope 'e does better when it comes to a proper bull and cow wiv Fritz.'

Harry shakes his head contemptuously and takes a deep lungful of smoke from his cigarette. 'I 'ate these black Sober-annies. I 'ear the toffs smoke 'em; I think they make 'em outta dog-shit an' black treacle! You got any Willie Woodbines?'

'Nah, these are all right, though. Got 'em orf an injured Fritz officer who woz brought through Locre. All he wanted for 'em was a drop o' rum.'

The snow is coming down heavily. It is depositing a thick coating on the hand-knitted woollen scarves, gifts from the Red Cross, which the two serjeants are wearing over their Standard Dress army caps. To his amusement, their headgear reminds Harry of a confectioner's pie. 'Fuck me, Mo, yer look like you've got a dollop o' cream on yer crust!'

'Very funny, and you look like a twat in a girl's bonnet!'

The laughter the two images creates is suddenly curtailed. They can hear hurried footsteps in the mud of no-man's-land; there is the heavy breathing of someone approaching only a few yards away. Is this a surprise attack? Someone clambers into the trench. They are only feet away, but it is impossible to identify who it is. Both men raise their rifles and aim at a shadowy shape coming towards them out of the blizzard. Suicidal Germans have been known to launch frenzied attacks in the middle of the night. But instead of the pickelhaube helmet of a German foe, they see the peaked cap of a British friend. Harry bellows at the intruder. 'Identify yourself, you bloody idiot!'

The reply is breathless and inaudible but clearly emanates from an Englishman; a well-spoken one at that.

An earnest young face appears. Maurice and Harry stiffen to attention as they recognize the three pips on the young captain's uniform. Maurice speaks before Harry, knowing full well that his comrade will have recognized the cavalry insignia and will be thinking: *Another clueless cherry bum!*

'You a bit lost, sir?'

'I might be, a little. I was going to our right but now realize that 3rd Division ends here. I did shout over to some of our lads further down the line and told them that I was looking for 3rd Division HQ.'

'What did they say?'

'Well, not to put too fine a point on it, they told me to fuck off, and that I was going the wrong way.'

'Well, sir; you've now found the end of the sector: we're it. I'm CSM Tait. This is CSM Woodruff, 4th Royal Fusiliers.'

'Very good, what a relief. Captain Aubrey Smythson, C Squadron, 15th King's Hussars.' Smythson's voice is breaking; he is in shock. 'I was doing reconnaissance on a small mound just beyond our trenches with my serjeant. The snow started to fall, so we took some cover in an old shed. A flare went up and – *bang!* – my poor serjeant, John Waddle from Gateshead, wife and three kids . . .' He pauses to fight back a tear. He tries to compose himself. '. . . shot by a bloody sniper. Killed him stone dead, with a shot just above the eye. Thank God he didn't feel a thing; he was dead before he hit the ground.'

Harry sees that Smythson's hands are shaking. He is very pale and has noticeable beads of sweat on his forehead. 'Are you all right, sir?'

'I'm very cold, Colour, and a bit ashamed that I had to leave Waddle out there. But he'd gone down a shell crater and, when I tried to pull him out, I couldn't get a good footing.'

Harry's annoyance has subsided. The lad might be another cherry bum, but he is a forlorn and frightened one. And Harry knows how that feels; every soldier does.

'You were right to leave 'im. That sniper would've plugged you for sure 'ad you tried to drag 'im.'

Maurice offers him one of his Sobranie cigarettes. 'Would you like one o' these, sir?'

'Good heavens, where did you get those? They're my mother's favourite.'

'Orf a Fritz officer, for a tot o' rum.'

'Not my style, I'm afraid. Have one of these – good old British fags, Capstan Navy Cut.'

Harry grabs one with relish. 'Thank you, sir.'

As Smythson tries to light his Capstan, his hand trembles so much he fails to get the match close to the tip of his cigarette. He realizes that the two fusiliers have noticed his anxiety, which only adds to his woes. 'Actually, I am a little off beam,' he says. 'I need to get back to HQ. Do you mind . . . ?' The young officer pauses, his knees buckle and he staggers forwards. '. . . I . . . need to . . .'

Maurice grabs Smythson under his armpits to steady him. 'Sir, where's your battalion? Is it near to HQ? You might be better off there – we can send a messenger to your CO, telling him that you're reporting sick.'

Smythson becomes a little incoherent, as if he's been drinking heavily. '. . . I'm not sure where they are, I only arrived in Flanders on New Year's Eve. I was sent up to HQ and they went into billets at Locre, but I think they've moved since.'

Maurice and Harry realize that, although Smythson has three pips on his epaulettes, he is but a boy in this horrific world of muck and bullets. Maurice asks a pointed question. 'Sir, if I might ask, if you're new to the Front, why are you out doin' a recce on a night like this?'

'My CO thought it would be good for me to get the lie of the land.'

Harry cannot resist passing comment. 'Then, if you don't mind me sayin' so, sir, the man's a right crown an' anchor.'

Smythson looks at Maurice quizzically.

'A wanker, sir; it's Cockney rhyming slang.'

'I see. CSM Woodruff says what he thinks, doesn't he?'

'He does, sir, always has. Hope you don't take offence.'

The young captain smiles for the first time. 'No, Colour, don't worry. Actually, his assessment is not far off the mark.'

Both Harry and Maurice smile back. Maurice takes the young man's arm. He seems calmer. ''Ave a sit down 'ere, Captain. So, are yer from the Reserve?'

'No, India. I served with the Duke of Connaught's Lancers in Bombay for six years, where I made Captain. I came home in December and got myself a transfer to the Hussars.'

'Tot o' rum, sir? I 'ave a little 'ip flask 'andy.'

'Have you now? Don't s'pose I'll be missed at HQ for a while . . . Thank you, most kind.'

Harry cannot resist another barbed remark. 'Not in this blizzard, you won't. They'll all be sittin' on their fat fifes an' drums, warmin' themselves on loverly warm braziers an' scoffin' Maconochies.'

Smythson looks puzzled again. Maurice clarifies.

'Fifes and drums, sir – bums.'

'How amusing. You must teach me more, it will go down very well in the mess after dinner.'

'I'm sure. 'Arry will always come an' do a turn for yer, won't yer, 'Arry?'

'Bollocks I will!' Harry looks up to a clearing sky. 'Come on, sir, we need to get you back. The clouds are breakin'. This isn't a safe place to wander around in with that sniper abaht; he's got eyes like a bleedin' 'awk.'

'But it's the dark of the moon?'

'I know, Captain, but he'll see yer if yer stick your ruby red above the parapet.'

Maurice begins to translate again.

'No, wait, Colour. Ruby red – head; is that right?'

'Spot on, sir, we'll soon be makin' a Cockney outta yer. Come on. I'm going back to C Company, my Gates of Rome. Stay close.'

'Gates of Rome?'

'Got yer that time, sir: Gates of Rome – home.'

'Of course! Very good. I do like your rhyming slang.'

Smythson shakes hands with the two fusiliers. 'Gentlemen, thank you for the rum and the lesson in linguistics.'

Now Harry looks bemused. 'What's lingistics, sir?'

'Lingu*i*stics, Colour – languages. But, most of all, thank you for straightening me out. I was a bit Mazawattee for a while.'

Harry smiles at the officer in an earnest, fatherly way. 'We all get that way from time to time. I do almost ev'ry bleedin' day.'

Maurice and Smythson begin the long, awkward traverse of the trench towards the north-west. It is impossible to move at any speed or with any steadiness. There is almost a foot of water in the pit of the trench and, beneath that, almost the same depth of cloying mud. There are duckboards in certain places, but timber is in short supply and most are ramshackle at best. There is an all-pervasive stench that is all but unbearable, created by improvised sanitation and the putrefying bodies which still lie in no-man's-land. To make matters worse, after the fall of snow the clear skies are allowing the temperature to plummet to well below freezing.

As the two men navigate one of the zigzags of the trench bulwarks, less than 50 yards from where they left Harry, they see the red glow of a fire.

Maurice shouts as loudly as a hushed voice will allow: 'Who's lit a fuckin' fire? Douse it, you twats!'

Both men begin to run towards the glow. As they get closer they see that a group of men have turned an old grease tin into a small brazier.

Maurice rushes forwards and kicks the tin and its contents into the bottom of the trench, extinguishing the flames. 'You cunts! Fritz can see that for miles.'

'Sorry, Colour, but Fritz can't see this little glow down 'ere – unless he can see round corners!'

Maurice raises his fist to strike a fresh-faced corporal, the most senior man there, who cowers in terror. As he is about to strike, a bullet splats into the trench just in front of him.

'Down! Everyone down!' Maurice ducks as low as he can in the trench, then looks around to check that everyone has done the same. It is only then that he realizes that Captain Smythson is still standing. He grabs the officer's belt and pulls him on to his knees, which splash into the muddy water, sending waves halfway up the trench wall and soaking everyone to the skin.

Squinting through the gloom, the veteran Fusilier peers at Smythson. His eyes are wide open in a fixed stare; his impassive face seems frozen in time but his knuckles are white with strain. They are at his throat, as if he is trying to strangle himself. But it is not an act of suicide, it is a desperate act of self-preservation. The bullet that just missed Maurice had already found its mark. It had entered

Smythson's neck marginally to the right of his spine and exited to the left of his Adam's apple, severing both his carotid artery and jugular vein and destroying his larynx.

His life force floods through his fingers and, propelled by an involuntary vomit, spews out of his mouth, covering himself and Maurice in a shower of blood. There is just one more cough, ejecting yet more blood, as Smythson falls into Maurice's outstretched arms. The young Hussar's head lolls on to Maurice's shoulder, where it rests as if he is in a contented slumber. Maurice holds him for a while, feeling the warmth of his blood soaking through his tunic, before laying him down on the trench firing platform.

Maurice's fury at the stupidity of the men who lit the fire has subsided. He speaks calmly and quietly. 'Corporal, send for the orderlies an' get a messenger to Division HQ. This officer is Captain Aubrey Smythson, 15th King's Hussars – an' get his fuckin' name right. Finally, ask CSM Woodruff to join us 'ere.'

When Harry arrives, the orderlies have already taken Smythson away. Maurice is holding his head in his hands. Harry has never seen his old friend shed tears, not even when they were boys together. Mo never cried: not when he got hit in the face by a cricket ball as a boy, and never during all the hardships, sadness and terrors of their years as soldiers. But he is crying now.

''Arry, I've 'ad enough. Now I know 'ow you felt in Vailly last September.' Harry had lost both his company serjeant major, Billy Carstairs, and his commanding officer, Captain James Orred, in the battle. His loathing and dread of shelling and his rage at what had happened had led him into the town for a binge of drinking and cavorting. He could have been court-martialled for going AWOL, but although he lost his commendation for a DCM he kept his stripes. 'You said it was all bollocks then. And you woz right, it *is* all bollocks.'

Harry puts his arm around his comrade. 'Come on, Mo, stay strong, mate. You're the one who keeps me goin'. Don't buckle on me now.'

'I'm fuckin' cold an' 'ungry; fuckin' fed up o' tom-tit nosh in these khazis we live in like rats in a sewer; an' fuckin' fed up wi' fightin' Fritz – who seems to be a decent fella, just like us – in a war that no one can win!'

'I know, but at least Fritz is gettin' the same. If 'e can stick it, so can we.'

Maurice wipes away his tears with the cuff of his sleeve. It is covered in Smythson's blood and leaves a crimson smear across a face dirtied by the daily grime of life in the trenches and the stubble of a man unable to shave because no such luxury is possible. He points down the trench indignantly, in the direction of Smythson's departing corpse.

'That lad 'as only just fuckin' got 'ere. He thought soldierin' was policin' the wogs in Bombay, so then he volunteers to come to this shit'ole.'

Harry lifts up his life-long friend. 'Come on, mate.' He tries to be as mordantly cheerful as he can. 'It's only a war: blood an' guts; misery an' sufferin'; then we die. Nothin' new.'

Arm in arm, Maurice and Harry stagger through the mud to the small recesses cut into the side of the trench where the men sleep.

'I think we both need a swig o' rum, a couple o' fags an' a good nosh. A willin' young filly from the Mile End Road would be even better, but she's not on the menu tonight.'

Maurice smiles through his misery. 'Are you sure abaht that?'

''Fraid so.'

'Fuck! Na'er mind, tomorra's another day.'

Tuesday 19 January

Prince and Princess of Wales Dock, Royal Navy Dockyard, Gibraltar

Tom Crisp is staring out across the harbour of Gibraltar, a huge expanse of water full of British battleships, cruisers and destroyers, almost too many to count. Their new camouflage – swirls and zigzags in multiple shades of grey – seems to be at odds with the spectacular setting beneath the 1,400 feet of soaring limestone that is the Rock of Gibraltar, the European column of the Pillars of Hercules.

Gib is, like Hong Kong, Singapore and Cape Town, a home from home for Britannia's all-powerful fleet. Many of its residents are more British than the British and proud to be part of its immense empire. Although few have ever been to Britain and most are ethnically Mediterranean and speak Llanito, a form of Andalusian Spanish, the locals think of their little spit of terra firma at the tip of the continent as if it were Dorset's Portland Bill or Yorkshire's Spurn Point.

It is a beautiful afternoon; the fierce winds of winter that usually howl through the nine-mile channel that separates Europe from Africa have abated. The sea is calm and the sun as warm as on an English summer's day. Tom smiles to himself; for the first time in many months, he is relatively content.

The battlecruiser HMS *Inflexible* has been in Dock One of Gib's Royal Navy Dockyard since she returned from the Battle of the Falklands in mid-December. She has been undergoing repairs and refit ever since. One of the grand old ladies of the Royal Navy, she attracts large crowds, especially at weekends. They come to gaze at her immense scale and her new 'Dazzle' camouflage plumage, designed to make it difficult to detect her range at sea.

Fitters, carpenters and gunnery engineers swarm all over her with added urgency, as word has just been received that she is to put to sea in two days' time. The destination is not officially known, but the word below decks and in Gibraltar's bars and brothels is that it is the Eastern Mediterranean, where the ship will feature in a major new theatre of operations. A landing in Palestine is frequently mentioned, but the more informed gossip is an attack on the Turks through the Dardanelles and onwards to Constantinople.

For a young man from Presteigne, a small Welsh town in Radnorshire set hard against the English border and almost encircled by it, Tom has travelled a long way in a few short months. Having left his home, destroyed by his fiancée, Bronwyn's, affair with an older man, he found work as a carpenter, and was working on *Inflexible* when Winston Churchill, Lord of the Admiralty, ordered her to the South Atlantic in an emergency on 10 November, with all the craftsmen working on her. Chief ship's carpenter Cornishman William 'Billy' Cawson, an old sea dog with thirty years' experience in the navy, noticed his skills and when most of the artisans were put off at

Gibraltar, Tom was asked to stay on. In early December Tom was in the treacherous waters of the South Atlantic, taking part in a memorable naval encounter, the Battle of the Falkland Islands.

Here in Gib, Tom turns as he hears Billy's familiar whistle behind him. As usual, the old mariner is on about the 'good old days'.

'No matter what they reckon about trickin' the enemy, you'll never get me to agree with it. When I started out as a lad, ships were built of finest oak; lovely dark brown they was, like a gorgeous brunette. It took me a long time to get used to cold cast iron; made the old girls look cold and ugly. Then, ten year ago, they started paintin' 'em grey. I liked that; they looked well out at sea. But look at this lot.' Billy throws out his arms in despair, gesturing to the fleet in the harbour. 'It looks like a child's been let loose with a paintbrush! Bloody criminal; makes us look like a bunch of buffoons in toy ships. I ran into a bunch of Yanks the other day – laughing their socks off, they was! Had to turn round and walk the other way.'

'Oh, it's not too bad, Mr Cawson. I don't mind it, especially if it puts off Fritz's gunnery crews.'

'Well, you can keep it, as far as I'm concerned. Bring back plain battleship grey for our ladies. Anyway, we're off agin soon. I hear it's the Dardanelles.'

Tom looks blank.

'The Bosporus, lad, a bit like 'ere, between Europe and Africa, except it's between Europe and Asia. Constantinople; the Turks; they're in with Fritz.' Billy laughs. 'At this rate, young Tom, you'll have seen all the world's continents and not stepped foot on any of 'em.'

'Well, I'm in Europe now.'

'No, you're not. This is Britain, part of the empire. Britain's not in Europe.'

'That's not what my teacher used to say.'

'Your teacher sounds like a traitor! Must be a socialist!'

Tom is not as excited about putting to sea as he would have been a week ago. Since then he has fallen for a local Gibraltese girl, Violeta Robba, a waitress at the Horseshoe, a pub in the old town owned by her father. Small and dark with a well-rounded figure, she is not unlike Bronwyn, except her hair and complexion are even darker. He has seen her three times since he first asked her to stroll along Main Street with him after her morning shift at the café.

All his carnal appetites have returned, especially since Violeta allowed him to fondle her breasts at the end of their last encounter. He was certain that more of her delights would be on offer the next time they met, but that may now be a long time in the future, as *Inflexible* will soon take him far away from Gibraltar. Then again, it may not be so bad. A common phrase among Jack Tars is 'a girl in every port'; not too gloomy a prospect for a healthy young sailor.

'So, are we invading Turkey, Mr Cawson?'

'I don't think so, lad. There's no sign of troop ships. I think we're to force the Dardanelles from the sea and go on to blockade Constantinople.'

'Sounds dangerous.'

'It is. Johnny Turk will have artillery on both sides of the Straits, and the little buggers know how to use them.

They're not afeared of a scrap if it comes to it – tough little blighters, them Turks.'

The Duke's Head Hotel,
Market Place, King's Lynn

'Not a bad supper, given that we're in the middle of nowhere.'

'Oh, Kitty, I thought the lamb excellent and the pud very well done. I do love sticky-toffee! And, darling, I don't think King's Lynn's the "middle of nowhere". The middle of Norfolk, yes, but not the middle of nowhere.'

'But isn't Norfolk the middle of nowhere?'

'Oh, don't be so haughty, Kitty. You sound like a snotty duchess!'

'Really! Well, I'm not a snotty duchess just yet, but I soon will be.'

In order to discuss plans for 1915, Katherine Furse, Commander-in-Chief of the Voluntary Aid Detachment, has agreed to meet Kitty, Lady Katharine Stewart-Murray, one of her committee members, at a halfway point. Kitty, who normally resides amidst the splendour of the family home at Blair Atholl, is living at the home of family friend, Matthew, Viscount Ridley, at the far-from-modest Blagdon Hall in Northumberland. From Blagdon, her husband, Bardie, Lord Stewart-Murray, heir to the dukedom of Atholl, can be close to his regiment, the Scottish Horse, which is undertaking coastal defence duties.

'Any more news of your brothers-in-law?' asked Katherine.

'Dearest Geordie is gone, I'm afraid. It looks like he was killed in September. I doubt we'll ever find his body.'

'I'm so sorry, Kitty.'

'The Duke is in such a frightful state as a result. He spends his time locked away with his mistress in a tiny cottage on the estate. Hamish is somewhere in Germany, in a camp. But we did have a letter from him the other day. He's allowed to tell us that he's in a disused oil factory. All the other prisoners are officers, thank goodness; mostly Russians, some French and a few Belgians. He's learning Russian and playing patience!'

'What a miserable, worthless existence. It would try the resolve of any man.'

'Indeed! Capricious Frenchmen, cowardly Belgians and smelly Russians – truly awful!'

'You're exaggerating, Kitty. The French are charming, and the Belgians are holding their own. As for the Russians, I'm sure they don't smell; I'm told Petrograd is very sophisticated.'

Kitty is in a bad mood because she is disappointed about the midway rendezvous with Katherine. In a mutually agreed 'free' marriage, Kitty has made frequent trips to London for VAD work, which have allowed her to carry on a rumbustious affair with George Grey, a major in the Grenadier Guards. Since losing an eye and the use of his left arm to shrapnel in France, Grey is doing desk work for Lord Kitchener at the Ministry of War. Kitty found the dashing Grenadier irresistible when they first met at a reception at the St John Ambulance headquarters in St John's Gate, Clerkenwell. Ten years younger than her, tall, handsome and a war hero with a Military Cross to his name, he provides the kind of sexual exhilaration she lost with Bardie long ago.

Almost forty now, Kitty feels like a twenty-year-old after a tryst with her young lover. They meet at his flat in Pimlico whenever she is in London but take care never to be seen together, even at the most modest of Pimlico's eateries. Their very satisfying routine involves sex before and after a home-cooked supper and another pre- and postprandial session the following morning: an early morning 'loosener', as George puts it, and an after-breakfast 'goodbye kiss', as Kitty puts it.

Furse has just returned from France, where, after initial rejections and not a little hostility, the VAD has won its spurs as a worthy medical and welfare support operation. She is now desperate to expand the work of the VAD.

'Since we've been recognized and affiliated to the Red Cross and the St John Ambulance, things have improved dramatically. But there is so much to do. We need so many more recruits.'

'Well, lots of my friends are joining all the time.'

'Yes, but they're all independently wealthy aristocrats. We need middle-class women — even working-class girls.'

'Is that wise?'

'Why not? Most of the men we are caring for are working class.'

'But how will they be paid?'

'The trade unions. I've spoken to Harry Hyndman and others. He thinks it's feasible.'

'Good God, Katherine! Hyndman's a bloody socialist!'

'Indeed he is, but a nice one.'

'No such thing!'

'Well, he can bring us lots of girls. We need drivers, cooks, cleaners – skivvies of all sorts. Are your friends prepared to be skivvies?'

'Yes, of course. Some are doing it already.'

'But are they any good? I'd rather have girls who are professional skivvies.'

'It's crazy, if you ask me. If Hyndman sends them, they'll be socialists, suffragettes and dangerous. Do we want women like that in our –'

Kitty's tirade is cut short by a loud bang that shakes the foundations of the Duke's Head; glasses smash to the floor and one of the barmaids screams in alarm.

'What on earth was that?'

There is a look of terror etched on Kitty's face as she gets to her feet and rushes to the door. Outside, in King's Lynn's pretty Georgian market square, a crowd, many in it screaming and very distressed, gathers as people empty from pubs, restaurants and homes. Sirens begin to wail from fire engines, ambulances and police cars. Several people point to the sky. Overhead, emanating from a very large but distinctive silhouette partly hidden by the clouds, there is the low drone of an engine. Bewildered, Kitty turns to Katherine.

'What is it?'

A huge black shape moves across the night sky above them. In its wake are bright-red glows from the flames of the devastation it has wrought.

'It's a bloody Zeppelin! It's dropping bombs. They're attacking from the air!'

'God, do you mean they're invading?'

There has been talk of a possible German invasion on the East Coast since the war began and rumours that they would use their airships as a weapon to begin the attack.

'I suppose so. The coast's not far.'

People start to run, some towards their homes, shouting concerns for their loved ones; others back inside buildings, fearing that more bombs are about to drop on them. There has not been any kind of military conflict in the town for over 270 years, when it was briefly besieged during the Civil War. Now, bombs are dropping from the heavens. There are at least three red glows low in the sky, two to the west and one much closer to the north, near King's Lynn's old dock area.

Kitty begins to tremble. Like many around her, she is terrified. She has heard gunfire before, having been on many grouse shoots and even on a firing range when Bardie's Scottish Horse was training. But bombs falling from the sky in the middle of a small Norfolk town is an utterly horrifying experience. Breathless and tearful, she grasps Katherine tightly.

'I need to get back to Bardie. If they're invading, he'll be in the fighting straightaway.'

'Kitty, it's too late for the trains. Besides, if it's an invasion, the army will commandeer the railways.'

'Then I'll get a car. I must get to Blagdon.'

'No, not along the east coast. It will be crawling with Germans. Come with me to London in the morning. That's much safer.'

'I don't care. I have to go north.'

'Kitty, calm yourself. It's like this every day in France, but much worse.'

Almost hysterical, Kitty shouts, 'We're not in France! This is England. They wouldn't dare invade us!'

Katherine pushes Kitty away and holds her at arm's length.

'Come on, Kitty, get a hold of yourself. There are people around. You're the wife of the colonel of a regiment and a leader of the women of the VAD. Get a bloody grip!'

Katherine's forthright words make an impression. Kitty begins to take deep breaths and fight back the tears.

'Sorry, so sorry; you're right. No way to behave.'

The immediate panic in the town dies down a little. The drone of the airship engines has passed, and the noise of sirens and emergency vehicles has stopped. There are no more explosions and, on a still night, there is no sound of distant gunfire or artillery. Even so, thirty minutes later, a large and anxious crowd is still gathered in the centre of King's Lynn. Policemen begin to circulate among it, telling everyone to disperse to their homes. A large, moustachioed serjeant bellows the loudest.

'Come on, everyone! Off to bed. They're gone now; the raid is over. It was a German Zeppelin, but it's on its way home now, just like you should be. Come on! On yer way!'

Some in the crowd, still badly shaken by what has happened, bristle at the serjeant's tone. One woman shouts at him, reminding him that King's Lynn is their home and if they want to stay up to find out what has happened, they will. Another, an older man, tells him that he is a former soldier and wants to know if anyone has been killed and what the government has not told them about the German threat. The serjeant takes a more conciliatory approach and slowly ushers away the anxious crowd.

Katherine Furse speaks to him in a hushed tone. 'I'm Katherine Furse, C-i-C Voluntary Aid Detachment. This is my colleague, Lady Stewart-Murray, Marchioness of Tullibardine. Is this an invasion?'

The serjeant is initially surprised and sceptical about the identity of the two women. He looks closely at their clothes and particularly the large diamonds of their engagement rings, before deciding to salute both ladies deferentially. 'You're a long way from home, mum.'

'Indeed, Serjeant, but King's Lynn is a convenient meeting place for us. So, having been an appropriately inquisitive police officer, will you now answer my question?'

'Yes, mum, but I had to ask – 'ave to be careful these days. No, mum, we don't think it's an invasion. We've had no reports of any landings; no firing heard. We've called Hunstanton, Cromer and Boston – nothing – but there has been a raid over Great Yarmouth: a few casualties there. It looks like they've dropped a few incendiaries and one or two explosives, one nearby, in Alexandra Dock. They may have been making for the docks on the Humber and been blown off course.'

'What about Sandringham? Where are the Royal Family?'

'We've checked. They're in London, safe as 'ouses, mum.'

'Any casualties here, Serjeant?'

'We think a couple on the edge of town.'

'Can we help?'

'Very kind, mum, but everything's under control. Are you staying at the Duke?'

'Yes, we are.'

'Then, beggin' your pardon, ladies, I should get yourselves a stiff brandy and get yer heads down.'

Wednesday 20 January

Admiralty House, Whitehall, London

London is wrapped in a thick blanket of early-morning fog. The air is acrid, infused with the smog of thousands of domestic fires, factory furnaces and vehicle exhausts. From the Admiralty it is not possible to see across Whitehall to Gwydyr House, the home of the Welsh Office, let alone up to Trafalgar Square to the Royal Navy's greatest hero, Horatio Nelson, atop his column.

The din of horns and horses and buses and trams and the rhythmic tread of countless footsteps seems even louder than usual as people make their way to work through the murk. Accompanied by his Special Branch guardian, Serjeant John Gough, Winston Churchill has been to the Home Office for a breakfast meeting with Reginald McKenna, the Home Secretary. There is a mutual loathing between them, but the Zeppelin raid on Norfolk the previous night compelled them to meet and to try to be civil to one another. Both will be asked searching questions about how the attack was allowed to happen and, as crafty politicians do, they conduct their business together in terms of their mutual self-interest. Winston will take the lead in the Commons; McKenna will talk to Fleet Street and report that the attack was an abject failure, thanks to the diligence of the Royal Navy and the fortitude of those manning the coastal defences.

Winston and his serjeant are about to enter the Admiralty gates when Winston looks up Whitehall to where Nelson should be in sight. 'Wretched morning, Mr Gough.'

'It is that, sir.'

'Old Horatio would be able to see bugger all, even with his good eye.' Winston strides forwards, talking to himself. 'Similar weather in about a month's time might be very useful for what we have planned in the Mediterranean.'

'Is it all approved, sir?'

'Indeed it is. I'll spare you the details, but it is not going to be like a jolly weekend at the Henley Regatta.'

After several weeks of debate and argument over the correct choice for a new front against the Axis Powers, the War Council approved a major naval operation in the Dardanelles on 14 January. The decision sanctioned an attack in the Eastern Mediterranean against Turkey, which would not only open a new theatre of the war but also lend significant support to Russia, currently struggling on the Eastern Front against German and Austrian forces.

Before his breakfast meeting with McKenna, Winston had sent a detailed telegram to Victor Augagneur, the French Minister of the Navy, outlining the British plan and requesting the support of the French Navy under British command: 'The Royal Navy will attack the Turkish forts and force a passage into the Sea of Marmara. There will be a naval bombardment lasting two to three weeks, using 15 battleships or battlecruisers, 3 light cruisers and 16 destroyers, including the 15-inch guns of HMS *Queen Elizabeth*. The fleet will be assembled between 7 February and 15 February, with the attack to follow immediately thereafter.' At the beginning of the war, it was agreed that the French Navy would take the lead in the Mediterranean, so it is not going to be easy to get them to commit ships to the operation but at the same time relinquish command to a British admiral.

Winston's doubts about the operation without army support remain and he still maintains his preference for an attack across the North Sea. But his advisers, especially Admiral Carden, are confident that the Dardanelles can be forced and that the operation can succeed. So, he has thrown himself into the venture with his usual unstoppable determination.

As Winston turns to walk through the Admiralty's gates, a large truck trundles up Whitehall. Its bulky presence makes the Lord of the Admiralty pause to watch the convoy pass. The truck and its trailer are hauling a large agricultural steam tractor. The tractor is propelled by caterpillar tracks rather than wheels.

'Mr Gough, what do you make of those?'

'What do you mean, sir?'

'Those tracks on that tractor.'

'Oh, yes, sir; very useful in a ploughed field.'

'Indeed, Mr Gough.'

As soon as Winston reaches his desk, he writes a hurried note to his Prime Minister:

Dear Prime Minister,

An observation for you that might prove useful in the medium to long term. It would be quite easy in a very short span of time to fit up a number of steam tractors with small armoured shelters, in

which men and machine guns could be placed, which would be
bullet-proof. Their caterpillar system of propulsion would enable
trenches to be crossed quite easily and the weight of the machine
would destroy all barbed wire entanglements. I will give the concept
more thought and refer back to you.

Ten minutes later, the letter is delivered to Downing Street by a Royal Marine, where it is filed in the Prime Minister's 'Winston' in-tray, a repository already overflowing with months of copious correspondence from his Lord of the Admiralty. At his desk, across Horse Guards, Winston has more pressing matters to deal with and, for the time being, his imaginings about an 'armoured tractor' are put to the back of his mind.

That evening, alone for dinner with Clemmie, he is in pensive mood. 'Cat, darling, I had a couple of terrible shivers in the War Council this morning.'

'What about, Pug?'

'Well, first I had to report on a Zeppelin attack on Norfolk. Two people killed in Great Yarmouth and two in King's Lynn. Bombs from the skies, my darling. They must have flown right over our cottage in Overstrand. Nobody said anything in Council, but I'm sure they were thinking: *Where was the bloody navy?!*'

'But is it the navy's job?'

'It is while they're over the sea. But the buggers make almost no noise and, on a cloudy night, you can't see them. We need to black out our towns and cities if this continues.'

'How do they drop their bombs?'

'Not very accurately. They prefer cloud to avoid fire

from the ground. They lower a chap on a rope through the clouds, and he telephones back to tell them when to drop their bombs.'

'Hell's bells, that sounds precarious!'

'Not as precarious as being underneath him.'

'True. So what was the second shiver?'

'It was a bit alarming. Old Block was scribbling away to Venetia, as usual. I'm not sure he was even listening properly. Eddie Grey was very enthusiastic in advocating an offensive against Zeebrugge to help prevent submarine attacks – something about which he's quite right and which I would support wholeheartedly. Anyway, and bless the man, he didn't realize what he was saying; he was in full flow when he said it had to be worth an attempt and might *only cost eight thousand lives*!'

'Oh dear, but Eddie's a good man, isn't he?'

'Yes, he is, but his somewhat callous remark certainly stopped Asquith's jottings!'

'Did he say anything?'

'No, but he gave him one of those reproving looks like he does; you know, the one as if you're in the headmaster's study and you've been caught smoking in the dorm. Eddie didn't notice and carried on regardless.'

'"Only eight thousand lives." Winston, what an awful position we've come to.'

'I know, dearest one; men have become no more than cyphers in the arithmetic of this dreadful war. It was ever thus, of course, but the scale of the numbers is horrifying.'

'So, are we to attack Zeebrugge?'

'No, LG said it was too insignificant an action and not worth the effort.'

'That's a relief. Eight thousand lives saved, then!'

'Only for the time being, Cat.'

Saturday 23 January

Cant Clough Reservoir, Widdop Moor, Burnley, Lancashire

'Tell yer wot, Mick, we're nearly in fuckin' Yorkshire up 'ere.'

'Feels more like t'Arctic t'me, Tommy. I'm freezin' me nuts off!'

'Sat'day afternoon; it's a good job t'lads are laikin' away at t'Spurs, or I'd be reet moithered.'

'They'll get a reet seein'-to down there if thi laik like thi did agin City last week.'

Tommy changes the subject from Burnley Football Club to their predicament as volunteer soldiers in Kitchener's Army. 'Is'ta still thinkin' o' packin' it in, Mick?'

'Aye, am reet fed up wi' it. I want t'feight Germans, not bugger around up 'ere like little lads in t'Boys Brigade.'

'Well, wi'v med us bed, we'll 'ave t'lie in it fer now, especially if Cath and Mary go down t'London like they reckon.'

'Aye, s'pose so. I just wish they'd get on wi' it.'

Mick Kenny, Tommy Broxup and their comrades in D Company are on exercises high on Widdop Moor above Burnley. They are almost on the Pennine watershed, close to the Yorkshire border. January's weather has been atrocious. Today is no different, except that at this altitude, almost 1,000 feet, the rain that yet again is soaking the town below is an icy sleet that often turns to thick snow.

With Mick and Tommy in the same platoon are close friends Twaites Haythornthwaite and Vinny Sagar and their mentor, former club steward and local cricketing legend John-Tommy Crabtree.

Following the harrowing reports from France about the appalling conditions in the trenches, D Company's officers have decided to disperse their men across Lancashire's bleak moorland in an attempt to prepare them for what they will face at the Front. Not that their deployment overseas is imminent. Their battalion, 11th East Lancs, is still some weeks from going off to their formal military training camp in Caernarvon and months from being deployed to fight.

In command of Mick and Tommy's platoon are Lieutenant Arnold Tough, an alumnus of Sedbergh School and now a dentist in Accrington, and Captain Raymond St George Ross, an old boy of Giggleswick School and now an analytical chemist in Burnley. Insofar as the primordial chasm between officers and men will allow, Mick and Tommy have become very friendly with Tough and Ross. They know each other from local sport, where they played together as equals, and all are passionate about football and cricket. Tough and Ross love boxing and especially contemporary legend Bob Fitzsimmons, and are teaching renowned street-brawlers Mick and Tommy how to fight within the gentlemanly rules of the Marquess of Queensberry.

Not far away, doing their rounds of the various platoons of volunteers, are previously retired regular training officers Serjeants Jimmy Severn and George Lee, both Englishmen, and Andrew Muir, a Scot, who has just returned from compassionate leave after losing his son, John, at the Battle of Mons. They are trying to bring military discipline to unruly weavers and colliers and to instil in them the ability to fight and kill. Most men take to it, some do not; either way, the regime demands obedience and that they do their duty for King and country.

The men of the battalion are camping in canvas tents and cooking on open fires. They have carried their own packs and equipment on to the moor and, other than the proximity of their homes and the fact that they have been spared the waterlogged trenches, the conditions are not too dissimilar from the rigours of the Front in Flanders. To make matters even more authentic, orders to start digging slit trenches have been issued, with a promise that the men will be lying in them for most of tomorrow, no matter what the weather brings.

John-Tommy Crabtree comes over to where Mick and Tommy are standing. 'You two moitherin' agin?'

Tommy is quick to respond. 'Aye, we are, John-Tommy. Aren't you? Look at me: ave got icicles on me 'tash; I can't feel me toes, an' me fingers 'ave gone blue. Other than that, am reet as ninepunce!'

'Tha moans t'much, our Tommy. As'ta read t'casualty figures in t'*Burnley Express*?'

'Aye.'

'It's them lads at t'Front who 'ave a reet t'moan. Think on that – every bit as wet an' cald as us, but much worse, fer days on end; no Keighley Green an' a pint o' Massey's of a neet fer them. An' wi' thousands o' Germans tryin' to

94

blow their heeds off or put a bayonet in their bellies. Think on, our Tommy, and you, Mick.'

Both Tommy and Mick look a little sheepish. They would not take such a rebuke from many men, but John-Tommy is different. He has earned the right. Warming to his paternal task, he points to the platoon's two officers. 'Sken yon two, Tough an' Ross. They look like a pair o' school officer cadets, but don't be fooled. They luv it, the harder the better; they'll match yer in any test you like. Think on, both o' ya. Proper men, those two. Gents, but 'ard as nails.'

Tommy nods in agreement. 'Aye, they're alreet. Don't mind bein' led b'men like them lads. Mick an' me call 'em Rough an' Toss.'

''Ow's t'boxin' comin' on?'

'Alreet. Mick gets it better than I do. I reckon it won't be long afore he fettles Serjeant Severn.'

'That's summat I'd like to see if it 'appens!'

The next morning, a bitterly cold Sunday, when it is just possible to hear the church bells of nearby Worsthorne, the Pals complete their slit trenches. The sky is crystal clear and deep blue; the moorland air is breathtakingly pure. But it has snowed heavily overnight and the ground is covered by a half-foot-thick blanket, glistening as if littered by thousands of gemstones.

Clothed only in their uniforms and greatcoats, the men of D Company, just like their equivalents in France, spend the day simulating the mindless monotony of manning trenches. Tommy is not impressed.

'I reckoned marchin' up an' down on t'rec wer

95

bollocks, but this is fuckin' worse. Me knob's shrivelled up like a prune. I'll ne'er produce childer at this rate!'

Mick is also unimpressed by their circumstances but is full of admiration for the men in the trenches at the Front, knowing what they have to endure.

'By 'eck, Tommy, thi reckon t'trenches at the Front are eight feet deep, 'alf full o' water, an' run frae English Channel fer 'undreds o' miles; ferther than fra' 'ere t'London. Fuck me, that's a lotta diggin', even fer top colliers!'

'Is ta sayin' we should be countin' us blessin's?'

Mick smiles ruefully. 'Aye, s'pose I am. Reckon t'trainin' is a piece o' piss compared to wot them lads are puttin' up wi'.'

Then comes a welcome relief in the monotony. The orders are given for target practice for each platoon. Numerous oil drums are placed at intervals of 200, 400 and 600 yards. Three 'mad minutes' of firing are ordered for each set of targets, with a prize of a half-day's leave for the most accurate platoon. The noise is heard echoing around the moors for miles around.

'John-Tommy's Platoon', as it is known to the lads, manages to exceed an average of twelve rounds per man for each target and is by some margin the most accurate. To everyone's surprise, Twaites proves to be the best shot, followed by John-Tommy, whose eye for a cricket ball stands him in good stead. The winning platoon opts to take its prize the following Saturday afternoon, when Burnley will be at home in the FA Cup against Southend at Turf Moor.

After the target practice competition, the temperature plummets as the sun begins to fall rapidly to the horizon, but to the relief of all concerned orders arrive from Captain George Slinger, Battalion Adjutant, that the exercise is over. Lieutenant Arnold Tough confirms the command.

'Right, lads, if you get a move on, you can fill your bellies with a gallon of ale before closing time. Serjeant Muir, get them on their way!'

Three hours later, after a rapid march which ends in darkness and still in their uniforms, Keighley Green Working Men's Club is full of 11th Battalion volunteers. The men are trying their best to respond to Lieutenant Tough's invitation to fill their bellies with Massey's ale. They have been joined by Tommy's wife, Mary, and Mick's wife, Cath. Mary pulls no punches with her menfolk.

'You buggers stink; tha smells like tha's been livin' in a pigsty!'

Tommy is indignant. 'Nay, our Mary, if we'd loitered t'ave a wash, we'd 'ave lost good drinkin' time! It's no good bein' clean an' thirsty; much better t'smell like a badger than be as thirsty as a parched donkey!'

'So, did tha learn owt t'day?'

'Aye, John-Tommy fettled us about t'lads at t'Front.'

'How d'ya mean?'

'Told us to stop moitherin' an' count our blessin's!'

''E's champion, that lad. Am reet glad 'e's lookin' after you lot. Mebbe he'll get tha through it in one piece.'

Cath carries on with the teasing. 'So, tha's been diggin' trenches; dost that mean tha's proper soldiers now?'

Mick responds with a grin. 'Aye, except wi don't get shot at t'end o' t'day, we come ere an' get lathered!'

Locre, West Flanders, Belgium

The men of 4th Battalion Royal Fusiliers have just enjoyed another three nights in billets in Locre. Harry Woodruff and Maurice Tait are enjoying a beer in their increasingly comfortable serjeants' mess in the vestry of Locre's L'Église St Pierre. More and more scraps of furniture have been added by each battalion billeted there, and the walls are now festooned with incongruous military memorabilia from the fighting at the Front and bric-a-brac from the local area.

Pickelhaube helmets retrieved from no-man's-land hang next to family photographs rescued from destroyed Belgian houses. There are shelves full of old ration tins, the remnants of Red Cross parcels and empty beer and wine bottles, some with candles in them. Graffiti covers every inch of the bare walls, most of it totally inappropriate for a priest's vestry. Almost anything is utilized in an attempt to transform a stark and alien environment into a familiar home from home. There is even the frame of a bicycle against one wall, astride which is a naked female mannequin – christened 'Big Marge' by Harry, after his favourite 'lady friend' back home in Leyton.

Locre's 'Big Marge' is minus her left leg, has only half a right arm and has lost the index finger of her remaining hand. She also has two bullet holes to the head and her torso is the canvas for much graffiti, none of which is either chaste or reverential.

It will be Harry's and Maurice's last beer for a while, as the Fusiliers will be relieving their colleagues, 1st Battalion Honourable Artillery Company and 2nd Battalion South Lancs, early tomorrow morning, but not in the best of spirits. The Fusiliers' morale is being severely eroded, not by battle, but by worsening sickness and incessant sniping. The German marksmen are lethal and seem to grasp every opportunity to kill or maim any man who strays into a vulnerable position. On the day they left the trenches they suffered six casualties, three men killed outright, during the morning of their pull-out, and three more as they were being relieved. All were hit with unerring accuracy in the head; one or two particularly skilful snipers seem to be doing most of the damage.

The battalion's new colonel, Fraser Campbell, is just one of the many sick and injured. Campbell, who has now got a bad knee to add to the ankle he sprained inspecting the trenches, has not inspired much confidence so far, having twice gone sick within days of taking command. Lice, vermin, insanitary conditions, sodden trenches and ferociously cold weather are slowly wearing down even the doughtiest individuals, leaving the battalion with only about 60 per cent of its men fit and able to fight.

Maurice's and Harry's companies have not fired a shot in anger for several weeks and are frustrated that the German snipers are gradually reducing their number, as if the men were coconuts on a fairground shooting range. In an attempt to fight back, Harry has devised an audacious plan. Not only that, he has decided it will have to be executed without the consent of their officers, who, were they to ask them, would almost certainly refuse him permission.

'Next Thursday, Mo, the last night of our next stint.

It'll be the dark of the old silver spoon. We'll take four top blokes and see if we can nail at least one of those Hun twats.'

'An' how'll we do that?'

'The old soldiers' way: tunic an' boots orf; strip to the waist . . .'

'Wot, in this bleedin' cold! It'll be the death of us.'

'No, we grease oursel's up against the cold; black up wiv dubbin'; bayonet between the teeth like the Gurkha boys; crawl up close to the Hun position; wait till we see his rifle flash; then cut the fucker's head orf!'

'We'll 'ave to be sharp about it.'

'Yer, but it'll be worth it if we can do for one of 'em.'

Maurice thinks for a minute, trying to decide if Harry's plan could work. Then he smiles at him. 'Right, I'm in. Next Thursday it is.'

As Harry and Maurice raise their beer bottles to one another to confirm their clandestine mission, 4th Battalion's new serjeant major, Eddie Fothergill, walks into the mess and makes a beeline for them.

'You two been suckin' the adjutant's dick or wot?'

Harry does not like Fothergill and, rather than take the suggestion with its intended humour, bristles at the comment.

'Wouldn't dream of it, Mr Fothergill. Too many 'ave sucked it already!'

Fothergill stares at Harry and leans forwards in an attempt to intimidate him; not an easy manoeuvre, given that the top of the battalion's senior NCO's head only just reaches Harry's chin. The volume of laughter and chatter in the mess diminishes as several men realize that two old stags might be about to lock horns. Maurice sees what is coming and intercedes.

'Beer, Mr Fothergill?'

Fothergill likes a beer, and relents. 'Thanks, Colour Tait. That'll do very well.'

Maurice beckons to Harry to go and get Fothergill a bottle of the local Belgian beer, a brew that is growing in popularity in the mess. Fortunately, Harry takes the hint and wanders off to the lance corporal behind the make-shift bar, who is keeping a tally of the mess bills.

'So, Mr Fothergill, wot's our reward for suckin' O'Dowd's dick?'

'You're goin' 'ome. Two weeks' leave, the pair of yer. Not Armentières, not Paris, but Blighty.'

'Fuck me!'

'Exactly! Apparently, only an 'an'ful of senior NCOs 'ave made it this far. So you're on yer way to Calais in the morning. You jammy pair of bastards!'

Harry returns with Fothergill's beer, another for himself and one for Maurice, who continues to placate his superior: 'Your good health, Mr Fothergill.'

Fothergill swallows his beer in one gulp, salutes crisply, turns and leaves.

'Little cunt! I could swing fer 'im.'

'Yer might change yer mind, 'Arry, given the news 'e's just brought.'

'Wot's that, then?'

'We're gonna 'ave to postpone next Thursday's little mission.'

'Why, wot 'ave we done?'

'Nothin', fer a change. We're goin' on leave; two weeks, to Blighty, first thing in the mornin'.'

'Fuck a duck!'

'Too right, mate!'

'You know wot, Mo?'

'Wot's that, 'Arry?'

'Yer see Big Marge over there on 'er bike?'

'Yer.'

'Well, after a skinful in the Drum with me old fella, I'll be round to see the real Big Marge. Talk abaht saddle-sore – she won't be able to sit darn fer a week!'

'So wot do wi do abaht the Hun sniper?'

'We nail 'im when we get back!'

Gallipoli: The Nightmare Begins

Tuesday 9 February

The Cabinet Room, 10 Downing Street, Whitehall, London

The War Council has been sitting all afternoon. Sir John French, Commander-in-Chief of the British Expeditionary Force in France, has travelled from his HQ in St Omer, Normandy, to attend. Dinner appointments have been cancelled and sandwiches are being served, as the meeting is unlikely to end until late evening. Winston is in his element. The previous two weeks have gone well for him and the Royal Navy.

On 23 January, making use of a German naval code book sent to them by the Russians and an intercepted German signal revealing that twenty-six ships of the Kriegsmarine's High Seas Fleet were to sail that night, Admiral John Jellicoe was ordered to attack. The next day, off Dogger Bank in the North Sea, battle was joined. It was an impressive victory for the Royal Navy, as the German armoured cruiser *Blücher* was sunk with the loss of over a thousand men and the rest of the Fleet fled back to port.

Most importantly for the military strategists, and the Admiralty in particular, there now seems to be unity about the wisdom of a new theatre of operations in the Eastern Mediterranean. Jacky Fisher's increasing stubbornness has abated, his changes of mind have ceased and he now supports the plan. Also, the French have agreed to play a major role and to do so under British command.

Winston's star seems to be in the ascendancy, with much public praise for what the press called a 'glorious' victory at Dogger Bank, and a private audience with the King to brief him about the planned action in the Dardanelles, which was followed by a handwritten letter of thanks.

Best of all, the War Council seems to be coming round to the idea that, should the navy's forcing of the Dardanelles be successful, the need for a significant army presence to secure the Gallipoli Peninsula will be crucial. Encouragingly, apart from Winston's own well-trained Royal Naval Division, there is talk of a large force of Australian and New Zealand troops and the excellent 29th Division, a mix of five battalions of various Fusiliers, three of Borderers battalions, along with 2nd Hampshires, 4th Worcesters, 1st Essex and 5th Royal Scots.

Winston, after holding court for a major part of the evening in the War Council, especially in trying to persuade Kitchener and French to commit the army to the Dardanelles cause, has the last word, just as the clock strikes ten fifteen.

'So, Prime Minister, to conclude. As I said to His Majesty the King last evening, our preparations could not be better. The first wave, led by the *Queen Elizabeth* and her eight 15-inch guns, will consist of six battleships; the second wave will also be six battleships, including four from our French comrades. The third and final wave will consist of four more battleships. Sixteen battleships in total, gentlemen; 196 guns at 6-inches or better! The Turks will not know what has hit them, but will know only too well from whence it came, because only the Royal Navy could deliver such a mighty blow.'

After the Council members disperse, Asquith asks Winston to join him in his study for a drink. Venetia Stanley is there, who finds Winston to be a bit like a curate's egg. She loves his kindness, wit and energy, but loathes his vanity and political ambition.

Although Venetia is ten years younger than Winston and over thirty years younger than the Prime Minister, she acts like a matriarch to both. As she hands Winston a tumbler of malt and smiles warmly, she begins what Winston is certain is going to be a reproach.

'How are Clemmie and the family?'

'They are well, thank you. It is such a comfort to have them with me at the Admiralty.'

'It must be. How does Clemmie cope with three little ones? She is a marvel.'

'She is. I am a fortunate man.'

'Henry tells me that, as usual, you held centre stage today.'

'I hope, Venetia, that I did so eloquently.'

Asquith interrupts. 'You were stirring, as always, Winston, but perhaps at times it was more like a speech in the House than a factual account in Council.'

Like a concerned mother, Venetia puts her hand on Winston's arm. 'Dearest Winston, your talents are so obvious and so prodigious, you don't have to remind us about them quite so often.'

'Perhaps I did get a little carried away. But I am enthused

by the fight. What we are about is not for the faint-hearted; if leaders don't go into battle with the bit between their teeth, how can we expect our sailors and soldiers to do the same? I wouldn't say this to too many people, but so many of our generals and admirals are old men, who have perhaps lost the spark they had as young officers. Yet they are commanding young men, who need inspirational leadership; vitality and verve; vim and vigour!'

Asquith frowns. 'Most of them are about the same age as I am. Does the same argument apply to prime ministers?'

'Not at all, and forgive me if that's what I implied. Politicians have a different role. They need experience and wisdom, not dash and elan; that's for the battlefield . . .'

Venetia and Asquith exchange glances as Winston goes into detail for several minutes about the qualities needed by political leaders as opposed to military leaders. They listen intently until Asquith, yawning very pointedly, gets up from his chair and says that he must get some sleep.

After Winston leaves, Venetia pours Asquith another malt. She smiles as she does so. 'It's hard to tell Winston not to be so arrogant and pompous when he is so entertaining with it.'

'Quite.'

Venetia pours herself a drink and goes to sit on Asquith's lap, where she purrs contentedly. 'How much of a risk is this Dardanelles operation, my darling?'

'Not much, I hope. Everyone is confident; the theory is good. I suppose a lot depends on how much resistance Johnny Turk puts up.'

'And Winston? Didn't he want an invasion across the North Sea?'

'He did, but he's now fully embraced the Dardanelles. He wants an army to go as well, of course, but I'm not sure K will let him have one.'

'He so wants to be in charge, doesn't he? To be at the Front, leading us all to victory, sword held high, breast-plate gleaming in the sun?'

'He does; you describe it so well. It rankles with K and the generals, and with many of Winston's own admirals, especially when he wears one of those silly uniforms he likes to concoct.'

'Would you make him Minister of War if Kitchener went?'

'Yes, without even blinking. If any man can win this war with, as he puts it, "vim and vigour", it's him, but he might put me in my grave in doing so.'

'Could he ever be Prime Minister?'

'No, never; he's too much of a maverick – a brilliant one, but also an infuriating one. He makes too many enemies.'

'So what of his future?'

'I suspect he'll burn himself out.' Asquith pauses to savour a mouthful of his drink, warming to his description of Winston. 'Yes, like a beautiful summer butterfly, a Red Admiral: so vibrant and colourful, then it's gone.'

'Do you mean an early death?'

'Not necessarily, although his family is not long-lived. But his energy might turn to bitterness if he doesn't get his way. He can get very moody, even morose. He'll prob-ably end up on the back benches, eventually as a Tory, for that's what he is deep down. He'll snipe from the wings, go to fat and write withering articles about the government of the day, full of clever verbosity and flowery prose. But he'll still be on everyone's dinner-party list, until he upsets them one by one.'

'Oh dear, what a sad picture you paint.'

'Perhaps, but I've got him in his prime and I'm going to make full use of him.'

When Winston returns to the Admiralty he finds Clemmie has waited up for him with a nightcap in hand.

'How was it, Pug, darling?'

'Very good; all is in hand. I think French is relieved there'll be another front for people to worry about.'

'And the plans for the Dardanelles are all in good order?'

'Yes, I might even get some infantry – the tide is turning in Council on that. Largely because it's blindingly obvious.'

'I hope that doesn't mean darling Jack will be going?'

'No, he will stay with French in St Omer. But Bardie Stewart-Murray may get his wish. I think there's a good chance the Scottish Horse will be on K's list to support the 29th Division.'

'That will be a big relief. Guarding the north-east coast will be driving Bardie to distraction, and I'm not sure Kitty enjoys travelling up and down from Northumberland every week. How was the Old Block?'

'On very good form. Venetia was there, so he was very relaxed. He's absolutely besotted; like a youngster in love for the first time.'

'Poor Margot. That woman's a saint. Do you think she knows?'

'I'm sure she does.'

Winston takes a mouthful of his malt before laughing out loud.

'I nearly forgot. After Council, OB asked me to his study for a dram. I was to receive some paternal advice about my demeanour, I think. You know, "Winston's vanity", and so on. I felt like I was back in my house at Harrow with my housemaster and his wife. My God, Venetia is only a child herself!'

'So did you take it in good part?'

'Not really, I gave a brief acknowledgement, then carried on as usual, with, of course, an extra portion of vanity. I even hinted – very obliquely, mind – that Asquith might one day have to bow to a younger man.'

'Be careful, Winston; OB's a good man and a good friend.'

'Yes, I know; I was only teasing him.'

'Even so, as they say, pride comes before a fall!'

'As who says? I loathe that expression, it's silly, Cat. Besides, if I have to take a fall, my pride will help me get back up again.'

Friday 19 February

HMS Inflexible, *off Cape Helles, Dardanelles*

'So, Mr Cawson, is this it?'

'Aye, lad, she's getting up speed. Constantinople, here we come!'

Ship's Carpenter Tom Crisp and Chief Carpenter Billy Cawson are on HMS *Inflexible*'s deck as the battlecruiser steams forwards into the mouth of the Dardanelles. The Dardanelles is a deep channel between Europe and Asia, a little more than two miles wide at its mouth, which leads eventually into the Sea of Marmara, over 40 miles away. Further up the channel, at The Narrows, the gap is less than a mile. It is a place of maritime legend and has been one of the most dangerous routes in naval history.

Currently, the Turkish defences consist of two major forts at the mouth of the Dardanelles Channel, Sedd-el-Bahr on the European side and Kum Kale on the Asiatic shore. There are also two major fortifications at The Narrows: Kilid Bahr on the European bank and Chanak Kale on the opposite side.

The Channel is also festooned with German-manufactured artillery pieces: 75mm Krupp field-guns; 75mm Schneider mountain guns and a few 150mm Krupp and Schneider-Creusot howitzers. All in all, the British ships will have to run a gauntlet of artillery all the way to the Sea of Marmara.

The battlecruiser HMS *Inflexible* is line abreast, third from the right amidst her five sister ships. She has *Prince George* and *Triumph* on her starboard side, and *Lord Nelson*, *Agamemnon* and Admiral Sackville Carden's flagship, *Queen Elizabeth*, to her port. They have sailed from Mudros Bay on Lemnos, 50 miles to the west, the island which the Greek government has granted as a base for the operation.

The weather is fine and the sky clear when, just before 10 a.m., the bombardment of the Turkish defensive gun emplacements begins. The plan is to destroy systematic-ally the Turkish defences, leaving the route through to Constantinople open to an unopposed attack from land and sea. The assumption is that, with their defences gone, the Turks will either capitulate, or there will be a pro-Allied coup in Constantinople which will welcome the Allies with open arms.

The attack is relentless. From the ships, it looks as if little – the defences of the Turks, or the Turks themselves – could survive such an onslaught. But surface explosions, with their thunderous noise, bursts of flame and billow-ing smoke, can be deceptive. Astutely designed defensive fortifications and defenders with resolve, dug in deep underground, can survive attacks that seem over-whelming.

The Allied planners may well have underestimated their foe. It will not be the first time, nor the last.

Tom grabs the ship's rail and gasps as volley after volley from *Inflexible*'s 15-inch guns make her entire superstructure shudder and her hull lurch sideways in the water. The noise is deafening as smoke swirls around the deck and the smell of cordite fills the air.

'Bloody hell, Mr Cawson, she's fair lettin' rip!'

'She is that, lad. But that's only a few early farts, wait till she really gets goin' and empties her belly. Those gun barrels will be red hot soon.'

The attack continues until dusk, when Carden orders the ships to withdraw.

Tom is feeling distinctly queasy by the end of the day. As a result of helping the armourers move shells to the gun turrets, he has not eaten and has had very little to drink. He is covered in oil and dust, and his eyes are red-rimmed and watering. His hearing has been reduced to nothing better than ringing echoes of the day's shelling. Billy puts his arm around the young sailor.

'Come on, lad, let's get you below decks and get some grub inside yer.'

'How did we do, Mr Cawson?'

'Not too well. Lots of explosions around the Turks' guns, but I don't think we hit much. None of their magazines went up.'

'But we sent enough shells over.'

'We need to get in closer, but old Carden's a bit too cautious for that. He's not Lord Nelson, that's for sure. He was Admiral Superintendent of Malta afore this lot kicked off, which is usually a job for old sea dogs past their prime.'

'I was told he was a good man.'

'He is, but that don't make 'im a good commander. You have to be ruthless to win battles. Below decks they all reckon Arthur Limpus should have got the job. Apparently, he used to be Naval Commissioner to the Turks before they threw in their lot with the Hun. He knows them and the Dardanelles like the back of his hand.'

'So why didn't they pick him?'

'Cos our ambassador in Constantinople thought the Turks would be upset if we chose him.'

'How do you mean? I thought the Turks were our enemies now. Besides, we're blowin' up their bloody artillery positions – that might upset 'em a bit too.'

'I know, daft ain't it? That's diplomats for yer.'

'So what will happen now?'

'Back to Lemnos, take on more ammo and come back for another crack.'

However, a severe gale and bad visibility postpone the bombardment, giving the Turks time to strengthen their defences and move many more men on to the peninsula. When the attacks resume, shells from the Turkish positions fill the air before the British guns can open fire, suggesting that little damage has been sustained in the first attack.

Tom can see the flashes of the Turkish guns onshore, then counts the seconds before the shells arrive overhead. Billy Cawson tells him that if you can hear their screech you are safe; it is the one you cannot hear that will kill you. Not clear how reassuring that information is, he watches with increasing trepidation as *Inflexible*'s neighbour, *Agamemnon*, is hit seven times in just ten minutes. Fortunately, the shells are small and little damage is caused. Even more fortuitously, *Inflexible* is spared altogether.

Tom is exhilarated by the battle; regrets about leaving Violeta back in Gibraltar are forgotten as he thinks of new adventures to come.

'What are Turkish girls like, Mr Cawson?'

'Big and hairy, lad, especially round the minge.'

'What, all of them?'

'In the main. You might get a slim one, but she'll still have a fanny like a forest.'

Tom's thoughts drift back to Violeta. Although he never got to the point of discovering how hirsute her nether regions were, he is sure they are not like 'a forest'.

Royal Navy Marines, in their distinctive blue uniforms, prepare to go ashore to consolidate the damage done to the forts and guns. The marines to be put ashore from *Inflexible* are eighty-four men from 11th, Plymouth Battalion, Royal Marine Light Infantry. Their exploits will be just one example of what will become Gallipoli's many legends. Tom helps them board their landing craft, handing them their equipment and wishing them well.

One of them, Johnny Donaldson, a burly Brummie serjeant as big as a house, nods in appreciation as Tom hands him extra bandoliers of ammunition.

'Thanks, lad. Hope we don't need all this – your navy guns are supposed to have made Johnny Turk run for the hills. Why do I have my suspicions he might just have gone to ground?'

'I'm sure he's scarpered, Sarge.'

'My granddad fought with the Turks when they were on our side in the Crimea. He said they were tough little buggers. So I'm not banking on it, make sure there's a tot o' rum waiting for us.'

'Will do, Sarge.'

'Good lad, I'll bring you back a kabalak, one of their funny-looking caps, as a souvenir. My granddad gave me his when he died. We keep our eggs in it at home.'

'Thanks, Sarge. I can wear it below decks. I'm always banging my head on something or other.'

As the marines go ashore, Tom watches intently, taking turns with Billy Cawson's field glasses. The landing is initially unopposed, as is the ascent up to the fort, but the Turks spring an ambush as soon as the marines come into the open. Four men are killed instantly by the Turks' lethal Maschinengewehr 08 machine guns; eight more are wounded. Tom watches them fall. At first there is no sound, making it seem unreal, like they are collapsing in slow motion as in a piece of amateur theatre. Then the delayed sound arrives: the sickening *rat-a-tat-tat*, making it all too real.

Johnny Donaldson's 15 Platoon becomes trapped in an enfiladed position between two machine-gun posts and over two dozen riflemen. The platoon is cut to pieces. A few manage to find cover, but Johnny is not one of them. He is hit several times in the chest, which explodes in a cascade of blood. Thankfully, it takes him only moments to die.

Tom can do nothing to help as men strive to find protection in any hollow in the ground, behind a pile of rocks or a small bush not even in bud. He watches as man after man is hit by accurate Turkish fire. They are like ducks in a fairground shooting stall, but have even less chance. Usually, shooting-gallery owners adjust the sights on their rifles so they do not align properly. The Turks have been trained by German sharpshooters, their sights are spot on and they are lethally proficient.

Knowing that sooner or later they will be hit, several marines make a dash for it across open ground. Most get no more than five yards before they are cut down. Some, weaving and crouching to make themselves less easy to hit, get much further, but their flight is futile. The intensity of fire is too great and, one by one, they succumb.

Everyone watching from the ships hopes and prays that each desperate dash will be successful, but none is. One man is hit several times, falls to the ground and is motionless. However, he is not dead. He waits for the Turks to look elsewhere for a target before hauling himself to his feet and resuming his escape. One leg is badly wounded and he has to use all his strength and courage to drag it behind him.

Cheers ring out from the ships as he makes it another 20 yards. He is now only feet away from the landing craft. Then he throws his head back and stops. He has been hit in the back. Another bullet strikes him and he half turns as the impact twists his shoulders to his right. The cheering stops and the stricken man falls into the sand for the last time.

Bob Jones of 13 Platoon is among the dead, as is George Dyter of 14 Platoon, two men Tom spoke to earlier to wish them luck. Another man Tom recognizes is Jimmy Dickinson, a renowned teller of dirty jokes and blessed with a good singing voice. His leg is all but severed above the knee by multiple bullets. Dragging Dickinson and several others as they go, the few surviving marines make their way on to the landing craft under the withering fire from above. Tom can see the thick trail of Jimmy's blood all the way along the beach and watches as he is bundled aboard. Jimmy is already dead. However, as a marine, there is one comfort: he will be buried at sea, not on foreign soil.

There are audible cheers from the Turkish defenders, which serve only to multiply the anger of the Allied observers. Nevertheless, even the most indignant onlookers know that war is war and, if the circumstances were reversed, every Allied man would, without mercy, shoot to kill, just as their enemies have done. Such is the horror of war.

Only fifty-nine men make it back to *Inflexible*, four of whom are severely wounded. Half a dozen more are carrying lesser injuries. As Serjeant Donaldson said, Johnny Turk had gone to ground, and the 'tough little buggers' can fight.

Ominously for the Allies' grand scheme in the Dardanelles, the Turkish defenders are increasing in numbers and their resolve is stiffening. Most significantly, carefully laid Turkish minefields, some mines newly placed under cover of darkness and unknown to the planners on the *Queen Elizabeth*, are hampering Carden's attack far more than had been anticipated.

Reports sent back to London begin to look increasingly gloomy. Carden, who is in his late fifties and has a severe stomach ulcer, is wilting under the pressure. The Admiralty wants progress soon, and Winston Churchill's impatience is growing. Kitchener has sent in General Sir William Birdwood, Commander of the Australian and New Zealand Army Corps training in Egypt, to reconnoitre the situation. His report makes it very clear that he believes it unlikely that the navy will be able to force the Dardanelles without the support of the army.

A simple, swift and decisive strike to open up a new theatre of the war is suddenly becoming complex, ponderous and inconclusive.

Saturday 20 February

Blagdon Hall, Seaton Burn, Northumberland

Blagdon Hall is an impressive Georgian pile just off the Great North Road, nine miles north of Newcastle. It has been in the White Ridley family for several hundred years. The current owner, Matthew White Ridley, 2nd Viscount Ridley, is Colonel and Commanding Officer of the Northumberland Hussars. His wife, Rosamund, is first cousin to Winston Churchill.

The White Ridley's have been playing host to Bardie and Kitty Stewart-Murray for the past six weeks while Bardie's Scottish Horse have been undertaking coastal defence duties. Annoyed that his regiment was not sent to France in the first place, Bardie has become more and more frustrated at being isolated in the north-east of England, 300 miles from London and even further from the Front.

But today his mood has changed dramatically. At eight fifteen this morning a messenger arrived in the middle of breakfast. Bardie and Matthew were all togged up, ready for a day of stalking, when a Coldstream Guards serjeant from the Army's Northern Command in York handed over a top-secret telegram from Lord Kitchener to Bardie. It read: 'Dear Bardie, His Majesty the King and I are coming north, May, inspection tour. Dates to follow from

HM's PS, Stamfordham. Inspection of Scottish Horse and White Ridley's N-Hussars on our list. Also, will have mission for you overseas soon thereafter. Get your men in tip-top shape. Yours, K.'

Even though it is only nine o'clock, a second bottle of champagne has just been popped as Kitty and Rosamund appear for breakfast, surprised to find that their husbands have not left for their shoot. Rosamund looks on sternly as Matthew fills Bardie's glass.

'Champagne before a shoot! I hope the ghillies have their wits about them.'

'The shooting is cancelled, darling. Bardie has had some splendid news. We're all going to the Royal in Newcastle for lunch to celebrate.'

Kitty is impatient.

'Bardie, for goodness' sake, stop quaffing champers and tell us the good news.'

'It's in two parts, Sweet Pea. First of all, the King and Kitchener are coming up in May to inspect my Scotty Boys and Matthew's Geordies.'

Rosamund's eyes light up. 'My goodness! Where will they stay?'

Matthew takes two more glasses of champagne from his butler and hands them to the ladies.

'Roz, don't get your hopes up. I think they'll stay with the Percys at Alnwick. Stamfordham will confirm the details in due course.'

Rosamund frowns. 'That little shit!'

Bardie is taken aback. Stamfordham is the King's Private Secretary, and he has met him several times in London and at Blair Atholl.

'Oh dear, Roz. I take it you're not fond of the old boy.'

'He's a trumped-up vicar's son from just down the road who smarmed his way into the old Queen's affections when she was in her dotage.'

Not interested in Rosamund's prejudices and keen to impart his news, Bardie interrupts. 'You haven't heard the best bit yet. K says he will have an overseas posting for me after the inspection.'

Kitty is delighted for Bardie. 'At long last, darling; absolutely splendid news! France, I assume?'

'Perhaps not. There's lots of scuttlebutt in York and Catterick about a new front, perhaps across the North Sea or in the Med.'

'Well, if it's in the Med, I definitely want to come too!'

'Darling, the days when wives went on campaigns are long gone. Wars are not fought by gentlemen any more, they are fought by the masses; no luxuries, no wives, no rules.'

A very liquid lunch ensues, followed by a very hairy drive home with a cross-eyed viscount at the wheel of his Rolls-Royce Silver Ghost. The four celebrants finally stagger back to Blagdon Hall at six thirty in the evening, when yet more champagne is consumed, followed by a supper as profligate as their lunch. Because they 'know how to behave', they remain polite to the butler and the servants despite falling into an ever more profound drunken stupor until Matthew brings the celebration to a close with a toast. He is barely coherent but somehow manages to get the challenging syntax past a tongue that seems to be at odds with his teeth.

'To the King and Kitchener, God bless them both!

May the Scotty Horse and the Geordie Hussars bring glory to Scotland and England . . . Oh, I forgot the Welsh and Irish . . .' He pauses for a moment, before giggling like a schoolboy. 'Well, bugger the Welsh and Irish!'

His outburst produces howls of delight as all four empty their glasses for the final time.

Sunday 21 February

Burnley Lads' Club, Manchester Road, Burnley, Lancashire

'Well done, Mick.'

'Thank you, sir.'

'No need to call me sir, Mick. It's Sunday, and we're at the club. Arnie will do fine.'

Mick Kenny, Tommy Broxup, Vinny Sagar and Twaites Haythornthwaite are, as usual on a Sunday, relaxing at Burnley Lads' Club. Mick has been in the boxing ring, where Arnold Tough has been coaching him in the subtleties of the Marquess of Queensbury's Rules and the nuances of ringcraft. Tough is there with his friend, Raymond Ross, another lover of the art of pugilism and a strong supporter of the club. During the week, Tough is a lieutenant and Ross a captain in the men's battalion, their officers, not their friends, and the men have to jump when commanded to do so.

Everyone in D Company is in good spirits because final orders have just been received from the War Office confirming that, on Tuesday next, the entire Accrington Pals Battalion will set off for its training camp in Caernarvon. As a consequence, Cath and Mary have already made their plans to travel to London to see if socialist leader Henry Hyndman can get them placed in the Voluntary Aid Detachment.

Everything is about to change for this small group of lads and lasses from Burnley.

As Mick towels himself, Tough and Ross take him to one side. Raymond Ross does the talking. 'Mick, are you still bored by all this military training?'

'Aye, I am. It's drivin' me daft.'

'Even though we'll soon be off to a proper training camp?'

'Aye, but it'll still b'trainin', not feightin'.'

'I understand. In that case, something's in the offing that might be of interest to you. The Germans have begun tunnelling under the trenches on the Western Front and laying explosives. Then they have withdrawn and detonated them. It's created mayhem in some sectors.'

'Sorry, sir, wot's "mayhem"?'

'A bloody mess, Mick.'

'That's feightin' dirty. Reckon that's not in t'Queensbury Rules.'

'Indeed it isn't. But the good Marquess's idea of a fair fight doesn't apply at the Front; it's more dog-eat-dog.'

'My sort o' feightin'.'

'Exactly.'

'So, what's tha sayin'?'

'Well, there's a senior officer doing the rounds up here. He's coming to see D Company tomorrow. I met him on Friday with the Accrington lads. He's called Major John Norton-Griffiths. He's quite a character, someone I think you would take to: an engineer, self-made millionaire, MP; he was adjutant of Lord Roberts' personal bodyguard during the Boer War in South Africa and has built bridges, docks, railways – everything – all over the world.

He's done the lot; they call him "Empire Jack". He's also called "Hell-fire Jack". I'll let you guess why.'

'So wot's 'e got t'do wi' owt?'

'You're a miner?'

'Aye, afore I got into this soldierin' malarkey.'

'Well, Major Norton-Griffiths is looking for miners. He's persuaded the War Office to give him a blank piece of paper to create a tunnelling company within the Army's Royal Engineers.'

'So that wi can dig tunnels under t'Germans an' tek feight to 'em under t'ground?'

'Yes, exactly.'

'Sounds reet enough to me.'

'Apparently, the major's own engineering company has built sewers in Manchester and Preston, and he's already recruited many of his former workers for his tunnelling operation in France. He calls them clay-kickers.'

Mick's eyes light up. He knows all about clay-kickers. 'Clay-kickin' is wot tha dos in a confined space in soft ground, when tha's no room to swing a pick. Tha uses tha feet to kick at t'earth to get it loose. We don't do it i' Burnley; it's different ground 'ere. We use t'pick an' shovel. Either way, it's fuckin' 'ard work.'

'Listen, Mick, if you're interested in the major's new company, you'll be in London on Wednesday: no training, no drill. You've already got all the skills you need: no bull, no spit and polish. You will be in France by the weekend and digging the following week.'

'Is tha serious?'

'That's what the major said. He took three Accrington lads, miners from Hapton, on Friday.'

'I know t'lads frae Hapton – champion colliers. It's a deep shaft; long roads, frae an' back.'

'So, are you interested?'

'By 'eck I am, but a'll ata talk t'Cath. An' then tha's t'other lads. They're weavers, not colliers. Tommy an' John-Tommy wouldn't be interested; not sure abaht Vinny an' Twaites. S'pose thi could be baggers.'

'What's a bagger?'

'Lads who do t'diggin' are called facemen. Baggers bag up spoil an' get rid on it.'

'Will you speak to them?'

'Aye, a'will. But a'll ata square it wi' Cath first. She's t'foreman-tackler, in our 'ouse. I'm just t'under-fettler.'

That evening the mood is sombre in the Keighley Green Club. There are thoughtful expressions on the faces of the seven friends sitting around their favourite table near the bar. They all know that it may be a long time before they are all together again. John-Tommy tries to lighten the mood.

'Stew an' 'ard all round? New steward sez that, as we're buggerin' off next week, it's on t'ouse.'

The traditional East Lancashire stew of minced brisket on top of oatmeal havercakes soon arrives, as do jugs of Massey's ale for the men, Cath's ginger beer and Mary's milk stout. There is more than a minute of hush as each of the seven reflects on their future, before John-Tommy, bewildered by Mick's decision to join the army's new tunnelling company, breaks the silence.

'Joinin' up to feight t'Germans is one thing, but to do it in 'oles in t'ground is summat else altogether.'

Mick smiles. 'Tha mebbe reet, John-Tommy, but I'll be fettlin' them Germans long before thee.'

Cath takes a nip of her ginger beer and, looking directly at her husband, shakes her head disapprovingly. ''E's a daft appeth. Crawlin' around in little tunnels – I can't bear thinkin' abaht it. Am washin' me 'ands o' 'im. At least if he pops his clogs, they won't ata bury the big bugger!'

John-Tommy turns to Twaites and Vinny. 'An' wot abaht you two oily rags. You're goin wi' 'im?'

Vinny answers for both of them. 'Aye, wi think so. We've 'ad a natter abaht it, an' Mick reckons 'e'll get us in as his baggers.'

'But tha's ne'er been down t'pit.'

'Nay, we 'aven't, but anythin' to get out o' this marchin' up an' down on t'moors. At least it's warm under t'ground.'

'Who told yer that?'

'All colliers tell yer that.'

'Aye, but they're a long way down. How deep, Mick?'

''Undreds o' feet, John-Tommy.'

'Tha won't be diggin' that deep under t'Germans. Tha'll still be cald an' wet, just like on t'moors, but tha'll be cooped up like badgers in a sett. But above yer it'll be wick wi' t'Germans droppin' bombs on yer! Think on, the pair o' yer.'

Vinny and Twaites blanch a little and stare at one another before Vinny takes a deep swig of his beer. 'We'll be alreet wi' our Mick. 'E'll look after us.'

Mary, suddenly fighting back a tear, looks down at her drink. 'Wot's to become on us? This time next week John-Tommy and our Tommy will be in Wales, these three silly buggers will be diggin' 'oles in France, an' Cath an' me a'll be in London, talkin' posh wi' them toff lasses. It's a reet to-do.'

Tommy almost chokes on his Massey's at the thought of his wife 'talkin' posh'. 'By 'eck, ad like to sken that. But don't come back t'Burnley talkin' like a toff.'

Cath comes to Mary's aid. 'Don't, Tommy. Mary's upset.'

John-Tommy tries to offer a bit of humble wisdom. 'Come on, let's 'ave another drink. Tomorra's another day. What will be will be.'

When Mick, Vinny and Twaites stand in front of Major Norton-Griffiths the next morning the recruiting process is as straightforward as Captain Ross said it would be. Hell-fire Jack is every bit as imposing as his reputation suggests. Tall, slim, straight-backed, he looks immaculate in his brushed khaki; his heavy moustache, neatly trimmed, sits on his top lip in perfect symmetry.

'So Private Kenny, you're a miner by trade, a faceman. These two, Sagar and Haythornthwaite, are your baggers.'

'That's correct, sir.'

'Have you ever worked in clay, Kenny?'

'No, sir, only coal, we work wi' pick an' shovel 'ere i'Burnley.'

'How many pits in this area?'

'Can't count 'em, sir; 'undreds. But tha's a lot more weavin' sheds. Burnley's not called King Cotton fer nowt. We just dig t'coal to fire t'mills' furnaces.'

'How do you get on with the local weavers?'

Mick looks at Hell-fire Jack with an ominous leer. 'Like yard-dogs feightin' o'er a bone.'

The major nods appreciatively. 'I hear you go by the name Mad Mick?'

'Aye, sir, ave bin called that.'

'Well, I go by Hell-fire Jack. We'll get on well. Are you happy to go tunnelling under the German lines – minimum of propping; timber will be scarce – because that's what you'll be doing in France?'

'Yes, sir, Captain Ross has told us all abaht it. And am used to getting by wi'out many props. Mine owners are as tight as ducks' arses when it comes to brass fer propping.'

'Very good. He tells me you're a bit of a pugilist.'

'A wot, sir?'

'A boxer, Kenny.'

'Aye, that's reet, sir, but am still learnin' 'ow t'feight proper, like t'captain can.'

Norton-Griffiths stands and shakes Mick's hand. 'Very well. You're in, Kenny, and your two baggers. We need baggers just as much as we need diggers. We call ourselves moles. The top brass think we're mad. Are you happy to be mad moles?'

'Bin called a lot worse, sir.'

'Sagar, Haythornthwaite, anything to say?'

In unison, both answer, 'No, sir.'

'Strange name, Haythornthwaite. What does it mean?'

'A "thwaite" is a field up 'ere, sir. So it just means "hawthorn-field". Me ancestors must a bin farmers.'

'Interesting. Well, a foreign field awaits you, lad – or at least the bowels of one. You'll all be in London the day after tomorrow, to be kitted out, and in France by the weekend, where we will meet again. *Bon voyage.*'

The three Burnley boys look perplexed. Captain Ross explains. 'It means, "Have a good journey". It's French; it's what they speak where you're going.'

Mick's brow furrows. 'But we don't ata speak it, do wi, sir?'

The major smiles. 'No, but you might have to speak a little slowly when talking with some of your tunnelling colleagues. They will be men from all over the country, and your Lancashire twang might be difficult for them.'

Mick answers with a broad grin on his face. 'We call it Lanky, sir. We'll try not to slark it on too thick. Unless, o' course, we don't want 'em to reckon to wot we're agate.'

Hell-fire Jack looks to Arnie Tough for clarification. 'It's a verb, Major. "Agate" means "saying".'

'Very amusing. You and your baggers will do very well. I look forward to some productive tunnelling with you.'

Kruisstraat, Wulvergem, West Flanders, Belgium

For the Royal Fusiliers on the Western Front February has brought significant changes. Since Harry and Maurice returned from their fortnight's leave in London, 4th Battalion has been transferred to a new division and has moved both to a new location in the trenches and a new billet. In doing so, much to their exasperation, they have had to relinquish to the Grenadiers of the Guards division their increasingly homely serjeants' mess in Locre.

The 4th Royal Fusiliers, one of the BEF's most formidable fighting battalions, London boys through and through, is part of 9th Brigade with three other equally well-regarded units: 1st Lincolns, 1st Royal Scots and 1st Northumberlands. But the 9th has now been moved from its original assignment in the 3rd Division of General Horace Smith-Dorrien's II Corps, to his newly formed 28th Division.

The 28th has been put together from various colonial battalions returning from duties around the empire, mainly from India, Singapore and Egypt. Having had almost no preparation in England, the division assembled at three camps in Hampshire in December 1914, arriving at Le Havre on 19 January. It was then sent straight to the Front, to neglected and waterlogged trenches south-west of Ypres between Bailleul and Hazebrouck. Within a week, over 60 per cent of the men of the 28th were sick with bronchial problems or trench foot. Most of the rest were 'demoralized', 'disillusioned', 'depressed'; each battalion adjutant's report had a different name for it, but if the men could have expressed it in their own words they would have said, 'Fuck this for a game of soldiers!'

Lancastrians and Yorkshiremen, all from distinguished regiments with military pedigrees going back to the Napoleonic Wars and beyond, they are not men known for lacking in spirit or resolve. But life in far more tranquil and much sunnier climes has been grossly inadequate preparation for the privations of Flanders' trenches in midwinter. Men more used to being colonial policemen than front-line troops in a kind of war the ferocity of which no one has experienced before, they have buckled under the pressure. As a consequence, 9th Brigade has been transferred to stiffen the wilting ranks of the 28th.

Harry and Maurice are far from happy about the move.

In particular, the loss to the Foot Guards, the detested Grenadiers – 'toy soldiers', as Maurice calls them; 'bum-boys in bearskins', as Harry more crudely puts it – of their cosy serjeants' mess in the vestry of L'Église St Pierre at Locre, is the cause of considerable annoyance. But their annoyance is, in part, ameliorated by the mirth derived from having been asked to straighten the backbone of Lancashire and Yorkshire regiments, men who wear their northern heritage and regimental hearts on their sleeves.

'Duke of fuckin' Lancasters, East Yorks – bloody northerners, Mo. They're always prattlin' on abaht "soft southerners". Look at 'em, whimperin' in their trenches like ribbons and curls.'

'It dun 'arf make yer larf, 'Arry; losin' us our mess, the tossers! It were a proper Robin Hood gaff that we won't see again in a while.'

The 4th Battalion's new trenches are 200 yards beyond some abandoned barns at a crossroads on Kruisstraat, a country road between Wulvergem and Wijtschate, about seven miles south-west of Ypres. The barns, or at least what is left of them, are serving as temporary billets.

Now the Londoners face the most gruesome of duties. The trenches they have taken over have been manned by 1st Battalion the Suffolk Regiment, another group of empire troops who have been rushed back to Europe *in extremis*. In October, the Suffolks were serving in Khartoum in the Sudan, where the average daytime temperature is 86 degrees Fahrenheit and where there is only six inches of rain in a year. When they arrived in Flanders only three weeks ago, the temperature was -2 degrees and it had been snowing for twelve hours. As a result of the subsequent decline in morale of the Suffolks, their trenches have become neglected and saturated. But that is the least of the Fusiliers' dilemmas. Much worse is the state of no-man's-land; it is a charnel house strewn with rotting corpses from several weeks of fighting.

Lieutenant Ralph Coates, commanding officer of Harry's B Company, and Lieutenant Walter Thornton, in command of Maurice's C Company – both new arrivals at the Front – have organized repair teams to work on the trenches and ordered burial parties to collect and dispose of the dead.

As Harry and Maurice look on, Coates and Thompson march into no-man's-land under the protection of a white flag, a symbol of peace that is, in fact, the vest part of a set of discarded long johns, insodoing earning great respect from the two London veterans. Fortunately for the two intrepid Englishmen, the German trench is not occupied by Jaegers, usually hard-nosed infantry units, but by Uhlans, 13th Mounted Rifles, a light cavalry regiment which has abandoned its mounts for life in the trenches. It is a traditional Prussian regiment, commanded by old-school officers who respond chivalrously, a virtue which has all but disappeared in this brutal war. They meet the British officers halfway.

Coates read Modern Languages at Cambridge and is fluent in French and German. But the two German officers also speak French and near-perfect English, so, after a polite exchange of salutes, the smoking of a cigarette each and warm handshakes all around, a one-day, daylight truce is arranged for the next morning. Harry and

Maurice look on incredulously. As usual, Harry pithily puts it into perspective in his best 'toff's' accent: 'I say, old boy, do you mind awfully if we have a little pause for a bit of tiffin in this spat? Shall we say we kick off again at dusk tomorrow?' He spits into the bottom of the trench and reverts to his East London vernacular. 'It's all fuckin' Tommy Rollocks, innit? Still wet behind the ears, those two; they think it's a fuckin' game o' cricket!'

Maurice has more sympathy for the young officers. 'Give 'em a chance, 'Arry; they've only just arrived. Neither one can be more than twenty-five. Coates don't look like he's been shavin' more 'n a month.'

'Yeh, an' he'll not need to shave where 'e's goin'. He'll soon be in an 'ole in the ground, like all the ones before 'im.'

During the daylight hours of the following day Harry gets the burial party job, Maurice the trench maintenance duty. While Maurice gets his men working in the trench with buckets, hammers and nails, Harry's men, with scarves wrapped tightly over noses and mouths and using shovels and improvised wheelbarrows and stretchers of several designs, begin to collect the decomposing remains. They find thirteen intact bodies that are clearly identifiable as British and bury them in a shallow communal grave just behind their trench. Whatever personal belongings they find are sent to the adjutant, Captain O'Donel, so that he can transport them on to Divisional HQ. The communal grave is marked by four pieces of timber, one at each corner and each topped by a khaki service cap, of which there is no shortage.

Harry's party also retrieves the fragments of at least two dozen more men. But because a festering arm in tattered khaki might rest next to an equally rancid leg in threadbare field grey, their nationality is not clear. They also find evidence of French dead: a fetid skull inside a poilu's pale-blue kepi; a knapsack, complete with a trenching spade and rotting rations, attached to a torso and head minus its limbs; and at least two separate arms. But there are not enough parts to put whole men together.

So, with the agreement of the German burial party working just yards away from them, which is also making a pile of body parts, two mounds of unidentifiable scraps of humanity are combined and entombed in a large pit halfway between the trenches. There are no prayers, no readings, no ceremony of any kind; it is too horrendous a task to prolong it any longer than necessary.

Lashed together with strips from an old shirt, a German Wachmeister fashions a rudimentary cross from the handles of two broken shovels and thumps it into the ground with his rifle butt. The day is all but over as he strikes the final blow, so there are quick salutes from both German cavalrymen and British Fusiliers and perfunctory handshakes between all involved in the grisly task. For men who have spent the day purging an abattoir, that is enough.

As a dense, chilling mist begins to fill the air, Harry gets back to his trench in the gloom of the evening. Within moments, he is as sick as a dog, repeatedly vomiting into a latrine pit and shaking uncontrollably. Maurice sees him in distress and rushes over to hold him around the shoulders. 'All right, mate?'

'Yer, must 'ave eaten som'in' that don't agree wiv me.'

'Right, come on, let's get yer head down.'

After a few moments Harry stops vomiting; his shakes subside a little and Maurice helps him to his makeshift bunk, dug into the side of the trench.

'Mo?'

'Yes, mate?'

'Let's go an' see that Welsh sniper when we're relieved.'

'Good plan, we're gonna be relieved day after tomorra; let's go an 'ave a butcher's at 'im.'

They are a few miles away from their previous position near Locre, but they have not abandoned their plan to go into no-man's-land and flush out at least one of the snipers who has been wreaking so much havoc in the British trenches. However, their plan has been modified following their brief stay in Poperinghe on their way back from leave in London.

There they heard about a young Welsh sniper who has been christened the Black-handed Assassin. He is one of the first recruits to a new army School of Sniping. Currently recuperating in Pop-Hop, one of the army's field hospitals in the town, Harry thinks he would be an ideal partner in their venture.

Sunday 28 February

British Army Field Hospital, Provost Lace Mill, Poperinghe, West Flanders, Belgium

After several weeks of relative quiet at Pop-Hop, during which most of the casualties have been caused by disease, neglect and squalor, the number of injuries from military activity is beginning to rise again. The hospital's doctors, nurses, orderlies and ambulance drivers know about changes in German tactics before Sir John French's HQ at St Omer. They just count the number of men on stretchers and the nature of their injuries. By calculating the balance between wounds caused by artillery, rifle or machine-gun and trench-fighting injuries like bayonet wounds and head traumas caused by improvised weapons, they know with some accuracy what kind of encounter has just taken place. Their statistics go back to the Royal Army Medical Corps HQ in London to help better prepare medical recruits and garner resources and supplies more accurately.

The most dependable planning for the number of incoming wounded to Pop-Hop comes from the arithmetic of artillery attacks. Seasoned medics can calculate with astonishing accuracy the number of likely arrivals, both dead and wounded, from the proximity of the shelling, its intensity and the duration of the bombardment.

With a margin of only a few minutes, they are even able to predict the timing of the first arrivals from the Front.

Pop-Hop's Captain Noel Chavasse has been listening and calculating. He has summoned Margaret Killingbeck, sister-in-charge of the night duty.

'Fifteen minutes, Sister. Artillery again; a heavy one this time: fifty to sixty stretcher cases; twenty-five for theatre. Check with the theatre sisters and organize the chloroform; alert the orderlies and ward sisters.'

'Will do, sir. Will you be operating tonight?'

'Yes, with Lieutenants McKinnell and Cunningham.'

As Chavasse gets ready to operate, Margaret prepares the emergency teams and sends Nursing Auxiliary Bronwyn Thomas, her friend and room-mate, on a vital errand to the outside stores.

'Bron, take two orderlies. We're expecting sixty but have only twenty-two beds. We need forty put-me-ups from the stores. Have them placed in the corridors on each floor.'

The first of a steady stream of wounded men begin to arrive barely two minutes beyond Chavasse's prediction. Chavasse has also been uncannily accurate about the number of casualties. Fifty-seven men are admitted. The operating theatres work all night and, by dawn, forty-nine men are still alive. There have been twelve amputations: eight legs, two arms at the elbow, one at the shoulder and a hand. Two men have lost an eye and one has been blinded. Twenty-six bullets have been excised and half a bucket has been filled with shrapnel. One piece, as big as a man's fist, was removed from the thigh of a Gordon Highlander. He lost the leg but somehow survived the ordeal and has a modest chance of recovery.

The time has passed quickly, the only saving grace on a typically busy night at Pop-Hop. The orderlies are sluicing the floors of the operating theatres and carrying away the residue of the night's work: the dead to the mortuary; the body parts to a lime pit dug for the purpose – unless, of course, the remnant belongs to one of the dead, in which case they try their best to add it to the right corpse.

The Monday-morning shift has already been working for over an hour when Margaret and Bronwyn finish all their tasks and find time for breakfast in the hospital canteen. Mushroom omelette is the dish of the day, a rare treat, and the two women are devouring it with an unladylike relish. They have already forgotten the names and faces of the men they have just treated, both the living and the dead. Apparent indifference is a necessary part of the defence mechanism of those treating casualties at the Front. If medical staff allow themselves to become emotionally involved with their patients, they will crumble within a week. Only rarely do casualties become more than yet another anonymous man in khaki. When they do – a particularly badly injured or brave warrior, or a victim not much older than a boy who charms those treating him – it is a dangerous indulgence for those who need to stay immune from normal human emotions. Badly injured men usually die and charming boys eventually go home to their mothers, bringing more sadness to what is already an almost unbearable burden.

As the two women finish their omelettes and begin to swig their mugs of tea, Bronwyn's brother Hywel joins them.

'Good, was it, girls?' he asks.

Bronwyn grins at him. 'Don't think it touched the sides.' She notices that Hywel is also smiling broadly. 'You look like you've either been touching up Nurse Jones again, or you've had some good news.'

'Both. I had some good news about an hour ago, so went round for a grope of Wendy's arse to celebrate.'

Margaret thinks she knows what the good news is. 'Dr Chavasse says you can leave Pop-Hop?'

'Correct, Margaret! Next Friday; can't wait.'

Both women grab Hywel by the neck and shriek, causing everyone in the canteen to turn around and offer their own congratulations. Many come up to shake Hwyel's hand, making sure to grasp the uninjured left hand he offers them. Hywel, now known as the Black-handed Assassin because of his reputation as a sniper, grins but is clearly embarrassed by the adulation. As all three have been working nights, breakfast is their supper, so Margaret suggests that they go into Pop to celebrate Hywel's news at La Maison de Ville, their favourite estaminet.

At 11 a.m., by which time they have consumed another breakfast and emptied a carafe and a half of wine, the need for sleep overcomes them. Bronwyn and Margaret make their way back to their room, while Hywel, somewhat the worse for wear, staggers back to his tiny bunk in Pop-Hop.

When he reaches the reception area he sees two formidable figures arrive at the doorway just behind him. Both colour serjeants, they are immediately recognizable as Fusiliers from their cap badges. Their craggy demeanour and the claret-and-blue ribbons of their Distinguished Conduct Medals suggest they are veterans, men of the first batch of arrivals of the BEF in France. The two men are Harry Woodruff and Maurice Tait, 4th Battalion, Royal Fusiliers. Maurice calls out to Hywel.

'Excuse me, son, we're looking for Colour Serjeant Thomas, Welch Fusiliers.'

'There are lots of Thomases in Welsh regiments.'

Harry bristles. 'Listen, laddie, you're supposed to answer "Serjeant" when addressing a senior NCO.'

'Sorry, *Serjeant*, and you're supposed to address me as "Orderly".'

'You cheeky little –'

Maurice intervenes to prevent an unnecessary altercation. 'We're lookin' for a Thomas who's a sniper. They call him the Black-handed Assassin.'

'That's me. How can I help you?'

Hywel is dressed in the plain khaki uniform of a medical orderly, complete with an embossed red cross on his sleeve. Maurice looks baffled.

'Sorry, Colour, we thought you was –'

'I am. I'm working as an orderly until my hand's healed.'

'So you're a sniper?'

'I am.'

Harry is always more blunt than Maurice and always prepared to say exactly what he thinks. 'Fuck me, you must be good to make Colour Serjeant at your age.'

'I am, but listen, I've had a bucket of grog and I'm on duty at eight tonight. I need to get some kip.'

'We need to buy you another 'alf a bucket before you do. Where's the nearest boozer?'

'You want me to do some sniping for you?'

'Exactly.'

'Don't you have any good shots in your battalion?'

'Not as good as you're supposed to be.'

'I don't think I can help. I'm joining the new army School of Sniping when I'm discharged at the end of the week.'

'In Blighty?'

'I think so.'

'Don't wan' another pop at Fritz before yer scarper?'

Intrigued and not a little overawed by the two East Londoners, five minutes later Hywel is back at La Maison de Ville, this time with a jug of beer in his hand. Harry continues his pointed questions: 'So, how can yer shoot wiv an 'ole in yer 'and?'

'Captain Chavasse is a magician as a surgeon; I've only lost the use of my middle fingers. Then he got a reinforced glove made for me in London. It's very simple, but very clever; I'm as steady as a rock with it.'

'But it's your right 'and.'

'I'm left-handed.'

Two more beers later, with many soldiers' stories told, and Hywel, now very drunk, admitting that he has a score to settle with a German sniper, Maurice comes to the point of their visit.

'You know you said you wanted to nail the Fritz sniper wot plugged your officer?'

'Yes.'

'Then we can 'elp yer get 'im, an' probably some of 'is mates. Like you, we 'ave our reasons to do fer at least one of those dead-eyed dickheads.'

'But how?'

'It's a full moon tonight, an' for the next three or four

nights. 'Arry an' me is gonna flush 'im out, an' you can pop the bugger.'

'Have you cleared it with your CO?'

'Definitely not; this is an old soldiers' operation. Strictly on the QT.'

Hywel is due to go back on the day shift on Tuesday; Harry and Maurice's offer gives him an ideal opportunity to deal with his unfinished business from November last year.

'All right, you're on. Tuesday or Wednesday, if we get a clear night.'

'Good lad!'

Maurice hands Hywel a piece of paper. 'We've just been moved to Rosendale Chateau, near Wulvergem. We're stood down, but in support. This is how to find us. There's a serjeants' mess in the basement; we'll meet you there, 21:00 hours.'

As the three colour serjeants are plotting their mission into no-man's-land, Margaret and Bronwyn are, even though it is only lunchtime, enjoying a nightcap. They have both become fond of pastis. For many of the medical staff at the Front, cheap French alcohol is one of the few ways of bearing the ordeal of long, exhausting hours in the midst of so much death and suffering.

They are both fairly tipsy and, led by Bronwyn's earthy sense of humour, are in fits of giggles, telling nurses' stories of bedpans, catheters and male appendages. Margaret is laughing so much she has tears running down her cheeks. She looks at Bronwyn's radiant face, and feels, as ever, a strong attraction to her. Despite the fact that she is petrified about what the answer might be, she asks a question she has been wanting to ask for some weeks.

'What became of that Guards officer who took you out a few times?'

In an instant, Bronwyn's face loses all its joyfulness. 'He's dead.'

An awful, gravid silence ensues until Margaret speaks. Now she is weeping tears not of elation but of anguish. 'Bron, I'm so sorry.'

'He was blown up last week; a direct hit into his trench. What was left of him was buried nearby. Thank God he didn't come here – I wouldn't have coped with that too well.'

'Had you fallen for him?'

'Not really. He was very sweet, but only a boy.'

'And you're only a girl.'

'Yes, but Philip spoiled me for boys; he was such a beast. I still think about him.'

They are both lying on Bronwyn's bed, side by side, still fully dressed. Margaret leans over to Bronwyn and kisses her. Bronwyn does not push her away.

PART THREE: MARCH

Granny's Boom!

Wednesday 3 March

Reform Club, Pall Mall, London

A very irate and worried Lord of the Admiralty has booked the Cabinet Room, one of the Reform Club's private dining rooms, for a late lunch with his old friend and colleague in the War Council, Chancellor of the Exchequer David Lloyd George.

'Winston, why are you so cross? You were rude to that hall porter.'

'Well, I booked the bloody room an hour ago! How dare he say I didn't!'

'He didn't say you didn't, he just said he hadn't got a booking. The office obviously hadn't told him.'

'Well, they bloody well should have!'

'Agreed, but that's not his fault.'

Winston pauses and stares at one of the few men he regards as his equal. 'You're right, of course, LG. I'll apologize when we leave.'

'Good. Now tell me the real reason for your grisly mood.'

'Kitchener! He's just put me in a very awkward position with the Old Block and enjoyed every moment of it.'

Before Lloyd George can sympathize, a waiter arrives with pre-lunch drinks. After serving them, he is told by Winston, who does not even lift his head, to bring lunch immediately. Unfortunately for the waiter, he suggests the Club claret to accompany lunch.

'No, certainly not; it's not good enough to put in a peasant stew!' says Winston.

Lloyd George intervenes and whispers an aside to his friend. 'Winston, it's Wednesday lunchtime, and there's a war on.'

'Quite. All the more reason to have a decent bottle.'

Winston turns to the waiter and snaps. 'Two glasses of Léoville-Barton, '05, and be quick about it.'

When the waiter leaves, Lloyd George again chastises Winston. 'You know, you really shouldn't speak to the staff as if they're skivvies.'

'They *are* skivvies! They're paid servants of the Club, and well paid too.'

Lloyd George loses patience. 'Good heavens, man! All too often it becomes patently evident that you're the grandson of a duke, and a conceited one at that.'

Winston pauses as he scrutinizes the scowl on Lloyd George's face. 'Point made, LG. You're right again. Don't worry, I'll leave the man a handsome tip.'

'Good, but thank him as well. And look him in the eye and smile when you do it; that will make his day.'

Winston, chided like a juvenile, accepts the rebuke. 'Do you know, David, if your political star ever comes crashing to earth – not that I see any prospect of that, you understand, but should it ever come to pass – you would make an inspirational head of a prep school. The two I had to suffer as a boy were cruel and stupid in equal measure.'

'I'm sure that's a copious compliment but, at the moment, I'm not contemplating moving to the comforts of the Home Counties to minister to the snooty and snotty offspring of the great and good.'

By the time the two men begin their lunch, Winston's preprandial scotch has relaxed him. The two giants of British politics look a little meagre sitting either side of a table big enough to seat fourteen, but both are used to large tables and big rooms. Winston begins to get off his chest the frustrations of the morning.

'I was summoned by the PM at eleven and told to be at Downing Street in fifteen minutes. I checked with Jacky Fisher as I left: as far as he knew, nothing was brewing or had boiled over. When I got to Number 10, to my consternation Kitchener was with OB in his study. K's tash, freshly waxed and very erect, like the horns of a prize bull, twitched as I sat down. He smelled blood.'

Lloyd George never resists an opportunity to belittle Britain's most famous soldier. 'A prize bull! The old sodomite! I can't understand why he doesn't want to send troops to the Dardanelles. If he did, he could reacquaint himself with his old acquaintances, the Ottoman bumboys he met in Cairo.'

'LG, don't interrupt, this is important. K had a telegram in his hand, from Birdwood, a general he has sent to check what Carden is up to.'

'Isn't that a bloody cheek?'

'Not really. If I'm asking him to send troops, then he's entitled to know how the navy is paving the way.'

'So, who is this cove Birdwood?'

'One of K's coterie, on his staff in South Africa, where I met him briefly. Not a man of great consequence, in my opinion.'

'What did he have to say?'

'Well, he's not very complimentary about the navy or about Admiral Carden. K read out the telegram, the gist of which was that he doubted that Carden could force the Straits, at least in the short term. It seems that the Turkish forts are being dealt with, but that they have brought in mobile artillery pieces. Carden can't pinpoint them from his ships and can't get his reconnaissance planes in the air to locate them because of the weather.'

'It sounds ominous.'

'I'm concerned, LG. The portents are not good. The Turkish Army is flooding the peninsula with infantry, who are digging in. Carden has telegrammed to say that he has sent some marines ashore, and they got a bloody nose!'

'I thought the view was that Johnny Turk would capitulate if the Dardanelles were challenged and that there would be a coup in Constantinople.'

'That was the intelligence from the diplomats.'

'So much for their intelligence! I have the feeling that their information is no more profound than the gossip of washerwomen. So, what do you think of our prospects in the Straits?'

'To be frank, LG, it's not going as expected.'

'Bugger! I thought Carden said it could be done?'

'He did. He's blaming bad weather for the delay.'

'Is he looking for excuses?'

'He might be.'

'Is he any good?'

'Jacky Fisher and Tug Wilson said he was the right man. Now, I have serious doubts.'

'Bugger, bugger and buggery! What did the PM say?'

'Nothing at first. K asked me if Carden was up to it. I didn't answer but stared back at him, making it clear it was a highly improper question, to which he said, and I quote, "Birdwood says Carden would hesitate if he saw a bag of gold sovereigns in the gutter."'

'A pithy comment, if I may say so. What did you say?'

'I said, "Who the hell is Birdwood to be passing opinions about an admiral of the fleet?" I tried to sound indignant, but I'm not sure I carried enough conviction. Then Asquith intervened to ask the obvious question: "So where do we go from here?"'

'And?'

'I said, "Let's get the army mobilized before the whole thing falls apart. I made a particular case for the 29th Division, the only crack troops we have in reserve.'

'Let me wager a guess: the gallant earl said no.'

'Indeed, that's what he was waiting for. He knew I had a weak hand, so only had to play a weak trump to win the rubber.'

'So, where *do* we go from here?'

'A glass of port with our pudding, LG.'

Winston's comment makes Lloyd George smile. His friend's anger has subsided, to be replaced by his customary tenacity. He has been challenged and bettered, but only temporarily.

'A glass, or two, of Warre's best Vintage will do very well. Should we order a bottle?'

The suggestion produces a wide grin on Winston's face. 'Why not? It's only three o'clock. The afternoon is young.'

Half an hour later, during which most of the

conversation has been humorous, if a little inconsequential, Lloyd George's tone, perhaps as a consequence of the alcoholic trimmings to lunch, becomes severe again: 'Do you know the biggest threat to the security of our islands at the moment?'

Winston thinks he does. 'The possible collapse of the Russians on the Eastern Front.'

'No, that's a lesser concern. The greater threat is the War Council itself. Most of them cower like cornered animals. They see danger everywhere; they have challenges they can't face, questions they can't answer; they are frightened men. Asquith is the biggest culprit. His contrived, urbane Yorkshire facade hides a man afraid of his own shadow. He doesn't know what to do. He listens to everyone's opinion but still can't see fact from fiction, truth from myth.'

Winston scrutinizes his friend. He knows what must soon happen. 'When will you make your bid?'

'For what?'

'Don't be coy with your old friend. We both know that the Old Block is as wise as Old Father Time in normal situations and a consummate politician, but in these unprecedented days we need a leader who can take passionate command: lead the dispirited leaders, stir the nation and inspire the army and navy to rise to its many challenges.'

'As usual, you put it so eloquently.'

For once, Lloyd George seems to lack self-belief; he needs Winston's reassurance. 'Do you honestly think I could do all those things?'

'I do. When the time is right – and I think it will be soon – I will be at your side.'

Winston adopts one of his more endearing guises: the gallant King's champion: 'And you will need me when the time comes. Together we will make a powerful force, sweeping all before us.'

Lloyd George roars out loud. 'You certainly have your ancestors' blood in your veins. Do you always see the world and its future as a succession of battles in the waging of war?'

'Yes, of course. It was ever thus.'

'Then, you're right, I will need you at my side. I will be the King; you will be my Prince Rupert.'

'But that ended in defeat, and Charles Stewart lost his head.'

'That's very true, but you and I can and will rewrite history.'

Irish Benedictine Convent, Rue St Jacques, Ypres

All but one of the Irish Benedictine nuns left Ypres for the relative safety of Poperinghe long ago. Having survived the ordeal of occupation by the Germans at the beginning of the war, they rejoiced when the town was liberated by the Allies during the Battle of Ypres in October. But incessant bombing since and the destruction of large parts of the fabric of the convent eventually forced the nuns to leave at the beginning of January. All, that is, except for Sister Philomena.

Sister Philomena arrived from County Kerry as a girl of fifteen; she is now in her seventies. To call her formidable would be a significant understatement. She has only rarely left the precincts of the convent and has not set foot beyond Ypres' ancient walls since the day she arrived. She is not going to change her ways now. The devout Benedictine, who adheres closely to the precepts of the Rule of Saint Benedict – peace, prayer and work – now sleeps in a small, damp storeroom in the cellars, watched over by the convent's ancient caretaker, Edmund, who has no teeth, little conversation – even in his indecipherable Flemish – and a very short temper.

Much to Sister Philomena's fury, the convent is now one of hundreds of Flanders buildings used as a billet for the BEF. A staunch Irish Republican, she does not like the British and especially its English soldiers. Even though she tries hard to keep to the Benedictine commitment that silence be enjoyed where possible, she often launches into a tirade about the convent's British 'guests'.

When she sees Mad Mick Kenny's size-twelve army boots sticking out of the end of a pew and his puttees draped over a nearby crucifix in what remains of the chapel, she bellows like a Killybegs fishwife: 'Will yer get those big fat feet off that pew, you heathen Englishmen!'

Mick almost jumps out of his skin, as do, lying on the next pew, Vinny Sagar and Twaites Haythornthwaite, and all the other men of the army's new tunnelling company. When Mick comes to and remembers where he is, he looks at the nun, clad in her black Benedictine habit, in amazement. The last time a nun bellowed at him was when he was a little boy at St Mary's Catholic Primary School in Burnley, which was run by the Sisters of Mercy, an Irish order he always thought inappropriately christened, given the number of beatings they meted out to their charges.

'Sorry, Sister, but we've only just landed frae England and wi'v 'ad no sleep.'

'Well, go and sleep in yer bunks, the lot o' yer. Clear out.'

'But Sister, we 'ave no bunks, we were told to kip in 'ere. Oh, an' am not English. My parents are frae Galway.'

'Are they now? So what are you doin' fightin' for the Brits?'

'I thought Ireland was part o' Britain. Isn't t'King o' England t'King o' Ireland as well?'

'He is, but he's a usurper and will not get away with it for much longer. Wait till this war's over!'

Sister Philomena turns and, with a purposeful stride a woman half her age would be proud of, stomps off to find a British officer to berate about the arrival of yet more soldiers.

It is noon. After a tortuous journey, Mick, Vinny and Twaites arrived at the convent only five hours ago. They took the train in relative comfort from London to Dover, then crossed the Channel in atrocious weather, a journey so rough that even some of the crew were sick. Another train followed, but this time a freight train with nothing better than cattle trucks for accommodation. They were fed in Béthune, a bowl of potato soup and stale bread, before facing over 60 miles of frozen, rutted roads in the back of an open-topped, solid-tyred lorry. Even though it is the beginning of March, it snowed all the way. By the time they arrived in Ypres they looked more like snow-men than soot-caked miners.

As promised when they were recruited, their journey to the Front has happened with extraordinary speed. Now they can hear the rumble and see the flashes of artillery all too distinctly. Vinny is not impressed.

'Is this wot we volunteered us'sels fer? Am starved, frossen, wi'v bin told off like schoolchilder be an Irish nun and thu's bombs goin' off all ova t'place.'

Twaites is also concerned by the proximity of the enemy. 'Them big guns reet moither me. Ave ne'er heard owt like it.'

Only moments after Twaites finishes his sentence, a blinding flash of light sears everyone's vision and a thunderous boom shakes the convent to its foundations. Shards of glass fly through the air, anything not fastened down crashes to the ground and clouds of dust billow up into the roof-space. The newly arrived tunnellers are thrown to the ground, some cut and bruised; all are deafened and disorientated.

Vinny begins to scream and run around in a blind panic. 'Fuck, fuck, fuck! What was that?'

Mick and Twaites, helped by some of the other men, grab him and sit him down in the pews. Mick shakes his friend and stares into his eyes. 'Vinny, it were a shell, a bomb. This is t'Front; it's a fuckin' war. It's wot 'appens. T'Germans a'tryin t'd' fer us cos we're tryin' t'd' fer them. So get 'old o' tha'sen.'

Mick's blunt words calm Vinny. He takes a few deep breaths and nods at Mick appreciatively. Men begin to gather themselves, check their cuts and bruises, shake off the dust; there are no serious injuries, but the men are severely shaken. They have been in Flanders for less than six hours.

Mick and some of the older miners, several of them wizened, grey-haired veterans of pits, tunnels and sewers, go in search of the source of the explosion. When they walk from the chapel into the refectory they witness a scene that will haunt them for the rest of their lives. The shell has breached the east wall of the building, leaving a hole as big as a terraced house. Amidst a large heap of brick and stone piled against the opposite wall are all the refectory's furniture and paraphernalia of food and eating. Small fires smoulder and crackle in the debris.

There are one or two moans of pain within the rubble but, mainly, there is an ominous silence. The room had been full of men eating lunch: two platoons of the Black Watch, one of Scotland's finest regiments; over fifty weary men relieved from the trenches only last night.

Mick squints, trying to focus through the dust and smoke. At first he thinks the colourful smears on the walls, the piles of slime and the pools of liquid on the floor, are the residue of lunch. But he is mistaken. They are the remains of noble Scotsmen. He begins to see more and more pieces of British Army khaki and the distinctive navy-blue and green of Black Watch tartan. Their uniforms and kilts, moments ago whole and worn with pride, are now shredded into tiny pieces. The same has happened to the men inside the khaki and tartan. Their humanity has been reduced to blood and tissue, their individuality lost amidst the remains of their brothers in arms. Mick turns away, appalled at the sheer horror of the scene.

Forcing himself to look back, he sees, lying in a heap, a shredded, blood-soaked nun's habit. Of its wearer, only a few mounds of unidentifiable flesh are left in the folds of the once-black, now-crimson, garment. Mick knows immediately that he is looking at the corporeal remains of Sister Philomena, the last of the Irish Benedictines of Ypres. Next to her are old Edmund's remains. For once, he could not keep her safe.

Mick turns around. Vinny, Twaites and several other men have followed him into the refectory. They stand motionless, ashen-faced, wide-eyed; Twaites begins to retch. Mick swallows hard, trying to gather himself, and beckons to his fellow tunnellers.

'Come on, yer buggers, tha's colliers, aren't tha? Tha's lads alive in there. Let's get 'em out.'

Some men hesitate, but most follow Mick's lead and start to pull at the rubble to find the source of the cries of the living. An hour later, by which time all the miners have joined in, eight men have been released and are alive but only four have any chance of surviving.

Members of the Red Cross and VAD have arrived. The survivors are stretchered away and the tunnellers taken to the convent's cloisters, where they are given cups of tea, bowls of broth and have their cuts and bruises taken care of. Most of them, hardened miners and tunnellers, are in shock; some are shaking and are being wrapped in blankets. Although pit accidents are commonplace and some of the older men have seen many a gruesome sight, what they have just witnessed has chilled them to the core. Nothing could have prepared them for this; they will live with the memory for the rest of their lives. The images will come back to them in their dreams. They will appear in flashes in the most mundane circumstances: the crackling of a fire in the hearth, a sudden noise, the smell from a frying pan, a nick of blood when they are shaving, the sight of fresh meat in a butcher's window. They will never forget.

Sitting between his two friends, Mick has an arm around Vinny and Twaites, trying to stop them trembling and offering words of support. Unknown to their fellow tunnellers, neither Vinny nor Twaites has been near a pit, and, other than a few minor injuries at work and a couple of broken bones on the sports field, neither has ever witnessed a traumatic death, let alone on this gargantuan scale.

Twaites is unable to speak, but Vinny is repeating the same words over and over again: 'Mick, I can't do wi' this! 'Ow do we get our'sens 'ome?'

Mick does not answer; he has no answer to give. Then, behind them, the sharp *click-clack* of boots on cobbles comes close, before it suddenly stops.

'Gentlemen, I am sorry that your arrival in Flanders has been met by this terrible tragedy.'

It is their recruiting officer and the new commanding officer of the Royal Engineers Tunnelling Companies, Major John Norton-Griffiths. He is an imposing presence, but his emerald-green eyes, usually fierce and determined, have a compassionate look in them and he casts a comforting smile as he speaks.

'I'm afraid this is a horrible war.' He looks down at his feet, remembering the many battles he has fought in Africa. 'It is not like other wars. So many men are dying every day and, as you have seen, in the most awful of circumstances. It's like being underground – something everyone here is familiar with. It's bad enough when things are going well, but much, much worse when things go wrong.'

All the men are now looking up, focused on what the major is saying. Even Vinny is listening, his shakes subsiding.

'That is why you're here: to stop this carnage. Yes, by meting out carnage of our own. But here is a simple fact: the war on the ground cannot be won by either side, at least not until we bleed one another dry of men. And not tens of thousands of men, not even hundreds of thousands, but millions. It will take years, and every day of all those years will be like this one, like what has just happened to you, here in Ypres – in a convent, of all places!'

He pauses. He holds his audience rapt. He is a consummate salesman.

'I want to wage a new kind of warfare, underground, using your special skills. We can break the stalemate in the trenches, go under the barbed wire, avoid the machine guns . . .' Like the perfect showman, he pauses again. '. . . and blow Fritz and the Kaiser to smithereens!'

Several men rise to their feet and begin to clap. Others shout their support; some even step forward to shake Norton-Griffiths by the hand. Vinny and Twaites are feeling better. In fact, Vinny has taken a shine to his new CO.

''E's alreet, that lad. If he's goin' down t'tunnels, then I'll go wi' 'im.'

Major John Norton-Griffiths has certainly taken to soldiering like he took to all life's other challenges. After persuading a highly conservative Lord Kitchener, the formidable Minister of War, of the merits of his plans (who immediately promoted him to Major and gave him carte blanche to implement his initiative), he used his presence and charm to do the same to the senior officers of the Royal Engineers at BEF HQ in St Omer. There, to a roomful of highly specialized sappers with engineering degrees from Cambridge and the like, using yet another vigorous demonstration of clay-kicking with a coal shovel from the fireplace, he convinced seasoned, technically gifted men that his tunnels could work.

Not only that, he got a cheque signed for £750 so that he could buy a brown-and-cream Rolls-Royce Silver Ghost. He filled its boot and the trailer it pulled with vintage port, fine cognac and Épernay's best champagne. He also loaded it with chocolates, cigarettes, leather gloves, woollen scarves, silk long johns and riding boots. All are intended as 'sweeteners' to persuade his fellow officers to release from their battalions men who knew how to dig. His Rolls-Royce has been shipped from England, as have, accompanied by their grooms, his two favourite horses, Hero and Mint, mounts he will use not for transport but to go hunting.

Norton-Griffiths looks, sounds and acts like an aristocrat with a centuries-old pedigree, but it is a clever facade disguising a tough, self-made man who uses his brawn, intellect and good looks to devastating effect.

Three hours later, the entire contingent of Norton-Griffiths' tunnellers is assembled in what remains of the cavernous Cloth Hall in the centre of Ypres. Sheltering from the rain under the one part of the roof that is intact,

Norton-Griffiths is on his feet again. The group that Mick, Vinny and Twaites travelled from London with has been joined by two more, one of which arrived only an hour ago. There are thirty-six men in all, the first instruments of the British Army's new weapon of war – moles!

'Tomorrow, you will be at the Front, which is but a few miles down the road. Soon, you will be in the trenches, then under them, then under the killing area between them, which has now been christened no-man's-land. We will be clay-kicking; the Germans still use mattocks. We will be able to hear them, but they won't hear us. Now, listen carefully to this: clay-kicking is four times faster than mattock-digging! You will soon be under Fritz's lines, so close that you'll be able to hear him making a brew, breaking wind and telling dirty jokes – but only in German!'

There are smiles all around. Once again, he has his audience under his spell.

'Let me outline where we stand. The Minister of War, Lord Kitchener, has personally authorized the establishment of tunnelling companies under the direct command of the Engineer-in-Chief of the Royal Engineers, Brigadier General Henry Fowke. Now, here is a man, I have no hesitation in promising you, you will like and respect. A big man who plays rugby like a bull in a china shop, he's a proper engineer who knows what he's about.'

Vinny cannot resist a whispered aside in Twaites' ear. 'Fowke! Wot sort o' name is that? Fowke me, it's dafter than Haythornthwaite. At least you're not named after a shag!'

Twaites starts to giggle, which immediately attracts the major's attention. 'Serjeant Major Cadwallader!'

'Sir!'

'The comedian there is called Sagar; the grinning idiot next to him is called Haythornthwaite: both Lancastrians – Burnley boys, baggers – music hall turns, comics! They think General Fowke's name is amusing. Field Punishment Number 2: one day; they're to march with us to the Front tomorrow in their stocking feet, no shoes.'

'Very good, sir – no comedians in this company!'

The major, his face now thunderous, continues. 'Let me be clear, I'm paying you six shillings and sixpence a day, three times the rate for an infantryman. You're spared drills and spit and polish, and you'll be better fed than the average Tommy Atkins. But, in return, I demand bloody hard work, strict professional standards and rigid army discipline. No "if"'s, no "but"'s – is that clear?'

Shocked by the change in the major's tone and by the issue of a rare Number 2 Field Punishment to two of their comrades, there are nods of assent and 'yes, sir's' from everyone in the room.

'So, to continue, I will liaise with General Fowke's second-in-command, Colonel Harvey, another first-rate engineer who believes in the same techniques as I do. If you come across him, listen and you will learn, but don't get on the wrong side of him. His nickname is Ducky Harvey not because he waddles like a duck or acts like a girl but because, when he's angry, you duck!'

Everyone laughs. The men like the sound of their officers.

'He and I will be responsible for recruiting new men, so that we will soon have nine tunnelling companies, each of at least two hundred men, commanded by a Royal

Engineer. We will be the size of two battalions – a for-midable force. You are the pioneers, the army's moles. Tomorrow we march to the Front. Try to keep together and look like soldiers. The rifles you've been given are the real thing; if you see any Germans, shoot them! Those of you who've come straight from a mine or a tunnel will be shown how to use them by Serjeant Major Cadwallader. Now, get some rest.'

As Norton-Griffiths leaves, Vinny tugs at Mick's sleeve. 'What's a Field Punishment Number 2 when it's a' 'ome?'

'Didn't yer reckon to owt in trainin'?'

'Not much.'

'Han'cuffs an' fetters; tha'll ata walk all way t'Front wi' 'em on.'

'D'ya mean like 'obblin' an 'orse?'

'Aye, that's reet. It'll learn yer to keep yer trap shut; an', Twaitesy lad, not t'giggle like a little lass.'

Kruisstraat, Wulvergem, West Flanders, Belgium

It is the last night in their billets at Chateau Rosendale for Harry Woodruff and Maurice Tait. Tomorrow they will go back into the trenches they vacated only a few days ago. But, if the audacious scheme they have planned comes to fruition, they will be back at the Front even earl-ier than that. The prospects for their nocturnal mission into no-man's-land are looking good. The moon is gib-bous, only two days before full, and the sky is crystal clear. They are rehearsing their tactics for the night while enjoying a beer in their serjeants' mess in the chateau's basement, a poor imitation of their previous abode at Locre.

The two London veterans are waiting for their rendezvous with Royal Welch Fusiliers sharpshooter Colour Serjeant Hywel Thomas. The two BEF originals look distinctly odd. To the amusement of their fellow NCOs, they are wearing wet-weather ponchos from neck to knee. Most of their colleagues know what they are planning, so there is not too much mickey-taking. Nevertheless, although not apprehensive about their venture, they still feel distinctly self-conscious. They know that their ponchos hide the other bizarre preparations they have made for their derring-do operation.

They have stripped to their waists, smothered themselves in goose fat, blacked up with boot polish and armed themselves with razor-sharp knives and bayonets. So as not to be the cause of too much mirth, they have left the blacking-up of their faces till later.

'Where's that Taffy boy? He's fuckin' late!'

While Harry is typically impatient, Maurice, as always, is more relaxed. 'We've plen'y o' time, 'Arry. It's only 'arf ten.'

Ten minutes later Hywel Thomas arrives and sits down next to them. He appears uneasy. 'Evening, Maurice, Harry. Is the Mess Chairmen here?'

Harry, surprised, is apprehensive. 'Why?'

'Don't get annoyed, but I've come with an officer. He'd like to help us.'

'Fuck me, Taff, this is strictly an off-limits op. You could get us all court-martialled!'

'He's a good bloke, he won't let on; he's not like that . . . He's, well, eccentric, but he can help us.'

Maurice adopts a more conciliatory tone. 'Who is this geezer?'

'Major Vernon Hesketh-Pritchard, explorer and big-game hunter. He knows everything you need to know about guns and shooting.'

Harry is now incensed. 'A fuckin' huntin' an' shootin' toff. Don't tell me, he wears a deerstalker?'

'No, a cowboy hat.'

Harry looks at Maurice; he is incredulous. 'You're fuckin' jokin', right?'

'No, he's outside, with his Buffalo Bill hat. He's the CO of the army's new School of Sniping.'

'Mo, ave gotta see this. Who's the senior NCO in 'ere?'

Maurice looks around. 'There's a Jock CSM over there, an' a Geordie in the corner. Both looked pissed.'

'Well, we won't be botherin' wiv them. Who else?'

'The two of us.'

'Good, then let's invite Buffalo Bill into our little drum! Hywel, son, get four Crimeas in, on my mess tab.'

'Four what?'

'Beers, son, Charlie Freers, Christmas cheers; Daily Mails – ales! What do they call 'em where you come from?'

'Beers.'

'Fuckin' Welsh – no imagination!'

Major Hesketh-Pritchard is well over six feet tall and broad-shouldered, an athletic man who played first-class cricket with W. G. Grace for the MCC and toured the West Indies. All conversation stops when he strides into the dimly lit basement room. Cowboy hat in hand, highly polished cavalry boots catching the lantern-light, and immaculately clean and pressed uniform contrasting with the dishevelled dress of the assembly of front-line soldiers, he is an impressive sight. He nods appreciatively to all and sundry and shouts over to the duty barman.

'Serjeant, a round for everyone, on me. Thank you for inviting me into your mess, gentlemen.'

His words, delivered with the haughty air of a music hall compere, break the silence to great effect. His greeting is reciprocated with nods and smiles from the gathering, many of whom raise their beer mugs in appreciation. As the animated conversation in the mess resumes, Hywel introduces Hesketh-Pritchard to the two Royal Fusiliers.

'Sir, Colour Serjeants Tait and Woodruff.'

'Good evening, gentlemen. I've heard a good deal about you from CSM Thomas. It is a privilege to meet two highly decorated originals, men who are now being called "Old Contemptibles".'

Maurice responds first. 'Good to meet yer, sir. Dunno about "contemptibles" – sounds like an insult.'

'It was intended to be; apparently, that's what the Kaiser called the BEF last year.'

Harry, as strident as ever, answers next. 'If you arsk me, sir, he's got an effin' cheek, old Kaiser Bill!'

'Indeed he has, Colour, a right effin' cheek.'

Hywel arrives with the beers, and the serious business of the evening begins with a pointed question from the major.

'I see you're prepared for a little expedition. What do you have in mind?'

Harry and Maurice look at one another, worried about

revealing their plans, but Hesketh-Pritchard reassures them.

'Gents, this is off the record: I'm in your mess, as your guest. King's Regs are waived for this op. I'm here to help for two very good reasons. First, Hywel here is an absolute natural; you can't teach what he's got. His scores on the range are unparalleled, and he's done it on the battlefield, not something that all crack shots can manage. Now that his hand is healed, I've got my first chance to see what he can do. The second reason is that I'm determined to beat Fritz at his own game. In their bountiful and extensive forests, the Germans are a nation of hunters and have no shortage of marksmen. Their elite battalions are called Jaegers, which is German for "hunter". Other than a few gamekeepers, who shoot with rifles, we shoot with shotguns, so have nothing like the same number of men to pick from. Their scopes are excellent. I estimate they have 1,500 in service, most of them pointed at the Allies on the Western Front, and they know how to use them. We only have a few scopes cobbled together from private sources, but they've been given to men without any training. I've been checking any I can find. Over three quarters are out of alignment to such an extent that the man using it couldn't hit a barn door at 50 yards!'

Harry and Maurice are hanging on every word Hesketh-Pritchard utters.

'Although we have the best rapid-fire infantrymen in the world, we are years behind the Germans in sniping. Some officers from the Guards Division told me the other day that they have stopped wearing their luminous watches, as they attract Fritz's beady eye. The word around the battalions is consistent: if you put your head where Fritz can see it, he'll put a bullet in it within moments.'

Maurice nods in agreement. 'That's definitely 'ow it is in our lot.'

'Let me give you one startling fact from BEF HQ in St Omer. Since the beginning of the year, each British combat battalion has lost an average of twelve to fifteen men a week to snipers, almost all of them clean head-shots.'

The three men at the table find that number incredible, as do those eavesdropping on nearby tables.

'Last week, one bored Fritz near Aubers Ridge, in between shooting British soldiers, spent the day carving out a crucifix on a barn door. The range was over 200 yards and, when he'd finished, the cross looked like it had been carved by a master craftsman. So you see, I'm here with very serious intent: instead of cowering in our trenches, your adventure and others like it are what we should be doing every day. So your laudable expedition is safe with me, and I'm happy to authorize it here and now.'

Maurice and Harry nod to one another. Maurice smiles as he outlines the plan.

'Very well, sir. We're gonna do it the old soldiers' way; we've greased up, blacked up, an' we're goin' in like Gur-khas, dagger in the belt, bayonet in the teeth. The Fritz snipers in our sector 'ave two or three men on their night shift. They're active until abaht 02:00 hours. We was gonna lie low in a shell 'ole or some other cover until we spot one of 'em in 'is 'ide. Then we'll crawl up to 'im on two sides an' 'ave 'im!'

'I see. Shame you don't have kukris.'

'That's what we thought, sir.'

'Well, I think I can help.'

Hesketh-Pritchard gestures to his batman, Private Greaves, who is sitting at the bottom of the basement steps. The young soldier picks up a large kitbag and brings it over to the table. Hesketh-Pritchard rummages around in it before producing two fearsome knives the size of a man's arm.

'There you are: a Gurkha kukri and a Malaysian golok.'

Harry is impressed. 'Does yer always carry round yer own personal arsenal?'

'I do. Well, my man Greaves does. You should see my collection of guns. I have a Holland & Holland Magnum in my car, an elephant gun that is accurate at over 500 yards. Thought it might be jolly useful; Fritz has taken to skulking behind steel plates, which a bullet from an ordinary Lee-Enfield won't penetrate. But my Magnum will punch a hole straight through it.' Grinning broadly, he pauses for effect. 'And straight through the bugger hiding behind it!' he resumes. 'I've also got a box of our new Mk III Aldis telescopic sights. They are excellent. If properly adjusted and in the hands of a top marksman, they can take out a sparrow's eye at a quarter of a mile. They're based on one that CSM Thomas acquired for us from a German sniper last year.'

Hywel's eyes light up at the thought of a high-velocity gun with a range over 500 yards. Harry's eyes are also full of admiration. He likes the officer with the double-barrelled name and the cowboy hat. To Harry, he is a proper gent and a proper soldier.

'Sir, your batman is welcome to a drink wiv us. He can put it on my tab.'

'Thank you, Colour. Now, how can CSM Thomas help you with your op?'

Maurice responds. 'As cover, sir. We thought that, if we got rumbled, Hywel could keep Fritz's head down so we can get back to our line.'

'I understand. Well, gentlemen, I think your ruse is a fine and brave effort, but very hazardous. I also fear your chances of success are not high. I think we can improve them, however, and that Thomas can do better than give you cover. I have brought something for you which will mean you don't have to get cold or put yourself at risk.' Hesketh-Pritchard smiles smugly. 'Shall we show them, CSM Thomas?'

Private Greaves, who was in the middle of a swig of his beer, disappears up the basement steps to retrieve something from Hesketh-Pritchard's car. Moments later, he returns with a large box, from which he removes an object covered in brown cloth, and hands it to his officer. Like a magician on stage, the major pulls off the cloth: 'There!'

Instead of a round of applause for the magician's trick, there is a stunned silence from Harry and Maurice. Several of the NCOs nearby also fall silent, then there are outbursts of sniggering and laughter.

The major is undaunted. 'So, gentlemen, what do you think? It's papier mâché, cheap to make; I am having dozens made.'

Harry does not hold back. 'It's a painted bald head, sir!'

'How perceptive of you, Colour. But it's a very clever bald head. We call him Tommy, after Tommy Atkins.'

So what? is the question Harry is asking himself.

'Your cap, please, and your fag.'

Still bewildered, Harry hands over his service cap and half-finished Sweet Caporal. The major places the cap on the papier mâché head and the lit cigarette into a small hole in its mouth. He then stands and asks that all except one of the mess lanterns and candles are extinguished.

'Thank you, gentlemen. This will only take a moment. Imagine a typical night in the trenches.'

He removes the cigarette to take a deep draw on it, and puts it back. Using the muzzle of his revolver, he then hoists the head high into the now dimly lit basement. The derision that accompanied the appearance of the dummy head is replaced by gasps of amazement. With a cigarette glowing in its mouth, its painted moustache and sideburns under its genuine cap look convincing, even from as little as ten yards it could easily be mistaken for a careless Tommy Atkins taking the night air while enjoying a quick fag.

'You see, Colour Serjeant Woodruff, it could be you, or any other British soldier who happens to put his head above the parapet.'

There are appreciative comments from all observers.

'But I have something else for you. I am having these made by the score as well.'

This time Private Greaves produces a long, rectangular box and hands it to Maurice.

'It's a simple periscope for the trenches. Again, cheap to make: three reflective mirrors allow you to see the position of a sniper without putting yourself in danger. And finally, Greaves, if you please.'

Private Greaves produces yet another surprise, this time a large bag, and passes it to his officer.

'This is my final contribution to your worthy mission.'

The major reveals a canvas, balaclava-style hood with sewn slits for eyes, nose and mouth. It is camouflaged with green, brown and beige paint and covered with foliage so that it looks like a small clump of wintry ground.

'They are made for me by a group of elderly ladies in Eastbourne. We call them Eastbourne Grannies. They can be tailored to different countryside and different seasons. With one of these on and a camouflaged rifle, it is almost impossible to see you in your lair.'

The major pauses to let the impact of his revelations sink in.

'So this is how we nail Herr Scharfschütze.'

'Wot's one o' them when he's at 'ome?'

'Our target, CSM Tait: that's what they call their marksmen.'

'Bloody darft language if you arsk me!'

'So, gentlemen, shall we get to work? CSM Woodruff, you're the dummy . . .'

Maurice cannot resist. 'Good choice, sir!'

'Forgive me, Colour, but someone has to be the dummy. You place the head where it can be seen. Now, here's the skill: you have to be subtle about it. Fritz will be suspicious if the dummy bobs around like a circus clown.'

Harry is a convert and hanging on every word. 'Understood, sir.'

'Now, CSM Tait, you and I have the vital job of trying to see the source of the sniper fire. To help with this, when Herr Scharfschütze hits Tommy, we can use the trajectory of the entry and exit points to help us source the origin of the bullet. While all that is going on, CSM Thomas and I will be secreted away, wearing our Eastbourne Grannies. CSM Thomas will use my Magnum – suitably camouflaged, of course, while I support your work with the periscope with my ship's telescope. We will be his spotters. By triangulating the bullet into the dummy and our sightings, we should be able to pin him down. Then we will be ready to plug Herr Fritz – perhaps two or three of them.'

Everyone in the mess, all of whom are now watching and listening to Hesketh-Pritchard's demonstration, is amazed.

'Any questions?'

Harry and Maurice answer in unison: 'None, sir.'

'Good, it's eleven fifteen. How far to the trenches?'

'Twenty-five minutes' walk.'

'Perfect. Gents, you can rub off your grease and boot polish and get dressed. Let's go to war!'

Thirty minutes later, with the moon casting deep shadows and the air as clear as a bell, all four men are in position. Except for the sentries on duty, the men of Maurice's C Company and Harry's B Company, 4th Fusiliers, have been told to get into their bivouacs and sleeping holes and to stay there in silence.

Silence also pervades the battlefield. Only rarely is the Front without artillery or rifle fire. But the quiet lasts only for a couple of minutes. Huge, soundless flashes to the south-east herald a bombardment by nearby French artillery. They are soon followed by a thunderous reverberating rumble that echoes around Flanders' empty landscape.

The Allied volley wakes up the battlefield. Single shots ring out; the German *Scharfschützen* are out hunting.

The four British men are determined to stalk their hunter and make him their prey rather than become yet more of his many victims. Maurice and the major position themselves as spotters ten yards either side of Hywel. He has disguised himself inside his camouflage balaclava and created a discreet firing position between the piled sandbags of the trench parapet. He has also donned his now-famous black glove, the first time it will be used in earnest. Harry has his dummy Tommy ready, replete with a casually cocked service cap and a brightly glowing cigarette.

In a hushed voice, Hesketh-Pritchard issues his order: 'Raise the target, CSM Woodruff. Keep it quite still for now.'

It does not take long for the Germans to respond. 'Tommy' is soon hit through the temple, sending him spinning into the bottom of the trench with a splash. His cigarette hisses as it is extinguished by the freezing water.

Maurice rushes to retrieve it to do the alignment trigonometry. He makes an excited but muted observation: 'He must be to the right. I can't see 'im through this bit of kit, but he must be near that pile of stones.'

With his powerful telescope and using Maurice's estimate, the major soon spots the German's gun-metal barrel in the bright moonlight.

'The blighter's hidden in the bottom of that pile of stones. I can see his muzzle; it's poking out on top of that half-empty sandbag. He's got a big Mauser sporting rifle.'

Hywel responds. 'I need to move a few yards to the left: my angle is wrong. He may have put his head down by the time I get there; let's put Tommy up again.'

As Hywel repositions himself Harry retrieves Tommy and moves ten yards down the trench. The major and Maurice move with him. Harry turns Tommy's head the other way round. He then pulls his service cap down to hide the bullet hole and inserts another cigarette. Hesketh-Pritchard quickly issues a new order.

'Wait a couple of minutes; only reveal a quarter-head, Colour, a back quarter. It mustn't be too much like the last target.'

The response from the German sniper takes longer this time, as if he is trying to understand why two easy targets have appeared so readily. But, eventually, the bullet strikes as truly as before. There is a hiatus of only a few moments before Hywel fires. The major exclaims, this time without any attempt to quieten his voice, 'My God, you got him! That's all of 180 yards, and at night! Astonishing!'

The four men gather to celebrate. Hywel remains calm but knows he has accounted for one possible assassin of his Welch Fusilier comrades. Hesketh-Pritchard produces a large silver hip flask from his tunic pocket.

'Drink, gentlemen? It's a rather good Armagnac. Drink well – Greaves is nearby with plentiful reserve supplies.'

They take a ten-minute breather before Hywel offers a challenge. 'One more – what do you call them, sir?'

'*Scharfschützen*.'

'Yes, sir. One more of those before we call it a day? I have a feeling I haven't got the one I'm after.'

They all nod in agreement. The major suggests a new position and target: 'A hundred and fifty yards to the west. Let's put up my Stetson – that will tempt Fritz; he won't be able to resist it.'

Fifteen minutes later the four assassins are in position again. A new cigarette is lit and the major donates his hat to the cause. Harry moves the dummy much more quickly this time, as if the man under the Stetson is in a hurry. Almost immediately, several shots ring out. All of them miss, and Harry pulls the target down beneath the parapet. Hywel puts up his hand, signalling for everyone to pause and be quiet.

The silence lasts for minutes on end. Hywel's three accomplices dare not move; their anxious breath fills the air around them. The artillery falls silent, adding to the eerie tension. It is so quiet they begin to think that their racing heartbeats are audible. They hear distant coughing from a man sleeping nearby and the scurrying of rats in the bottom of the trench, followed by Hywel whispering, 'I can see you, Fritz, but where's your mate?'

More silence follows. Harry needs a pee, but does not move a muscle. Maurice shakes his head at him as if to say, 'Cross yer legs!' Then another urgent whisper comes from Hywel.

'Now I see both of you!'

An instant later a single shot rings out, cracking in the night air. Two seconds later there is another. Moments after that Hywel's voice booms into the air. 'Got them! Two of the buggers! One behind his steel plate and another hidden in the timber of the parapet.'

His three accomplices rush over to congratulate Hywel.

'That was incredible, Colour – two in quick succession. I've never seen anything like it.'

'Your Magnum helped, Major. It cut through that plate like a knife through butter.'

'Have you got your man now?'

'I think so – the second one. I don't know why – hunter's instinct, maybe – but I think it was him. I feel better now.'

'So now I can have you at my new training centre?'

'You can. I'm all yours.'

Harry and Maurice shake hands with the major.

'Sir, your kukri and golok. Thanks to you, we don't need 'em now.'

'On the contrary, CSM Woodruff, I think trench warfare is going to get bloodier and bloodier. I'm sure you will make very good use of them in the future. Please keep them. I know where to get many more from my friends in the Far East.'

'Thank you for your 'elp, sir. Mo an' me appreciate it.'

'Not at all, Colour. It's been my privilege to meet the two of you.'

As Hesketh-Pritchard moves off down the trench, Harry and Maurice shake Hywel by the hand and slap him on the back. Harry is beaming.

'Where the fuck did you find 'im?'

'I didn't; he found me.'

'Well, 'e's a proper soldier. If only we 'ad a few more like 'im.'

While their comrades from Burnley – Mick Kenny, Twaites Haythornthwaite and Vinny Sagar – are coming to terms with the horrors of life at the Front in Ypres, Tommy Broxup and John-Tommy Crabtree are spending their second week at their new training base in Caernarvon, North Wales.

When it came to the time when the five Burnley volunteers had to go their separate ways, not much was said between them. Overt emotion is rarely seen among men who think tears are for children and women and that affection is a sign of weakness. Even so, beneath the facades of stoicism, each felt a great sense of loss at their parting and very real apprehension about the future that awaited them. They shook hands and told one another to 'tek care o' tha'sen', and off they went.

It was not much more affectionate when Tommy parted from Mary, and Mick from Cath. There were kisses, and the women shed a few tears, but they were in uniform, in the company of dozens of men who know them both as 'cocks of their middens', so too much sentimentality would break the mould. Mary walked away at the last moment, too upset to say anything, but Cath captured the mood perfectly when she shouted to Mick: 'And don't come back until t'Germans are on t'run.'

The Accrington Pals left their home towns in Lancashire on Tuesday 23 February. In celebration, in each of the towns the mills and pits were closed for the day, children were allowed out of school and thousands gathered to send the men on their way. There were brass bands in the vanguard of the marching men as they made their way to the three specially chartered trains. The people lining the routes, sometimes ten deep, cheered and waved. Many cried, but on the whole their tears were not of sadness but of pride. Over a thousand officers and men, looking immaculate in their khaki, kept time perfectly, their boots rattling the cobbled roads with the cadence of warriors seeking glory. It is a scene being witnessed all over the country as Kitchener's mighty New Army takes its first steps on the road to the Flanders fields.

Leading D Company, the Burnley lads, was Raymond St George Ross, recently promoted to Major. He sat tall in the saddle on his bay horse, his fellow officers mounted behind him, and led 274 men to Bank Top Station, where their train was waiting for them. Burnley's deputy mayor, Alderman Keighley, sent them on their way with a brief address, which concluded with a Lanky send-off for Lancashire lads: 'On yer way, lads. We're all proud on yer. Do yer bit over theer and come 'ome safe.' The train left just after 11 a.m. and, by mid-afternoon, after a warm welcome from the townspeople of Caernarvon, the men were in their billets in time for tea.

There have been several changes to 11th Battalion East Lancs, the most notable being the arrival of a new commanding officer, Lieutenant Colonel Arthur Wilmot Rickman, a career soldier who served with distinction in the Boer War with 2nd Northumberland Fusiliers. Colonel Sharples, a close friend of John Harwood, Mayor of Accrington and founder of the battalion, is far too old to continue to be Colonel of the Pals, so he has stepped aside. Rickman is the son of a general, a fine horseman and a respected soldier. His first address to the entire battalion in Castle Square at 8 a.m. on Monday 1 March went well, especially as he then dismissed the men and gave them the day off. He has been less generous since.

Despite the gloom and chill of March mornings in North Wales, parade now commences at 7 a.m. in Castle Square, after which the men return to their billets for breakfast. Drilling and exercises begin in earnest at nine fifteen, when the battalion marches across the Aber swing bridge to their training ground for long days of strenuous activity, including nine-mile forced marches with full kit to Penrhyn Park in Bangor. After lunch in billets, the men repeat the same programme in the afternoon. The exercises include communications and signalling, skirmishing, rifle and bayonet practice, and mock-attacks in both daylight and night-time against entrenched positions, a new army training exercise designed to respond to the current dire situation at the Front.

Rickman has also changed the names of the companies, for reasons that have baffled the rest of the battalion. A Company – the Accrington lads – has become W Company; B Company – Other Districts, mainly Blackburn boys – has become X Company; the Chorley men – C Company – is now Y Company; and D Company – the Burnley boys – has become Z Company. The new names have already led to much mirth; W has been called 'Where?', because you can never find them; X has become 'Illiterate', because none of them can write their name; Y has become 'Why?', because none of them understands why they are here; and Z has become 'Dozy' because they do not understand any instructions. 'Dozy' is thought to be particularly apt for the Burnley men. In the East Lancs pecking order, the folk of Burnley, as the most remote of the cotton towns, lost in the mists of the Pennines, are thought to be particularly inbred and backwards.

As an experienced soldier, Rickman knows what to expect in Flanders. Perversely, the War Office issues only vital pieces of field equipment when battalions are about to go overseas, so Rickman has given John Harwood a shopping list of things that are needed and can be incorporated into the training. It includes range finders, electrical signalling kits, extra binoculars, field telephones, police whistles and various medical supplies. The mayor has organized a public subscription to raise the £125 required, which has been achieved within three days.

While the battalion's thirty-one officers have been accommodated in considerable comfort in Caernarvon's best hotel, the Royal on Bangor Street, Tommy and John-Tommy have been billeted together in a modest boarding house further down the road at number 33. It is a street in two parts. Although the Royal is only a few yards away, set back and hidden by trees, lower down Bangor Street becomes a lively thoroughfare running north-east from the centre of the town and is noted for its many pubs, boisterous weekend evenings and as the haunt of ladies of the night.

But number 33 is a pillar of spartan respectability. It is run by four spinster sisters, the Ensors, aged between fifty and seventy-five: Mary, the eldest, Jane, Margaret and Hephzibah, the youngest.

Both Burnley lads like Caernarvon. The air is clean and

the wide vistas of mountains and sea contrast dramatically with the murk of Burnley's mills and pitheads. The local pubs serve beer a little maltier and sweeter than Burnley's hoppy bitters, but it's perfectly drinkable, except on Sunday, when, to the consternation of the Lancastrians, no beer of any kind can be found anywhere. As far as the East Lancs men are concerned, it is the town's only drawback.

And Caernarvon likes the Accrington Pals. Quite apart from welcoming the Lancastrians out of a sense of patriotic duty, the arrival of over a thousand unattached men with good money in their pockets and few household costs to bear is an economic windfall for the borough, especially out of season.

Concerts have been laid on; football, billiards and roller-hockey matches have been played. Tournaments have been held between companies, between officers, NCOs and men and against local teams. Tommy boxed in a series of bouts in the Caernarvon Pavilion, winning all his fights as a middleweight. But the star of the card was seventeen-year-old Harry 'Kid' Nutter from Rishton, who stopped all his opponents in less than a round.

The Ensor's boarding house is a modest abode which has seen better days, but it is clean and serves a good breakfast, lunch and dinner. Some men have taken to the local delicacy, laverbread with bacon and cockles, but not all. Burnley is a long way from the sea, so seaweed and cockles are an acquired taste. The ladies also make and sell highly thought of cakes and pastries, which are very welcome additions to the menu.

Tommy and John-Tommy share a room facing Bangor

Street, and there are two more pairs of Pals in rooms at the back. There is a communal indoor lavatory and a large bathroom with a big porcelain bath. Both are veritable luxuries for men used to an outside privy and a tin tub hanging on a nail by the back door.

Their accommodation also has other benefits. It is only 100 yards from Caernarvon's Castle Square and the six-hundred-year-old stone bastion of English rule that towers over it. The castle is thought to have been modelled on the mighty walls of Constantinople, and certainly casts a huge shadow across the town. Compared to Burnley, the town is quaintly picturesque and in summer attracts visitors from Liverpool, Manchester and even the English Midlands. Perhaps even more enticing for the Burnley lodgers at number 33 is the Royal Oak and the Prince of Wales, two popular pubs, one next door at number 35 and the other next door but one at number 37. For six nights a week the aroma of malt and hops and the babble of conversation and laughter waft up to the men's rooms, tempting them to walk just ten short yards to join the merriment.

''Ow dost think Mick an' t'lads are doin' in France?'

''Ope they're alreet, John-Tommy. I wouldn't fancy wot they're laikin' at. Feightin' in little 'oles in t'ground.'

'Nay, me nayther; if I'm gonna feight t'Germans, I'd ratha look 'em in th'eye.'

The two Pals have been seduced once more by the temptations of the adjoining building. They are savouring the Royal Oak's Welsh Dragon, a bitter made for the landlord by his brother, who owns the Black Boy in Castle Square, the town's oldest public house, and who brews on his premises. The pub is full of Burnley men, as it is every night. The beer is flowing in torrents and, like the landlord, the local professional girls are doing a roaring trade.

'Not bad, this ale.'

'Aye, I reckon to it. You know wot, John-Tommy, we've coughed up alreet 'ere. Good digs, good ale, trainin' in t'fresh air.'

'Tha's reet; it's champion; it'll do me. I'd be 'appy to stop 'ere fer a bit.'

''Ow long dost think we'll be 'ere?'

'Major Ross told me at least three month, mebbe until t'summer.'

'What dost mek o' t'landladies; queer owd biddies, aren't thi?'

'They're alreet, as spinsters go. Must 'ave bin comely lasses in their time; reet odd that no on'em's wed.'

'Aye, couple o' t'lads at t'back are single – mebbe they'll be tempted by older women. When all's said an' done, it's a nice little business they've got 'ere.'

John-Tommy laughs at the thought. 'Nay, lad. Youngest, Hephzibah, must be fifty-odd!'

Tommy shakes his head, acknowledging that his suggestion is unlikely to come to pass. 'I 'eard 'em talkin' Welsh to one another this mornin'. Reet daft tongue it is; can't understand a word on it.'

'That's cos it's a different language, Tommy. Margaret asked me t'other day to speak slow cos she couldn't understand me. So it cuts both ways, our Tommy.'

'S'pose so, but it still sounds reet odd t'me; it's like they're coughin' up phlegm.'

John-Tommy drains his jug of beer and asks the bar-boy

to bring two more. He then looks at the clock behind the bar.

'Last one, Tommy . . . Wonder 'ow Cath an' Mary are doin' in London. Wouldn't fancy that either. Ne'er been down south, but they reckon it's ten times bigger 'an Manchester; too many folk fer me.'

'Expect they'll be alreet, tha's nowt much bothers them two.'

John-Tommy has a sudden thought. 'Fancy goin' up Snowdon at t'weekend?'

'Yer mean on t'railway?'

'Nay, hikin' it.'

''Aven't yer 'ad enough marchin' in them 'ills?'

'Don't be a soft appeth, it'll do us good. If I can fettle it at nearly twice thi age, thee can.'

'How far is it?'

''Aven't a clue; I'll tell yer when we get t'top.'

'An' wot will we do when we get there?'

''Ave a slice o' parkin an'a glass o' beer.'

'Give over!'

'I'm not pullin' tha leg; th's a cakes an'ale cabin at t'top.'

'Reet. Yer on, John Tommy.'

St John's Gate, Clerkenwell, London

For Mary Broxup and Cath Kenny, the last thirty-six hours have been a bewildering whirlwind of new experiences. They felt like excited children on the train down to London from Burnley. They had only ever been in third class before, and then only twice, to Blackpool. Now they are enjoying the comfort of a second-class carriage, paid for by Henry Hyndman, on the very grand London and North-west Railway, seeing places, people and scenes unlike any they have witnessed before.

At Rugby Station, one of the nation's most important railway hubs, they spotted a lady in the most sumptuous fur coat and pearl necklace they had ever set eyes on. She carried a tiny dog, the like of which they had never seen before, and was followed by a younger woman in a neat, navy-blue, two-piece suit, who was organizing two porters pulling a trolley piled with a heap of leather luggage taller than they were. The group disappeared into the first-class carriage amidst a flurry of feverish activity as the station manager appeared, complete with top hat resting on his ears and two assistants trailing obsequiously in his wake, to ensure that 'Madam' got away safely.

At Watford, the platforms were full of hundreds of dark-skinned foreign troops. With the notable exceptions of a handful of Asian faces working as cleaners in the mills and a Black American harmony group that was performing in the music hall, the only dark-skinned people they had seen in large numbers were colliers on their way home from the pit, covered in coal dust and grime. But these men were immaculately turned out, their uniforms brushed and pressed, their boots gleaming. Many of them had elaborately waxed full beards and wore khaki-coloured turbans instead of army service caps. Others were smaller, more olive-skinned men who wore slouch hats with the brim turned over on one side.

The guard on Mary and Cath's train, a former regular soldier in the Indian Army, told them that the men were

Sikhs, Gurkhas, Jats and Bhopalis shipped in from India; all were destined for the Front.

When Cath, in her usual provocative way, asked the guard why men under British rule would fight for their colonial masters, he smiled and told them that they would do so without hesitation and at least as well as their British counterparts, in many cases better.

On the approach to London the two just sat and stared out of the window in wonder. They had always thought Burnley was shrouded in smoke, from the spewing chimneys of its countless mills, but London also appeared to be clouded, in a fug from endless rows of houses, each of which belched its own thick column of smoke. As they drew closer to the centre of the city, the houses grew bigger and had multiple chimney stacks and pots. Occasionally, through gaps in the rows of houses, they could glimpse some of London's elegant streets and squares. There they saw a plethora of two-wheeled hansom cabs, four-wheeled 'growlers' and the increasingly popular 'motor taxis'. Unlike the working men of the North, London's 'gents' were wearing bowlers and top hats, and its well-to-do women, instead of dowdy Lancashire shawls, sported elegant, wide-brimmed hats with feathers, bows and flowers.

Henry Hyndman met them at Euston and took them to his rooms on Baker Street for tea. There they met half a dozen more working-class northern women whom Henry had invited to London to join the Voluntary Aid Detachment. After tea, sandwiches and cakes, he told them that accommodation had been arranged at the YWCA off the Edgware Road and that he would introduce them to the senior women of the VAD at the St John Ambulance headquarters in Clerkenwell at ten o'clock the following morning.

Henry then made straight for Mary and Cath and invited them both to supper at the Beehive, a nearby restaurant on Crawford Street. There, after the renowned British socialist plied them and himself with large quantities of food and drink, Mary's prediction about Henry's amorous intentions came to pass. Cath nearly choked on her drink, but manages to put a broad smile on her face when she responds.

'Henry, tha's a saucy bugger, that's fer sure. Do tha ollus proposition young women tha meets?'

'Not at all, only particularly attractive ones like you two.'

Mary giggles at the absurdity of the proposition.

'And is it ollus two at a time?'

'No, of course not; it's quite rare to meet two such beauties at the same time.'

Cath gets up to leave. 'Listen, Henry, if tha's got us down 'ere for a quick one o'er brush in exchange for an introduction to t'VAD, then we're on t'next train 'ome!'

'My dear Cath. What do you take me for? I've asked; you've said no; let that be the end of the matter. I make no apologies for the proposition: you brought that upon yourself by being so gorgeous. It's got nothing to do with the VAD. I want you involved because you and Mary are the sort of intelligent young girls who can change the lot of working women all over the country.'

Cath sits back down. She is puzzled, so is Mary. 'Dost mean that if we don't g' t'bed wi thi, tha'll still give us t'introduction t'VAD and pay us a wage in France?'

'Of course. The two things are quite separate. I'm not a cad, just a man sorely tempted by beauty and the thrill of pursuing it. I trained as a mathematician at Cambridge; I'm good with numbers. The odds on both of you saying yes were perhaps a thousand to one; on one of you saying yes, much less, perhaps as low as a hundred to one. I thought it worth a flutter. But God forbid at the cost of your respect.'

'You know wot, Henry, tha's a dirty sod, but tha's got a nice way o' goin' abaht it.'

Cath brings the conversation to a close. 'Alreet, Henry; nowt more said abaht it. Now get us another drink in. Mary will 'ave a Mackeson an' a ruby port and, for once, after all your shenanigans, I'm breakin' t'pledge. I'll 'ave a brandy.'

'My pleasure. I would recommend a large fine champagne cognac.'

'No, a brandy, Henry.'

'Cath, cognac is the finest of brandies – in fact, the only one worthy of the name.'

'Oh, well, a large one o' them'll do nicely.'

After the drinks are brought over Henry proposes a toast.

'To the VAD and their work in France, to the future of British working women and to you two, my Burnley beauties. And not forgetting, of course, Mick, Tommy, Vinny, Twaites and John-Tommy.'

An hour later, after several more drinks, Mary and Cath walk arm in arm to their YWCA digs. Cath, who has only drunk alcohol a couple of times in her life, needs help to walk in a straight line.

'Dost think Henry gets many yeses.'

Mary laughs. 'Mebbe when he were younger; expect he were 'ansome then.'

'S'pose some girls tek to 'im cos he's a clever bugger, an' an important man.'

'Aye, but not fer me.'

Mary changes the subject. 'Is tha moithered abaht tomorra?'

'Aye.'

'So am I.'

When Mary and Cath arrive at St John's Gate, the HQ of St John Ambulance, Henry is there to meet them, as are the other northern aspirants. Henry is, as usual, full of enthusiasm and optimism and does not look in the slightest sheepish about the events of the previous evening. He reminds the women that St John Ambulance and the Red Cross have agreed to unite in their war effort and that both have taken the VAD under their wing to help it with its work.

'So, ladies, this morning, you will meet Katherine Furse, the head of the VAD. She is a passionate and very capable woman. As early as August last year, she went to the battlefields with a small group of women to help in any way they could. The BEF hierarchy didn't like it, but she won them over with her forbearance, despite the hardships. So, she's worthy of respect. But don't be intimidated: she's a woman, a mother, a widow – she's no different from all of you.'

'Except she's rich!'

Cath, who has a sore head from her indulgences of the

night before, cannot resist shouting out her prickly comment. Henry just smiles.

'That's true, Cath, but she's not that rich. Money doesn't buy courage, determination and generosity, and she has all of those as well.'

Cath is reluctant to accept Henry's point and shrugs her shoulders.

'You'll also meet Katharine Stewart-Murray, a VAD board member. She is a very accomplished pianist, highly intelligent and has a title through her marriage to the heir to the Duke of Atholl. She is already a marchioness . . .'

'Wot's one o' them, Henry?'

Cath's apprehension about the impending meeting is exhibiting itself in aggression. Again, Henry is undaunted. 'Her husband is the Marquis of Tullibardine, the second title of the dukedom.'

'Dost mean he's got more 'n one title; that's bloody greedy if tha asks me!'

'Oh, he'll have more than that when he's a duke. He'll probably have half a dozen.'

Mary, emboldened by Cath, adds a brief but pithy comment: 'Bugger me!'

The other women are incredulous, partly at hearing of the Stewart-Murrays' many titles but mainly because of Cath and Mary's outspoken comments. Henry tries to calm the Burnley women. 'I don't really know the marchioness, but I hope she doesn't have you standing on ceremony. If she does, the correct address is "Lady Katharine".'

Again, Cath cannot resist the temptation. 'I'm callin' 'er Katharine, whether she likes it or not!'

Henry smiles to himself; her comments reminding him why he so admires the feisty Lancastrian.

'As you please, Cath. Now, you'll all go in as individuals, or in small groups if you've come with friends. Finally, remember this: these are not job interviews. You are volunteers. The British Socialist Party will pay your way, so all they're interested in is your commitment to the cause of the war.'

Henry goes to the office door, opens it slightly and beckons to Cath and Mary. 'Cath, Mary, you're first. Good luck.'

The two Burnley lasses are suddenly on their own. Self-conscious in their Sunday-best ruffled white blouses and long, pleated skirts, thinking it the correct pose, they stand to attention like soldiers. Sitting behind the long mahogany table in front of them are two formidable women, pillars of Edwardian society. Neither smiles nor makes more than a token glance upwards. There are two chairs in front of them, and Katherine Furse nods at the two women to take a seat. There are several moments of silence as the two VAD senior officers scrutinize the paperwork in front of them. Cath and Mary look at one another, wondering whether they should speak first. Cath is just about to do so when Furse looks up.

'So, Kenny and Broxup, you are weavers from Burnley, Lancashire?'

Cath answers confidently, trying to soften her East Lancs dialect and strong accent. 'Yes, Katherine; I'm Cath and this 'ere is Mary. We're pleased to be 'ere.' She then looks at Kitty Stewart-Murray. 'You must be t'other Katharine; I'm a Catherine too, but call me Cath. Pleased to meet you.'

Mary then speaks out. 'I'm pleased to meet you as well.'

Furse and Kitty look at one another and raise their eyebrows. Neither Cath nor Mary can decide whether it is a look of surprise, horror or admiration. Kitty Stewart-Murray asks the next question.

'Cath, why do you want to join the VAD?'

'Oh, that's easy. Our Mick – me 'usband – he were a collier; he's gone off tunnelling under t'German lines at t'Front. So I want to do my bit.'

'He must be a brave man.'

'Not sure abaht that; he's as daft as a yard brush 'alf o' t'time.'

To the mild bewilderment and significant amusement of Furse and Kitty, both Lancastrians are slipping back into Lanky.

'And you, Mary?'

'Our Tommy's in camp in Caernarvon; 11th Battalion, East Lancs. He volunteered fo' Kitchener's Army last year. So, ratha than sit at 'ome on me arse doin' nowt, I want to 'elp t'lads at t'Front.'

'Another brave man.'

'He's an 'ard man in a fist feight, or when tha's some cloggin' goin on. Don't know abaht feightin' t'Germans wi' guns an' bayonets. He might run a mile!'

'Sorry, Mary, what's cloggin'?'

'It's when t'lads feight wi' hobnail clogs on; thi kick one another to buggery.'

'Really! Can he not find his recreation in other ways, like sport?'

'Oh, he plays football and cricket and a bit o' knur and spell.'

'Knur and spell?'

'Aye, thi laik at it on t'moors fer brass. Thi'av to 'it a little ball a long way wi' a bendy mallet; futhest wins all t'brass – money.'

'How interesting. Slightly more wholesome than brutal street-fighting.'

Cath is beginning to tire of the inquisition. 'Aye, but not as brutal as shootin' 'elpless bee-asts wi' a shotgun.'

Kitty bristles at Cath's unnecessarily prickly aside. 'You are a woman of strong opinions, Cath – perhaps too vociferous at times?'

Cath realizes that her comment was uncalled for. 'Sorry, Katharine, th's no need fer me to be rude.'

'Forgotten, Cath. I like to speak my mind as well. You said you didn't want to be at home, as you put it, on your arse doing nothing. What about your weaving jobs?'

Mary decides to intervene. 'We got sack from t'mill. Thi said we were troublemakers, which were reet; we are.'

'I see. Will you be troublemakers in the VAD?'

'Don't reckon so. We're being paid properly and, as long as we're treated reet, fair and equal like all other women, we'll be as good as gold.'

Cath adds her comment. 'It's t'lads feightin' t'Germans that's more important than us. Like Henry Hyndman sez, we can deal wi' t'other issues when war's over. Fer now, sendin' Germans packin' is all that matters.'

Kitty looks at Furse. They both nod to one another. Furse smiles at Cath and Mary.

'You two are the kind of young women we are looking for. We know you're not women of means, but Mr Hyndman has taken care of that. By the way, as a matter of interest, are you both socialists and supporters of the suffragettes?'

Cath answers quickly. 'Yes, and republicans.'

Furse swallows hard. 'I thought so, but we're a Catholic cause and welcome all shades of opinion – although you two seem to have the full set of radical views.'

The grin breaks first across Cath's face, but the other three soon follow as Furse's sardonic remark sinks in.

'So what can you do for us?'

Mary is strident in response. 'Wi can both drive, turn our 'ands t'most things; but better 'n that, we don't mind 'ow 'ard it is. We've lived wi' nowt – no coal fer t'fire, no brass fer candles, nowt t'eat 'cept tatty soup. No matter 'ow tough it is fer t'lads at t'Front, wi can fettle it.'

'Fettle?'

'Cope wi' it.'

'Very good. Do your driving skills include driving large trucks?'

'Them's all wi can drive.'

'Good, we'll have you in France by the weekend – probably in St Omer, near the headquarters of the British Expeditionary Force. There's a good deal to be done there. We have several routes to the Front in the south with vehicles going back and forth all the time.'

Cath and Mary are overjoyed and hug one another before shaking hands with their VAD superiors. Cath is bold enough to kiss both women on the cheek, who, although they try hard to hide it, are taken aback by her audacity.

'Thank you, ladies. We won't let you down.'

After Mary and Cath leave, Kitty Stewart-Murray and Katherine Furse reflect on the encounter. Kitty is thoughtful. 'Well, quite a pair; insolent in an endearing sort of way.'

'Aren't they? You were right – socialists, suffragettes – but the world is changing, and there's no doubt they are formidable women. I think we're right to take them, especially as Hyndman is funding them. What Kenny said at the end was ominous. The end of the war will be an interesting time for all of us. But I'm not sure I'm going to be kissing my servants!'

'That I would like to see, Kitty. But I agree: they'll do well for us. There is no doubt they're cunningly intelligent and will mature with time. More importantly, as they said, they'll handle the horrors at the Front better than most. After all, this is a "people's war" and they are certainly people! But am I ready for this new world Kenny and Broxup tell us is nigh? No – and I'm sure they'll not be on my dinner-party list this year.'

'Nor mine. But they're both pretty girls; I rather think they would raise the blood pressure of the men at my table!'

'Frightening, Kitty. Clever, pretty and angry; an awesome mix.'

Cath and Mary hold their own inquest as they stroll from Clerkenwell through Holborn on their way to the Edgware Road YWCA. Mary grabs Cath's arm and locks it into her own.

'So, our Cath, wot dost think?'

'Not a bad couple o' lasses fer toffs. Ave not met any before; funny that they're like anybody else.'

'Fer a moment I thought you we're gonna rise t'Marchioness' bait, or whatever she's called.'

'She did moither me a bit, but it were a fair feight.'

'Aye, it were. So, we'll be in France soon. Wot a t'do.'

'I know. I were full o' blather in there, but, t'tell t'truth, I'm reet windy abaht it.'

'So am I.'

Mary smiles, thinking of last night at the Beehive. 'So, Henry finally showed 'is 'and last night, Cath.'

'Wot yer mean is he tried to show us 'is little knob. At least he were honest abaht it.'

'Aye, s'pose he's not a bad lad.'

'No, he's alreet, just a lad, like all on 'em. None of 'em can keep their little willies in their trousers.'

Cath and Mary are enjoying their walk through London's famous streets – Clerkenwell Road, Gray's Inn Road, High Holborn and Oxford Street – before they reach Edgware Road, the ancient road to all points north. Partly because it sounds French – a culture they realize they are going to have to come to terms with – but mainly because it looks very tempting, they decide to indulge themselves in Joe Lyons' Maison Lyonses at Marble Arch. They order sandwiches, tea and cakes and, while they wait for their order to arrive, they gawp at the other customers. When it does, served by the ubiquitous Lyons 'Gladys', it is something of a curate's egg.

'Lovely cakes, Cath.'

'Should be, at that price. Tea's weak, like maiden's water.'

'Oh, stop moanin'. Look, they've cut crust off t'bread.'

'Waste o' a 'alf a good loaf. But they're reet tasty, I'll grant thi that.'

Cath becomes less and less critical of the food as she

devours more and more of it. ''Ave yer ever drunk coffee, Mary?' she asks.

'Never. I'm told it's reet bitter.'

'I'm goin' to 'ave one. I read thi drink it i' France; thought we should get used to it.'

'Well, I'll 'ave one an' all.'

When the coffees arrive, both women decide they will have a cognac to go with them. It's not quite as good as the brandy proffered by Henry Hyndman but enjoyable all the same. By the time the café clock strikes three and the volume of customers begins to decrease, Cath and Mary are content.

'Grand in't it, Mary? Shall we go out t'neet? One last fling?'

'Aye, let's enjoy it while we can. I think it'll all be different when us gets to France.'

Wednesday 10 March

The Cabinet Room, 10 Downing Street, London

London is enveloped in a dank morning mist, and the mood in Downing Street's Cabinet Room is just as gloomy.

The weekly meeting of the British War Council is attended by an unusually large group, including several guests. The Prime Minister is concerned about the progress of the war, both on land and at sea, and has invited his political opponents, the Conservatives Andrew Bonar Law, Arthur Balfour and Lord Henry Lansdowne. They are also there because the Council thinks that the Allied offensive in the Dardanelles will result in the future of Constantinople being thrown into the balance and, with it, much of the Eastern Mediterranean.

The meeting demonstrates power politics at its most stark and conceited.

The consensus among Britain's war leaders is that, once the Royal Navy and her French allies push through the Dardanelles and appear on the shoreline of the Turkish capital, the country's leaders will capitulate, or that there will be a *coup d'état*. This would then persuade Greece, Bulgaria and Romania to join the Allied cause against German and Austria-Hungary. Then, with the Russian, French and British fleets controlling the Black

Sea and the Mediterranean, a new front could be opened along the Danube, striking into the heartland of the Austro-Hungarian empire.

But the strategic dominoes are not as easily toppled as the theory suggests. First of all, the price required for the participation in the Dardanelles campaign of an army corps of 50,000 men from Imperial Russia is that it be granted possession of Constantinople, the Dardanelles Straits and the European parts of Turkey. At the same time, it demands that Greek participation and thus any territorial reward be denied. Secondly, and more significantly, the logic of the plan presupposes that 250,000 good-quality Turkish soldiers will melt away when the Allies attack. Never was conceit so blind.

Lord Kitchener begins the meeting with daunting statistics from the Western Front. He reports that the original BEF commitment to France in the autumn of 1914 amounted to 5,800 officers and 157,000 men, and that they suffered 113,000 casualties, killed or wounded.

Asquith fidgets as the numbers are read. He has already, the previous evening, written a long letter to Venetia Stanley and is now planning the next one, in which he intends to pen a long, self-deprecating fictional account of his own tribunal in front of Rhadamanthus, the mythological judge of men from Greek legend. His fidgeting and the peculiar flight of fancy about his own judgement day reflect his sullen mood, a worrying state of affairs for those around the table as they observe the leader of the nation. Ultimately, when Asquith's fictitious tribunal passes judgement, Rhadamanthus will decide that, because he has not used to their full extent the prodigious intellectual gifts that

God granted him, and which allowed his rise from modest beginnings to lead his nation, he will be denied the eternal peace of death when his time comes. Rather, he will be sent back to this earth but denied any gifts of intellect, insight or imagination and condemned to live a life of mundane obscurity: *From birth to death you will be surrounded by, imprisoned in, contented with, the Commonplace.*

As Asquith ponders his nightmarish daydream, the rest of the War Council shiver at the stark figures. Kitchener then offers more numbers, which are intended to offer reassurance but achieve the opposite effect, as they only too obviously hint at the future level of casualties. He announces that there are now over 15,282 officers and 446,467 men at the Front, supported by 1,105 artillery pieces and 1,011 machine guns. He also says that the army reserve is over 250,000, excluding the huge Volunteer Army he now has in training.

There is a self-satisfied look on his face as he finishes his headcount, a feeling that is not shared by the rest of the gathering, who, like the constituents they represent, are in shock about the sheer scale of the war and its ever-mounting death toll.

Winston gives a brief outline of the latest plan for an imminent naval attack through the Dardanelles, but even as he speaks he can detect doubt among his colleagues and barely disguised cynicism from his Tory opponents.

At noon the Cabinet disperses for a lunch of smoked-salmon terrine with cucumber and quail's eggs, served with an expensive Puligny Montrachet. It will be followed by crown of lamb stuffed with mushrooms, accompanied by an even more extravagant Gevrey-Chambertin. Pudding will be Eton Mess with clotted Devonshire cream, washed down by a Monbazillac dessert wine. The menu is chosen by Asquith himself and embraces three of his favourite dishes and wines. Unbeknown to the Council enjoying pre-lunch drinks, the first major offensive of 1915 has been raging in France for four hours. Kitchener and his senior staff at the War Office know that the attack is imminent but not the precise timing.

Sir John French, Commander of the BEF, is under considerable pressure from his French counterpart, the redoubtable General Joseph Joffre. Joffre is dismissive of the small scale of the British Army on the ground and its resolve to mount a determined frontal attack, so French has asked General Douglas Haig to plan the offensive. The attack has been carefully planned and designed in the hope of meeting the new demands of trench warfare. Aerial reconnaissance by the Royal Flying Corps has produced several photographs, which for the first time allow the planners to see the precise layout of the German trenches.

Almost four hundred powerful weapons, the greatest assembly of artillery pieces committed to the war to this point, have been carefully positioned under cover of darkness to destroy the barbed wire in no-man's-land, to neutralize the German machine-gun nests and to pulverize their trenches. Former residents of the locale have been interviewed about the layout of buildings, streets and houses, telephone cables have been dug deep underground and extra ammunition and supplies dumps have been created.

Haig has chosen a 2,000-yard-long section of the Front

just beyond the small village of Neuve Chapelle just inside the French border in Nord Pas de Calais. It is eight miles north-east of Béthune and 16 miles south-west of Lille. Neuve Chapelle was captured by the Germans in fighting in October but is now regarded as a weak point in the German defences, which could open the way to the strategically important Aubers Ridge beyond and, ultimately, Lille. Haig believes that the German trenches he plans to attack are manned by only one and a half German battalions, perhaps 1,200 men, against which he will hurl fifteen battalions, outnumbering them by more than ten to one.

The attack began at seven thirty with a single blast from the only 15-inch Howitzer available, nicknamed 'Granny'. It was said that 'Granny's Boom' of 10 March was heard in Ypres, almost 20 miles away. Granny is a formidable old girl, capable of launching a 1,500-lb Lyddite shell over six miles. Two and a half miles away, her opening salvo was aimed at the tower of the Église St Vaast in Aubers, which the Germans are using as an observation post. The shell missed by only a few yards but completely devastated the commune's town hall and immolated several civilians who had gathered there to plan their upcoming spring festival.

For thirty-five minutes the British artillery pounded the German positions. It was a ferocious assault, witnessed by the British infantry lying in wait. They had been told to keep their heads down but most could not resist watching the devastating outcome. Later accounts talked of timber, sandbags and body parts cascading into the air as the wire-cutting, all-but-horizontal shells screeched overhead barely six feet above them. It was said that the upper half of one German officer, complete with his pickelhaube helmet firmly fastened to his anguished face, and with his eyes wide open, landed, bolt upright, in the mud only a few yards in front of a company of 1st Battalion Sherwood Foresters.

On the order of their company serjeant major, the Nottinghamshire and Derbyshire men briefly removed their caps as a sign of respect. The Foresters are men who had been serving in the colonies and, although they have been in France since November, this was their first major battle. The sight of a dismembered enemy officer staring at them at the moment of his death was not an auspicious start.

Haig's infantry attacked at 8.05. The British Army's 4th Corps, six brigades of the 7th and 8th divisions, attacked from the north, and six brigades of the Indian Army's Meerut and Lahore divisions attacked from the west. By 10 a.m. Neuve Chapelle had fallen, but only with significant losses on both sides, after fierce hand-to-hand fighting in desolate open ground and in stifling trenches.

The British battalions pushed on beyond the village, but lines of communication began to break down, and confusion and misunderstandings hampered progress. The 5th Cavalry Brigade was committed to the attack to strike home the advantage, but General Henry Rawlinson hesitated. Several companies and platoons with open ground in front of them, and with no German defenders to be seen, are ready to push on, but no orders to advance arrive as communications between officers at the sharp end of the battle and their superiors at battalion, brigade, corps and BEF HQ break down. Chaos ensues; with telephone lines destroyed, messengers run or cycle with orders. Often they are killed in transit or their messages are rendered useless by new developments.

By one thirty German reinforcements have started to arrive and new defensive positions are being prepared. The artillery brigades are beginning to run out of shells and their use has to be rationed, meaning that infantry assaults have to be undertaken without the protection of adequate covering fire. The battle will continue into the afternoon, until the momentum subsides with dusk, leading Haig to halt the assault.

Just over a mile of ground has been gained and the deserted village of Neuve Chapelle 'liberated'. But casualties on this day and over the coming three days of attack and counter-attacks will total 11,200 men, at which point the two sides will have fought to the point of exhaustion. Afterwards, General Joffre declared himself satisfied that the British could, after all, mount an attack from a defensive position, but said disdainfully, *'Mais ce fut un succès sans lendemain'* ('But it was a success which led to nothing.').

The Battle of Neuve Chapelle brought back to all combatants and those observing from a distance the mass carnage of 1914. As then, there were many moments of sadness and madness. One of the saddest was the desertion of Private Isaac Reid, 2nd Battalion Scots Guards, on 11 March, the second day of the battle. He was found hiding in the rear area a few hours later. He was court-martialled and shot by firing squad a few weeks later.

Two of many moments of madness are worth recording. The first was the attack on the northern edge of the assault, close to what the planners called the 'Sunken

Road'. The defenders were two companies of crack German VII Corps troops, men of 11th Jaeger Battalion. They were unharmed by the early-morning British artillery barrage and were well protected in trenches bristling with machine-gun nests. The British attackers were men of 2nd Battalion Northants and 2nd Battalion Middlesex. Almost a thousand men left their trenches in the first moments of the battle; none was ever seen again.

The second, equally mad but less horrific moment was the story of Padre Wilfred Abbott. He appeared in the middle of a heavy German artillery barrage, cycling behind a line of trenches through a hail of machine-gun bullets, as if without a care in the world. When seen by an officer, who asked him what the hell he was up to, he apologized about the rickety state of his bicycle, saying that he used to own a much better one but that it had been stolen by a fleeing French refugee, for whom he now prayed every day. Moments later, a shell landed close by, obscuring the pastor in a cloud of dirt and debris. Certain that he was dead, several men rushed forward to retrieve what was left of him, only to see him emerge, still pedalling and whistling the hymn, 'Nearer, My God, to Thee'.

The Reverend Wilfred Abbott, Army Chaplains Department, continued to live a charmed life. He cycled to and fro along the Western Front for the next three and a half years and survived the war.

Friday 19 March

HMS Flexible, *off Cape Helles, Dardanelles*

The prospects for success in forcing a naval breakthrough in the Dardanelles have not improved. Damage caused to Turkish forts by day is being repaired by night. Mobile howitzers are still being moved around with skill and guile by the Turks, and their minefields have not yet been cleared. Mine-sweeping actions by British and French trawlers manned by sturdy volunteers have come to nothing because of the intensity and accuracy of artillery fire from shore batteries.

In a sortie over the night of 13/14 March four of seven trawlers pulling explosive charges on mine-sweeping cables were put out of action without causing any damage to the mines. Admiral Carden had run out of ideas. Pressure from the Admiralty was mounting and Winston's telegrams were growing blunter. Carden's stomach ulcers were becoming unbearable and his doctors declared that he was on the point of a nervous breakdown. He telegrammed his decision to step down on the morning of 16 March. Relieved, Winston immediately appointed Rear-Admiral John de Robeck as Carden's successor, a man who inspired much more confidence at the Admiralty and in those under his command.

De Robeck's promotion coincided with the arrival on

his flagship, the *Queen Elizabeth*, of Army General Sir Ian Hamilton, the newly appointed commander of military forces in the area. A good friend of Winston's since the Boer War, Hamilton was on the horns of a dilemma. Winston wants him to commit the army to a landing as quickly as possible to neutralize the threat from the Turkish forts. His superior, Lord Kitchener, wants him to wait until the 29th Division is ready.

In the wardroom of the *Queen Elizabeth* on the night of 17 March de Robeck and Hamilton, supported by their senior British and French commanders, decided to press ahead with the full-scale attack that Admiral Carden had planned for the following day.

It is 10.45 a.m. on the morning of 18 March. Tom Crisp and Billy Cawson are on deck on HMS *Inflexible* trying to lash together some boxes of rifle ammunition that have come loose behind one of the rear gun turrets. There is a sudden lurch as all eight of the ship's 12-inch guns fire in quick succession. Tom and Billy are deafened and knocked off their feet in the confined space between the turret and the superstructure.

'Bloody hell! They could've warned us!'

Billy is furious that, as a senior petty-officer, he has had to suffer the indignity of landing on the deck on his backside. Tom rushes to help him up.

'Here we go again, Mr Cawson.'

'Aye, Tom, this time we'll 'ave those Turks, mark my words.'

With the ammunition now secure, Tom and Billy gather their tools, ready to undertake any emergency repairs. It is a very warm day, with clear skies and little wind. *Inflexible* is line abreast with *Prince George*, *Queen Elizabeth*, *Agamemnon* and *Lord Nelson* to her port side and *Triumph* to her starboard. To their rear, a second wave of six battleships, four French and two British, is followed by a third wave of four more British warships. All sixteen vessels are pouring merciless fire on to the Turkish positions. Tom looks on in wonder.

'I wouldn't want to be under that lot, Mr Cawson.'

'Neither would I, lad. But it's what's underneath us that we should be afeared of. The word below decks is that all the Turks' minefields are undamaged.'

'How dangerous are mines?'

'Much worse than a shell. Shells almost always hit above the water line and, unless they hit the weapons magazine, they won't sink you. But mines hole you below the water, and can sink you in minutes.'

The clear skies of only minutes earlier are now clouded by pungent smoke from mammoth ships' funnels and heavy guns. Once-placid waters become a maelstrom whipped up by giant propellers. Barren shores, moments before peaceful, full of birdsong and the hum of insect life in the hot sun, are now dotted by flaming buildings, the ground beneath them quivering from the onslaught.

The three waves of the Allied fleet sweep through the Straits all the way to the Narrows, inflicting significant damage on all the Turkish forts along the way. Sedd-el-Bahr and Kum Kale at the mouth of the Straits are in ruins. Kilid Bahr and Chanak, which guard the Narrows, are heavily damaged. By 2 p.m. almost all fire from Turkish positions has ceased. It appears that the day has been won. But there is a nasty sting in the tail of the Turkish defenders.

Ten days before the attack, under cover of darkness and in total silence, the *Nusret*, a Turkish mine warfare ship under the command of Lieutenant Commander Tophaneli Hakki, laid a line of twenty mines parallel to the Asiatic shore under the guidance of German mine specialist Lieutenant Colonal Geehl. They were placed 100 yards apart and submerged 15 yards below the surface. The defenders had noticed in previous attacks that the Allied battleships turned to starboard when disengaging, so knew exactly where to lay them.

At six o'clock, with victory in the Allies' grasp, Allied ships turn to leave the Straits. Within moments the French battleship *Bouvet* hits one of Geehl's mines. It is directly in front of *Inflexible*, at a distance of about 1,000 yards. Tom and Billy hear the muted explosion and turn to see the great swell of water beneath her water line and watch it burst and cascade into the air like a sea spout. Billy brings his field glasses to bear on the stricken vessel.

'She's been hit amidships, beneath her starboard gun turret; that's not good, Tom.'

The young Welshman is horrified by what happens next. *Bouvet* begins to list almost immediately, trapping most of her crew below.

It is a scene of terrifying panic. There are the shouts and screams of men who know their end is nigh. Klaxons sound, whistles shrill and bells ring to add to the cacophony of boiling and hissing water.

Sailors know that death at sea is a price many will have to pay, but they prefer a clean and quick death – a shell or a bullet, or even exposure in an open boat – drowning is their worst nightmare, especially below decks, where the horror of claustrophobic confinement augments the agony of asphyxiation.

A few on *Bouvet*'s deck and some of those who can scramble out of the gun turrets make frantic attempts to hurl themselves into the water, but in less than two minutes all 12,000 tons of the vessel and 639 of her complement of 700 officers and men plunge to the sea floor.

As the *Bouvet* disappears in a great tumult of pluming smoke and hissing water, the *Inflexible* makes a similar turn. Billy rushes to the rail and looks down into the depths.

'Old Fidgety Phil must think the Frenchie was hit by a shell or a torpedo. He's turnin' us straight into the same minefield!'

Although Captain Phillimore has a derogatory nickname, he is a highly respected captain and well liked by his men. Billy rushes forwards towards the forecastle.

'Tom, keep your eyes peeled and stay on deck. I must get to the bridge and tell the skipper that we're steaming into a fuckin' mousetrap!'

Billy takes only four more steps when a deep-throated rumble from her bow signals that the *Inflexible* has also been hit. He is knocked sideways towards the ship's rail. He makes a desperate grab for the top bar, but his momentum is too great and he is flung overboard. Tom is also thrown on to the deck but jumps up and rushes forwards.

'Man overboard! Man overboard!'

By the time Tom reaches the rail, there is no sight of Billy. *Inflexible*'s spume and wake obscure everything.

There is chaos on board. Klaxons and whistles assault the ear. Men rush backwards and forwards: some bellow orders, others try to respond; some are confused, others know exactly what they need to do. *Inflexible* is moving at speed, and there is no chance of Billy being retrieved from the water. He is not wearing a life jacket, has fallen over 35 feet, off balance, and although the water is calm and warm he is a long way from shore, with a relentless current pulling him towards the open Mediterranean. His only chance is the remote possibility that another ship in *Inflexible*'s wake sees him. Even then, the most they can do is throw him a lifebelt, but that is an even more remote possibility, as the eyes of every sailor in the navy will be focused on their own well-being. Ominously, dusk is throwing its shroud over the scene.

Tom sees an officer run by. 'Sir, man overboard!' he shouts. 'It's Mr Cawson.'

The officer continues to run, shouting back as he goes, 'Sorry, lad, he's long gone. Get to your emergency station. We're holed for'ards; it's touch and go!'

Tom bursts into tears, something he has not done since he lost Bronwyn to the amorous Philip Davies. Billy had been his superior, but also his mentor and the only real friend he had had since the dark days of the previous year, when he ran away from Presteigne and everything he knew and loved. Why did a harmless, honest and generous man like Billy have to die? Why all those French boys – lads from ramshackle farms, tiny villages and the poorer districts of towns and cities – their lives cut short in an instant?

At another time or in another place, Billy would have

been a fisherman or a harbour-master; he would have lived to old age and watched his grandchildren grow up. Now a war that has nothing to do with him or those French boys has killed them all in the blink of an eye.

Billy Cawson, an old salt whose heritage was rooted in the glorious days of mighty ships of English oak powered by wind in their sails, should have retired months ago, to live out his days in his beloved Cornwall. But duty to his King and country persuaded him not to. Now, he will never see England again but die a lonely and agonizing death at sea. He was the naval equivalent of the Old Contemptibles, men from a different age the like of which will not be seen again.

The eighteenth is the dark of the moon and the sky is still clear, so Billy will have one comfort: the sky will be as he remembers those of his youth; on nights when he yearned to go to sea, full of lustrous stars, the Milky Way radiant like a stairway to the heavens.

Brilliant seamanship gets *Inflexible* back to its berth on the Greek island of Tenedos. But her sister ship, *Irresistible*, and the battleship HMS *Ocean* are badly damaged and eventually sink. The French battleships *Suffren* and *Gaulois* are also badly damaged, and limp home to Lemnos. Stunned by the sudden setback, de Robeck withdraws his ships and decides against further action until support can be provided by an amphibious landing by the army. What he does not know is that the Turkish defenders have run out of shells and mines and their morale is at a very low ebb. But twenty mines, carefully laid in a perfect position, have booby-trapped the entire enterprise and bought Turkey the time it needs to send masses of men and supplies to the Gallipoli Peninsula to defend against a landing they know is now inevitable.

When Winston gives his account of the situation in the Dardanelles to the War Cabinet on the morning of the 19th, the mood becomes hostile. He tries to hide his own misgivings about the operation and the calibre of Admiral Carden but knows that Kitchener has his own source of information through his emissary, General Birdwood, and could upstage him at any moment. Nevertheless, he reports as positively as he can.

'On the afternoon of 18 March the *Queen Elizabeth* entered the Straits and fired eight rounds with her 15-inch guns at Fort number 13, Rumilie Medjidieh Tabia, three of which were direct hits. As for the minefields, about which I know we all have concerns, Admiral Carden assures me that the cleaning up of these will take only a few hours, but that it cannot be attempted until the forts are destroyed, which he tells me may take a little longer than anticipated.'

Winston continues with more detail of the campaign but knows only too well that he has given an evasive and insipid summary of the facts. As he finishes, he glances around the room. His two Admiralty colleagues Tug Wilson and Jacky Fisher look pensive; they know that the true situation is looking increasingly problematic. Thankfully, Kitchener shows no hint of what he is thinking, but Winston knows that he has already reported to Asquith that the Turkish defenders are repairing the forts as quickly as they are being damaged, and that their mobile howitzers are impossible to detect.

Asquith is already beginning to scribble his missive to

Venetia, but the eyes of the Conservative invitees are sharply focused on Winston. They say nothing – now is not the time – but they smell blood. It may not yet be Asquith's, and certainly not Lloyd George's; it is definitely Winston's political life-blood their acute partisan senses can detect, that of the man they regard as a traitor to their cause.

Tuesday 23 March

10 Downing Street, Whitehall, London

Winston is delighted to be asked to dinner by the Prime Minister, but the composition of the gathering suggests that there is more to the occasion than conviviality. Clemmie, F. E. Smith with his wife, Margaret, and Margot Asquith are the only other diners.

It is midweek, and everyone is tired, especially Asquith, who is also worried that his passion for Venetia Stanley may not be fully reciprocated. He has already written two letters to her during the day, each many pages long, and is now contemplating a third, regretting the length of the other two and apologizing for being too demanding of her time and affections.

Winston is beginning to feel depressed: the events of the last twenty-four hours have worsened at every turn and he has just heard that his brother, Jack, has left Sir John French's staff at St Omer and is on his way to Lemnos to join the staff of Sir Ian Hamilton. Thankfully, F. E. Smith is as entertaining as ever and keeps everyone amused until the real purpose of the evening begins, after dinner in Asquith's study. Margot has taken Clemmie and Margaret off to drink coffee, leaving the three men to talk politics and war.

Unusually, Asquith comes straight to the point. 'Winston,

Margot tells me that Fleet Street is alive with stories of Cabinet plots against me and that you and Lloyd George are at the heart of them.'

Winston thought that the postprandial whisky would be a post-mortem about the attack on the Dardanelles the previous week, so is shocked by the Prime Minister's question. 'Henry, that's nonsense. I am not aware of plots and have had no conversations on the subject with anyone, and certainly not with LG. Everyone has the utmost confidence in you.'

Asquith turns to FE. 'Your ear is always close to the ground,' he says. 'What have you heard?'

'Well, as you know, Prime Minister, we Tories, the guttersnipes of British politics, as your Liberal friends like to call us, can't avoid having our ears to the ground.'

'Be serious, man. What have you heard?'

FE, not used to being upbraided, answers sharply. 'It is very simple. The Conservative Party is tiring of keeping quiet and toeing the line in the "national interest". Balfour is being goaded by Bonar Law, and both are being harangued from their own backbenches. Lansdowne is similarly berated in the Lords, if not more so.'

Asquith has had a lot to drink and his tongue is beginning to run away with him. 'Balfour is a man with a futile, feminine brain. When his party is in need, he takes his hat off, says he's ill and leaves his unfortunate friends to be led by a fifth-rate man like Bonar Law.'

FE bristles at the vitriol about the leaders of his own party. 'There is a lot of talk of shortages of shells and ammunition in France, and recent events in the Dardanelles have got the papers restless. They won't take too many more setbacks like Neuve Chapelle without kicking up a fuss.'

'But we won new ground at Neuve Chapelle and put the wind up their generals and the Kaiser!'

'Yes, I know that's the official line, but you and I both know that the outcome fell a long way short of what French and Haig intended.'

Asquith then rounds on Winston: 'So what of the Dardanelles, where do we go from here?'

'I am grievously disappointed.' Winston springs to his feet, thrusts his thumbs into his waistcoat pockets and stares at Asquith intently. 'And I smell a rat! Two days ago de Robeck was raring to have another go with our battleships. But now he's changed his mind and says he can't risk it without the support of a full-scale amphibious invasion. And, if I may say so, Henry, you have also changed your position, as has his lordship, Kitchener.'

'But, Winston, that's because Fisher and Wilson – your men – are advising against it.'

'Exactly. They also changed their minds overnight. Too many volte-faces in one day, don't you think?'

'What are you suggesting?'

'You asked me about a plot. It seems to me that several people are protecting themselves against any mud that may stick from the Dardanelles and that I'm the one being left out to dry.'

'Come on, Winston, you're imagining things.'

'Am I? With de Robeck deferring to Hamilton's invasion plan, the whole operation comes under Kitchener's remit and I lose control. But my name is on the original plan, so if anything goes disastrously wrong I carry the can.'

Winston looks to FE for support. His friend nods his agreement. 'Mark my words, Henry, a disaster is a distinct possibility. We underestimate the Turks at our peril. They are Ottomans – empire-builders; Constantinople has been at the forefront of history for fifteen hundred years. The place is running alive with Germans training their men, teaching them how to dig trenches, mount machine-gun posts and use heavy artillery. Our naval attacks over the past month could not have sent a clearer signal. The Turks know an invasion will be next and will be feverishly preparing, even as we speak. On the other hand, reports suggest that, at the moment, the defenders must be at breaking point and I suspect that they have few or no shells or mines left.'

Asquith begins to respond, but Winston wants the last word. 'We must strike now! But, without your support, I can't order de Robeck to attack.'

'Winston, you're repeating the same argument you've made for the last two days,' FE interrupts, as if making one of his renowned acerbic remarks to a judge.

'Then, sir, it's about time you listened!'

Asquith is furious. 'That's bloody impudent, and I won't have it!'

FE stands, tempted not to back down, but Winston flashes him a fierce look, and his friend relents. 'Sorry, Prime Minister, that was impolite, but Winston is right: several senior members of my party want a scapegoat, and they have a score to settle with my dear friend and your First Lord of the Admiralty. Fleet Street is being fed the morsels and is more than ready to devour them.'

Asquith ponders this. 'So part of this is to try to drive a wedge between us?'

'Exactly.'

Asquith thinks again. Winston and FE remain silent. Downing Street's clock strikes ten fifteen, prompting the Prime Minister to have another sip of his fifteen-year-old Macallan. Eventually, he responds.

'Very well, gentlemen, thank you for clarifying the situation. I think another malt is called for. Let's make sure we continue to enjoy Speyside's finest and keep a wary eye open for wedges.'

An hour later, F. E. Smith and Winston are enjoying yet more malt in Winston's Admiralty study. FE has to be at Dover at six in the morning to catch a ship back to France, so Winston has organized a navy car for him. He can sleep on the journey, so is happy to keep Winston company over one of his many sleepless nights.

'I'm worried about darling Jack, FE. HQ at St Omer was ideal. He was doing good work and was relatively safe. But this posting to the Dardanelles is fraught with danger.'

'I'm sure it's of great concern to you, but he's a resolute chap; he can take care of himself.'

'Of course he can, but he's my kith and kin and I feel responsible for him and the Jagoons.'

FE changes the subject, knowing that Jack's welfare always makes Winston fret. 'What did you make of Asquith's little fishing expedition?'

'Not sure, but you certainly gave him short shrift.'

'I know, I'm sorry about that, but he was very impolite about my party leaders.'

'With just cause and a canny level of precision?'

'I refuse to answer that, m'lud, on the understanding that I may be tempted to tell the truth.'

Winston pours them both another drink.

'You know, Winston, the Old Block is the consummate politician. If he thinks he can prosper through your downfall he will not blink an eye in sacrificing you.'

'It was ever thus, FE; from the Agora in Athens to Rome's Palatine Hill, intrigue is the stuff of political life.'

'Are there plots?'

'I'm sure the Tories are plotting and scheming every minute of the day. As for our own ranks, the only alternative leader is LG. He makes no secret of his ambition, so it is hardly a plot.'

'And you, my dear friend?'

'How kind of you to ask. Sadly, I fear my star, distant and weak as it is, is waning such that it is about to disappear from even the sharpest telescopes pointed at the celestial firmament.'

PART FOUR: APRIL

A Gasping Death

Monday 12 April

Hill 60, Zwarteleen, West Flanders, Belgium

'Do'st think wi' theer yet, Mick?'

'Another two yard, Vinny, then wi'll 'ave fettled it.'

'Twaites'll be chuffed; he's reet knackered.'

'Knackered! All 'e's doin' is lumpin' bags up an' down; I'm doin' all t'diggin'. Wheer is t'bugger?'

''E's comin', I can 'ear 'im snufflin' an' snortin' down t'tunnel.'

When Twaites appears, like his two fellow moles he is covered head to toe in Flanders' heavy clay. As the tunnellers say, it looks and sticks like pale shit. Mick pretends to be annoyed with his 'bagger': 'Wheer the fuck 'ave you been?'

'Stopped off in t'Wellington fer a pint.'

'Two, more like, yer lazy bugger; thu's three bags 'ere, waitin'.'

'Bollocks, Mick, am goin' as fast as a'can. I were gaggin' fer a tar, so 'ad to stop fer one.'

Vinny grimaces. ''Ave you 'ad another shit up t'tunnel?'

'Aye, I 'ad to. It's that bully beef, it gives me t'tomtits.'

'The wot?'

'Heeard it off some cockney lads in t'billets. Thi 'ave these daft words wot rhyme: tomtit – shit; brown bread – dead; granny grunt – cunt; meks me cow and calf.'

'Eh?'

'Laugh.'

'But that don't rhyme wi' calf!'

'It does t'way they sez it; they sez, 'larf'.'

Mick has almost finished the yardage he has been asked for on his shift. 'Will you two stop natterin'? Let's get these bags out an' we can knock off.'

It has been almost seven weeks since Mick, Vinny and Twaites arrived in Ypres. Their first day was a baptism of fire as they witnessed the horror of the attack on the Irish Convent. The day after the devastation there, the three men were assigned to the 171st Tunnelling Company and sent up the line to billets at Zwarteleen, just three miles south-east of Ypres. Vinny and Twaites survived their Number 2 Field Punishment with very sore, blistered feet but earned some very important kudos among the hard-bitten moles.

Almost every day since they left Ypres, they have seen similar horrors on the battlefield, as well as experiencing the back-breaking toil and sweat of digging.

Sitting above the small village of Zwarteleen is a large mound of spoil from the construction of the railway line in the nineteenth century. It is 60 metres high, thus its name, Hill 60. Since November of 1914 the hill has been held by the Germans, affording them a commanding position over the flat landscape of Flanders. Because of its strategic position, the British want it back, so it was chosen as an ideal proving ground for the new army moles.

But the task did not have an auspicious beginning. Shipped with great speed from England, specialist mining equipment soon arrived; a huge pile of shuttering, digging tools, air and water pumps, clothing and boots was made ready for work to begin. On close inspection, though, the tunnellers were horrified. All except some of the tools were rotten or antiquated, which was hardly surprising, for when the men read the shipping manifest they discovered that the items had been put into storage in 1856, at the end of the Crimean War.

Since then, the moles have begged, borrowed, stolen or made their own equipment, including the most important piece of all: air pumps. Theirs, although admittedly not sophisticated, are very effective. Made from blacksmiths' bellows, pumped by a man using bicycle pedals, they supply a hosepipe with clean, fresh air along the entire length of the tunnel.

The tunnels they have been digging are smaller than those they use in their normal working conditions. Not designed for the extraction of coal or as sewers, they need only be big enough for a man in a crouching position to pass through easily at his shoulders. This makes the work particularly claustrophobic; not a task for the faint-hearted or a man broad of beam. Mick, despite being tall and broad-shouldered, is used to confined spaces and, fortunately, after a few early shivers, Vinny and Twaites have become accustomed to long hours in narrow slits in the bowels of the earth.

After digging an access shaft 16 feet down, they have slowly made their way across no-man's-land. They are now more than halfway, 100 yards from their starting point. Their tunnel is designated M1. Running parallel to theirs is M2, dug by another team of moles, mainly ex-sewer clay-kickers from Major Norton-Griffiths's own company. Now that each has completed 100 yards of tunnel, they will both split into a two-pronged fork which will run right up to the German trench, creating four explosion chambers.

Besides the rigours of their daily toil, there are also the brutalities of war to endure. Shells landing nearby have come uncomfortably close, on one occasion collapsing a four-yard section of tunnel behind them. Vinny and Twaites panicked, but Mick made them lie still, close their eyes and breathe deeply, before slowly and methodically digging them out. Snipers are a constant menace at the beginning and end of their shifts, and two members of a tunnelling company nearby were killed on a single day; one on his way to begin his shift, another on his way back to his billet. Both were dead before they hit the ground.

In their third week of digging, after their eight-hour shift the three Burnley men decided to walk to the village of Zillibeke for a relaxing beer. The German trenches were some distance away and all was quiet. It was a warm spring evening, almost as if peace reigned after all. Fifty yards ahead, several groups of men from the Worcesters were strolling to the same destination. Mick, Vinny and Twaites did not hear the bullet but saw a lance corporal on the far side of the group recoil backwards before crumpling like a ragdoll. Blood spewed on to the road from a large hole in the back of his head. Everyone ran for cover.

A few minutes later, followed by a serjeant and two men, a Scots Guards captain, a man in his thirties, tall and straight-backed, who looked like a veteran, rushed from a nearby barn. He shouted his orders as he ran: 'He's in that large ash in the corner of that orchard! Fire at will; let's bring him down.'

Two dozen shots rang out within moments, followed by the cracking of branches and a heavy thud as a human figure fell from the tree. The officer, smiling widely, issued a new order to his serjeant.

'Serjeant, please retrieve our catch. Let's have a look at the bugger.'

As a large group of British soldiers from the road gathered around, the sniper was dragged through the field by his boots and deposited on the ground in front of the captain. He was still alive but bleeding profusely from a wound to his shoulder and another to the thigh. Strangely, the boots he had been dragged by were not German Army-issue *Knobelbecher* marching boots but peasant farmer's. Nor was he wearing a field-grey uniform, but the civilian clothes of a Belgian local. The captain spoke to him in schoolboy German, then in slightly better French, but got no response. He turned away and spoke quietly and calmly to his serjeant.

'He's dressed as a civilian; that makes him a spy. Recruit some of those Worcesters. I'm sure they'd be happy to form a firing squad.'

'Very good, sir.'

But before the serjeant does as he is bid he whispers in the captain's ear, 'Begging your pardon, sir, but he only looks about sixteen or seventeen. How can he be a spy?'

The captain stiffens, not used to any hesitation from those to whom he issues orders. 'I have absolutely no idea. Get on with it, man!'

'Yes, sir.'

As the serjeant gathers the men of the Worcesters, all of whom are more than happy to put an end to the life of the man who killed their friend, a shout comes from one of the Scots Guards standing over the stricken sniper.

'Sir . . . Captain, sir; come an' 'ave a look 'ere. He's got a collection of dog-tags round his neck; some Frenchie ones, but mainly Brits. There must be a dozen of 'em.'

The captain strides over, fury in his eyes. 'Take them off him.'

The serjeant takes the large collection of hunting trophies from the young assassin, bringing yet more pain to his shattered shoulder, blood from which has already turned his brown jacket the colour of old mahogany.

The captain bends down close to the young sniper. 'How many have you killed, Fritz?'

Through the gritted teeth of excruciating pain, the boy answers in excellent English, 'My name is not Fritz; my name is Daan . . . I'm a Flemish Belgian.'

The captain is shocked. 'So why are you killing Belgium's allies?'

'Because I don't like the Walloons . . . the Belgian French . . . and I don't like their French cousins.' The baby-faced killer lifts his head slightly and winces at the extra agony it creates before snarling at the British officer, 'I especially don't like you . . . because you're helping the French . . . and it's none of your business.'

'How old are you?'

'Seventeen.'

'Where did you get the rifle?'

'From a dead German, shot in the back while running away. He wasn't much older than me.'

'How long have you been doing this?'

'Since the beginning of the war.'

The captain realizes he is talking to a ruthless killer driven by a profound hatred. 'How many?'

The young assassin forces a leering smile through his agony. 'More than you can count!'

With that chilling answer, the captain draws his revolver, places it between the young man's eyes and pulls the trigger. 'Today you've killed your last victim, Daan. May you rot in hell.'

Without a hint of remorse, the captain strides back towards the barn, issuing another order as he does so: 'Serjeant, get the men to drag the body down the road and throw it in the ditch. And make sure that poor chap from the Worcesters gets a proper burial.'

The three Lancashire lads have watched the drama unfold wide-eyed. Vinny's pithy comment speaks for all of them: 'Fuck me. I thought we laiked 'ard i' Burnley. But wherever yon captain comes frae, thi laik fer keeps!'

By the evening of 17 April all four chambers for the explosives have been completed and packed with their charges. The task has been undertaken by engineering officer Lieutenant Lionel Hill, who has placed half a ton of explosive into each one. It has been a delicate business, involving the dogged manhandling along the narrow tunnels of almost a hundred bags of gunpowder, each weighing 100lbs. After being double fused and wired back to the firing plungers, each chamber has been tamped along 30 feet of its access with a plug of wet sandbags to ensure that the blast goes upwards and forwards towards the Germans, rather than backwards towards the British trenches.

Hard-bitten tunnellers and their engineer officers do not always see eye to eye. The men doing the digging and humping often resent the more comfortable surroundings of their superiors above ground. Nevertheless, the one area where the engineers earn the respect of their men is in the calculation of the quantities of explosives required and how they are placed to inflict the maximum damage on the enemy at the minimum risk to their own men.

Miscalculations can be catastrophic. Everyone knows that getting it right is subject to very fine margins. Soil or rock composition, levels of ground water, quality or type of explosive being used and diligence during the tamping process may all make a significant difference to the outcome of a blast.

During the last two days of preparation German tunnellers have been heard directly above tunnel M1. If the German tunnels and explosives are ready before the British ones, all will have been in vain.

But the British detonation cannot happen until the infantry is ready.

To everyone's great relief, 1st Battalion Royal West Kents and the 491st Home Counties Field Company, Royal Engineers, are in position. Their orders are to attack immediately after detonation, even if debris is still falling. Major Norton-Griffiths could not have put it more succinctly when he addressed the men earlier in the afternoon.

'I'd rather the odd one or two of us be killed by

German dead falling from the heavens than hundreds of us mown down by their machine guns. And when I say "us", I mean what I say. I have the permission of your CO, Colonel Westwood, and I will be going over with you when the time comes.'

It is five minutes past seven. Mick and his baggers look on nervously. For the time being, their work is done, but it has little value if what happens next comes to nothing. Major Norton-Griffiths, every inch of him looking more than worthy of his moniker, 'Hell-fire Jack', smiles as he nods to the three sappers holding the explosive plungers. There is then just a moment of delay before the thunderous tremors coincide to make the entire area heave, as if a massive meteor has struck the earth. Almost at the same time a chasm as big as a football pitch is hewn out of the top of the hill. Earth, sandbags, trench timbers, rifles, myriad bits of equipment and soldiers' paraphernalia are flung hundreds of feet into the air. The ground on to which they fall becomes a field of debris 300 yards across.

Of course, German soldiers, or parts of them, form part of the debris. Mick looks at the scene. Blood, flesh and pieces of German field grey are all too visible. Thinking back to what happened at the convent when they first arrived, he steels himself against the revulsion he is feeling. He looks at Vinny and Twaites, who both have a look of horror on their faces.

'It's them or us, lads. Tek a good sken. We 'as t'do that to them, or they'd d'sem to us.'

Vinny looks doubtful. 'Ata sure, our Mick?'

'Aye, lad; certain. C'mon, let's get our tackle fettled.'

Only seconds after the explosion, as the East Kents

and the 491st Field Sappers go over the top and begin their steady climb up Hill 60, British and French artillery pieces open up to keep German support troops in the rear at bay. Unlike almost every other attack in the entire war, the men of 13th Brigade achieve their objective with minimal casualties. Their opponents have either been buried alive or blown to pieces around the hillsides and, by midnight, Hill 60 is under British control.

As the infantry at the top of the hill consolidate their ground and begin to prepare new trenches, Mick, Vinny, Twaites and the men of 171st Tunnelling Company, having decided that they will celebrate tomorrow, are fast asleep in their billet, a large barn close to Zwarteleen crossroads. But the barn door creaks open, accompanied by the bellowing voice of Company Serjeant Major Morgan.

'Attention! Come on, you lot! Wakey-wakey! Major Norton-Griffiths wants a word.'

A great deal of expletive-laden muttering ensues until the men finally get themselves into some sort of order. Mick is one of the moles about to confront Hell-fire Jack but sees that he is smiling directly at him.

'At ease, gentlemen.'

He produces a bottle from behind his back. It is a bottle of Haig's Dimple whisky, a brand well known to every man in the company but one that few can afford, except on rare occasions. The major then turns and shouts for his batman, who appears immediately, with a large wooden case. The smile on Hell-fire Jack's face becomes a mischievous grin.

'Gentlemen, providence always provides for the righteous and, miraculously, this case of one of Scotland's finest exports has just appeared in the boot of my car. As you may have heard, HQ takes a dim view of me driving around with booze in the back of my Rolls, so I thought I had better get shot of it. Do any of you know of a good home for it?'

The men crowd around the major as the bottles are distributed. Handshakes are exchanged and backs slapped.

'A toast – to all of you. Thanks to your great skill, courage and tenacity, Hill 60 is ours. The first victory for the moles!'

Norton-Griffiths makes a beeline for Mick and his two baggers and puts his hand on Vinny's shoulder. 'How are your feet, Sagar?'

'Alreet, sir. I used to go barefoot as a little lad, so it didn't moither me much.'

'And you, Haythornthwaite?'

'Same, sir; me mam ollus sez wheer thu's no sense, thu's no feelin'.'

He then turns to Mick and shakes his hand vigorously. 'I now understand why they call you Mad Mick. Your rate of digging is 8 per cent better than any man in any of my companies. Very well done.'

'Pleasure, sir. It wer a reet grand sight when it blew!'

'Indeed it was, Kenny. But I'll soon be calling you Mr Kenny. Your serjeant's stripes will be issued in the morning. Congratulations.'

Friday 23 April

British Army Field Hospital, Provost Lace Mill,
Poperinghe, West Flanders, Belgium

'What the hell is it?'

'I've no idea. They're suffering a reaction to a chemical of some sort.'

When the orderlies at Pop-Hop open the doors of the first ambulances to arrive during the evening of 23 April they know a different kind of horror has reared its ugly head.

It is the drivers who tell them the repugnant details: 'It's gas of some kind; it came from the German trenches on the far side of Ypres. They said it was like green fog. It got in the trenches and shell holes. The German machine guns were banging away, so either the gas got you or you took a bullet in the back. The worst of it was last night among the French darkies. They ran for their lives. Hundreds never made it. They were foaming at the mouth, eyes bulging, rolling around. They couldn't breathe – it was horrible!'

Another driver continues the account. 'This lot are Canadian boys; they copped for it this morning.'

One driver pulls an orderly to one side so that he can whisper in his ear. 'These are the unlucky ones. Their mates – the lucky ones – died quickly and are lying all over Kitchener's Wood. Most of these will slowly choke to death, unless the docs have got a magic potion.'

At 5.30 p.m. on 22 April the German Army introduced a new form of killing on the Western Front. Using a slight easterly breeze, 168 tons of chlorine gas in 5,730 cylinders was released near Langemark-Poelcapelle, north of Ypres. It formed into a grey-green cloud that drifted across positions held by Zouaves, French colonial troops, who broke ranks in sheer terror, creating an 8,000-yard gap in the Allied line. However, the German infantry were taken by surprise at the potency of the gas and, lacking reinforcements, failed to exploit the opportunity. The 1st Canadian Division and more French colonial troops reformed the line before they too suffered gas attacks. It was the beginning of the 2nd Battle for Ypres.

By the time Surgeon-Captain Noel Chavasse arrives after an emergency call to his room in Pop-Hop, it has been confirmed by RAMC HQ in St Omer that the French medics in Paris have verified that chlorine is the gas that is being used in the German attacks. When it comes into contact with water in mouths, eyes or lungs, it creates hydrochloric acid, an irritant to soft tissue in diluted form but lethal if concentrated.

Chavasse orders that the men struggling to breathe should be put in the open air, not in wards, and that sore eyes should be treated with castor oil, not water. Sister Margaret Killingbeck is put in charge of the arrangements. 'Bron,' she says. 'Go to the stores. Bring all the bottles of castor oil and cotton wool you can find.'

The next three days become one of the most traumatic episodes yet experienced at Pop-Hop. Over three quarters of the men who are admitted die a slow and agonizing death as their lungs dissolve. Those who survive will have breathing difficulties for the rest of their lives, quite apart from the mental trauma caused by their ordeal.

Bronwyn is now fulfilling the role of a qualified nurse and has been given due recognition and the pay and uniform of a member of Queen Alexandra's Imperial Military Nursing Service. While Noel Chavasse and the other doctors administer sedatives, Margaret and Bronwyn spend their time comforting men in their death throes. First it is the Canadians, then British boys from battalions already all but obliterated at least once before by bullet, bayonet and shell. They are now being decimated yet again, this time by a silent killer which invades the air they breathe.

As Bronwyn looks across the rows of stretchers laid out in the yard of the old lace mill, she cannot help but think of floundering fish marooned in the bottom of a fishing boat suffering a gasping death. She looks across at Margaret, the woman she admires so much. She is going from dying man to dying man, holding their hands, offering words of comfort, being the angel any man would like to be there as he took his last breath.

Since what happened between them a few weeks ago, something that Bronwyn had vowed would be a one-off, Margaret and she have become more and more intimate. For Margaret, their affair is the realization of a dream of fulfilment and happiness; for Bronwyn, a riddle of emotions and sensations but, for the time being, a satisfying one. For both of them, it makes days like the last three in Pop-Hop just about tolerable.

There has also been a moment of profound sadness for Bronwyn. Her brother Hywel, the army's star recruit to its new School of Sniping, has been sent to the 29th Division, which is preparing for an overseas posting to an operation in an undisclosed destination. After being reconciled to Hywel after the family's trauma of the previous year, she has become close to him again during their time together at Pop-Hop, and to lose him now is a big blow.

When she hears that the QAIMNS is asking for volunteers for hospital ships that will support the operation, she begs Margaret to recommend her. Margaret is mortified. 'Would you leave me so readily?' she asks.

'Of course not. Come with me.'

'But I'm needed here. So are you.'

'Mags, I don't want to lose Hywel again. You'll be needed wherever you go. Please come with me. We've become so close.'

'But we've no idea where the operation is.'

'I know, but if they're sending Hywel and hospital ships, then it's going to involve fighting and casualties.'

Bronwyn's eyes fill with tears; her expression pleads with Margaret, who cannot resist her young lover's entreaties.

'All right, Bron, let me talk to Captain Chavasse. I'll also have to clear it with Matron McCarthy. She's a tough nut, but I think she'll agree.'

'Oh, Mags, it will be such a new adventure for us.'

*

The German attack of the 22nd and the subsequent attacks and counter-attacks over the next month become the 2nd Battle of Ypres. The effectiveness of chlorine gas diminishes with time as the Allies realize that improvised protection can be achieved with a wetted piece of gauze or linen to the mouth and face, and that men's urine is even more effective than water. They also discover that, as chlorine is heavier than air, the men should avoid the bottom of their trenches during attacks and climb to their firing steps.

Having seen the futility of repeated frontal attacks, on the evening of the 24th General Horace Smith-Dorrien, hero of the Zulu Wars and veteran of the Western Front since his daring at Le Cateau in August, drives to see Sir John French in St Omer. He pleads with him not to order more assaults. His words fall on deaf ears, and Smith-Dorrien is sent home to England, which in effect relieves him of command. The next morning, in broad daylight, 15,000 British and Indian troops are ordered to go over the top and attempt to cross no-man's-land against German machine-gun fire that is so fierce the bullets fly like hailstones.

Men in the first wave carry yellow flags tied to their webbing. They protrude above their service caps to allow the British artillery to identify them and thus avoid them with their fire. Ostensibly, it is an attentive gesture, but its architect fails to realize that the flags also render the wearers ideal targets for the German riflemen and machine-gunners.

By the end of May the Germans, exhausted and out of artillery shells, call off the attacks. They have managed to reduce the 'bulge' of the salient around Ypres to a little over three miles, bringing it within range of so much artillery that it is soon reduced to rubble and becomes deserted. In order to gain just a few hundred yards of muddy fields, some drainage ditches and two small streams, German losses are over 35,000; Allied losses in trying to defend them are over 70,000 dead, wounded or missing British, French, Canadian and Indian men.

Sunday 25 April

HMS Implacable, *off Cape Helles, Dardanelles*

It is 06:00 hours. Hywel Thomas grips his Lee-Enfield firmly. He checks his sniper's paraphernalia once more. Everything is there and everything is camouflaged. He pays particular attention to his Aldis telescopic sight, his pride and joy; his instrument of death, based on the trophy he won in his duel with a German opponent. He has painted his own summer camouflage on his rifle and side-mounted sight: swirls of pale green, beige and cream to resemble the terrain on to which he is about to step.

When he gets to the beach he will be on his own. His reputation has won him the right to pick his spot to carry out his lethal mission. It is a simple objective: to kill any Turkish defender who puts himself in harm's way. The only other requirement is to report to his commanding officer, Captain Richard Willis, the CO of C Company, 1st Battalion Lancashire Fusiliers, at the end of each day, either to be told to carry on or to be given new orders.

Hywel has been assigned to the Lancastrians who form part of the 29th Division, men from North Manchester and district, headquartered at Bury. A regiment with a fine pedigree, they are the men Kitchener hopes will make the difference in the assault on the Gallipoli Peninsula and allow the navy to force the Dardanelles Straits.

The Fusiliers have just disembarked from HMS *Implacable*, an aging battleship, and have boarded thirty-two small coastal cutters, which are being towed towards the Turkish beaches. Their objective is Tekke Burnu Beach at the very tip of the peninsula. The men are so tightly packed into the cutters there is no room to move. Although it is early morning and quite cool, the cramped conditions make the men hot; some feel claustrophobic; a few get angry. Tension and the rolling of the waves causes many men to vomit, the spew covering neighbours as well as the spewer. This in turn makes more men sick. It is not an auspicious start to the day. A colour serjeant tries to calm his men in a gentle, paternalistic way: 'Steady. Steady, lads, nearly there.'

There are no lights visible on the shore, which looks bleak and inhospitable in the gloom of pre-dawn, and the sea is still shadowy from the black of the night.

The shortage of supplies and facilities on the Greek Aegean islands has meant that preparations for the army landings have had to be done in Egypt. This has cost time and made the intentions of the Allies all too apparent. The Turkish defences have been put under the control of German general Otto Liman von Sanders, an efficient and astute soldier who has spent the five weeks since the disaster of the 18 March attack making the peninsula a formidable fortress. He has 80,000 men at his disposal; they are expertly positioned, well provisioned and well armed.

Sir Ian Hamilton commands what is now named the Mediterranean Expeditionary Force. He has under him 17,649 men of the 29th Division; 10,007 men of the Royal

Naval Division; 16,762 French troops, including Zouaves, Senegalese and men of the Foreign Legion; and 30,638 Australians and New Zealanders, the cream of their armies, who will soon immortalize the appellation 'Anzac'. Hamilton should have over three hundred guns but has only been given 118. He is short of shells and has no high explosives, just shrapnel. The logic is that the peninsula will fall quickly under the massive Allied assault and therefore he will not need much heavy armour as he drives north, conquering all before him.

So haphazard has been the preparation that officers who should have been planning the details of the landings have been scouring the Mediterranean for equipment missing from their inventory. A motley collection of support ships has had to be turned into an invading armada: tugboats, converted cruise ships, colliers, trawlers – anything that floats, in fact. For the army, donkeys, mules and packhorses are bought at exorbitant prices. Water and petrol tanks, wire-cutters, torches, ladders and cooking utensils have had to be found. But nobody thought about mosquito nets or summer clothing, and only at the last minute has someone thought about the provision of hospital ships.

Surrounded by antediluvian cavalry officers grown fat in far-flung parts of the empire, Hamilton is something of a Renaissance man. Sixty-two years of age, he has seen service in India, in the Boer War and the Russo–Japanese War, where his actions suggested he is a man without fear. A poet and prolific writer, he has, over port and cigars, planned the campaign through debate, consensus and conciliation, perhaps not a technique best suited to what will become one of the most ruthless battles in modern warfare. Scholarly generals write well about wars, but ruthless generals win them.

Two days before the landing the poet Rupert Brooke, a sub-lieutenant in the Royal Naval Reserve, is on his way to land on Gallipoli when he is stung by a mosquito. He develops blood poisoning from the bite and dies aboard a French hospital ship on 23 April. Winston Churchill, a great admirer of Brooke's writing and who arranged his commission into the Royal Naval Reserve, writes his obituary for *The Times*:

> *Joyous, fearless, versatile, deeply instructed with classic symmetry of mind and body, he was all that one would wish England's noblest sons to be in days when no sacrifice but the most precious is acceptable, and the most precious is that which is most freely proffered.*

Sir Ian Hamilton immediately reaches for his diary to write:

> *Rupert Brooke is dead. Straightaway he will be buried. The rest is silence . . . Death grins at my elbow. I cannot get him out of my thoughts. He is fed up with the old and sick – only the flower of the flock will serve him now, for God has started a celestial spring cleaning, and our star is to be scrubbed bright with the blood of our best and bravest.*

But Hamilton is a soldier, not a poet, and although his reports are lucid and eloquent he is overawed by his superior, Lord Kitchener, and fails to challenge any of his judgements. He is also surrounded by men who have been given senior appointments made by Kitchener, none of whom he feels he should overrule and almost all of whom will be found wanting when the time comes.

On the other hand, the leader of the Turkish forces, von Sanders, has on his staff a thirty-four-year-old divisional commander, who will, despite his relatively junior position, have a crucial impact on the outcome of the battle and, in years to come, the modern history of Turkey. His name is Mustafa Kemal. Charismatic, a brilliant strategist and an inspirational leader of his men, he will make several decisions, often way beyond his level of authority, which will alter the course of the brutal encounter against the Allies.

Like the men around him, Hywel is apprehensive. They are almost at the beach and freedom from their sardine tin. But is their arrival going to be as tranquil as it appears? Hywel turns to look at Captain Willis, who nods reassuringly. There is still no movement, light or sound coming from the beach. But dawn has broken and, through the half-light, heavy entanglements of barbed wire can be seen on the beach. However, the men are unable to see the tripwires below the water line, or the land mines they are attached to, nor can they see the 2-lb pom-pom cannons hidden out of sight. Despite the unnatural doings of mortal men that are about to be released, nature has provided a perfect day. It is warm, fresh and clear; there is not a breath of wind. Insects buzz and hum and the birds sing and spiral into the air – but not for long.

The Fusiliers have been assigned to W Beach, at the southernmost tip of Cape Helles. The beach itself,

350 yards long and 50 deep, is relatively flat and sandy, ideal for a relaxing day at the seaside, but is overlooked by a steep, rocky cliff, perfect for entrenched positions and offering a textbook line of fire on to the landing site.

Just one crack from a single bullet breaks the silence and heralds the beginning of the battle. One of the dozen sailors straining with their oars to row the cutter the last few yards to the shore falls forward, blood pouring from an exit wound in his back. There is hardly time to realize that he has been shot before the entire vessel is riddled with bullets.

Wood cracks and metal pings as bullets land and ricochet all over the cutter. But bodies make different sounds when they are hit. They squelch like a stone hitting mud or, if bones are shattered, there is a sickening snap like a twig being broken, followed by faint echoes as fragments tear into surrounding tissue. But the most nauseating impact is the splash of cerebral matter when a bullet explodes someone's head. These noises are heard many times over as the Lancashire Fusiliers are slaughtered like fish in a barrel. A few leap overboard in the hope of salvation but, with 70lbs of kit attached to them, plummet straight to the bottom.

Captain Willis is shouting orders, as is his surviving lieutenant and the two NCOs who are still standing, but no one can hear them above the firing and the screams and cries of dying men.

After thirty seconds the cutter is close enough to the beach for men to wade ashore. Most stumble as they jump, some drop their rifles, others get clogged by sand. Then the mines are detonated, blowing a dozen men to pieces and flinging their torsos and limbs into the air. The pom-pom shells land in little clusters, maiming anyone close by. Those who make it to the beach struggle to cut through great swirls of barbed wire. Yet more men are killed as they try to crawl under it or cut their way through, their bodies caught up like a macabre line of washing on a clothes line.

Hywel is lying prone just above the water line. He has piled up the bodies of three of his comrades and is using them as cover and support for his rifle. His targets are the three machine-gun positions which are wreaking most of the havoc. He has also seen several snipers, but the machine guns are his priority. Captain Willis, who is rallying his men and working his way up the beach slowly and methodically, has sent Hywel a lance corporal with extra ammunition and given him his field glasses so that he can help identify targets.

'What's your name, Corporal?'

'Shutt, Colour. Bert Shutt.'

'Well, Shutt, grab a couple of bodies, get behind them, keep your head down and see what you can see with those bins.'

Hywel's Lee-Enfield can take five rounds at a time and he has reloaded four times.

Lance Corporal Shutt is impressed. 'That's twenty rounds you've got away. How many 'ave yer plugged?'

'At a guess, sixteen. There's a drift of wind that has started to run along the back of the beach that's difficult to read.'

'Bugger me — sixteen; that's a bloody miracle!'

'No, it's not. It's four bullets wasted and four Turks still alive to kill more of us.'

Hywel pulls the trigger on another round.

''Eck! I can see the little bugger tumblin' down yon cliff like a ragdoll. Yer got him good an' proper.'

'Keep that ammunition coming and keep your trap shut, Shutt. I'm trying to concentrate.'

It takes Captain Willis and his men over an hour to get over the beach and around the cliff to drive the Turks out of their trenches and secure their objective, Hill 114, which is 450 yards beyond the ridge at the top of the beach. In doing so, his company has been reduced to 67 men from an original force of 256. First Battalion's overall strength has been reduced from 1,029 to 410.

When Hywel and his young spotter/ammunition quartermaster, Bert Shutt, reach Hill 114, the first to greet them is Captain Willis. The CO is dripping with sweat and shaking from the exertion of battle. He has a graze to the side of his head, where a bullet came close to blowing his brains out, and a gash to his left arm, the result of a bayonet thrust or a slash from a Turkish officer's sword. He gathers himself.

'Colour Thomas, we couldn't have done it without you. Very well done.'

'Thank you, sir.'

'How many did you bag?'

'A few, sir. The drift along the beach was a little tricky.'

Shutt is taken aback. 'Excuse me, sir. "A few" is twenty-seven by my count, including two of their snipers.'

'Twenty-seven! That's extraordinary shooting. Where did you learn how to shoot like that?'

'On my farm, sir, but Major Hesketh-Pritchard says I was born with a gift.'

'So you're one of his Sniping School boys?'

'Yes, sir, I'm proud to say I think I'm the first.'

'Well, I'm not surprised. You have a remarkable eye.'

The captain looks down at Hywel's gloved right hand. The glove is no longer black; Hywel has bleached the black out of it, making it as pale as he can to blend with his camouflaged rifle.

'So, Colour, why the glove?'

'Sir, I had a bullet through my palm in Flanders, but a surgeon, a wonderful man, Captain Noel Chavasse, rebuilt my hand and got this glove made for me in London. It's reinforced with copper rods and gives me a stable supporting hand.'

'How bloody ingenious. May I see your hand?'

Hywel takes off his glove to reveal his disfigured palm and wayward digits, and Willis examines them closely.

'I'm lucky, sir, I'm left-handed.'

'You're not lucky, Colour, you're a phenomenon. I pride myself on being a good shot and did well in the Army Championships a couple of years ago, but with two good hands. I'm going to get you a medal for today, Colour Serjeant Thomas. I'm going to recommend you for a Distinguished Conduct Medal.'

'Thank you, sir, but I'm not sure that I deserve it.'

'Oh yes, you do; you saved many lives this morning.'

Besides Hywel Thomas's DCM, for their bravery on the morning of 25 April six Victoria Crosses will be awarded to 1st Battalion Lancashire Fusiliers, one of the most decorated regiments in the British Army, including a VC for Captain Richard Willis. They will become known as the 'Six VCs before breakfast'. That evening Sir

252

Ian Hamilton orders that Tekke Burnu Beach will henceforth be known as 'Lancashire Landing'.

Hywel walks away for a quiet moment of reflection. He has, in the cold-blooded way that is the modus operandi of the sniper, just killed many men. Not for the sniper the hot blood of an infantry charge or the adrenalin of hand-to-hand fighting; he has to kill by stealth, his pulse calm, his heartbeat frozen as he pulls the trigger. He cannot afford to be squeamish about his prey; they are just targets to be killed as clinically as possible. His is a pragmatic business; there is no room for morality or regret. If ever either appear, the game is up.

From the top of the hill Hywel can see most of the assault beaches. The shoreline of the once-remote, wind-swept peninsula is alive with men and their instruments of war. He is surprised how close the other beaches are: the whole spit of land is less than three miles across. It seems to his untrained eye that the beaches are secure, with very few Turks to be seen. He looks north-east along the hinterland, which appears to be deserted: no columns of men; no artillery pieces on the move; no vehicles of any kind. With many hours of daylight remaining, he asks himself the obvious question: Why do we not advance? But he puts it aside, assuming that the generals know what they are about.

He looks back to the landing beaches. It is an extraordinary sight. At sea, the great battleships are pounding away at the Turkish positions, each shell producing a thunderous rumble and plumes of yellow-grey gun-smoke which billow up into the clear sky. Around them, destroyers and support ships linger like bees around their queen while the landing craft go backwards and forwards like workers bringing nectar to the hive. But the men on the beaches look more like ants scurrying across the sand, thousands of them, and, as under the brutal laws of nature, not all of them survive.

On W Beach, the Worcesters are landing as the second wave of the attack. Spared, by the bravery of their northern comrades, the slaughter meted out to their predecessors, a thousand sturdy Mercians are wading ashore and making their way across the beach.

On the opposite side of the Straits, the French Senegalese Tirailleurs of the 6th Colonial Regiment secure the fort and village of Kum Kale with relative ease.

Fifteen miles away in the far north, the Anzacs have been put ashore a mile further up the peninsula than intended because of unexpected currents. The terrain they face is very difficult to manoeuvre across, and poor communication makes progress haphazard. The peninsula is wider here, more than five miles, but there is little opposition and they have the chance to dash across its breadth and isolate the Turks to the south. However, other than in small, isolated groups led by the more audacious of junior officers, who then become marooned from one another, there is no coordinated thrust forward.

Also, by sheer chance, the Turkish commander, Mustafa Kemal, is in the vicinity. He realizes the threat and, in a masterstroke of bravery and ingenuity, manages to gather a large enough force to mount a counter-attack. Kemal's subsequent order uses language far less poetic than the florid prose of Sir Ian Hamilton, but it proves to be much more effective:

Every soldier who fights here with me must realize that he is honour bound not to retreat one step. Let me remind you all that, if you want to rest, there may be no rest for our whole nation throughout eternity. I am sure that all our comrades agree on this, and that they will show no signs of fatigue until the enemy is finally hurled into the sea.

Bitter hand-to-hand fighting in the narrow gullies and steep ravines lasts all day, as the small groups of Anzacs are attacked and forced to retreat. Eventually, the Turkish 57th Regiment regains all the high ground around the Anzacs' landing ground, leaving them with no more than the precarious toe-hold of a beach-head.

X Beach is attacked by 2nd Battalion Royal Fusiliers. It is a 200-yard-long strip of sand with a high ridge behind it, just to the north-west of their fellow Fusiliers from Lancashire. When they land, they find only a handful of defenders and make it to the ridge almost unopposed, and are soon able to join forces with the luckless Lancastrians to their right.

Put ashore by HMS *Cornwallis*, 2nd Battalion South Wales Borderers, who, under their previous title, 2nd Battalion, 24th Regiment of Foot, were the heroes of Isandlwana and Rorke's Drift in the Zulu Wars, command S Beach, three miles to the right of the Lancastrians. Unlike on the other beaches, the Turkish trenches here are visible from the ships off the coast, and thus the bombardment is successful in depleting Turkish numbers and resolve. By ten thirty all the Borderers' objectives have been achieved, digging of defensive positions has started and counter-attacks have been repulsed.

V Beach is a different story. Less than a mile to the

right of the Lancastrians, it is also festooned with barbed wire and guarded by two companies of Turkey's 26th Regiment – veteran troops, disciplined men and well led. An hour of artillery fire precedes the landing, scattering the defenders far and wide, but as soon as it ceases they rush back to their trenches to wait for the attack. Machine guns and breeches are loaded and men pick out their targets in light that improves by the minute as the sun rises higher and higher.

The landing is to be led by 1st Battalion Royal Munster Fusiliers, 2nd Hampshire Regiment and 1st Royal Dublin Fusiliers. The Munsters are aboard a collier, SS *River Clyde*, purchased only two weeks earlier and adapted for the landing by having sally-ports cut into her hull so that the men can disembark.

By 6 a.m. the Dubliners have been put in small landing craft and are being towed ashore. There is silence as the flotilla of little boats reaches the shore. Those aboard are convinced that, other than the three lines of barbed wire they will have to stride over, their landing will be unopposed and effortless. Their miscalculation becomes all too apparent as soon as the first Dubliners' serjeant jumps from the lead boat. He is hit by a hail of bullets, which catapult his body several different directions at once, before, lifeless, it collapses and is swallowed by the shallow water. All the remaining men in the first boat are dead within moments; those in the other boats fare little better. The only survivors are a few who slip over the side and find cover. The sea turns from Mediterranean turquoise to muddy red within minutes as the complement of Dubliners is reduced from 700 to 300, half of whom are wounded.

The *River Clyde* is deliberately run aground at 6.22, but the intensity of fire is so great from the ramparts of Sedd-el-Bahr Fort above that the Munsters cannot use the sally-ports to disembark. Several incredibly brave sailors, notably Commander Edward Unwin, the skipper of the *River Clyde*, attempt to build a bridge of small boats to allow the infantry to rush the beach. For over three hours, with bullets hissing and spitting into the water all around them, the sailors try to lash together enough boats to reach the shore.

The Munsters make three attempts to run the 150-yard gauntlet from ship to shore, which can be attempted only in single file. One in ten makes it. Eventually, late in the morning, all further attempts are abandoned. A mere 200 men are ashore, skulking wherever they can find shelter. Their comrades, mainly the Hampshires, wait, safe behind *River Clyde*'s steel hull. Only when darkness comes can the collier disgorge her haul, not this time a consignment of inert coal but the remnants of three brave battalions of Britain's army. This final landing is unopposed – the Turks know they cannot see their targets at night – and there is not a single casualty.

Y Beach most typifies the day's mismanagement, mistakes and miscalculations. Slightly less than four miles up the west coast from Cape Helles, it is more a cliff than a beach but is totally undefended. The landing is made by 1st Battalion Scottish Borderers and Plymouth Battalion, Royal Marines. They make landfall unopposed and climb the cliff with ease. By the time the sun is fully up, with their comrades being slaughtered just a few thousand yards away, 2,000 men are relaxing, drinking tea. Their commander, Lieutenant Colonel Godfrey Matthews, the clement sun of a spring morning caressing his back, strolls across an agreeable plateau of Turkish countryside until he can see, less than 500 yards in the distance, the minaret of the mosque of the small town of Krithia, the only significant settlement in the area.

Krithia is empty of both civilians and soldiers and thus at the mercy of the Allies. Matthews has more men at his disposal than all the Turkish troops to his south and can, with a single act of daring, take Krithia and the surrounding high ground. This would secure enough of the bottom of the peninsula to create a much more defensible bridgehead and probably forestall much of the horrendous suffering that is to come. But, without direct orders, he decides against a precipitous act and ambles back from whence he came.

Even though Sir Ian Hamilton sails past Y Beach at eight thirty and sees the Borderers and Marines at leisure, he issues no fresh orders. So, at 3 p.m., Colonel Matthews decides to withdraw his men to the top of the ridge above the beach and to dig in. It is an order that has been issued far too late. While British commanders fail to grasp any initiative presented to them, the Turkish leadership acts differently. Lieutenant Colonel Khalil Sami Bey, commander of the 9th Division, rushes troops southwards to halt any further advances. He issues a blunt order: 'It is quite clear that the enemy is weak; drive him into the sea, and do not let me find an Englishman in the south when I arrive.'

Even though they are outnumbered two to one, a battalion of Sami Bey's men attack Matthews' men on the ridge at Y Beach at 17:40 hours. The fighting, soon in darkness and driving rain, is ferocious. The Borderers and the Marines have been able to dig only shallow slit trenches, but they have more cover than the advancing Turks, who attack relentlessly across open ground. Turkish reinforcements arrive at 23:00 hours, by which time the British position is perilous. Between midnight and dawn Colonel Matthews sends four messages to Major General Aylmer Hunter-Weston, begging for more men, more ammunition, and pleading that his situation is dire. He receives no reply.

At 07:00 hours Matthews counts the cost. He has lost almost a third of his men: 627 dead or wounded. With daylight, panic sets in and, without orders, men run from their meagre cover and make for the beach, especially the Marines to the right. When groups of men arrive at the beach they signal to the ships, which send in boats to get the survivors off. When Matthews realizes that almost the whole of his right flank is undefended, he decides to make the impromptu retreat an official one and orders a withdrawal. By eleven thirty he and the remnants of his force are back at sea, leaving the beach and surrounding countryside strewn with bodies and equipment.

Later that afternoon a naval officer goes ashore to see if any wounded have been left behind. There is an eerie silence; not a shot is fired. The Turks have left to fight on the other beaches.

Thirty thousand Allied troops have been put ashore, but the grand scheme to open a new front against the

Central Powers is already doomed to failure, on the very morning that it has begun.

As men on both sides die in droves in the awful reality that is the Great War the fantasy world of geopolitics continues in the smoke-filled rooms of Europe's political rulers. Should the Allied attack succeed, it has already been conceded that Russia will acquire Constantinople and the Dardanelles Straits from Turkey, but, in a secret treaty signed on 26 April, Italy, encouraged by the scale of Allied ambition, agrees to join their cause. In the treaty she gets the paper-price her leaders demand. From Austria-Hungary, she will be granted Trentino, the South Tyrol, Trieste, the counties of Gorizia and Gradisca, the Istrian Peninsula, Northern Dalmatia and numerous islands in the Adriatic. She will also be given territory in North Africa and several concessions in Albania.

But the real price will be paid by Italy's young men, as they add their lives to the bill already being paid by many others across Europe.

On 28 April and again on 6 May the Allies launch massive attacks to break out of their bridgeheads and take Krithia and the high ground around it. Both attempts fail, at the cost of almost ten thousand Allied casualties. The plan that was designed to end the stalemate on the Western Front produces a stalemate of its own. Jack Churchill writes to his brother Winston.

PART FIVE: MAY

A Hideous Spectacle

Sunday 9 May

Laventie, Pas-de-Calais, France

Both the Churchill brothers witness the horrors of the Great War on the second Sabbath in May. Jack is on Sir Ian Hamilton's staff on his new command ship for the Gallipoli campaign, the *Arcadia*, but has gone ashore at Cape Helles to observe the Allies' attempts to break out of their bridgeheads. When he returns to his cabin he writes an impassioned letter to Winston.

My Dear Winston,

It is hard to know where to begin. The French are jittery, but our chaps are, on the whole, doing well. But we need to make progress, or I fear we might get into a terrible mess. Here we are at the tip of this little appendage of Turkey, with more and more of the little terriers, for that is what they are, coming our way.

More of our men arrive all the time, some Lancashire Territorials today, a sturdy lot, but we need more! Perversely, the weather is splendid, but it does little for the corpses that still lie around. They make for a most disagreeable assault on one's nostrils. The poor Turks have so many to bury, they don't put them in very deep, and, in extremis, neither do we.

By the way, the great exploits by the Lancashire Fusiliers have led Ian H. to order that their beach be called Lancashire Landing. He's a thoughtful cove.

Terribly sad about Rupert Brooke. He had a very moving funeral. French and English officers carried his body about two miles by torchlight up a beautiful gully on Skyros Island. It was a spot he much admired a few days earlier – how romantic and how appropriate.

But on a more serious note. The Turks are so well dug in. Their 'Jack Johnsons' and shrapnel attacks are ferociously accurate. Did somebody suggest they'd run for the Bosporus as soon as we landed! I have seen some terrible sights. Row upon row of stretchers; the men on them mainly beyond saving. Blood and bandages everywhere; not enough nurses and doctors; only two hospital ships, which are full to the gunwales.

We are getting far too many injuries to fingers and toes, many of which are clearly self-inflicted. It is a worry, but many of the new arrivals are reservists, not battle-hardened men. I have heard at least two reports of men shot on the battlefield for desertion.

From my trench, I saw the French caught in a terrible ambush to our right. The Senegalese were distinctive in their dark blue, the sweat on their coal-black faces gleaming in the hot sun. Oh why does Hunter-Weston insist on attacking by day – I wish he'd come ashore and see what it's like – and why does Ian H. let him? At least H. does come and see for himself. The French were in their pale blue, officer's swords waving, catching the light. Suddenly, the Turks in front of them got up and ran like hell. The French picked up the pace and ran after them, thinking the day was won, but it was a deadly ruse. As soon as the French got within distance, a ferocious artillery barrage got up and covered the whole field in smoke. When it cleared, I saw only a handful of men still on their feet. The rest had been obliterated, including many Turks, who, their generals must have decided, had to be sacrificed!

My God, Winston, it's just like Flanders. May the Almighty help us all.

Your loving brother,
Jack

Winston is desperately saddened by Jack's letter. He knows that it is bad news for the nation's war effort, but also for his political future. Any further setbacks, especially in the Dardanelles, will threaten Asquith's government. The Conservative opposition will push for changes in the government, and they, fuelled by their friends in Fleet Street, will demand a scapegoat for any and all failures. Their prime target will be Asquith's young firebrand, and Tory traitor, Winston Spencer Churchill.

The First Lord of the Admiralty is also missing his family. After spending many months with him at the Admiralty while Clemmie nursed their third child, Sarah, who was born in October, he has rented Hoe Farm at Hascombe, Surrey, for the spring and summer. He never functions well when away from Clemmie.

He has been in Paris overseeing the secret negotiations with Italy for her to enter the War on the side of the Allies. Under his usual alias, 'Mr Spencer', he stayed at the Ritz, which, despite the exigencies of war, still provides a uniquely luxurious experience, one that he enjoys with his usual gusto. Never one to see a contradiction between war and pleasure, he relieves his increasing gloom with French cuisine and fine wines. The Ritz management knows only too well of his liking for Pol Roger champagne, and a bottle awaits his arrival, as does another to accompany his departure. He also indulges his love of the French language and bounds through its nuances with abandon, if not always with great fluency and not always to the exact comprehension of his audience. Amused by his bluster, the French generally welcome his well-meaning mauling of their language, preferring it to the approach of most other English visitors, who think that if they increase the volume of their English diction and reduce the speed of their delivery, their French hosts will eventually understand what they are saying.

But Winston is now in a very different place, high in the bomb-damaged steeple of the church of St Vaast, Laventie, a small town on the French side of the Belgian–French border. On his journey back from Paris he paid a visit to his friend, Sir John French, Commander-in-Chief of the BEF, who in turn has invited him to witness yet another attempt to end the stalemate on the Western Front.

From his elevated position he can see the entire battlefield. The attack he is about to witness is the British component of a combined Anglo–French offensive, the 2nd Battle of Artois. French Commander-in-Chief Joseph Joffre has asked Sir John to provide British units to support a French offensive to capture the heights of Vimy Ridge, a vital escarpment five miles north-east of Arras, on the western edge of the Douai Plains.

The British, under the command of Sir Douglas Haig, Commander-in-Chief 1st Army, will attack near the village of Laventie. Their objective, across the dreary and waterlogged terrain, is Aubers Ridge, an area of slightly higher ground marked by the villages of Aubers, Fromelles and Le Maisnil.

Winston is appalled by what he sees during the day. Although he has fought in several wars and seen his fair share of their terrors, what he observes as a consequence of the attack on Aubers Ridge on Sunday 9 May 1915 will live with him for the rest of his life. On his journey home to London, he writes to Clemmie:

Darling Cat,

I fear that what follows may depress you. But I hope that the lovely surroundings of Hoe in May and having the little Kittens at your feet will assuage some of the awfulness in what you're about to read.

Dear Jack has written a long missive from the Dardanelles. The situation seems worse than I imagined. I think I know Kitchener's game. He seems to want it to fail so that he can be proved right in the end. As for me, I hope you take great comfort in knowing that soon I may be spending much more time with you in Sussex than previously. My days are numbered. Jacky F. is going to leave me high and dry by resigning, claiming that he was against the whole enterprise from the start. Infuriatingly, he's now saying that he preferred Borkum, which is somewhat galling in that the bloody island was my idea and he said it couldn't work! I think his irascibility and tenacity have turned into lunacy!

But, darling, I must talk about what I have seen today. It chills me to the bone, but I have to share it with you, as you're the only one I can confide in. You know I have little regard for my own safety and that war fills me with a perverse thrill. Few understand that, but it is my nature. That is my personal relationship with the gods of war, but others are gentler souls, who serve our king and country out of duty, not because they crave the danger and the adventure, as I do. I pity them; they suffer so much and often with naked fear coursing through their bones. How do they do it?

As for the battle itself – a great coming together of mighty armies – I saw nothing other than shells and smoke and heard nothing other than the boom of their Big Berthas, the whistle of their whizz-bangs and, of course, the awful rat-a-tat-tat of their deadly machine guns. Haig (it was his op) was kind enough to me, but I sensed that he thought my presence was a bloody nuisance! We climbed a tall steeple and got close to the trenches, but it was all deafening noise and choking smoke. It is little wonder the generals are at a loss to know what to do. In the great days of the past, Napoleon or Wellington could see the whole scene and direct their forces accordingly. Now generals are blind, and blindness can inhibit even a military genius, but when it's combined with incompetence . . .

It is what I saw later that shook me the most. I visited a large hospital at Poperinghe, Pop-Hop, which more resembled a slaughterhouse than a medical facility. There were over a thousand poor souls lying outside waiting to be admitted, line upon line of them. Pierced, torn, seared, choking and dying. The ambulances kept coming, each with four or five tortured innocents in them. The orderlies deposited the men into crude but necessary holding areas, which, in simple terms, were: those who had no chance of survival, those who had a small chance of survival, those who would survive with care and those who would survive regardless of care. As you might guess, little regard was paid to the first and last categories. Of the other two, most attention was paid to the men for whom care might make a difference. The rest had to wait.

Nearby, burial parties were working incessantly to clear the accumulation of corpses. It was medieval in its revolting simplicity – men thrown into pits, side by side, then on top of one another. Good men, many hardly men at all, farm boys, factory hands, clerks, postmen, railwaymen.

I went past an operating theatre. It was not a good moment. A man was undergoing a trepanning. I could see nothing of him, just those tending him, covered in his blood from head to toe, and, at their feet, a mountain of bloodstained bandages.

In the middle of it all, calm, professional, but weary to the point of exhaustion, were the remarkable doctors, nurses and orderlies. My host was a Captain Noel Chavasse. A fine fellow, son of the Bishop of Liverpool, good rugger player and ran for us in the Olympic Games in London. He has been in France since the beginning. I could see the sadness and the exhaustion in his sunken eyes. He was pale and thin, but never once did he complain or badger me, he just thanked me for coming.

I also met some of the remarkable girls of the QAIMNS. Just splendid! They are in the middle of it all. One of them, Sister Margaret Killingbeck, a northern girl of some spirit, had no hesitation in telling me what I could see with my own eyes. She said that Captain Chavasse had told her who I was, so asked me very pointedly if anyone on the War Council had any idea what is going on at the Front. I answered that I thought so. Her response was very apposite.

'Well,' she said, 'are you all monsters? If you know, why do you keep sending men to their certain deaths?'

I was taken aback, and those around me shuddered. But as a sister she carries the rank of captain, so is entitled to speak her mind. I hadn't given a very good answer, so I deserved the rebuke. I tried to change the subject and asked when she was due some leave. Her answer was equally to the point.

'Not for some time, sir, Nurse Thomas and I travel to Marseilles tomorrow. We've been assigned to a hospital ship supporting the Mediterranean Expeditionary Force.'

Nurse Thomas was standing next to the sister, a striking-looking girl, a picture of Celtic beauty, no more than 20 years of age; she could have been the raven-haired Guinevere herself. She perhaps thought Killingbeck had been too harsh with me; she looked at me with an intensity that could have melted stone and said, 'Sir, Sister Killingbeck is a saint; she's saved dozens of lives. Wherever there are men suffering like these, she'll be there . . . And I'll be with her.'

She then did a remarkable thing: she got on her tiptoes and kissed me on the cheek and said, 'I hear you're a good man, sir. When you see Mr Asquith and Lord Kitchener and the rest of them, tell them what you've seen today. It will help us to know that what is happening here is not lost on them.'

I was moved to tears by her resolve and promised to make sure that anyone and everyone knew what the war is really like. Then she was hurried away by Sister Killingbeck with the words, 'Come on, Bron, we've got work to do.' I took careful note of their names so that I can have the Admiralty find out which ship they're on and make sure Jack makes a fuss of them when they arrive in Gallipoli.

As I left the hospital late in the afternoon, the darkening of which made the scene yet more hideous, the guns were still firing in the distance, the drumming thunder of a cannonade, every beat of which proclaimed that the process of death and mutilation was still raging.

Forgive the callousness of this note, but I needed to put into words what I have seen and felt. Now I feel a little purged.

So, my darling, I am now onboard ship heading for Dover. There is a War Council on Friday, which promises to be volcanic,

so I will try to clear my desk tomorrow and Tuesday and get down
to Hoe on Wednesday. I think I will need the sustenance only you
can give to face what lies ahead.

Much love to the Kittens,

Your devoted and loving,
Pig

The Battle for Aubers Ridge proved to be an unmitigated disaster. The British bombardment of German positions started at 05:00 hours. Thirty minutes later the British infantry attacked from their trenches but immediately came under withering machine-gun fire. German trench work was far too good to be severely damaged by even the heaviest British howitzers. In some places trenches ran in double or triple lines with deep, reinforced, boxed shelters to protect the defenders against bombardment. Communication trenches were deep and well concealed and huge coils of barbed wire were dug into ditches in front of the trenches, sometimes two yards deep and five wide. Machine-gun posts placed at regular intervals were protected by reinforced concrete and faced with steel plate cut with firing holes.

The lead assault battalions to the south of Laventie were 1st Northants, 2nd Royal Sussex, 2nd Royal Munster, 2nd Royal Welch, 2nd Gurkhas, 7th Sikhs and 4th Seaforths. To the north the attack was led by 3rd Northants, 2nd East Lancs, 2nd Rifles, 1st Royal Irish Rifles, 14th Londons and 6th Jats. It was a roll call of the best of Britain's empire, an army whose bright-red tunics symbolized an army that conquered half the world. But the army was no longer in imperial red, and this would not be a day that would be remembered with pride, only with grief and ignominy.

The infantry was left severely exposed by inadequate artillery support. Shell production in Britain, jealously guarded by Major General Sir Stanley von Donop, Master General of Ordnance, and limited by antiquated contracts to a few accredited suppliers, led to a severe shell shortage. The scarcity led to rationing, which on the day of the attack on Aubers Ridge was eighteen rounds per battery per day. Sadly, when those precious shells were used they were fired from guns in need of repair or replacement. Many misfired, killing their crews, or released lethally short rounds.

In some places in the British attack in the southern sector men never got beyond the first yard before being mown down. Those who made it further were impeded by the swathes of barbed wire, making them easy targets for the German snipers. The few who made it to the German lines were slaughtered in hand-to-hand fighting in the trenches, or taken prisoner. At 06:00 hours the order was given to halt the attack, leaving hundreds of men pinned down in no-man's-land.

Events in the northern sector told the same story, but some units did manage to take the German trenches in three limited areas. The new tunnelling companies had laid mines under the German positions and their detonation at 05.40 hours made for a successful attack on the heavily fortified Delangre Farm. It was one of the few successes.

When he received reports of good progress by the

French on Vimy Ridge, but without a full picture of British losses, Haig ordered a fresh attack in the southern sector beneath Neuve Chapelle. The Allied bombardment started at 15:20 hours. The Black Watch went over the top seven minutes later. Miraculously, some reached the German front line, but only to be killed or captured. A handful even reached a second line of trenches before being massacred by the defenders.

By the evening and encroaching darkness, chaos reigned. Communications between HQ and officers at the sharp end of the attack had completely broken down. In part it was because roads and paths to the rear were blocked by men carrying equipment and searching for rendezvous points, but mainly because most company commanders lay dead. At dusk Haig called off the attack.

The Battle for Aubers Ridge lasted but one day. There were 11,161 British and Indian casualties. It gained no ground and did not aid the wider French offensive in any discernible way.

Saturday 15 May

St Omer, Pas-de-Calais, France

Although St Omer is as distinctively French as anywhere else in the nation, it has taken on some very British features. Indeed, Britain could easily be an occupying power. Street and road traffic signs in English have been put up. The shops sell a whole range of British goods; York ham, whisky, American cigarettes and Cheddar cheese are to be found everywhere. However, not all translated signs are entirely accurate. One that has amused British guests is a poster for concerts at the hôtel de ville which asks those attending to arrive on time and addresses them as 'the comings tardily'.

Forty-two miles north-west of Lille and twenty-eight south-east of Calais, St Omer sits on the main route to the Channel from the French heartland. It is the home of the HQ of the British Expeditionary Force and the Royal Flying Corps, and base to dozens of other organizations related to the war effort. In fact, the British have requisitioned large parts of the town and are filling its coffers and those of its shopkeepers and restaurateurs to excess. It is like a frontier town, with men and equipment moving in all directions at once, day and night. Despite the often drab uniforms, droves of injured soldiers in a multitude of hospitals, strict rationing and the general exigencies of war, the bars, brothels, cafés and restaurants are full every night.

The mood is frivolous, the drinking prodigious, and brawling, sometimes en masse, is commonplace. The scarlet-covered service caps of the military policeman – 'Cherry-nobs', as the men call them – who patrol in quartets are conspicuous every night of the week. The Provost Marshal deals harshly with repeat offenders, as evidenced by the large number of men in St Omer's two Field Punishment centres. Two weeks ago a reservist from the Royal Fusiliers was court-martialled and shot at dawn for killing another soldier in a drunken fight at his billet south of St Omer.

Other draconian restrictions have been instituted. Drink can be served only during the limited hours set by the Defence of the Realm Act in Britain, and absinthe, *la fée verte*, or 'green fairy', of legend, is banned altogether. Prostitution is regulated, at least in part, but has become a growth industry all the same.

The most popular haunt, especially for young officers needing to let off steam, is Café l'Harmonie on the Grande Place. Besides the raucous atmosphere and modestly priced alcohol, its leading attraction is Jeanne, the eighteen-year-old daughter of the owner, M. Vincent. Jeanne is a very fetching brunette, lavishly endowed, her figure made even more feminine by corsetry that defies the laws of engineering and high heels that defy the laws of gravity. Jeanne captivates all who see her as she flounces between the tables carrying a huge tray of drinks high above her head with one hand. M. Vincent has a simple rule: you may wave, blow kisses, sing to her, whistle at her, or offer her endearments in French or English (but *not* in Flemish or German, and *no* suggestive observations of any kind), but you must *never* touch. Touching means a lifetime ban for a man of any rank. It is said that the rule would apply to Sir John French himself, but the great general has yet to cross l'Harmonie's threshold.

Rumours abound that Jeanne has been known to take the occasional fortunate fellow to her room after hours so that they can discuss the situation at the Front or work out how to release her from the tortuous bondage of her corset, so every man who walks through the door lives in hope. However, there are cynics who suggest that the rumours were begun by Jeanne's very protective but equally entrepreneurial father, who would never dream of letting anyone near his beautiful daughter but is more than happy that his customers carry on drinking and imagining that he might.

Sitting at a window table of l'Harmonie are Mary Broxup and Cath Kenny. They are trying to gawp in two directions at once: through the window to the Grande Place, where throngs of people mill around the many drinking and eating places, and through the cigarette fug of l'Harmonie itself, alive with laughter and excited conversation.

The dominant colour on this Saturday night in St Omer is khaki, but there are also French blue and the copious red, pink and purple worn by the ladies of the night, some of whom look well coiffed and expensive; others less so. A few of the women are dressed very conservatively: the British nurses, Red Cross girls, FANYs and others who are arriving in ever greater numbers. Other than the gorgeous Jeanne and the ubiquitous *filles de joie*, local French women are nowhere to be seen. They know it is better to stay at home in the evenings while the British indulge their penchant for drink and debauchery.

'Sken that lass there, Mary, the black one? She's got an arse like a balloon! D'yer fancy 'avin one like that?'

'No, ta; am 'appy enough wi' t'one ave got.'

'Do'st reckon she meks a lot o' brass?'

'She must 'ave; ne'er skenned so many tarts in one place! It's more like a whorehouse than a pub.'

'Don't think thu's much difference round 'ere, our Mary.'

Cath turns as Jeanne sashays past, her lips as red as a postbox, her eyes made up like Cleopatra's.

'Na-then, that's a figure to die fer. No wonder this place is packed!'

'Aye, not bad, our Tommy'd get reet 'ot an' bothered if 'e wer 'ere. Mind you, yer 'ave to wonder wot 'appens to all that flesh when she teks off that contraption she's strapped into.'

Mary pauses to survey the room. 'Any dacent-lookin' lads?'

Cath has already seen one and has been staring at him for a while. 'Thu's one o'er yonder, a pretty blond lad, blue eyes. 'E's got three pips; wot does that mek 'im?'

'Oh, 'e's a captain. Very 'ansome. Wouldn't mind once round t'maypole wi' 'im.'

'Me too. A bet 'is pole is long and thick!'

'Steady, Cath, tha's givin' me ideas.'

'Ave bin 'avin those ideas ever sin wi got 'ere. Do'st reckon wi can get by wi'out a seein' to fra our lads? Bet they're not goin' short.'

'Don't, Cath.'

'It's men's nature, Mary. Face up t' it. Am beginning t'think it's my nature too. All ave been doin' this last few week is ticklin' me little button. Ave even bin thinkin' abaht three in a bed wi Henry Hyndman.'

'Bloody 'ell, Cath! Wot's to be doin' wi yer. I 'ope I'm not included in that little trio?'

'Course, y'are, yer silly bugger.'

'At'a tellin' me, tha fancies me?'

'No, yer daft 'appeth. Am just tellin' yer am feelin' as randy as buggery!'

'That's alreet then. Tha got me moithered fer a minute then. Come on, let's away, wi'v got them two toff lasses t'see, t'morn. We need clear heeds.'

'Aye, s'pose so; I wager them two do a fair bit o' button ticklin' when t'fancy teks 'em!'

'Doubt it, bet thi've both got a young stallion tucked away somewheer.'

Mary walks off, muttering to herself. 'Henry bloody Hyndman ... You poor lass, you must be bloody desperate ...'

The next morning, a day that has dawned clear and fresh with a promise of warm sunshine to come, Cath and Mary walk from their lodgings just off the Grande Place to a large town house on the Quai du Commerce, which fronts St Omer's Canal de Neuffossé. It is the headquarters of the VAD in France. It is 9 a.m. to the second when, accompanied by two very trim and upright women in VAD uniforms, Katherine Furse and Kitty Stewart-Murray walk into the large belle-époque reception room on the ground floor.

This is Kitty's second visit to France to see the work of the VAD in action at first hand. She has left Bardie, whose euphoria about an overseas posting has long since evaporated, as no word has been forthcoming about when it might happen, at Blagdon. She has also left George Grey, her young lover, in London, but only after spending a very raucous night with him en route from Northumberland.

There are almost thirty young women in the room: bright eyed, well scrubbed, if a little apprehensive. Most are well-to-do, wives or daughters of landowners, the nobility or rich businessmen; some are the offspring of barristers, doctors or civil servants; and four of them, Cath and Mary and two girls from Bermondsey whose fathers are dockers, are distinctly working-class.

It is relatively easy to tell them apart. Breeding is not visible but money is. Clothes, hair, make-up, shoes and complexion give the game away. The four 'ordinary' lasses sit next to one another, like four peas in a not very comfortable pod.

'This is a very proud moment for Lady Stewart-Murray and myself and, of course, for the Voluntary Aid Detachment. You ladies are the eighth group we have sent off to duties in support of our brave men since the beginning of April. Our numbers are growing all the time, as is the acceptance that we are of value, which wasn't always the case.

'Now, some of you have done some nursing training or first aid. You will be assigned to various hospital duties by Sister Smythson here, who is from the Red Cross. She will also issue you with standard Red Cross nurse's uniforms.

You will be addressed as "Nurse" and be treated, hopefully even by the army, as having the rank of an NCO.

'Others among you are qualified drivers or have volunteered for kitchen or catering work. You will be assigned by Miss Shuttleworth, who is from the First Aid Nursing Yeomanry, or FANY.'

There are a few titters from the ranks of women and Cath laughs out loud.

'Yes, I know, but you'll get used to it, and a lot worse. Miss Shuttleworth will issue you your uniforms: standard khaki culottes. Why, you may ask? Well, because it was originally intended that we would collect the injured on horseback! But times have changed. You will have a standard tunic and belt, not unlike an army officer's jacket, and our own distinctive baggy caps – very smart. You will also be given a greatcoat, which have been very useful, but hopefully will not now be needed for a while. You, too, will be designated as "Nurse" – it is easier for the men to come to terms with – and as NCOs, which is perhaps not as easy for them to accept, but we live in hope.'

Furse moves a little uneasily before continuing. 'Now, ladies, a few issues of some delicacy, but we're all adults here. Some of you are married, some are not, but all of you have chosen to enter a brutal, threatening and dangerous world. Men are dying in droves in the most awful of circumstances. You will be at risk yourselves and will see things that you will wish to forget. Steel yourselves for things that you will find hard to bear. Also, as a woman, you will be a rare sight for men a long way from their own womenfolk. You don't need me to tell you what circumstances will arise as a consequence. Those are also things you will have to deal with. As for your own behaviour, to those of you who are unencumbered, I would say just two things. First of all, we like to think of ourselves as living by the same military code as our menfolk, so we adopt the same "fraternization" rules as they do. Secondly, I would say be vigilant about your own behaviour. Set an example that will make everyone in the Red Cross, FANY and the VAD proud.'

She shuffles involuntarily in her seat once more.

'I would add one thing. Venereal disease is a significant problem not only in the ranks but also among the officers, even senior ones. How can I put this? . . . They are a long way from home; respectable French ladies have long gone to Paris and elsewhere. The women who are left are professionals; they carry every conceivable disease. The French military are realists in the matter and our HQ has taken, let's say, a passive position. So prostitution is rife, and you must know the risks if a man approaches you and . . . perhaps I can put it this way, begs that you help him in his hour of need.'

There are one or two sniggers around the room, while Cath, unable to resist, mutters audibly, 'Bugger their hour of need, what about ours!'

There are several 'tut-tuts' but also a few wry smiles from the women. Furse chooses to ignore the comment.

'Finally, if at any time you have a problem or want to talk to anyone, you must come back here to St Omer to Sister Smythson or Miss Shuttleworth, or, if we're here, to me or Lady Stewart-Murray directly. Any questions?'

Cath, unable to resist the temptation to be provocative,

jumps to her feet. 'Hello, Katherine, it's Cath Kenny, fra Burnley. We met i' London at St John's Gate.'

There are some intakes of breath from the women in the room at Cath's strong Lancashire accent and because the convention is to refer to their leader as Mrs Furse rather than Katherine.

'I remember very well, Mrs Kenny. How are you?'

'Am alreet . . . Now, about this "fraternization" malarkey. When tha ses "rules" an' reckon we 'ave t'status of NCOs, do'st mean wi can only *fraternize* wi' NCOs, but not t'ordinary lads and certainly not t'officers?'

'Well, Mrs Kenny, I'll leave that to your better judgement.'

Furse thinks she has given a good answer, but Cath stays on her feet, despite having her skirt pulled by Mary. Furse's brow furrows. 'Did you have another question, Mrs Kenny?'

'Aye, well, not a question, more a comment. An' please call me Cath; Mrs Kenny makes mi sound like a keep a boardin' 'ouse. A just wanted to say that if we're all out 'ere wi' bullets flyin' an' all that, then I reckon a'll fraternize wi' whoever teks me fancy.'

Furse smiles through gritted teeth and does not rise to the provocation but stands to leave the room. 'Thank you, ladies,' she says. '*Bon chance* in wherever you go and whatever you do.'

Mary looks mystified. 'What the buggery does that mean, our Cath?'

'It's French. It means "good luck".'

'How do yer know?'

'Burnley Central Library, Mary. Ave bin learnin' some French. It's 'ard, though, as me English is not t'best.'

''Eck, Cath, I reckon you're gonna get me in a lot o' trouble sooner or later! Come on, let's go an' see that Shuttleworth lass t'find out what we're lettin' us'sens in fer.'

As Cath and Mary collect their uniforms and the details of their assignment, Katherine Furse and Kitty enjoy a cup of tea in Furse's office.

'Good God, Kitty. I think we made a mistake with that Kenny woman. She's dangerous – a communist for sure – and, I suspect, she has the morals of a guttersnipe.'

Kitty, conscious of her own illicit relationship with her Grenadier Guards lover, tempers her words. 'She's quite a character, I'll grant you that. Not sure why, but given that she has no education, absolutely no breeding and talks in that comical dialect, I admire her devilment. I agree she's dangerous, but there's something about her; she's shrewd and courageous. Something tells me we may not have seen the last of her.'

'You surprise me, Kitty. Sometimes you sound like a crusty old duchess but at other times you could be a Pankhurst! Anyway, I told Shuttleworth to put Kenny and Broxup on the Poperinghe-to-Ypres run and to keep a very close eye on them. That will soon tell us what they're made of.'

Friday 21 May

The Houses of Parliament, London

Winston told Clemmie that the War Council gathering on Friday 21 May would be 'sulphurous', but events have moved so quickly during the week that it has been cancelled. The Conservatives, inspired by a desperate Sir John French, have been feeding Fleet Street the information about the shortage of shells, which has led to a growing storm around Asquith's government. The party whips have read the runes in Parliament, both in the Lords and the Commons, and the political cards have been dealt. Now the hands are being played out.

Realizing what is about to happen, and knowing that he stands to benefit from the turmoil, Lloyd George has withdrawn his support for Winston. Jacky Fisher, whose recent behaviour has bordered on insanity, has left his superior exposed in a most brutal way. He has resigned, this time with proper intent, and gone to ground in London. Not even a direct order from Asquith written in his own hand in the name of the King can persuade him to return. Not only that, Fisher has told Bonar Law that he has resigned, giving the Conservatives the final card they need to bring down Asquith's government.

Asquith, not as swashbuckling as Lloyd George but equally pragmatic, is doing what he does best: preserving his status and political future. His own mood is as black as thunder. He has heard that his epistolary obsession, Venetia Stanley, has decided to accept a marriage proposal from Edwin Samuel Montagu, a liberal MP. Even though he is crestfallen, he still knows how to survive in public life, no matter what the cost.

On the evening of the 21st there is, at least on the surface, an impromptu gathering in Asquith's offices in the House of Commons. All the senior figures are there for what soon becomes an unofficial council of war. Men are seated haphazardly around the room. Almost immediately Alfred Bonar Law, sitting in a window seat and appearing to watch the Thames flow under Westminster Bridge, turns and confronts Winston, who is seated close by.

'Would the First Lord of the Admiralty like to explain the position taken by his First Sea Lord, who seems now to be saying that the whole Dardanelles operation is a fiasco and was doomed to failure from the outset? Not only that, would Mr Churchill confirm that he sanctioned that cavalier adventure against the advice of his admirals?'

Bonar Law's short, blunt question, regardless of the fact that it is based on a false premise and an untruth, is a fatal blow delivered before the bell to begin the fight has been rung. Winston is incandescent, but to reveal his rage will only give yet more satisfaction to those who are gathered to see him suffer. He takes a deep breath. He suspects the meeting may have been deliberately arranged so that his *coup de grâce* can be inflicted publicly. As this is not supposed to be a formal meeting, he looks to Asquith inquiringly. Is he required to respond? The Prime Minister nods, indicating that he is, and hinting even more strongly that a deal has already been struck. Winston decides to go down fighting.

'Prime Minister, I beseech you and my esteemed colleagues gathered here to consider the broader canvas we have laid out before us, a canvas that does not show a picture of political intrigue and the machinations of power but one that depicts the reality that our soldiers and sailors face at this very moment.'

Former naval intelligence officer Colonel Maurice Hankey is in the room. He has begun to take minutes of War Council gatherings, so, instinctively, he raises his pencil. He has heard Winston in this mood before and knows that the oratory will be compelling and the argument overwhelmingly sound. But he also knows that it will not alter the course of events. Winston's Ides of May will not be forestalled. He puts his pencil back in his pocket.

Five minutes later Winston is still in full flow. Brutus, Cassius and the other assassins look down, shame-faced.

'So, Prime Minister, never have our Hearts of Oak been stronger. We have the Kaiser's Grand Fleet cooped up in its riverbank burrows like water rats that have had their tails bitten off. I have no doubts that our cause, no matter where it is being pressed, will triumph.' Winston gets to his feet. He is close to tears, but resists them. 'But we will have victory all the sooner if we here show the same resolve as our brave warriors – the young men of Britain and our empire, at Aubers Ridge only last week and on the inimical beaches and desolate scrubland of Gallipoli at this very moment – and fight as a team without jealousy or rancour. I welcome this government of all our people – of political friends and foes – but it will not work if you conduct it in the same scurrilous way which led to its creation.'

He pauses and looks in turn at Asquith, Kitchener and Lloyd George. They all avoid his stare. Only the Conservatives look at him, and not with expressions of warmth.

'God help our men in their hour of need. Be their faithful companion to victory and their guardian for a safe return to home shores.'

There is a long silence. Hankey decides to write a short memo to himself but thinks it diplomatic to précis the exchange with the banal entry 'Mr Bonar Law asked Mr Churchill to summarize the situation in the Dardanelles. Mr Churchill responded by describing in some detail the current position and its prospects for success.'

Winston walks from the room, upright and dignified. There is still not a sound behind him. As he strides down the long halls of the Palace of Westminster, through the Queen's Gallery, with its enormous paintings of the battles of Waterloo and Trafalgar, he is certain that he will never again walk the corridors of power in earnest. He has always felt that, like his ancestor John Churchill, 1st Duke of Marlborough, his deeds would one day adorn the walls of the Mother of Parliaments. Now he is certain that his dream is over.

That evening Clemmie writes to Asquith, pleading her husband's cause, suggesting that losing his services could grant victory to the Kaiser. In one of his last letters to Venetia Stanley, Asquith, in an astonishingly cruel comment, describes Clemmie's missive as the 'letter of a lunatic'. Winston also tries to salvage the situation by writing to Asquith, begging him to let him carry on: 'Let me stand or fall by the Dardanelles – do not take it from my hands.' He adds a postscript: 'I have not come to see you, though I should like to; but it would be kind of you to send for me.'

The Prime Minister does not send for him but writes a terse note telling him that the matter is settled. Winston, desperate and humiliated, writes again the next morning: 'I will accept any office – the lowest, if you like – that you care to offer me, and I will continue to serve in this time of war until the affairs in which I am deeply concerned are settled.'

The only solution to Asquith's dilemma is to make a deal with the Conservatives to form a national government. But Winston must pay the price and leave the Admiralty, which will be given to Arthur Balfour. Lloyd George will be made responsible for a new Ministry of Munitions, which will directly address the shell crisis. Winston is offered, and accepts, the role of Chancellor of the Duchy of Lancaster, an ornamental position of little power, but he is allowed to continue to attend the War Council.

The next day, heartbroken and fully in the grip of one of his bouts of severe depression, his 'black dogs', as he calls them, he, Clemmie and their children move into his brother's home at 41 Cromwell Road, a busy street opposite the Natural History Museum in Kensington. Jack's service in the Dardanelles means that Lady Gwendoline and their two young sons, John and Peregrine, the 'Jagoons', as Winston has christened them, are only too happy to have their company.

The same evening, Winston, Clemmie and Goonie – the family's pet name for Lady Gwendoline – relax after supper. Both women are concerned about Winston's state of mind. In an attempt to bring him some cheer, Goonie reads J. L. Garvin's editorial from the *Observer* Sunday newspaper published that morning: 'He is young. He has lion-hearted courage. No number of enemies can fight down his ability and force. His hour of triumph will come.'

Winston interrupts. 'James is a fine fellow. He hails from Birkenhead, like FE. You know, there must be something very wholesome in the water supply there. Although he doesn't have FE's wit, he does have a remarkable intellect and is a prodigious journalist. The son of an Irish labourer who died when the boy was two, he is an inspiration to us all.'

For a moment, warmed by his reflections, it seems as if Winston's mood has lifted, but he turns away to stare out on to Cromwell Road. 'He has always been kind to me. But not even James's fine endorsement gives me any comfort at the moment. The truth is I'm finished, Goonie. Clemmie knows it, and I know it. I'm finished in respect of all I care for – the waging of war and the defeat of the Germans. That is what I live for.'

'Oh, Winston, that cannot be true. You're so young.'

Clemmie begins to cry, and Goonie goes to comfort her. Winston, whose eyes are also teary and reddened, gets to his feet, his voice trembling with emotion. 'I think I'll stroll up to Hyde Park for some air. It's a lovely evening.'

Clemmie rushes to hug her husband. 'Winston, it's not a fine evening; it looks like rain! Do you have to go?'

'Darling Cat, I would like to, if you don't mind. I'll go via the Albert Hall and the Memorial. They are inspirational, and I need a little of that at the moment.'

They hug one another; both have tears running down their cheeks. Clemmie takes some deep breaths and gathers herself. 'If you must,' she says, 'but please be careful, it's quite late.'

As Winston leaves, Goonie takes hold of Clemmie, who is at the point of collapse. 'Goonie,' says her sister-in-law, 'I can't bear it. I think he might die of grief!'

Winston composes himself and crosses Cromwell Road. It is very busy as people begin to move westwards to their homes after spending Sunday evening in town. As he reaches the pavement on the opposite side of the road, he is startled by a large figure moving towards him, his face obscured by a dark shadow cast across his face by a homburg hat.

'Good evening, sir. Would you like me to walk with you for a while?'

'Good heavens, Serjeant Gough, how nice to see you. Now that I'm going to the Duchy, I thought I would lose the pleasure of your company.'

'You will, sir, tomorrow, but this is the weekend. My wife is out at her mother's tonight, so I thought I'd pop round to make sure all is well.'

'Well, that is very thoughtful of you. I'm going to walk up to Hyde Park, and to have you stroll with me would be much appreciated.'

Winston puts his cigar in his mouth and, with his cane striking out his steps, marches up Exhibition Road, with

Serjeant John Gough, his Special Branch security man, trying to keep pace.

'Serjeant, did I ever tell you about the time I escaped from the Boers in South Africa?'

Serjeant Gough has heard the story more than once but answers no, knowing full well that it will improve Winston's state of mind to let him tell it again.

When the story ends, by which time they are deep into the gaslight gloom of Hyde Park, Gough turns to Winston. 'Sir, no matter what anybody says now, they all wanted to go to the Dardanelles. And if it's been buggered up, one thing's for sure: it wasn't your fault.'

Winston turns away, anxious lest Gough sees new tears forming in his eyes, and tries not to let him hear the anguish in his voice. 'You are so kind . . . and perceptive! I should have had you on my Admiralty Board instead of those ancient mariners calling themselves admirals.' He increases his pace. 'Are you armed, Mr Gough?' he asks.

'I am, sir. My Webley is tucked away discreetly.'

'Good. You never know what we may find in Hyde Park – Zulus, Fuzzy-Wuzzies, the Kaiser's spies . . .' Winston pauses and turns to see Gough two yards behind him. 'Come on, Serjeant, keep up. No slacking.'

Gough smiles. He knows that Winston will be content if he can turn their casual stroll through Hyde Park into a do-or-die military mission.

'Now, Serjeant, Omdurman – that was a battle to chill the blood. There was I, sabre drawn, my Mauser C96 revolver primed – we called them "broom handles", you know, a very powerful weapon, saved my life more than once . . .'

Heat, Dust and Diarrhoea

Friday 4 June

RMS Essequibo, *Dardanelles*

After a relaxing journey by train to Marseilles and an equally pleasant crossing from France to Greece via Malta and Salonika, Margaret Killingbeck and Bronwyn Thomas have gone from the frying pan of the Western Front into the fire that is Gallipoli. The naked, searing heat of the flame will be much worse than the hiss and spit of the pan.

They are about to board the *Essequibo*, a packet steamer that has been requisitioned from the Royal Mail Steam Packet Company. Packet steamers have been hired for the military operation on Gallipoli because they are small enough to get close to the shallow shores of the Dardanelles Peninsula. This will, in theory, make it easier to get the sick and the wounded transferred from the beaches to the large hospital ships at anchor in nearby Mudros Bay on the Greek Island of Lemnos.

They had an all-too-powerful taste, or, more accurately, smell, of what they are about to confront when they boarded the *Essequibo* in Salonika, where the harbour was covered with endless neat rows of men on stretchers waiting to be put on board hospital ships bound for Alexandria, Malta or Cyprus. The men were suffering from all the injuries and ailments they had witnessed in Pop-Hop but, in the hot, cramped, fly-infested and insanitary conditions of their minuscule bridgeheads on Gallipoli, dysentery and enteric fever have become the biggest killers.

They are relieving Sister Mary Fitzgibbon, who has been working non-stop for over a month. She is physically and mentally exhausted and is being given leave in Egypt. When Fitzgibbon first sees Margaret and Bronwyn clambering aboard the *Essequibo*, smiling and cheerful, she is sceptical.

'Welcome, Sister Killingbeck, Nurse Thomas.'

Margaret and Bronwyn respond jauntily, but Fitzgibbon looks at their pristine QAIMNS uniforms with disdain. 'Have you just come from England?' she asks.

Margaret senses the resentment and smiles as broadly as she can as she offers Fitzgibbon her hand. 'No, Sister, Belgium. A major trauma hospital near Ypres.'

'I see. Since when have you been there?'

'Since the beginning.'

Fitzgibbon's face softens; her voice loses its English stiffness, allowing her soft Irish brogue to blossom. 'Then you don't need me to tell you what you've let yourselves in for.'

'No, Sister, please don't do that – just your medical report.'

'Yes, well, where to begin? I have no notes. No time for that.'

Margaret notices that Fitzgibbon's hand is trembling and that she is looking very thin and pale. 'Come on, Mary . . . May I call you Mary?'

'Yes, of course you can.'

'Come on, let's sit and have a cigarette.'

Margaret and Bronwyn help Fitzgibbon to the benches that line the outside of the cabins on *Essequibo*'s deck. The cigarette helps her relax.

'You've chosen a bloody awful day, that's for sure,' she begins. 'There's going to be another big push at lunchtime. It'll be their third crack at Krithia, a little town just inland, a place they were supposed to take on the first day! It'll fail, of course, every bugger knows that, except the silly sods back on Lemnos giving the orders . . .' She pauses to look at her nurse's fob watch. 'Ah, nine o'clock. They'll just be having breakfast at HQ: scrambled eggs, bacon (shipped in specially from Gib), orange juice; no smoked salmon – there's a war on, you know – but fresh coffee from the French and lots of nice pastries baked this morning. Bloody generals!'

She takes a deep draw on her cigarette and throws her head back. 'Where are you from, Margaret?'

'A little valley in Yorkshire called Swaledale.'

'Thought so. Didn't think you were a swell. And you, Nurse?'

'I'm a farmer's daughter. I'm Welsh and proud of it.'

'Good, then I can say what I really think. I'm Irish, from Cork – proper Ireland, not that bloody English city, Dublin. My father's a vet and a staunch Fenian. He says England's like a cow's arse, nothing but shit and hot air comes out of it. So, let me tell you, the truth is the generals are fucking useless. Tosspots, the lot of them!'

All three laugh loudly. It is not often that they are able to break free from the strict conventions by which they have to live every day.

'So, we're quiet now. We've unloaded our last lot and

will wait here to see what this afternoon brings. The orderlies, most of whom are very good, are cleaning up below decks. It's taken us three weeks to get rid of the horse shit down there.'

Margaret and Bronwyn look puzzled.

'The *Essequibo* brought horses and mules from Egypt – mangy things, but very useful. You can't use motor ambulances on the mainland – too hilly, no roads – so everyone has to be carried by wagon or on stretchers. We lose orderlies to snipers and shellfire almost as quickly as we lose soldiers. You've seven nurses. They're all good girls: five Brits, three a bit snooty but not bad; and a couple of Irish lasses. They've been here for three weeks. Three more to go before they get a break. We have no doctors. They're on the hospital ships. Our job is to dress them as well as we can and give whatever medication is necessary. The orderlies and sailors help. Some of the Jack Tars have become very good. Our biggest problem is fresh water, especially now it's hot.'

Margaret is horrified. 'We have to have water in these temperatures!'

'You know that, I know that, but the bright sparks in Alexandria didn't get their chain of supplies right. They sent five big lighter-ships full of thousands of gallons of fresh water. Two were sunk by submarines; two more couldn't get close enough to shore because of the shelling. One that did get fairly close got stuck on a sandbank and had no means of bringing the water ashore. Like everybody else, the quartermaster's planners assumed that all the bridgeheads would be taken with ease, allowing the water to come ashore by hose from jetties.'

Bronwyn has taken to carrying a beautiful, oval-shaped, silver and crocodile-skin hip flask in her bag. It was given to her by an injured officer just before he died. The flask has a simple inscription on it, 'PD' in copperplate, and several dents from the same shrapnel that killed its owner, Major Peter Dawson of the Green Howards. Its contents, replenished many times with whatever is to hand, often revive Margaret and her. 'Have a gulp of this, Sister,' she offers.

'What is it?'

'French brandy – not cognac, just brandy . . . Actually, it might be Spanish brandy.'

'That's very kind of you . . .'

'Bron. Short for Bronwyn.'

'Bron, right now, a swig of poteen would do!'

'So what happened to the water?'

'They tried to run the hoses as close as they could to the shore, four of them. The lads on the beach saw them and waded out with their little canteens, buckets, whatever they had. There was chaos; most hadn't had a proper drink in three days. Their officers couldn't keep order. Most of the serjeants were as bad as the men. Fights broke out; shots were fired. The hoses were too big for their containers, so most of the water went straight into the sea. When they saw what was happening, other men ran further up the hoses and starting cutting holes in them with their bayonets. Eventually, they lost the lot.'

The weary sister's hands have stopped shaking quite so much.

'We now have our own water on board, but it has to come from Lemnos every time we make a delivery. We're good for painkillers and bandages, but blankets are a nightmare because of the dysentery – but I'll come to that. So, this afternoon you will get what you are used to: a lot of injured and dying, shot, blown up – the whole textbook of injuries. But when you get them off in Lemnos and come back, if the fighting has died down, it'll be back to enteric and dysentery. And they're just bloody awful.'

Margaret tries to sympathize. 'We've had some of that in France and Belgium, and it's getting worse.'

'Well, here it's a curse. You're going to need strong stomachs, girls. Johnny Turk has no use for latrines, so his trenches are swarming with flies and maggots. It's like one of the Plagues of Egypt! Our lads try to dig latrines, but there's no room, and the ground is hard. Then, of course, no-man's-land is full of corpses putrefying in the heat. In some places, the Turkish trenches are only a few yards away. It's a scene out of hell itself. Dysentery has taken control.'

'How do you treat it?'

'We don't! We just try to nurse the men, give them as much water as we can and keep them cool. The strong ones live; the weak ones die.' Fitzgibbon looks up to the sky, shaking her head. Tears begin to form in her eyes. 'It's an awful, terrible thing. Their insides turn to liquid; first their faeces is like porridge, then cloudy beer, then blood. When the orderlies bring them in they tie string round the bottom of their trousers to stop their innards covering the stretchers and everything else. It's all they can do. We strip them down, cut off their trousers with scissors and wash the men in the sea. The sailors run hoses for us, pumped from the engine room. It works well and the men are so relieved to be clean – not that it lasts long!' Her tears roll down her cheeks.

'There's not much dignity for us. I use a sailor's boilersuit – no underwear, because you'd never wear them again – and wash it every night. Whatever you do, be careful with your own hygiene. Keep your hands away from your face when you're working and wash from head to foot in saltwater at the end of every shift. The sailors will arrange that for you in your cabins, which are not bad and have portholes facing away from the shore. But I'm afraid you may never get rid of the pong of diarrhoea in your nose. When you eat, don't eat anything with a fly on it. If you do, the odds are it's just left a bloated corpse on the mainland! The men can't avoid eating the flies; they're into everything as soon as a tin is opened. That's what's carrying the enteric.'

Even Bronwyn, who has emptied more bedpans and cleaned more soiled men and beds than she could ever count, shivers at the thought.

'They don't get any clothes after that. There's no point,' Fitzgibbon continues. 'We just wrap them in blankets and put them on deck. Those who can bear it go below decks, in with the horse shit, but now that we've got rid of it you can put more down there if you need to. But, be warned, it's like the Black Hole of Calcutta.

'It's a painful death right to the end. It's as if they're being desiccated like a prune; they have so much pain in their bellies, shitting is agony, but they can't stop. Even the strongest ones scream and cry at the end. If they were horses, they'd be shot to put them out of their misery. By Jesus, at times I've been tempted to borrow an officer's revolver and put an end to it for them, especially when they beg me to!'

Bronwyn tries to lighten the gloom. 'So, what about the good news? Saturday night at the pub, a few beers, shove-ha'penny, darts, a sing-song?'

Fitzgibbon laughs for the first time. 'Afraid not, sweetheart. There's drink to be had in the messes on Lemnos, but stock up when you're there – this place is a desert in more ways than one. There is one highlight, if you like that sort of thing: we sometimes get a few Turks if they've been captured. They think British women – and Irish, it seems – are fair game because we're prepared to wash naked men. So be warned, they tend to take out their little willies – and sometimes not so little . . .' She winks mischievously.

'. . . Sometimes several of the men at once, and masturbate in front of you.'

Margaret grimaces. 'How charming!'

Bronwyn smiles. 'Anything to pass the time of day!'

'The British boys don't like it, of course. A Turkish *çavuş* – that's one of their serjeants – was doing it the other day. A big, hairy brute; he stood straight up in front of me, grinning all over his fat face. He had such a big belly I could only just see the offending organ. Anyway, a corporal, a Lancashire Fusilier, went up to him and shot him through his nether regions, then put one through his head. We didn't have any more problems for a while after that.'

'Did the Fusilier get into trouble?'

'No, Bron. There were several officers nearby. Most were not very well, but one of them shouted out, "Put another in him for luck, Corporal!"'

Margaret and Bronwyn are beginning to think that volunteering for the Mediterranean Expeditionary Force may not have been a good idea. Fitzgibbon sees the concern on their faces.

'There is one compensation. These men are suffering a living hell out there. When they see you, it gives them hope. There's no finer thing you can do than that.'

The two women smile at one another. Margaret touches Fitzgibbon's hand. 'Thank you for being so frank with us, and enjoy your rest in Alexandria,' she says.

'I will, thanks. I'm going down to Cairo to see the Pyramids. I've always wanted to.'

'One last thing: who do we report to?'

'Ah, that's the other bit of silver lining: no one, really. The doctors ashore are young, inexperienced and too busy to be worried about you; those who survive, that is. The skipper here is a good old stick. He likes the ladies, so you can charm him into giving you whatever you want. Get young Bron here to show him a bit of Welsh ankle and he'll swoon. So that leaves Captain Fothergill on Lemnos. He's your CO, but you won't see him; they're swamped back there. In other words, you're your own boss. You can suit yourself.'

'What about going ashore? They must need nurses?'

'Men only, orderlies only – strict orders from the top. "Too gruesome, too dangerous".'

Margaret and Bronwyn exchange a look. Bronwyn says what they're both thinking. 'Better than shovelling shite on this old rust-bucket!'

The attack on Krithia began just an hour after Mary Fitzgibbon left for Lemnos. Counting the initial battle for the settlement on the day of the landings, it is the third Battle for Krithia. The second assault took place over three days, between 6 and 8 May. Australians and New Zealanders were brought in to help the beleaguered Lancashire Fusiliers, but it made little difference. One third of the men committed to the battle were killed or wounded. One battalion of Kiwis, the Auckland Battalion, lost 732 of its strength of 1,000, with only two of its officers still standing. Only a few yards of ground were gained, and at a cost of 6,300 British, Anzac and Indian casualties.

Despite the enormous losses of early May, the attack of 4 June follows a similar pattern. It is not that Sir Ian Hamilton and his staff are buffoons or heartless men; it is simply that they do not know what else to do. As in Europe, war and its weaponry have changed so quickly that they have outpaced the wisdom of those charged with leading men into battle.

In the middle of a beautiful, blue-sky Mediterranean day, Margaret and Bronwyn stare wide-eyed from the deck of the *Essequibo* as the British battleships pour fire on to the Turkish positions. But they are short of shells and have recently lost their sister ships, HMS *Triumph* and HMS *Majestic*, to submarine attack, significantly reducing British firepower. It is, nevertheless, an awesome sight, one that the two women have never seen at close quarters before. In between the huge boom of their launch and the even louder crash of their explosion, they can hear the deadly Lyddite shells fly just over their heads with a piercing whistle.

Bronwyn gasps as the hillside below Krithia erupts with multiple explosions. 'Bloody hell, Mags, those poor Turkish boys.'

'Yes, I know, but every one of them killed is one less to kill our men.'

British HQ introduces a new but not necessarily desperately clever tactic. They pause the bombardment after thirty minutes: a clear signal that the attack by the infantry is imminent, which makes the Turkish defenders rush from their deep shelters to their trench firing steps. However, as soon as the Turks are in position, the bombardment is resumed, catching at least some of them relatively unprotected. The second barrage lasts for twenty minutes, until, with just a thirty-second pause, officers' whistles, clearly audible from where Bronwyn and Margaret are standing, herald a mass over-the-top attack by the Allies.

To the centre and the left of the attack the women can see flecks of British khaki swarm across Gallipoli's parched countryside; to their right, pale-blue French dots flow over the ground. They can even see the garnet-red turbans of the Ferozepur Sikhs and the cherry-red Chechia fezes of the Senegalese Tirailleurs.

However, the initial free-flowing movement of the men does not last long. The British artillery bombardment has done little damage to the Turkish trenches or the men in them. The chilling echoes of rapid rifle and machine-gun fire soon fill the air. They turn a smooth tide of men washing across the landscape into a macabre ballet in which bodies stagger, contort and fall until the specks of colour lying motionless on the ground far outnumber those still moving.

Bronwyn and Margaret have only seen men die after

battles; now they are witnessing the horror of death on the battlefield itself. It is a slaughter, like every murderous battle since the war began nine months ago. During those battles, 5 million men have been killed and 8 million wounded, an attrition rate of 43,000 casualties every day since hostilities commenced.

The British men falling before the tear-stained eyes of Margaret and Bronwyn are adding to the 900,000 British casualties sustained since the first fatality, seventeen-year-old John Henry Parr, a private in 4th Battalion Middlesex Regiment who was killed at Mons on 21 August 1914. A former butcher's boy, he had lied about his age when he joined up in 1912. He said he was eighteen and, although he was no more than five foot three inches tall, they believed him. In fact, he was only fifteen.

Margaret draws in a deep breath. 'Bron, let's get our sleeves rolled up. This is going to be a long day.'

Despite previous failures, Aylmer Hunter-Weston has been promoted to Lieutenant General and continues to send massed ranks of men – five for every four yards – across open ground in broad daylight. He commits 30,000 men to the attack: the Indian Brigade – the Gurkhas and Sikhs – to the left; Lancashire Fusiliers, Hampshires, Worcesters, Scottish Borderers, Royal Fusiliers and Manchesters in the centre; and the Royal Naval Division and the French to the right.

Other than the Manchesters, no one makes any headway against withering fire, especially on the right, where the French Senegalese retreat, leaving the Royal Naval Division cruelly exposed to enfiladed fire. Having arrived from England only four days ago, the RND's Collingwood Battalion is all but wiped out, sustaining 600 casualties out of 1,000, including all its officers except one. The Collingwood Battalion will never be re-formed and becomes yet another part of the growing Gallipoli legend.

The first of the battle's 6,000 casualties begin to arrive on tugs and fishing boats mid-afternoon. They have to be hoisted aboard the *Essequibo* one at a time, secured in coffin-like boxes constructed by her ship's carpenter. The delay, for men packed like sardines in the blistering heat, is agony, but it gives Margaret time to decide what each patient needs.

It is a baptism of fire for her, the first time she has had to cope without senior medical staff and the resources of a hospital environment, but she issues her orders calmly and clearly: 'These three must go under cover. The corporal needs a tourniquet on that leg and is a priority for surgery on Lemnos.'

Followed by a second group of nurses, she moves on. 'These four can walk. Get them up and get their stretchers back to the tugs. Give them canteens of water and tell them to help give it to those below decks.'

One of the four, a private in the Hampshires, hears what Margaret has said. 'Can't do that, Nurse. I've been shot in the leg.'

Margaret barks at him. 'First of all, I'm a sister, and I'm in charge here. Your leg wound is a graze and you have dislocated your elbow. Now do as you're told, or you'll go back to the beach on the next tug.'

Bronwyn has the gruesome task of checking the seriously injured to see if they are still alive. They have been put in the hold close to the bow, where an area closed off by a curtain of blankets serves as a mortuary. Any who die have their blankets and stretchers taken from them and their bodies added to those awaiting an overnight burial at sea. In the last hour she has helped the orderlies add eleven more to the growing heap of corpses. She is on her way to check the port side of the *Essequibo* when she feels a tug on the hem of her uniform. The hand responsible belongs to an officer from 9th Battalion Manchester Regiment. Not older than twenty, he is ashen-faced and sweating profusely. He finds it hard to speak coherently and Bronwyn has to lean forward to hear what he is saying.

'Nurse, would you reach into my top pocket? I have a little notebook and pencil in there.'

Bronwyn pulls back the young lieutenant's blanket and shudders at what she sees.

'Yes, I know, I'm a bit of a mess, aren't I?' he says.

His right arm is missing from below the elbow, his left from just above. His legs are intact but are fully bandaged, with tell-tale spots of blood where he has been hit by shrapnel. His face, once handsome, with striking green eyes beneath a mane of thick brown hair, is now pockmarked with bloody craters, each containing a fragment of shrapnel. One piece has gouged a quarter-inch incision in his scalp from front to back. Bronwyn tries, not too successfully, to reassure him, but he just smiles.

'You're very kind, Nurse . . .'

'Just call me Bron.'

'Well, Bron, I've been keeping a diary for my fiancée since I left Manchester and I'd quite like to finish it. Do you mind doing a couple of sentences for me?'

''Course I will, but my writing's not the best.'

'Neither is mine. I was never much good in school. My father is a publican – he runs the Cheshire Cheese in Hyde.'

'Where's that?'

'Near Ashton-under-Lyne, east of Manchester. Ninth Battalion is Ashton's Reserve Battalion; we're part of the Manchester Regiment.'

Bronwyn tells the orderlies with her to carry on checking the men and tries to extricate the notebook from the lieutenant's breast pocket.

He suddenly winces with pain, and blood begins to seep from the bandages that bind his chest. His tunic has been put back over his shoulders after his wounds have been dressed. Bronwyn decides to turn him a little so that she can remove it. When she does, she sees so much blood on his back that it has turned the blanket he is lying on into a sodden puddle.

Bronwyn is astonished that he is still alive. She is reminded once again how strange it is that some men die surprisingly quickly from their wounds, usually from shock, while others with much more appalling injuries seem to survive for hours, or even days. Realizing that he has little chance of surviving the night, she rests him back down again.

His precious notebook is soaked in blood, too, but Bronwyn wipes it on her apron and opens the front page. It reads, 'To 2nd Lieutenant Allan Harrison Hudson, with love from your loving mother and father, Ann and Jervis, May 1915.'

Bronwyn places her hand on the lieutenant's forehead.

Although wet with perspiration, it is deathly cold. His end is near. Bronwyn whispers to him, 'What would you like me to write, Allan?'

His breathing has become very shallow, but he suddenly convulses in pain; blood spews from his mouth, soaking Bronwyn's face and uniform. He tries to speak, but cannot; his airway is full of blood, choking him to death. His head turns towards Bronwyn, his expression imploring her to help him. But there is nothing she can do except hold him tightly until his life slips away.

One of the orderlies comes over and asks Bronwyn if she would like a clean apron and if she would like him to help her wipe the blood from her face. 'No, thanks, I think I'll leave it for a while. It's still warm.'

She begins to leaf through his notebook. It is full of little anecdotes and sketches, and Bronwyn decides she would like to read it before handing it over to the Manchesters' adjutant.

Even though the lunchtime attack has made little progress, General Hunter-Weston decides to throw in nine more battalions in a second-wave assault. It also fails, with severe losses and many tales of heroism and senseless brutality.

Brigadier-General Noel Lee, Commander of the Manchester Brigade, is shot through the throat by a sniper. His wound is so severe he cannot speak but, after hasty surgery on the beach, he refuses an evacuation stretcher, preferring to mingle with his men, encouraging them to fight on, until he falls to the ground unconscious. He later dies of his wounds at the Blue Sisters Hospital on Malta.

On the evening of 4 June Lieutenant Dallas Moor of

the Hampshire Regiment shoots several soldiers for retreating in the face of the enemy. His action prevents a wholesale flight by his company. In due course he will be awarded the Victoria Cross for killing his own men. Lieutenant Moor is eighteen years old.

As dusk falls Hunter-Weston orders his men to dig in. Almost no ground has been gained, and in most sectors the Allied troops are back where they started from.

At two in the morning, except for the pervasive coughing, spluttering and moaning of her stricken cargo, an eerie silence has descended over the *Essequibo*. The halfmoon has not yet risen, so the night sky over the Dardanelles Peninsula is pitch black, the gleaming Milky Way so bright its intensity is almost audible. From the days of Ancient Egypt, Phoenicia, Greece and Rome, countless warriors have passed this way, but the heavens remain the same. The celestial deities have no regard for the armies and navies of mortal men; they are as nothing in the aeons of time they have witnessed. However, today, they have observed a tragedy that even they will have rarely seen.

The *Essequibo* has buried her dead at sea, including the wretched Lieutenant Hudson, and she is about to up anchor and sail for Lemnos. Margaret and Bronwyn are on deck enjoying a cigarette and a swig from Bronwyn's hip flask, a flagon she refills every night from her supply of Spanish brandy. An orderly appears in the gloom.

'Sister, one last shipment is on its way – a dozen or so.'

Margaret is so tired she can hardly speak. 'Thank you; we're on our way. Tell the captain not to sail until they're all aboard.'

She turns to rouse Bronwyn. She has fallen asleep with the drooping ash of her half-finished cigarette perilously close to falling on to her blood-spattered apron. Her hip flask, although held in her fingers, is in an unconscious grasp, and its position is precarious.

'Come on, Bron. There's more!'

Bronwyn wakes with a start, dropping her flask with a loud clang and sending grey ash cascading on to the deck. She rubs her face to wake herself and realizes that it is still covered with Lieutenant Hudson's blood.

It takes over an hour to deal with the new shipment of men. The last one, the least seriously injured, is sitting on deck staring at the night sky. He has a large bandage covering half his head and the right side of his tunic is drenched in blood. However, Bronwyn can see the cross-swords, bugles and stripes of his rank of colour serjeant.

'Colour, it's your turn. What have you been doing to yourself?'

'Fritz has shot my –'

As the serjeant turns, there is a sudden look of amazement on his face. 'Bron! What the hell are you doing here?'

Bron screams for joy. 'Hywel! Good God, I can't believe it! Are you all right?'

'Yeah, fine. But, as I was about to say, Fritz has shot my ear off.'

'Margaret! It's Hywel! He's over here.'

Margaret rushes over to help Bronwyn take off Hywel's bloodsoaked bandage. He has been very fortunate; a bullet has excised the middle part of his earlobe from front to back, leaving the top and bottom parts totally unconnected.

'It didn't half hurt, Bron. I must have just been turning away – otherwise he would have got me between the eyes! He's been after me for a week; definitely German-trained; I nearly got him a couple of times.'

'How long have you been here?'

'I came over with the Lanky Fusiliers at the end of April. You two?'

'Just arrived.'

'If I were you, I'd go straight back again. This place is a nightmare. If Fritz doesn't get you, the Gallipoli Trots will.'

Margaret starts to re-dress Hywel's wound. 'Well, neither is going to get you for a while. You're going to Lemnos until this ear heals, or it will become infected for certain. Bron, pass me the iodine.' She pours some on to a ball of cotton wool. 'This will sting but should clean up that wound.'

'Sorry?'

'I said, this should clear up this nasty wound.'

'Sorry, I can't hear you; I've been shot in the ear'ole!'

Margaret realizes that Hywel is play-acting. 'Very amusing. Be careful I don't box you on your other ear.'

The three of them laugh out loud, bringing a fleeting moment of happiness at the end of yet another horrendous day in the endless trauma that is the Great War.

Wednesday 16 June

Cambridge Road Trench,
Bellewarde Ridge, Hooge, West Flanders Belgium

'It looks like this is the real thing, 'Arry.'

''Ope so. Can't remember the last time I did for a Fritz.'

'Bloody silly time to be up an' about, though. It's the middle of fuckin' June, and there's no sign of the old currant bun yet.'

'That's because it's 'arf two in the bleedin' mornin'!'

'Wot a fuckin' silly time t'start a ruck!'

'I know. I'm off to get my lads sorted. Good luck, mate.'

'And you. See you tonight for an old nag.'

Since their escapade in no-man's-land with Hywel Thomas and Major Hesketh-Pritchard at the beginning of March, when they shot three German snipers, life has been far more tedious than dangerous for Colour Serjeants Maurice Tait and Harry Woodruff of 4th Battalion, Royal Fusiliers.

Fourth Fusiliers have been alternating between billets and trenches on a regular basis and have changed locations several times. Life has been monotonous, except for the adrenalin caused by the menace of sniper attacks, the relief of a few beers in the mess and the occasional night in Pop to partake of some female company. Mercifully, improved weather has changed life in the trenches from a living hell to just a nightmare.

Major battles have been fought nearby but, even though the men have heard huge volleys of gunfire, seen blinding flashes of explosions, sometimes at close quarters, and witnessed streams of dead and wounded, 4th Battalion has been spared.

At the end of the 2nd Battle of Ypres, the German trenches between the Menin Road and the Ypres–Roulers railway formed a significant salient bulging into the British line. From Bellewarde Ridge, on the eastern side of Lake Bellewarde, the Germans are able to overlook the greater part of the ground east of Ypres. So British High Command has decided to attack the salient and take possession of the ridge. The attack is to be carried out by 9th Brigade, 3rd Division, with 7th Brigade in support.

Dawn is not far off. It is exceptionally quiet and the ground is shrouded in a thick mist, reducing visibility and creating an eerie calm. Across a very narrow section of no-man's-land, German troops of 248 and 246 Reserve Infantry Regiments (Wurtembergers from Stuttgart) – and 132 Sub-Alsace Infantry Regiment (Alsatians from Strasbourg) are also swathed in mist. Except for their sentries, the German defenders are asleep. As all soldiers in this most terrible of wars, they have few comforts, and sleep is the most treasured – except for those whose slumber induces nightmares worse than the horrors they experience by day.

*

Beneath no-man's-land a parallel war is being fought. All along the Front, German, French and British tunnelling companies are making underground warrens that are almost as extensive and complex as the trenches above them. 'Hell-fire Jack' Norton-Griffiths is still dashing around in his Rolls-Royce, recruiting men with or without their commanding officer's permission. Corporal Basil Sawyers is a case in point. He has just been recruited to 177th Tunnelling Company. Only a week ago he was a Canadian corporal sitting in a tent just south of Ypres, and Norton-Griffiths, looking much more like a general than a major, jumped from his cream-and-brown Silver Ghost and asked for the twenty-three-year-old from Vancouver.

The subsequent conversation lasted only a couple of minutes.

'Sawyers?'

'Yes, sir.'

'I see from your records that you studied engineering at McGill?'

'Yes, sir.'

'It's an excellent university. You got an upper second?'

'Yes, sir.'

'I'm recruiting for new tunnelling companies to undermine the German defences. Are you up for it? There's a commission in it . . .'

'Yes, sir.'

'Good, your CO will get a billy-do in a couple of days. Give this to him with my compliments.'

'Yes, sir. Thank you, sir.'

Norton-Griffiths handed over a bottle of vintage Burgundy and clambers back into his car. He then turned back to Sawyers with an afterthought.

'I assume your vocabulary extends to more than "yes", "sir" and "thank you"?'

'Not really, sir, I'm an engineer.'

'Good answer; you'll do for me.'

Two days later a billy-do arrived for Sawyers' CO. It read, 'Second Lieutenant Sawyers to report, RTO Steenvoorde, for transportation to 171st Tunnelling Company, RE.'

Despite the inducement of a Nuits-Saint Georges Premier Cru from Clos des Argillières, Sawyers' CO is furious. Nevertheless, not even his plea up to divisional level to have the transfer blocked can prevent Hell-fire Jack from getting the man he wants.

Sawyers is now deep underground at the bottom of a shaft that leads to a tunnel under the German trenches on Bellewarde Ridge. He is with Mick Kenny, one of 171's originals, and several other clay-kickers, waiting for a report from a listening team at the clay face. Some of the men thought they heard German tunnellers on the last shift, so two ex-miners from Barnsley, a pair of case-hardened, barrack-room comedians called Laughton and Bickley, have been sent forward with a new listening device, a geophone, to try to detect German digging.

When the two return, young Sawyers is anxious to hear the news from the grey-bearded colliers, men more than twice his age: 'So, gentlemen?'

'Aye, we could 'ear 'em. Sounds like they're 'avin' a fuck, sir.'

'What, the Germans?'

'No, the rats!'

Much to Sawyers' embarrassment, Mick cannot stop laughing.

'Give me a break, Serjeant Kenny. A week ago I was a corporal with a degree in engineering, but my speciality was civil engineering – roads and railways – now I'm down a hole the size of a sewer pipe commanding men twice my age.'

'Sorry, sir. Mebbe tha can build us a road o'er no-man's-land.'

Mick's caustic comment only makes matters worse, and the laughter gets louder. He begins to feel sorry for the young officer. 'Alreet, you lot, button it. Let's get up t'shaft.'

Serjeant Bickley, a burly Tyke with several scars that attest to his ruggedness, takes offence. 'Who the fuck are you to be givin' orders?'

'Kenny's the name, you Tyke twat. Now get movin'.'

His face reddening, Bickley does not move; his colleague, Lance Corporal Laughton, bristles and positions himself at Bickley's shoulder. Mick stares at the two men impassively. Then he throws a punch with lightning speed. A short right jab, it catches Bickley just below the left eye; he falls backwards, pushing Laughton to one side. Laughton staggers but is able to swing with his left. Mick ducks, just as he has been coached to do by East Lancs pugilists Captain Ross and Lieutenant Tough, and the punch catches Sawyers plum on the side of the jaw, knocking him to the ground, unconscious. Mick is at Laughton immediately, hitting him with a combination of punches that put him on his back in some pain.

Bickley has got back to his feet and rushes at Mick with a shovel. Unfortunately, Mick's arms are now being held by two powerful clay-kickers who are trying to stop the fighting. Bickley seizes his chance and takes a wild swing at Mick's head. At the last moment Mick manages to heave the two men restraining him sideways, and the edge of Bickley's shovel slices into the back of the head of one of them, just behind the ear. There is a sickening noise of fracturing bone and spewing blood, and the man, one of Norton-Griffiths' Manchester sewer-builders, hits the wet ground with a squelch. Blood is pouring from the back of his head and everyone there knows the man is dead. There is a sudden silence, broken by Mick: 'Reet, let's get this fettled. Is Sawyers out cold?'

Bickley, his anger now replaced by fear of the consequences of what he has done, answers with a rasp of anxiety in his voice. 'Aye, a think so.'

'Reet, get 'im up top afore he comes round. Haul him up wi' a rope if tha 'as t'.'

As Bickley and Laughton begin to pull the stricken Sawyers to his feet, Mick tells everybody his plan. 'Look, we've a lad who's punched an officer; another's been killed wi' a shovel. We're lookin' at court martials 'ere – firing squads fer sure. Sawyers won't say owt about fisticuffs, but wi'v got to get this dead 'un into a tunnel, bury him under a roof-fall and make his wound look like 'e's been clattered by some timber.'

Laughton, still wincing from the punches to his body inflicted by Mick, asks how.

'Lie 'im on t'ground, crack 'im on t'back o' th'eed wi' a big piece a timber; then leave it restin' on his heed. Then collapse t'tunnel on t'top on 'im. Thi'll probably ne'er find 'im anyway, cos this lot's goin' up t'neet. But just t' b' certain.'

Mick looks around. 'All in fer it?' he asks.

There are nods all round.

'Reet, let's crack on afore this Canadian lad comes round.'

An hour later the deed is done. Mick goes to see Lieutenant Sawyers in his quarters, a refuge deep in the side of a trench not much bigger than the tunnelling shaft out of which they pulled him.

'You alreet, sir?'

'Not bad, Serjeant. You miners pack a hell of a punch.'

'Aye, but tha knows it weren't meant fer thee?'

'I know. Don't worry, the incident won't be mentioned; it's already forgotten.'

'Thank you, sir.'

'Call me Bas when there's no one around, I'm not used to this "sir" business. By the way, thank you for standing by me down there.'

'Well, I spoke out o' turn; shouldn't 'ave.'

'Did everyone get out?'

'No, one of t'lads, Postlethwaite, one of the Manchester boys, went back to check the fuses. There was a collapse, only a few yards, but he copped it.'

'Oh dear, the fuses all right?'

'Yes. All fine.'

'Did you dig his body out? He was one of Hell-fire Jack's men.'

'No, reckoned as tunnel's bein' blown t'neet there were no point.'

'Yes, I suppose so, but it would have been better to have given him a Christian burial.'

'Aye, but it's only two hour t'detonation.'

'Is it? How long was I out for?'

'Not long, but then tha slept fer a bit.'

The Canadian offers Mick a swig from a bottle of Canadian whiskey he keeps by his bed. 'So, our job's done here,' he says. 'We're off to Hooge next, a big one.'

'Wheer's that?'

'Just up the road. Hell-fire Jack says he wants the biggest bang in history!'

'That'll tek a lot o' gunpowder!'

'He's not using gunpowder. Our new CO, Lieutenant Cassells, is bringing ammonal from London.'

'Wot's that?'

'Deadly!'

Mick's Burnley mates Vinny Sagar and Twaites Haythornthwaite have not been with him since early morning. They have been sent to try to rescue a large group of 5th Battalion 1st Lincolnshire Regiment who have been buried alive by a German mine near Ouderdom. With a dozen more tunnellers, they have been working for over twelve hours without a break. So far, they have dug out eleven men, all of them dead, but they are not giving up. A distinct sound of tapping has been coming from below since they started the rescue. Every few minutes they stop, and listen. It's growing fainter but is still just audible.

'It's right under me feet, Twaites, a can still 'ear it. It's Morse code – SOS – am certain on it.'

Vinny shouts over to the Lincolnshire's officer supervising the dig. 'It's tappin' out SOS, sir.'

'Very well done, that man. Keep digging, boys. Let's have two more over here to help Sagar and Haythornthwaite.'

The pattern of tapping changes. Vinny shouts out again. 'It's different now, sir, and stronger again. Dash-dot-dot; dash-dot-dash-dash; dot-dot-dot; dash-dash-dash; dash-dot. That's it, sir, over an' over agin.'

'Excellent work, Sagar.' The officer checks in his notebook. 'It's D-Y-S-O-N, Lieutenant Dyson. He's alive!'

Cheers go up from the diggers, and from the Lincolnshires who are watching.

Less than five minutes later Twaites' shovel strikes something metallic: a piece of corrugated roofing. Faint cries can be heard from underneath, and the men scrape the earth frantically from it. A voice, weak and desperate: 'Quickly, lads! As quick as you can. I'm nearly done for.'

Several men rush forward to help. Together, and aware that every second counts, they quickly but carefully work at the corrugated sheeting. They can't risk any collapse. They dislodge it without any earth fall and draw it aside.

Beneath is a pitiful figure. So contorted are the khaki torso and limbs, it takes a moment to recognize which part is which. The lower legs are pressed tightly against the upper legs. Above them, like another sardine in a tin – and with its arms pressed hard against its side – is the victim's body. The head is cocked to one side, its fixed eyes staring out in dread.

Lieutenant Eric Dyson had been speaking on a field

telephone when the mine exploded. The roof above his head collapsed on him, pushing his head between his knees and breaking the chair he was sitting on. He ended up on the floor, bent double, winded and unable to move. Tons of earth pressed down on him, but the roofing bore some of the brunt and had saved his life. But for how long? Was his initial survival only a prelude to a slow and agonizing death?

He was in a small pocket of air, but he had no idea how long it would last. Was he to die here, entombed, asphyxiated? He could see nothing, hear nothing. In agony from his contorted position, he was sure his back was broken and he had little feeling in his legs. His torso was clamped close to his legs, his chin only inches from his knees. Unable to see how much space there was around him, he had to rely on his instincts, but the messages his senses were sending him were grim. He felt cocooned in soil; earth above his forehead and under his chin, everywhere. The only air hung dense in the small space between his bent knees and the beaten-earth floor. After a while, his blind panic subsided a little and he was able to assess his position. It was hopeless. If he could have reached his revolver, he would have used it, but there was no possibility of him reaching his holster.

Then he heard a distant noise, which, after what seemed an eternity, he identified as the sound of digging. He could move his right hand a couple of inches, so began to tap the telephone handset still in it against the corrugated roof. He remembered his training and turned his frantic tapping into a measured SOS signal. He knew it was only a matter of time before the diggers reached him. But would they come soon enough? He felt crushed, claustro-phobic, terrified.

When Lieutenant Eric Dyson is finally pulled from his tomb, he has survived for over fourteen hours. He is very weak and severely traumatized but, apart from some bruising, he has no serious injuries and his back is not broken. The battalion medical officer thinks he will be able to walk properly in a fortnight or so. As for the mental scars, it is hard to know if, or when, they will ever heal.

He is offered the chance of leave, but declines. He asks instead for a large room with windows in the rehabilitation hospital in St Omer. As he is taken away, still curled in a foetal position, he holds out his hand to Vinny and Twaites.

'Thank you, lads. Your names?'

'Sapper Sagar, sir, and this is Haythornthwaite, 171st Tunnelling Company, Royal Engineers.'

'Your CO?'

'Captain Bliss, sir.'

'I owe you a huge debt of gratitude. I could hear every strike you made with your shovels – you were relentless. I'll never forget.'

'All in a day's work, sir.'

'Perhaps, but Captain Bliss will be receiving a crate of Belgium's finest ale on your behalf. It's the least I can do to help quench your thirst from today's digging.'

When 171st Tunnelling Company's mine under Belle-warde Ridge is exploded at 02:50 hours the whole area heaves into the air, like a chest taking a lungful of air, before settling again. But, close to its epicentre, the blast is much more violent, sending trees, machine guns, trench timbers, sandbags and men, careening into the sky. It is an awesome sight, the like of which Maurice and Harry in their Fusiliers' trenches have never witnessed before. The sky is still mostly black but, to the east, a rich heliotrope turning to yellow and red marks the first hint of dawn. The half-light, edging them with a soft glow, lends a strange, surreal quality to the silhouetted shapes rising into the sky.

Hundreds of German defenders are killed in a moment. More follow as, seconds later, the British howitzers begin their onslaught. Harry looks around. He feels alone. He is used to having Maurice at his side in battle, but he is many yards away, with his own company. So Harry talks to himself: 'About bloody time. I thought those hamptons at HQ were gonna wait till it was broad bloody daylight!'

Despite Harry's cynicism, for once the British attack has been well planned. Three duplicate lines of telephone communications have been laid. Each man has been issued with two extra bandoliers of ammunition and double rations, and each company has been allocated good supplies of wire-cutters, shovels, empty sandbags, signalling flags and Mills grenades, a new invention which the men value highly.

The pre-attack artillery barrage, in three phases, with ten-minute gaps in between, appears to have been a success. It is now 04:25 hours and Harry can see that the German barbed wire has been shredded in several places and that their trenches, in some areas only 50 yards away, appear to be in disarray, having taken many direct hits.

Harry checks his watch again: 04:28. Another artillery attack will begin in two minutes, or the signal to attack will send him and the men of his B Company over the top. From where he is, he cannot see his new CO, Lieutenant Brian Edmund Warde. He is just twenty years old, from Kensington, London. The son of a career soldier who was a major in the same regiment, he was educated at Lancing College and Oxford University, before leaving his college to fight. Harry thinks Warde is a nice enough young man and will no doubt serve with distinction, but he feels sorry for him. He is about to be exposed in the most challenging of circumstances but has had no real training and has no credentials to justify his leadership of professional soldiers in battle.

In the distance, Harry can see the battalion adjutant, Captain O'Donel, clamber to the top of the parapet, whistle already in his mouth. This is it. Harry shouts as loudly as he can: 'Stand to!'

The piercing shrill of O'Donel's whistle cuts across no-man's-land, followed by countless others. Then come the roars and cries of thousands of men asserting their lust for battle, their anger, their fear. Just behind his new CO, Lieutenant Charles Wilfrid Bannister, a twenty-two-year-old from Tunbridge Wells, Harry can see Maurice at the head of his company, just part of a huge wall of men moving across the bare ground of no-man's-land. The German defenders open fire within moments, punching holes in the solid wall of khaki. Harry looks left just as Lieutenant Warde is thrown back over the parapet by the impact of several bullets that strike him simultaneously. His head is jerked backwards, knocking off his service cap. Blood cascades from an exit wound at the back of his neck; his whistle tumbles through the air. His grip on his revolver loosens, and it falls into the trench behind him, quickly followed by his lifeless form. He has made only one step and managed just one strangled toot of his whistle in his first battle. Now his war and his brief life are over. Harry turns away.

'Steady, lads, heads up!' he shouts. 'Keep moving: look for your objectives.'

Bullets cut through the air with whistles and whizzes, except those that strike targets. Then there are thuds and splashes, followed by the screams of dead and dying men. A rake of machine-gun fire strikes the ground in front of Harry. Moving from right to left, the bullets squelch into the ground, making small craters in the clay. He knows that the machine-gunner will adjust his trajectory on his next sweep, but there is nowhere to hide. All he can do is shout to his men: 'Keep moving!'

Maurice and his company reach the German trenches with relative ease. In the area of his objective, the British artillery has destroyed the barbed wire and 171 Company's mine has killed most of the Alsatian defenders. Ironically, many of the men from Alsace are native French speakers whose grandparents would have thought of themselves as French. Now they are dying for a country that is attempting to annihilate their motherland. The few German survivors of the explosion soon surrender, so Lieutenant Bannister orders C Company to move on to its second objective. It is only 07:00 hours; the attack is going well.

Again the Fusiliers make good progress, but it is soon

halted by the thunder of artillery fire. Maurice turns; the fire is coming from the wrong direction. They are British howitzers: 9.2-inch-calibre monsters, which can make a very big hole in the ground. Maurice dives for cover; the British barrage is falling short, right on top of the advancing British infantry. Either the Fusiliers are moving too quickly – or the gunners' trigonometry is dramatically askew.

Maurice shouts orders that their signal flags be driven into the ground to indicate their position but soon realizes that there is too much smoke and early-morning mist to allow them to be seen by the range finders. Now his only defence is to force himself as close to the ground as possible and put over his exposed head the shovel he is carrying. The ground beneath him trembles as the massive Lyddite shells rupture Flanders' fields. The explosions assault his head and ears, as if they are being struck by a blacksmith's hammer. The barrage lasts for many minutes; he loses count of how many. When it is over, he is covered from head to toe in earth. The dirt is mixed with human remains: the red and pink of flesh, bleached white bone fragments and light grey brain tissue.

Maurice jumps to his feet. C Company is no longer with him – at least not as the group of able-bodied men with whom he left their trench. Most of them have been obliterated, strewn over no-man's-land like ground meat. He can see the remains of Lieutenant Bannister, but only because he glimpses a sleeved arm with an officer's braid on it. He recognizes the mangled bodies of army stalwart Serjeant Billy Berry from Hounslow, wily Private Henry Burns from Bethnal Green and hard-bitten Private Charlie Hankin from Isleworth, a thirty-five-year-old Old

Contemptible, a dogged veteran with twenty years' experience. Maurice had liked Charlie: he was a proper soldier, a man so resolute, so strong, he seemed indestructible . . . until today. Now he is a smoking pile of khaki and blackened skin.

The remnants of C Company gather around Maurice, a dozen humbled, ragged souls. Stretcher-bearers appear and begin the search for survivors of the bombardment.

Maurice gathers himself. 'Come on, lads; let's get the fuck out of this khazi.'

Fifty yards away, Harry is still encouraging his men onwards. 'Keep moving, lads. Keep –'

But his order is stifled by an intensity of firing that fills the air with overwhelming sounds and sensations. His men are being cut to pieces all around him. There are more stricken comrades on the ground than still moving. The bullets, like hailstones, hit his men again and again, causing sickening injuries. Harry feels nothing in the maelstrom but, in the midst of its ferocity, for Harry, time slows down; the noise of battle recedes. Then there is silence; the light fades. And nothing – a black void.

''Arry, it's Mo. Wake up, mate.'

Harry hears the same voice over and over again. He is returning to consciousness. Eventually, he recognizes the voice of his life-long friend.

'Mo, what the fuck! Where am I?'

'You're in a dressin' station with the Liverpool Scottish boys. This 'ere is Captain Chavasse, the doc we talked to at that hospital in Pop when we was looking for that Taff sniper Hywel – remember?'

'Yeah, I remember – you sorted out the Welsh boy's 'and, right, sir?'

'That's right, Colour.'

'So, wot yer doin' up 'ere?'

'Liverpool Scottish is my regiment. When I heard they were part of the push today, I took leave from Pop-Hop to set up this dressing station. Good job I did: we've had a lot of casualties.'

'Bad is it, sir?'

'Terrible, Colour. By my calculations, I'm the only officer left from those I came over with last year, and that's because I've been at Pop-Hop most of the time.'

'So, sir, what 'ave I done to meself?'

'Can't you remember?'

'Can't say I do, sir. Everything went black; I just keeled over.'

'I'm not surprised. You've been machine-gunned in several places. One through your right forearm, one through the right thigh, another under your collarbone, and one hit you on top of the head. You must have a thick skull, because it appears to have bounced off! You have a bit of a hole where your parting ought to be.'

'Bloody Nora. I was lucky then.'

'Very fortunate: no arteries hit, no major damage to bones or vital organs, but you're going home, that's for sure. You'll be invalided out to Blighty in due course.'

'No, sir, not for me. Wot the 'ell am a' gonna do at 'ome when every other bugger's out 'ere fightin'?'

'But you'll be a hero and get a good pension.'

'Bollocks. Excuse my language, sir, but wot's the good

o' that if Fritz is marchin' up an' down Piccadilly by Christmas!'

'Do you mean you don't want to go home?'

'Correct, Doc. Can't you patch me up and get me some lovin' care from some of your lovely nurses till I get better?'

'Well, most men go home with half the wounds you've got – plus, it's expensive on staff and resources to fill up beds in France when there are plenty of convalescent hospitals back home. Besides that, your recovery will be long and painful. Then it will be back in those awful trenches. Have you got the bottom for that?'

'I 'ave, Doc. Better than bein' wheeled up Leyton High Street in an invalid's wheelchair bein' kissed by old ladies with stubble on their chins.'

'But what will I do with you here?'

'Wot abaht one of them nice little 'ospitals on the coast. I hear Boulogne is nice an' dandy this time of year.'

Chavasse smiles. He finds Harry's attitude heart-warming. 'It will take three or four months to get you into a state so that you can go into the line. Let me have a think about it.'

'Thanks, Doc.'

Harry turns to Maurice. 'So wot about your lot, Mo?'

'Blown to buggery by our own artillery.'

'Fuck me! All of them?'

'Most of them.'

'And the attack?'

'Not sure.'

Chavasse, who is still examining Harry's wounds,

answers for Harry. 'Well, it looks like we have gained some higher ground, but at a very high price. At this rate, every man in Britain and the empire will have to be sacrificed to get us to the German border, never mind Berlin.' He pauses. 'The last man I agreed not to send home was Hywel Thomas, the sniper you met. He's now back to killing Germans in large numbers, so perhaps I should do as you ask.'

Maurice cuts in. 'I think you should, sir. 'Arry is very good at killin' Fritzes; he's got a DCM an' bar for it.'

'Really? A double DCM; then that settles it. It's recuperation by the sea in Boulogne for you, Colour. I'll sort it with your colonel.'

'Thank you, sir, but yer'll 'ave to wait till we get a new one – we're gettin' through 'em like hot cakes. Colonel Hely-Hutchinson is going home, seriously wounded.'

'You make it sound like a curse, Colour.'

'Your words, not mine, sir.'

Wednesday 30 June

Rugeley Camp, Penkridge Bank, Cannock Chase, Staffordshire

John-Tommy Crabtree and Tommy Broxup had left Caernarvon on 13 May. It was a sad parting on both sides. The Lancastrians and the North Walians had grown fond of one another. There had been no trouble, no incidents, a little drunkenness but nothing to threaten the harmony between the Royal Duchy and the principality. In fact, there was more than one tender embrace on the platform of Caernarvon Station to signify the warmth that had been generated between the locals and the visitors. Handkerchiefs and Union flags were waved, cheers were bellowed and songs sung. There were also a few tears, not least those shed by the local publicans, hoteliers and retailers, whose recent income will now be matched only by a bumper summer season of holidaymakers.

After a parade in Castle Square it took two hours to get the massed ranks of the Accrington Pals on to their trains for the Midlands. Colonel Rickman led the way, with Battalion Serjeant Major Jimmy Shorrock keeping the men in proper marching order.

Little was ready for them at Rugeley. The land has been given to the war effort by Lord Lichfield and an army of carpenters had built wooden accommodation huts, but when the Pals arrived there was no running water or electricity. It also rained for three days, in contrast with Caernarvon, where the weather had been searingly hot. The men did not like the remote location, there were no pubs nearby to quench their thirst in and no local girls to catch their eye.

Their only company is other Pals Battalions. Two battalions of Barnsley Pals are also residents, as are the Sheffield City lads. There are few distractions. A heath fire on Whit Sunday, 23 May, threatened the entire camp and took 4,000 men eight hours to put out and damp down. Football has been a godsend. Z Company, the new designation for the Burnley men, has swept all before it and, with seven players in the battalion team, the Accy Pals beat the Barnsley men 2–1 in front of 500 spectators. Many men have taken advantage of Whit Weekend railway passes to go home to their loved ones but, with Mary away in France, Tommy decided to stay in camp. John-Tommy did take up the offer and went home to Wynotham Street to see his wife, Mary, and their children, Jack and baby daughter, Eileen.

Perhaps the highlight of their first few weeks at Rugeley occurred on 31 May, when a ceremonial parade in front of Brigadier General Bowles was held on the parade ground to mark the formal handover of the battalion to the War Office. It did not mean that the Pals were ready to fight at the Front, but it did mean they were now regular professional soldiers. Everyone was very proud, especially John Harwood, Mayor of Accrington, who had launched the battalion almost nine months earlier.

Following a route worked out by the thirstier men at

the camp, Tommy and John-Tommy have walked the mile and a quarter across the Chase to the Horns Inn on Slitting Mill Lane, the nearest pub. It is an easy walk in daylight, but less so at night, when a Tilley lamp is required to illuminate the whitewashed tree trunks painted by the battalion's more resourceful drinkers.

'Not a bad drop this draught Bass, John-Tommy?'

'Aye, not bad, but gimme a pint o' Massey's any day o' t'week.'

''Ow were Wynotham Street an' t'family?'

'Champion, thanks, Tommy. Little Eileen's doin' alreet; she'll be a year old this next September.'

'Why do'st thi call it Wynotham Street?'

'No bugger 'as any idea. Mary reckons tha's an old wives' tale that, years ago, one o' Burnley's mayors went to a civic reception where thi served cheese sandwiches instead o' 'am and 'e were supposed to 'ave shouted out, "Why not ham!" Thi reckon t'story went in t'*Burnley Express* and it stuck. Later that year, t'Town Council were voting on street names an' every bugger thought it were a good idea.'

'Do'st yer believe it?'

'Not a word – it's all eyewash!'

'I 'ear we're off to a new camp soon.'

'Wheer's that?'

'Ripon.'

'Bollocks, that's in Yorkshire. Can't be doin 'wi' that; it's full o' Tykes.'

'Well, at least wi can gi' 'em a hiding at cricket.'

'An' football.'

'Aye, tha's reet. Tha's nowt like beatin' a Tyke to remind 'im who's Cock o' t'North.'

The Horns is full of soldiers, Lancastrians and York-shiremen, and the volume of the conversation is getting louder and louder as the evening wears on and the level of alcohol consumption rises. A popular local down a country road, it is usually full of farmers and agricultural labourers and men from the slitting mill nearby. Although the locals are annoyed by the commotion created by the boisterous northerners, they forgive them for the sake of King and country and, in the main, only sit and scowl at them. The landlord, on the other hand, is more than happy to share in the men's King's shillings and keeps his doors open as long as the Staffordshire Constabulary will allow.

Colonel Rickman's training regime has extended to the digging of trenches, and mock-battles to attack and defend them. The heavy rain that often falls on the Chase has added to their resemblance to the real thing at the Front, much to the enhancement of the men's pride in being 'proper soldiers'.

Tommy takes a deep swig of his draught Bass. 'At least our trainin's lookin' up. RSM Shorrock sez it's just like reel thing at t'Front.'

'Mebbe, but we get to go 'ome for a wash an' a kip at neet.'

John-Tommy changes the subject. 'As'ta 'eard fra' Mary?'

'Not much. I got a letter to say she were in St O'Mare, or some such place, drivin' lorries, buses an' ambulances an' t'like.'

'And Cath?'

'Aye, they're workin' together.'

'Wonder 'ow Mick an t'lads are goin' on?'

''Spect they're chasin' t'French lasses a merry dance.'

'Don't expect we'll get a letter fra' them.'

'Reckon not; not one fer letters, our Mick.'

The beer has had the desired effect on Tommy and John-Tommy.

'Come on, lad. Let's be on our way across that heath, wi'v a battle to feight t'morn.'

'Aye, Le Cateau agin – Rickman loves it: "Hold the line men, stand firm; give them another mad minute." "Triumph of British Musketry!" He just loves it, old Rickman.'

PART SEVEN: JULY

Flammenwerfer

Saturday 3 July

Marble Lodge, Blair Atholl Estate, Perthshire

The Stewart-Murrays of Blair Atholl have gathered together for a rare family weekend, but not at Blair Castle. The old duke has refused to leave the security of Marble Lodge, Maud Grant's humble estate cottage. So, cooked on her small kitchen range, Saturday lunch is being served by the redoubtable Mrs Grant, the duke's only comfort in the depths of his melancholy.

High up Glen Tilt, Marble Lodge in July presents a fine picture of the Glens in all their glory. Red kites and golden eagles soar overhead, and the green of the hillsides is so bright it almost assaults the eyes. The Tilt river teems with salmon and the hill lochs with brown trout, making Mrs Grant's choice of lunch menu a predictable process.

'Lady Helen, will you ask everybody to come through and help themselves. It's all arranged on the kitchen table,' she says.

'Thank you, Mrs Grant, but please call me Helen. This is a family gathering.'

Lady Helen's comment makes Maud smile. Calling the lunch a 'family gathering' is tantamount to normalizing Mrs Grant's relationship with Helen's father, an acceptance that has taken a long time.

After the family have helped themselves to oven-baked salmon with tarragon, homemade fresh bread and butter and home-grown salad, they spread themselves around the fire in the lodge's tiny sitting room. Bardie has brought up some dry white Gewürztraminer from the castle cellars and pours out a glass for everyone.

There is an embarrassing pregnant pause as everyone thinks about how to start the 'family' conversation. Bardie decides he ought to be first.

'Father, any more news from Hamish?'

The duke, closest to the crackling fire that is kept lit all year round, is well wrapped up in a pullover and scarf, even though it is a warm summer's day. He would have preferred not to go through the ordeal of the gathering but has been forced into it by Helen's and Maud's insistence that he must resume his duties as head of the clan and the family. It is now three months since the death of Geordie became a brutal reality for the family, but the most titled man in the land still has not come to terms with it.

'He's been transferred to some god-forsaken place called Bischofswerda, in Bohemia. He could not be further away; it's apparently far to the east, near the Czech and Polish borders.'

'But very agreeable in the summer, Iain.'

Maud, as always, tries to get the Duke to look at things positively.

'I suppose so. He says the food and sanitation are much improved, but they have few orderlies so are having to do everything for themselves.'

'That won't do him any harm.'

David Tod, Lady Helen's fiancé, whose politics are significantly more radical than those of the family he is marrying into, cannot resist making this pointed remark – much to the annoyance of Dertha's husband, Colonel Harold Ruggles-Brise. He is not an aristocrat by birth but is very pleased with himself for having married one.

'You do talk rot, David. Do you have a housekeeper in your Edinburgh flat?'

'I do, but I can, and do, iron my own shirts and polish my own shoes. I don't need a servant to do those things for me.'

'More fool you!'

'Who would like some more?' Maud gets up to change the subject. 'I've made us a raspberry cranachan and been generous with the whisky. And, as this is a family gathering, Iain asked me to make a jug of Atholl Brose, and again I've not been mean with Blair's own malt.'

The duke's mood has not improved. 'Inglis wrote to me a fortnight ago to tell me that the army tents we've allowed on the Black Island might be visible from Blair's drawing-room window. I told him to tell the regimental quartermaster concerned that he had to move them forthwith, or I would come down personally and stick my 12-bore up his arse – bloody cheek! Then he told me that our chief clerk is joining the Seaforths. Yesterday was his last day. Inglis says that, because of the war, he might have to get a woman in to do the bookkeeping. What's the world coming to!'

Helen tries to soothe her father and goes to sit on the floor next to his chair. 'Papa, there is a war on, and I'm sure most women can add and subtract just as well as men.'

'Helen, I know only too well that women can do arithmetic. Your mother was a genius at adding up her allowance and knew to the penny how much I should write a cheque for to cover her debts at Binns of Edinburgh. That's not the point: a woman will be a bad influence in the estate office; if the young office boys get a sniff of her quim they'll not be able to concentrate.'

'Father, don't be so disgusting!'

'It is disgusting, I agree, but the smell of a woman in heat is a fact of life; like stags and does in the forest. And, by the way, I know there's a war on. I've lost two sons in it – have you forgotten?'

The old man's eyes fill with tears and he starts to rock in his chair. Dertha rushes over to help Helen comfort their father.

Bardie jumps to his feet. 'Father, let me get you some cranny and brose. I know they're your favourites.'

The duke tries to compose himself. 'No, thanks, Bardie. The wine's gone to my head. I think I'll go and lie down for a while. I hope it was a French Gewurzi not a Hun one?'

'Good point. I didn't think.'

Bardie grabs the bottle. 'Bugger me, it is a Rolly Gassmann – bloody German!'

'Pour the rest in the Tilt, Bardie. I can't have Hun wine on our tables when the bastards are killing my family and putting them in prison camps!'

Maud takes the duke up to bed, after which everyone settles down to enjoy the raspberry cranachan.

'Bloody good, Mrs Grant.'

'Thank you, Colonel Ruggles-Brise. Please call me Maud.'

'Only if you promise to call me Harry. My name is such a mouthful.'

Ruggles-Brise turns to Bardie. 'The old boy is very lucky to have such peace and quiet up here, to say nothing of Maud's cooking. Talking of peace and quiet, how's your Scotty Horse in Northumberland? I thought there was talk of a posting overseas?'

'There was. I assume it was Gallipoli, but nothing came of it – very dull.'

'Don't know, old boy. I think you're well out of it. I'm told it's a buggers' muddle, with Delhi Belly thrown in for good measure.'

'Well, I'm sure Kitchener will get it sorted now that Winston's heavy hand's not on the tiller at the Admiralty.'

'Not a fan?'

'I am, actually, he's a good man, although he rather forgot the promises he made over the aeroplanes we built up here. But he's a politician with dreams of being a general. I prefer them like Wellington, who did it the other way round.'

'I agree. Lloyd George is the same. Now he's interfering with munitions. The boys at the War Office know what they're about, but he's got his hooks into them. Mark my words, Asquith will be next; the little Welsh socialist will be Prime Minister soon. God help us all – we'll be taxed to buggery.'

'Well, it won't be Winston in Downing Street. I suspect he's blown his chances for good now.'

Harry leans forward so that no one can overhear. 'How are you and Kitty getting along? Any better?'

'Not really. I'm afraid I'm still partial to a bit of rough and ready, if you know what I mean. There are a couple of game girls near Blagdon I see from time to time. One, in particular, loves a hard ride on the moors, which loosens her loins somewhat, then she enjoys an even harder ride in the stables afterwards. And I'm pretty sure Kitty's got someone in London. She gets very scrubbed when she leaves for the train and is full of vim when she comes back. So we're both quite grown up about it.'

'What do you make of Mr Tod, the grocer who's soon to be your brother-in-law?'

'Rum sort – not sure what H sees in him.'

'Good sculptor, isn't he?'

'Yes.'

'Perhaps he's got a big chisel!'

'Don't know, and I'm not about to ask H! But I do know Father wasn't delighted when he pitched up to ask for her hand. Maud said he chased him down the Glen, waving his Purdey at him and shouting that he'll give him both barrels if he touches his daughter.'

'Oh dear. It was a no then.'

'It was, but H came up and squared it.'

'How?'

'Oh, she can wrap him round her little finger if she wants to. I'm sure she pointed out that his chisel had already made its mark. Besides, Father knows full well that she will do just as she pleases in any case.'

'She's quite a girl, your sister.'

'She is – absolutely spiffing sort. You and Dertha seem happy.'

'We are. I think I'll be back in harness soon. I've been told that, when I'm fit, I'll get the 40th Division, part of Kitchener's New Army.'

'Congratulations.'

'Thanks. That'll make me a full general. But the 40th are the bantams, under regulation height – odd little chaps. Fit enough, strong enough, but under five foot three.'

'S'pose they make smaller targets when they go over!'

Both men laugh loudly, attracting the attention of the others. Lady Helen gestures to everyone to be quiet.

'Shush, everyone. I just wanted to say, on behalf of all of us, that we really appreciate Maud's hospitality today and her marvellous Blair lunch – very fitting. But, much more importantly, I wanted to express our gratitude to her for all that she is doing for Father, who relies on her so much.'

Helen goes over to Maud and kisses her warmly on the cheek. 'Maud, thank you so much for all the love and kindness you show him.'

'He's worth it, Helen, he's a lovely gentleman. A bit old-fashioned, but nice with it.'

'Well, we're all very grateful.'

'I'm pleased to meet your intended. He's a very nice man, so he is.'

'I'm glad you like him. Father doesn't approve.'

'I know. As I said, he's old-fashioned. He knows the world's changing, and he doesn't care for it. But, as I keep telling him, you can't stop progress.'

'Is it progress, Maud?'

'Aye, 'course it is. When I were a wee girl, when Iain's father was Duke, we were told never to look him in the eye; it wasn't done. Now I do more than look Iain in the eye!' She giggles. 'We'll have the vote soon. That will change things.'

'Really, you're a suffragette?'

'Of course, aren't you? But don't tell your father.'

Sunday 11 July

Vlamertinge, West Flanders, Belgium

'Sure you can fettle it, Cath?'

'Aye, just needs t'spark plugs tekin' out an' cleanin'.'

'Well, 'urry up; am freezin' me bits off.'

'Am goin' as quick as a can, lass.'

Cath Kenny closes the ambulance's bonnet with a flourish. 'Right, turn her over.'

As soon as Mary Broxup turns the ignition, the Ford Model T Army Field Ambulance springs to life with a satisfying clatter of pistons and exhaust.

'Next job is t'find us way back t'Pop.'

'I told yer not t'pull off t'main road.'

Mary and Cath have been carrying wounded men backwards and forwards between Poperinghe and Ypres for two months without a break. They are exhausted, but enjoying enormously the challenges they face and relishing the freedom of being their own boss.

Their eight-mile route is not easy; the road is heavily rutted when it is dry and a quagmire when wet. Shells fall frequently, making the road even worse, quite apart from the threat to life and limb.

This is their last run of the day. They have four Somerset Light Infantrymen in the back, one of whom is in a bad way.

'Come on. This is t'way.'

Mary drives off towards the west, knowing that the setting sun points the way home to Poperinghe. After only a few yards they pass a group of Welch Fusiliers, who have clearly been drinking. They are singing the rude, soldier's version of 'Inky Pinky Parlez-vous' at the tops of their voices. One of them, a heavily built lance corporal, staggers in front of the ambulance, forcing them to stop with a screech of its brakes. He has a bottle of Belgian brandy in his hand.

'Hey, boyos, a pair of posh FANYs to join our party . . . Come on, girls, we've been given leave in Paris. You can drive us there.'

Cath pulls to one side the canvas that acts as a door to the ambulance's passenger seat. 'Fuck off, Taffy, we've got work to do!'

'Ooh, a FANY that swears – naughty girl. I'll have to put you over my knee and slap your fanny, FANY.'

'You and whose army? Fuck off, you big git.'

Cath's venom changes the mood among the men.

'Come on, boys. Pull 'er out. She needs 'er dirty mouth washing out, and I know what with!' says the lance corporal.

Several of the men rush forward, grab both women and pull them on to the road. Mary's uniform is ripped in the process, revealing her petticoat.

'Look, boyos! Haven't seen a pair of drawers in a month o' Sundays!'

Cath takes a huge swing with her right hand, a blow that travels directly towards the lance corporal's chin, but he puts his hand up and, with nonchalant ease, grabs her clenched fist.

'A scrapper,' he says. 'I like it when they fight back.'

He grabs Cath's arms roughly and twists them up her back, making her scream, then throws her over his shoulder. She can smell the drink on his breath and the odour of a body that has not been washed in many days.

'Mary, kick the bugger! Do summat!'

Mary tries to come to Cath's aid, but is hemmed in by two men, who, despite her punches and kicks, force her into the same position as Cath.

'Over there, boys! That barn'll do nicely for our little lesson in manners.'

Cath tries to think of a way out of their dilemma. 'Listen, lads, this is a court-martial offence. But let us go, an' we'll forget all abaht it.'

'Not a chance, darlin'. No one calls me a git an' gets away with it.'

The two women are thrown on to the floor of the barn.

'Gareth, go and move that ambulance into the yard. Tell the men in the back that we're getting some fuel.' The lance corporal leers at the two women, slavering like an animal. 'Now then, girls, let's get your kit off. Either you do it, or we do it for you.'

Cath looks at Mary. Tears are running down her face and she is trembling with fear. Cath tries to save her friend.

'Look, lads, I'm the one with t'big mouth. I'll tek care of all on yer, but leave her be . . . please.'

'Very noble of you – Cath, is it? But I like the look of Mary too. But you can go first. Come on, get those drawers off.'

Cath does not respond.

The sneering Fusilier pulls out his bayonet and sticks

its point under her chin. 'Do as you're fuckin' told, or I'll stick this up your arse!'

Cath knows from the look on the man's face that he means what he says. Resigned to her fate, she starts to remove her clothes as the Fusilier fumbles with the buttons of his flies.

'Come on – everything; it's a warm evening. I don't want you sweating all over me.'

Cath looks around, desperate for an escape route, as she removes her last piece of clothing.

'Well, you're a fine figure of a woman, I'll give you that. Hope your hubby does right by you.'

'He does. He's got a lot more than that little bit of gristle in your hand.'

The lance corporal brings his free hand across Cath's face with a fearsome crack, knocking her to the ground. 'Now, get up, you little cow. I thought of making you suck my dick, but I reckon you'd bite it off, you little vixen. Instead, I'm gonna fuck the fight right out of you. You won't walk for a week!'

Mary tries to intervene but is held firmly by her assailants. Cath is dragged across the barn floor by her hair and thrown over some bales of hay. A heavy hand is laid across her back and she can feel the man trying to enter her from behind. She lets out a cry of despair.

'No! Please, no! *Mick!*'

A male voice seems to answer. Not Mick's, but a gentle Welsh voice.

'Mae hynny'n ddigon, yr wyf yn meddwl.'

The Welch Fusilier turns, giving Cath the chance to pull away and run to her pile of clothes.

'Who the fuck are you?' snarls the lance corporal.

'Private Morgan Thomas, 1st Battalion Royal Welch Fusiliers.'

'But you're in civvies, lad, and that's a farmer's shotgun . . .' He pauses, puzzled, before continuing. 'Of course – you're a deserter. Now, you'd better hand over that gun and scarper, or the Red Caps'll get yer.'

'Not until the ladies are dressed and back in their ambulance.'

The lance corporal laughs wickedly. 'Look, there's five of us. You might get two, but then we'll 'ave you and, believe me, we'll make you pay. Then we'll finish our business with these little ladies. So think about it. What's to be gained? You can give 'em one as well if you want.'

Thomas begins to panic, not sure whether there are any cartridges in the shotgun. Then one of the men holding Mary speaks to the lance corporal.

'Come on, Johnny, let's get off to Paris. This has gone too far.'

Thomas looks at the man talking to the lance corporal, which gives the big Welshman a chance to rush him. Morgan Thomas sees the lunge too late and the barrel of the shotgun is knocked up in the air. He manages to pull the trigger, sending a volley of shot through the barn roof, but the gun is then pulled from his hands.

With a self-satisfied smirk on his face, the lance corporal then turns the shotgun and uses its butt to bludgeon Morgan to the ground. He manages to deflect one blow, but a second catches him on the shoulder; a third lands at the nape of his neck, knocking him to the ground.

'Get up, you bastard, or I'll blow your fucking brains

out. Get over there with those two tarts. You can watch me fuck them like the bitches they –'

Corporal Johnny is unable to finish his sentence, because Cath has driven a pitchfork through his back. He screams. 'You fucking bitch!'

One point has gone in just under his left ribcage; the other has struck bone and barely broken the surface. He turns and staggers towards Cath, the pitchfork dragging along the ground behind him. But he is stopped in his tracks by Mary, who has picked up the shotgun and blasted him in the chest and face with the second barrel. Both women scream while the other Fusiliers run towards the barn doors.

Their way is barred by a company serjeant major from the Somersets. He has his Lee Enfield in his hands.

'Not so fast, boys. I think you'd better go and sit over there.'

He beckons to the side of the barn with the muzzle of his rifle, then shouts to Thomas. 'You got more cartridges for that shotgun?'

'Yes, over there.'

'Then get it loaded and keep it pointed at these boys.'

He looks down at the stricken corporal on the floor, his face and tunic a mass of bloody flesh.

'He's a goner. Don't have to worry about him. You all right, ladies?'

Cath is getting dressed, she and Mary are both sobbing, but they nod to the CSM and Cath mutters tearfully, 'Yes, thank you, Serjeant.'

'I wondered what was going on, especially when I smelled the breath of the lad who came over to tell us about the fuel. Anyway, you ladies did well, you gave him what he deserved, the pig!'

Mary goes over to the CSM and takes him by the arm. 'Come an' sit down. You've had a bullet through that leg, an' it's bleedin' agin.'

'Oh, it's not too bad, it didn't hit anything important. You're a north country girl – whereabouts?'

'Burnley, Lancashire.'

'My goodness! My father were born in a place called Barnoldswick.'

''Eck, that's not far. We call it Barlick – it's nearly in Yorkshire. Funny folk, Barlickers. But I'm sure your dad's alreet.'

'He was – he's been dead ten year; killed by a baling machine.'

'I'm reet sorry.'

'Aye, well. Let's get these buggers to the Red Caps.' He turns to Thomas. 'What about you – what's your name?'

'Morgan Thomas, 1st Welch Fusiliers.'

'Sounds like you've got a story to tell. Do you want to tell it in Pop over a beer?'

Thomas looks around uneasily.

'Don't worry. What you did today for these ladies was very brave, so you're safe with us.'

'All right, over a beer it is.'

'Right, keep that shotgun on them. I'm going out on to the road to stop some transport and find an officer who can take this lot into custody.'

Two hours later, with the Fusiliers in Pop's Military Detention Centre, the other wounded Somerset boys in Pop-Hop and with the serjeant's wound re-dressed and heavily strapped, the quartet are enjoying a beer in the Maison de Ville in Poperinghe's Grande Place.

'So, I'm Vic Chubb, from Winsham in Somerset.'

'Cheers, Vic. I'm Mary Broxup, and this is Cath Kenny. We're Burnley lasses.'

Cath smiles mischievously. 'So now you know me name. Funny, in'it, first time I skenned yer both I wer bollock naked wi' me arse in t'air!'

Vic smiles. 'And, if I may say so, a fine posterior it is too. Me dad always said northern girls were tough and said exactly what they thought.'

'Aye, wi do. We call a spade a spade an' a fuckin' shovel a fuckin' shovel.'

Given what they have been through together, Vic's risqué comment and the ribald conversation is cathartic. Statements have been taken and the Military Police, who seem happy that justice has been done, have reassured them that the surviving miscreants will be dealt with in due course by a court martial. The Red Caps did not ask Thomas anything other than his rank and regiment, largely because Cath and Mary had found him a discarded uniform to wear at Pop-Hop, making him look like any other soldier. But they did commend him for his bravery.

Cath leans across and gives him a kiss on his cheek. 'That's fer savin' a girl fra a fate worse than death today.'

'I nearly messed it up, though.'

'No, what you did took some doin'; I wer terrified.'

Vic brings some beers and hands them around. 'So, Thomas, tell us your story.'

Thomas looks apprehensive. 'Well, it's a long one.' He

takes a mouthful of his beer before starting. 'I came over with my brothers, Geraint and Hywel, at the end of October last year. We were farm boys, from a little place called Presteigne, in Radnorshire. We did well after we joined up and got picked out to come over before the other volunteers, largely because of Hywel; he was a crack marksman on the range, the best they'd seen in years.'

'Of course – I've heard the name: Hywel Thomas, Welch Fusilier, the Black-handed Assassin. He's a legend in Pop.'

'Really, you must tell me more.'

'I will, and about his gorgeous sister, Bronwyn. They called her the Welsh Angel at Pop-Hop.'

'Bron! I thought . . . Well, it doesn't matter. Are they both at the hospital?'

'No, I don't think so. I think they both went to Gallipoli. Carry on with your story.'

Thomas, distracted by the dramatic news about Hywel and Bronwyn, pauses for a while before continuing.

'Not long after we arrived, we attacked the German line near here at Zwarteleen. I'll never forget, it was a Sunday, early November. Most of us copped it in the open fields – it was a slaughter. I kept my eyes closed most of the way, and just prayed. I could hear bullets all around me and felt a few wing past my head. Only a few of us made it to their trenches. Then it really started – hand-to-hand stuff, vicious, dog-eat-dog. There were all sorts of weapons: timber with nails in, stevedore's hooks, knuckledusters – everything. Our captain, Orme, was a sight to behold, going at them hammer and tongs. I think he got out, but I didn't. Geraint got a bayonet in the guts.

Blood spewed everywhere. I tried to stop it with my hands, but it was useless.'

He takes another mouthful of beer to compose himself.

'He died in front of me. I could tell, because the blood stopped pumping and he went very still. I was so angry. I tried to get up, I was going to kill every German in sight. Then I got my skull cracked by a big Fritz. I can see him now: I turned my head as he raised his arm. He had a cudgel in his hand, like the root of a tree, and a madness in his eyes, like a mad beast. I've seen it on the farm when an animal is cornered, or when you get between a cow and her calf. The lights went out.'

Cath puts her hand on his thigh. 'You poor thing.'

'Not really – he saved my life. When I came to, I was in a Fritz hospital. I had been unconscious for a week and had bayonet wounds in my legs, back and shoulder. I must have been bayoneted while I was on the ground. Apparently, they only realized I was alive when they threw me into a pit to bury me and my hand moved. I had been lying in the bottom of the trench for several days and it was very cold and wet, so I was in a bad way. I was in a Belgian hospital in Ghent, commandeered by the Germans. They were wonderful and got me better, but it took a long time.'

Vic does his calculations. 'So, this is July. You must have been assumed dead by your regiment months ago.'

'I know. Anyway, I got close to this Belgian nurse. I became fond of her, and she seemed to like me.'

Cath smiles. 'Oh, aye! A bit of 'ow's yer father durin' t'bed-baths!'

'Something like that. Anyway, when I was fit enough,

they wanted to send me back to a POW camp in Germany, but Riet – that was her name – she didn't like the Germans much; she got me some civilian clothes and packed me some food and gave me directions to her room in Ghent. I stayed there for a couple of months, but I couldn't work or bring in any money. It wasn't right that she paid for everything, so when the summer came she arranged for me to work on her dad's farm, where I could earn my keep and she could come to see me when she had days off.'

Mary is charmed by the story. 'Very cosy.'

'Yes, it was, very! As a farmer, I was a big help to her father, Pieter. But the Belgian police came looking for me. They must have worked out that Riet might have helped me get away. I managed to hide in one of the barns. Then it got tricky. The police took Riet in for questioning, and there was a German officer there. She was petrified. They made it clear that I would be shot if they found me, as would anyone who helped me escape. The family weren't sure if they could trust their neighbours. Most locals were collaborating with the Germans. They didn't really have a choice.'

Vic interrupts. 'So where is their farm?'

'Not far from here. It was near a village called Kruipuit, which is between Ghent and Bruges, about 45 miles east of Ypres. Trouble was, there was an airfield nearby, full of German planes doing reconnaissance, so everyone was very edgy.'

'So you had to leave?'

'It was a terrible wrench. I had learned some Flemish and was happy with Riet and her parents, who were lovely people, but it had to end. It was too dangerous for them. So they stocked me up with provisions and gave me a bicycle, and Pieter gave me a shotgun, and off I went.'

'Thank God for the shotgun!' says Mary, thinking back to the first time she ever pulled the trigger of a gun.

'Funny thing was I never checked if the thing was loaded. I covered it in hessian and strapped it to the frame of the bike then forgot about it until this afternoon.'

'So how did you get across no-man's-land?'

'It wasn't easy. But near Diksmuide, to the north, the Front is the Yser river, which the Belgians have turned into a drainage dyke. The locals opened the dykes at the beginning of the war and flooded the lot. There are some trenches there, but they're not like round here. There are gaps because of the water. So I waded across the fields and swam the Yser at night, then started moving south. I remembered Pop and hoped my regiment would still be nearby, so I made my way down here. I was hiding in that barn, trying to think of what I would say and whether I needed a uniform or not, when Mary and Cath were dragged in. I couldn't believe it was happening – Welshmen from my own regiment!'

Vic shakes his head. 'A lot has happened since you were captured, Thomas.'

'So I gather, and to my brother and twin sister.'

'Twin! So Bronwyn's your twin sister?'

'Yes, but I'm the older one.'

'What are you going to do now?'

'Rejoin the Fusiliers. I'm fit and strong again, thanks to good food and hard work on the farm.'

'Well, let's fix that in the morning. We'll find the Royal

Welch and I'll come with you to the adjutant and vouch for what's happened. Enlisted men aren't required to try to escape, so they might pin a medal on you, especially when I tell them about today.'

Cath empties her glass. Her teetotalism ended when they arrived in Flanders, and she has developed a liking for strong Belgian beers, as has Mary.

'And you can stay with Mary an' me t'neet. Wi'v got a sofa yer can 'ave. Me an' 'er bunk up together in t'double bed, but thu's not room fer three – shame, tho'!'

They all laugh out loud and Vic limps off to get more beer.

'Aye, let's celebrate!' shouts Cath. 'It's not every day a girl is saved by a 'andsome young Welshman with a big shotgun! And one wi' two barrels!'

'And by her best friend, who actually did the shooting,' adds Mary indignantly.

Later that night, with Pop's clock striking midnight, Mary is woken by Cath slipping out of the bed they share.

'Wheer yer goin'?'

'Fer a pee.'

'But the's a pot under t'bed.'

'Aye, a know, but thought ad go an' see if Morgan's alreet.'

''Course 'e's alreet. Get back in bed, yer 'orny cow.'

'Can't 'elp it. T'lad saved us both today. Those bastards wud 'ave slit our throats once they'd done wi' us. Reckon 'e deserves a goodnight kiss, if nowt else.'

'Bloody 'ell, Cath. Wot abaht Mick?'

'Oh, Mick knows wot am like. He knows a can't do wi'out it fer long.'

'Well, don't mek too much noise. I need t'sleep.'

'I'll try not t', but can't promise!'

Cath bends down and kisses Mary on the forehead. 'Come an' join us if yer want, but give me ten minutes first.'

'Bugger off, you old tart!'

Sunday 25 July

Hoe Farm, Hascombe, Surrey

Although he still has a seat in the War Council, Winston's voice is frequently heard but rarely listened to. His mood continues to become more and more sombre. He writes to his brother Jack frequently, keen to receive letters in return, which give him a much better understanding of what is happening in Gallipoli than official War Office memos.

He and Clemmie have taken Hoe Farm for the spring and summer, a Tudor house recently renovated by Sir Edward Lutyens. It is an idyllic, quintessentially English house, surrounded by meadows, woodland and a beautiful garden. Moreover, it is keeping Winston sane. During the week, he uses a room at 19 Abingdon Street, yards from the House of Lords, where he has been allowed to retain Eddie Marsh as his private secretary and Harry Beckenham, his Admiralty shorthand writer. However, his weeks are a misery as he watches from the periphery as the war drags on with no end in sight. In one of his letters to Jack he writes, 'The certainty that the war will not end this year fills my mind with melancholy thoughts. The youth of Europe – a whole generation, will be shorn away.'

But weekends are different. Amidst the flowers and butterflies of an English summer, the horror of war is a long way away, and his heart begins to beat normally as he is driven along the Portsmouth Road to Surrey every Friday evening.

'Goonie and the Jagoons are here, Winston. Just coming up the drive.'

'Excellent! Time for a Pol Roger! Eddie, would you oblige? And apple juice for the little ones.'

Winston rushes into the garden to greet the children, who are already halfway across the lawn. He makes a sound like he has been shot and falls on the ground.

'You got me, you English *Schweinhunde*!' he shouts, which persuades his children and Jack's to jump all over him, celebrating their kill.

Clemmie is furious. 'Winston, don't you dare use that language. I don't want the children to end up like you, unable to resist a battle.'

'But we're in a battle, a battle for our lives!'

Clemmie ushers the children into the house and helps Goonie with her things. Winston is fascinated by the easel she has under her arm. 'I didn't know you painted.'

'Just started. It's wonderful therapy now that Jack's away.'

Inevitably, the conversation over dinner turns to Gallipoli. Goonie is worried about Jack. 'He says it is horrible beyond belief, and getting worse.'

Winston frowns. 'I know, and Kitchener is planning a new landing and a big push next month. But I fear the Turks are getting more men into the field, and more quickly than we are, so every time we attack we're outnumbered and outgunned. We need at least twenty thousand more men, and many more guns. If they're not available, we should wait until they are. But they won't listen to me any more.'

Goonie pats Winston's arm. 'Poor you.'

'Poor Jack; he's out there. K asked me to go out and give him a detailed report. I could have spent some time with darling Jack. The Old Block and Arthur Balfour said yes, but word got back to Bonar Law, who kyboshed it.'

'The old sod!' Clemmie never had liked Bonar Law.

Winston is in full flow. 'The trouble with the War Council is that there are too many powerful and talented people in there. Their arguments cancel one another out. Also, the OB listens to them all but never chooses the best argument and then endorses it, so nothing ever gets decided, except by political expediency, usually to save his own skin. His decisions are not based on logic or balanced judgement but on self-interest.'

The next morning Winston rises late to find Goonie already at her easel in the garden and goes to greet her.

'Good morning, Winston,' she responds. 'Look at the light; it's so wonderful.'

Winston looks towards the meadow and the fringe of trees behind Hoe, which seem to be the subject of Goonie's picture.

'Yes. Very pretty.'

'More than pretty, Winston. Look at the sun playing on the buttercups; they're sparkling, like yellow diamonds on a dappled green carpet. Splash on the turpentine, lots of yellow and white. Make yourself the master of your brush and your canvas, make them cower before your assault;

wide, wild brush strokes. Then you have the scene under your spell, and it doesn't answer back.'

Winston smiles. He likes Goonie's choice of words and her description of what he always thought was a rather dull pastime. He looks at the scene again, then watches as Goonie tries to capture it. After about fifteen minutes he exclaims, 'Goonie, you're a darling. Now I know how to relax amidst this dreadful war.'

He marches off towards the kitchen, where Clemmie is clearing breakfast. 'Clemmie,' he announces. 'I'm going to get Harry B. to drive me to Guildford. I'm going to buy some paints and an easel.'

'Whatever for, darling?'

'So that I can start painting, of course!'

Clemmie, thinking nothing could be more unsuitable for Winston's temperament, humours him. 'Very well, Pug. Don't be long, and no detours via the White Horse.'

'What a good idea. Where's Eddie? Eddie, come on! We're going shopping!'

Two hours later, with the painting materials safely lodged in the car, and several glasses of beer to the good, Winston, Eddie Marsh and Harry Beckenham get up to leave Hascombe's White Horse.

As the pub door closes behind them they hear a voice from within, followed by much laughter. The voice issues a cry that Winston has heard only once before, when he was crossing the road from Abingdon Street to the Houses of Parliament, but it is one that will haunt him for the rest of his life: 'What about the Dardanelles?'

Eddie Marsh tries to be sympathetic. 'Ignore them;

they don't know anything, except what they read in the *Daily Mail*.'

'I shall, don't worry. I'm more concerned about the future. Our boys need leadership, not sloth and folly. If only K would commit the kind of numbers he'll send into battle in Flanders, we'd be in Constantinople and the eastern world would be ours. The men facing death out there deserve a plan.'

Winston looks to the exhaust of the car, which Harry has just started. 'Gas is the answer, Eddie; shiploads of it. The Turks shoot our men in cold blood when they try to surrender; they have massacred over a million Armenians, Greeks, Assyrian Christians. Let's gas the buggers! The Germans are happy to gas us. What's the difference between chlorine gas and a high-explosive shell?'

Eddie is shocked. 'The Geneva Convention of 1906, Winston.'

'Bugger the Geneva Convention. We're in a fight to the death, a fight to save civilization. God will forgive us if it brings the slaughter to an end. And if he doesn't, then I for one will pay the price in hell!'

Winston, having been castigated for being late back for lunch, spends the rest of the afternoon and the next day at his new easel. He copies everything that Goonie does and paints feverishly.

That evening, he is alone with Clemmie. 'Cat, the Laverys,' he says, 'they both paint, don't they?'

'Of course. Sir John is very highly thought of.'

'I know, but he's too clever for me. Doesn't Hazel paint as well? She could give me some advice.'

'Yes, she's very good. She's also very beautiful .... that wouldn't have something to do with it, would it?'

'Of course not; it's her skill with a paint brush that intrigues me. Let's invite them over next weekend.'

Winston is hooked; painting is a passion he will enjoy for the rest of his life.

Thursday 29 July

Hooge, West Flanders, Belgium

With Harry Woodruff in a military hospital in Boulogne, Fusilier CSM Maurice Tait is going into battle without his friend for the first time in his nineteen-year military career. It is a strange feeling. As far as 4th Fusilier comrades are concerned, Maurice is the last of the Old Contemptibles, the last of his species, part of a regular soldier tradition stretching back over a hundred years to the Peninsular War.

As no one has had time to replace Harry as Company Serjeant Major, Maurice has been asked to take charge of both his company and Harry's. They are both acting as support companies in the trenches at Hooge, south-east of Ypres. The small village has become strategically important because of a huge crater created by a British mine ten days earlier which allowed the Middlesex Regiment to capture the village. In this tragically bizarre war, the protection from direct fire which the crater offers has meant that a hole in the ground has become something over which it is worth fighting.

With Maurice are two reservist serjeants, Joe Smith and Kenneth Bryce, both Winchester men from the 2nd King's Royal Rifle Corps. It is their first week at the Front. In the advanced trenches in front of them are men of 8th

Battalion, Rifle Brigade, mainly from Kitchener's New Army, among the first to arrive in France.

'Right, boys, Fritz's guns have started. Get your heads down.'

A terrible whining begins, followed by short bursts of explosives. A look of dread plays across Joe Smith's face.

'What the fuck is that, Colour?'

'That's a Fritz heavy trench mortar, a *Minenwerfer*; we call them Moanin' Minnies. Nasty little bastards.'

The bombardment continues for several minutes before there is a sudden silence.

'Right, fellas, Fritz will be on his way any minute. Let's hope those Rifles boys up front have been well trained.'

Pandemonium breaks out in front of Maurice and the two serjeants. From their vantage point they can see a wide sweep of ground before them, and the men of 8th Rifles pouring rifle and machine-gun fire into a phalanx of field-grey German infantry running across no-man's-land. The Germans lose many men. Then the nature of the assault changes dramatically. Maurice has never seen or heard anything like it. Serpent-like, powerful hisses echo across the scene, followed by jets of flame, like jets of water from a fire-hose.

'Fuck me! Stand to, lads!'

Realizing that he is seeing something new and lethal, Maurice orders his companies to stand ready. 'Kenny, go an' find Captain Downin' an' tell him to get his arse over 'ere!'

Moments later Maurice's new CO arrives. 'What the hell are they, Colour?' he asks.

'They've got cylinders on their backs, sir – must be full

of petrol. There's a nozzle at the front with a trigger. It's spitting flame nearly twenty yards!'

As Maurice describes what they can all see, the British riflemen in front of them begin to pile out of their trenches in droves and run pell-mell towards the Fusiliers. The trenches they leave behind have become pits of burning fuel; many men, screaming in agony, are being burned alive. Some of the men running for safety are also ablaze. They do not get very far before succumbing to the heat and pain, and fall to the ground in heaps. Only ten yards from the Fusiliers' trench one poor soul, lying on the ground in an inferno of flame, feebly waves his hand, begging for help. Maurice raises his rifle and shoots him in the head. Captain Downing appears to be frozen in horror, so Maurice bellows at his men. 'Pick your targets, lads! Let's nail those fuckin' flamin' things!'

Galvanized by Maurice's order, the men unleash a hail of bullets which cuts down the German attackers, including all but one of their *Flammenwerfer*. The only one still standing is heading straight for Maurice's position.

Maurice takes steady aim at the encroaching German and hits him square in the chest. He recoils backwards but does not fall at first. Instead, he stumbles forwards, pressing the trigger of his weapon as he does so. A jet of flame squirts along the ground and into the Fusiliers' trench. Maurice, thinking quickly and using all his experience, clambers out of the back of the trench, yelling as he goes: 'Get out! Everyone out!'

His cries are too late for the two serjeants and Captain Downing, who are soon up to their waists in flames. Maurice rushes back and manages to help Downing out by grabbing the shoulders of his tunic. Other men rush forwards to pull out Bryce and Smith. Maurice takes off his own tunic and begins to attack the flames on the men's uniforms. He rolls them along the ground in an attempt to extinguish their burning clothing.

The last of the *Flammenwerfer* is now dead, but there are many more infantrymen still jumping over the deserted British trenches.

'Colour, leg it! They're all over yer!'

Maurice hears the warning from his men just as he feels a bayonet in his midriff. It feels like he has been stabbed by a hot poker. He turns in fury, grabs his assailant's rifle and uses it to throw him to the ground. But as he does so the German presses the trigger, propelling a bullet into Maurice's shoulder, shattering his collarbone. He falls to one knee. He has made a mistake no soldier should ever make: in his haste to get out of the burning trench, he has left his Lee-Enfield behind. He looks around in desperation.

'Take this, Colour.'

The thin, plaintive voice is that of Captain Downing, at his feet. He is offering him his Webley service revolver. Maurice grabs it and empties it into the Germans around him. Others are hit by his own Fusiliers, who have formed up in a rear trench 20 yards away.

'Keep firin', boys!'

Despite the deep wound to his side and his shattered collarbone, Maurice manages to get Captain Downing to his feet and helps him back to the rear trench. Then, with two lance corporals to help him, the three of them go back to collect Serjeants Bryce and Smith. Under Fusilier covering fire from their trench, they manage to get the two KRRC serjeants back but, as they are helping them down into the trench, Maurice feels a searing pain in his left buttock. He has been hit in the backside and knows the bullet has shattered his pelvis. He falls head first into the trench and loses consciousness.

'You're a strong man, Colour Serjeant Tait, DCM.'

'Sorry, sir?' Maurice can just about see the outline of a white-coated doctor.

'It's the chloroform. You'll be able to see straight in an hour or so. I said, you're as tough as old boots. You'll survive.'

'How bad is it?'

'The wound to your side is deep, but it missed your lung and your liver. Your collarbone will heal, but your pelvis is a mess. It will take a long time.'

'But I can go back to my battalion?'

'Certainly not. I'm talking about a long time before you can walk again, and that might always be with a limp and no small amount of pain. Your fighting days are over. By the way, your colonel's been through: you're getting a bar to your DCM. The three men you pulled out have all survived. Very bad burns to their legs. They're going home too, but they're alive.'

'Listen, Doc. My mate, Colour Serjeant Harry Woodruff, is recoverin' in Boulogne; we've been together since South Africa. Couldn't send me to his gaff, could yer?'

'But that's for men who can come back into service.'

'Yeah, he was pretty badly shot up too, but he's a tough old bird, an' old Captain Chavasse let him try to get fit again.'

'Noel Chavasse, MC, the hero of Hooge?'

'Yeah, that's the man. Top geezer.'

'Well, anything Chavasse can do, I can do. I'll see what I can arrange. I think your friend will be in Red Cross 7, that's in Boulogne. Good hospital – full of lots of pretty Red Cross volunteer nurses, VAD, and all that lot.'

'Thanks, Doc, that'll suit old 'Arry down to the ground.'

Maurice notices the decoration on the doctor's uniform. 'I see from your ribbons, Doc, that you've got an MC as well.'

'Yes, earlier this year.'

'Where, sir?'

'Second Ypres.'

'Tough one, that. And your name, sir?'

'Fred Davidson, Cameronians.'

'Thanks again, sir.'

PART EIGHT: AUGUST
Mustafa Kemal

Friday 6 August

Suvla Bay, Gallipoli Peninsula, Turkey

It hardly seems possible, but for Allied troops on the Gallipoli Peninsula, conditions are even more harrowing than on the Western Front. For the men in Flanders, summer has brought relief from the miseries of the wet and cold of winter. In the Eastern Mediterranean, high summer has brought searing heat for sixteen hours a day, desperate water shortages, the curse of plagues of flies and the onslaught of excruciating disease.

At the beginning of August the standard water ration is three pints a day for all purposes. The men's daily rations are melting in their tins and putrefying before they can be eaten. Conversely, the Turks, although no better fed, do have fresh springs on their higher ground. Worst of all, dysentery is now blighting almost the entire Allied Army, including an increasing number of medical staff, and in many cases it is proving fatal.

Bron is worried about Margaret. Although she is loath to admit it, it is obvious that she too is suffering from dysentery.

'It's just a tummy upset, Bron,' is her constant answer, but Bron has seen too many cases not to know the difference.

It is early morning, already 90 degrees Fahrenheit in the shade, and very humid.

'Margaret, you must rest,' says Bron.

'I can't. There's to be a big attack today. It will be chaos. I have to keep going.'

'You'll fall over. You've lost so much fluid, and you're running a temperature.'

Margaret does not answer. She has had to make another dash to the staff WC on the *Essequibo*, her fourth visit of the morning. There is blood in her stool, confirming that Bronwyn's diagnosis is accurate.

Essequibo is empty of patients and has been made ready for a new influx of men. Medical preparations have been meticulous for an attack Sir Ian Hamilton has been planning for weeks. He has over 100,000 men at his disposal, but they are either untried New Army recruits, or territorials, whose leadership is, at best, questionable.

There will be two diversionary attacks, one, led by General Harold Street at Cape Helles at the bottom of the peninsula, where 26,000 men – four British divisions and two French – will repeat the three previous attacks on Krithia and one at Anzac Cove, where the Anzacs, reinforced by Britain's 29th Division, will try to break out of their claustrophobic bridgehead. General Birdwood will be CO for the attack and will have 40,000 men at his disposal.

The main, disguised, attack will be north of Anzac Cove at Suvla Bay. The landing will be led by General Sir Frederick Stopford, a senior army officer but one with no major battle experience. He will have 30,000 men at his disposal. Opposing them will be only a small force of Turkish defenders, less than 1,500, and many of them gendarme units. Unfortunately, Stopford vastly overestimated the strength of the Turkish deployment.

Although it is not a pretty sight and resembles a piece of leather which has been chewed by a dog, Hywel Thomas's wounded ear has healed. He has been assigned to 11th Battalion Manchester Regiment and has landed with them just south of Nibrunesi Point, on what the Allies have named B Beach. Nearby are his old friends, 9th Lancashire Fusiliers, from the landing at Cape Helles at the end of April. Except for some sniper fire, the Manchester's landing has been almost entirely unopposed, and they have marched inland to take a small hillock called Lala Baba. Captain Oliver, CO of C Company, tells Hywel to find his own ground and to wait for the Turkish counter-attack.

'But, sir, wouldn't it be better to move on to Hill 10? It's barely a mile.'

'I don't think so, Colour. It'll be dark soon, and I have no orders to move on from Lala Baba.'

'But it's a clear night, sir, and a half-moon. The men will move better in the cool of the night.'

'Are you trying to tell me my business, Colour Serjeant?'

'Not at all, sir. Sorry.'

'You stick to sniping, and I'll give the orders.'

'Very good, sir.'

Hywel knows he is right, but he also knows not to push the point any further or he will be put on an insubordination charge, and that could lead to a field punishment.

He finds a spot on the top of Lala Baba, a mound not much bigger than a large sand dune, and digs a hide for himself. Unable to sleep, he uses his telescopic sight to watch the Turks moving more and more men into position for a counter-attack in the morning. The officers with the East Lancs and the Manchesters debate what to do next, but no orders come from General Stopford, who is still at sea, so, assuming they have done their job by taking the high ground, they agree to stay where they are.

On board *Essequibo*, Margaret is feeling better. She has been drinking water by the gallon and is feeling more hydrated. 'Bron, I've had a word with the captain,' she says. 'We can go ashore tonight with half the orderlies and help set up the dressing station on the beach.'

'I thought that wasn't allowed?'

'It isn't, but I smiled sweetly and he agreed.'

'I don't want to sound negative, but aren't there bombs and bullets on the beach?'

'Yes, but I'm fed up with cleaning and re-dressing wounds that have already been infected by sloppy practice at the dressing stations. I'll go on my own if you like, and I'll leave you in charge here, Sister Thomas.'

'What do you mean, "Sister Thomas"?'

'I got the telegram this morning from Matron-in-Chief McCarthy: you're promoted to Sister, QAIMNS.'

'Good God, Margaret, but I've had no training.'

'What do you call this? Besides, this is a war. Formal qualifications are forgotten about; experience is what counts. Anyway, it's up to you. You can stay here in charge of *Essequibo*, or come with me and I'll put Griffiths, the senior orderly, in charge.'

'I'm coming with you; wherever I can be of most help.'

'Thanks, Bron.'

While the main attack at Suvla Bay is wasting a golden opportunity, thanks to the caution of the junior officers on the ground and the failings of high command to issue clear orders, the men in the diversionary attacks are locked in bloody hand-to-hand combat. The most intense is the breakout at Anzac, where much of the fighting takes place in narrow approach tunnels dug in secret by Australian and New Zealand sappers. Some open only yards from the Turkish trenches; others exit directly in the walls of their trenches. The result is not unlike two swarms of rats fighting for territory.

Bodies fill the narrow burrows three or four deep as a vicious encounter with bayonets and hand grenades rages. The Turkish grenades have an eight-second fuse, so, on occasion, the same bomb is thrown back and forth three times before it explodes. Some men lose a hand but carry on fighting with their other one. One Australian serjeant, a proper Digger – surly, quarrelsome and as strong as an ox – battles on with the remnants of his right eye resting on his cheek. Men use whatever is to hand in the tunnels and fight like animals. They scream, kick, punch and bite for most of the night, until there is no one left alive to carry on.

At Cape Helles another frontal assault with heavy casualties gains the Allies about 400 yards of ground, still well short of Krithia, before they are thrown back to where they started.

The morning of 7 August dawns with a barrage of Turkish artillery on all three of the Allied attack groups from the previous day. Margaret and Bron are already ashore and have brought some order to the dressing station on B Beach. The three junior doctors at the station are very uneasy about their presence and have sent for the senior RAMC officer available, Captain John Sutherland, Battalion Medical Officer. When he arrives, he is already furious, and bellows at the top of his voice, 'Where are those two bloody nurses?'

Margaret hears him loud and clear. 'The two *bloody nurses* are here!'

Sutherland throws back the flap of the tent where Margaret and Bronwyn are organizing the orderlies' preparation for the first casualties. 'What the bloody hell are you two doing here?'

Margaret turns to him with a withering look. 'Don't you dare rush in here kicking up sand; this is a sterile area. And close that flap; you'll let more flies in!'

'You've got ten minutes to get off this beach or I'll have you carried off.'

'Don't you dare speak to me like that. What's the date of your commission?'

'What the hell has that got to do with anything?'

'As a senior nursing sister with QAIMNS, I carry the equivalent rank of Captain. I joined on 2 August 1914 and was made Sister straight away. I think that means I outrank you. I'll ask you again, when were you commissioned?'

Margaret is bluffing. Very few male officers, especially at the War Office, accept the QAIMNS claims about the equivalence of ranks between the Regular Army and QAIMNS. But, in this instance, the bluff seems to be working.

'Twenty-fifth August. But Sister, women are not allowed in forward positions, whether you're nurses or not.'

'Piffle! The dressings coming off the beaches are

appalling. So we've come here to sort it out. Now, please get about your business, and we'll get on with ours.'

'Are you making the impertinent suggestion that we are not doing our dressings properly?'

'Yes, and I've been asked for a full report by the Surgeon General in Egypt, General Richard Ford.'

Sutherland has heard of Ford and knows he is a fanatic about hygiene and clean wounds. He does not know that Margaret is blagging even more outrageously than before. Outwitted and embarrassed, he struts out of the tent, muttering to himself. Bron cannot stop herself from giggling.

'Margaret, you've got the cheek of the devil. How do you keep a straight face?'

'Practice, Bron. Living in a man's world all my life!'

It is not long before a steady stream of stretcher-bearers begins to bring in the dead, dying and wounded. Margaret has insisted that wounds are immediately doused in antiseptic carbolic acid from the buckets she has had put in key places. While Margaret oversees the triage stage, Bron, in charge of this antiseptic stage, is in her element, feeling so proud in her new sister's uniform and badge, which Margaret has made sure arrived from Lemnos. Every so often Margaret glances at her and smiles to herself. She admires Bron's strength, courage and her devotion to her cause. Occasionally, Bronwyn looks back at Margaret, and they exchange smiles. Their love for one another is a great source of strength for them both.

Margaret feels another bout of diarrhoea beckoning and makes her way to the latrine she has dug for herself behind the dressing-station tent. When she returns, Captain Sutherland is waiting for her.

'I'm sorry I was so rude to you earlier,' he says.

'It's forgotten, Captain.'

'Thank you. Now, I want to speak to you as a doctor. This time you *will* be leaving this beach, not on the orders of an officer but on doctor's orders. You've got dysentery.'

'No, it's a stomach upset.'

'I don't think so. I've seen enough dysentery to recognize it when I see it.'

'There's too much to do. I'll be fine.'

'No, you won't. You'll fall over soon; then you will be no use to anyone. Besides, you're putting your life at risk.'

Margaret sighs. She knows Sutherland is right.

'So, when this spate of casualties has cleared, you must go to Lemnos. You need rest and proper care. Sister Thomas can take care of things here. Is that clear, Sister Killingbeck?'

'Yes, Doctor. When the *Essequibo* docks on Lemnos, I'll stay.'

Up above the beach, Hywel Thomas is still in his hide on Lala Baba. The Turkish counter-attack occurring in front of him is ferocious. Driven on by pride in defence of a country and tradition that has been centuries in the making, the Turks throw themselves at the invaders of their homeland. Hywel has lost count of how many men he has killed, but he has only one rifle and the Turks are advancing in such vast numbers they are rapidly extinguishing the opportunity the Allies had at the beginning of their attack.

A Turkish officer suddenly appears in the crosshairs of his sights. A sturdy, trim figure with an eleven-a-side moustache, he looks immaculate in his tailored khaki uniform, knee-length brown leather boots and officer's enverieh – his Enver Pasha cap. He has recently been made a full colonel and awarded the Iron Cross, First Class, by his German allies. He has emerged over a ridge and stridden out into the open on his own. Before him is a slit trench of Loyal North Lancs, all of whom are men of Kitchener's New Army and none of whom have ever been in battle before. As bullets ping the ground and fly past him, he turns back to his own men, 20 yards behind him, and raises his hand. As he does so, a huge phalanx of Turkish infantry rushes forward at the signal of its leader.

Hywel still has the Turk in the cross-hairs, but something makes him hesitate. He admires the courage of the man and does not pull the trigger. Moments later, with their leader at their forefront, sword in hand, the Turks fall upon the Loyal North Lancs, who are cut to pieces with bayonets and grenades. Hywel, realizing that he has missed the chance to put an end to the kind of leader who is making the difference between the resolute Turkish defenders and the vacillating Allied attackers, tries to find his quarry again but, in the chaos of the melee, he cannot identify him.

With Hywel's hide now under threat from the counter-attack, he decides to withdraw down Lala Baba to find a new position on the beach, should he need to cover an Allied withdrawal to the boat.

Only later will Hywel know that the figure who has been in his sights is the man who will become Kemal Atatürk, the father of modern Turkey, the legendary Mustafa Kemal.

Sunday 29 August

Red Cross Stationary Hospital 7,
Hôtel Christol, Boulogne, France

Maurice Tait and Harry Woodruff are enjoying life in Boulogne. Hôtel Christol, commandeered by the British in 1914 as a military hospital, sits on the waterfront, just opposite Le Pont Marquet, which fords La Liane, Boulogne's main waterway to the Channel. Once a grand seaside hotel, it is now a little run-down, but for men recovering from wounds on the Western Front it is paradise. There are countless bars and cafés in the area, all of which are full of Allied servicemen, and the two-francs girls stand at every corner in twos and threes.

Harry has been in Boulogne almost two and a half months, Maurice just over one. Both are healing well. Maurice still needs to be pushed around in a wheelchair but, with Harry in charge, they are regular visitors to the bars along the waterfront. Word has got around that they have declined the chance to be invalided home, and visiting generals and dignitaries, both British and French, have come to see them several times. Indeed, both have been awarded the Croix de Guerre, to add to their DCMs and bars.

It has been possible to remove the bullet that had

lodged against Maurice's pelvis and, fortunately, it had caused only minimal damage to the pelvic bone. His bayonet wound has healed, but his collarbone is still troublesome and may well give him pain for some time to come.

August at the Front is proving to be a quiet month, just the usual daily quota of sniping and light shelling. Only thirty casualties a day, on average.

Mick Kenny, Vinny Sagar and Twaites Haythornthwaite are deep underground near St Eloi. They have been there since the end of June. They have no idea what the tunnels are for; they just know that there are lots of them and that they are very deep. They have been transferred to 172nd Tunnelling Company and are under the command of Lieutenant Horace Hickling, a mining engineer much admired by 'Hell-fire Jack' Norton-Griffiths. Hickling's solution to the water encountered at higher levels is to go deep, to at least 60 feet, where the thick blue clay is dry and easy to dig. However, at this depth, the tunnels take not weeks but months to dig. It is going to be a long autumn and winter for the Burnley moles.

August on the Gallipoli Peninsula is far from quiet. The disasters of 6 August, and indeed the entire campaign, are revisited more than once during the long, hot days. Jack Churchill, ever more disheartened by what he is witnessing, keeps his brother, Winston, briefed in a series of letters.

On 8 August Jack went ashore with Colonel Maurice Hankey, who has been sent to Gallipoli to make a report in Winston's stead, and Colonel Cecil Aspinall, a member of Sir Ian Hamilton's General Staff.

It was extraordinary. There were thousands of our men fighting hammer and tongs to get across this scorching salt lake. But they had no clear orders, and Stopford, for reasons beyond comprehension, is still out at sea . . .

. . . Apathy is everywhere and has spread from the officers to the men. We walked some distance inland. There was no shelling, no machine guns, no firing of any sort. I almost felt that we could have walked to Constantinople unmolested . . .

On 10 August Stopford, under pressure from Sir Ian Hamilton, finally issued orders to advance. Jack tries to explain what he thinks has gone wrong.

These men are not cowards. They are fit and strong, but their training has been based on the horror of the trenches, so they dig. And they think that if they gain 500 yards, it is a victory, so they dig!

Two days later Jack went to Lemnos to visit the wounded.

. . . By the way, I met the two nurses you asked me to see, Killingbeck and Thomas. What splendid girls. They went ashore at Suvla Bay, strictly against orders – how brave. I'm afraid Killingbeck is not very well – severe dysentery. The doctors think she'll recover in due course, but it's a worry. Thomas is going back to the Straits on her own – pretty little thing, doesn't seem old enough to be in the middle of a cesspit like the Dardanelles. Things we're asking our womenfolk to do! They both deserve medals. I'm going to get Hamilton to get them a Royal Red Cross.

After receiving Jack's letters, Winston caused a storm in the War Council meetings of the 19th and 20th. Stopford and two of his generals had already been recalled to London in disgrace, but Kitchener objected to Winston's suggestion that half the 50,000 troops in Egypt should be sent to Gallipoli at once, but under the command of a general who knew the meaning of the word 'attack'!

Kitchener preferred to launch another huge offensive on the Western Front, pointing out that the French troops were becoming restless in their trenches and that a Peace Movement was gaining ground among the rank and file. Once again, Winston lost the argument, and it was decided to wait until September to review the situation on Gallipoli.

On Sunday the 29th Winston wrote back to Jack.

Infuriating! I've heard through John French that K is planning a new offensive with Joffre for next month, despite the fact that LG and the Old Block think that it has been agreed with French High Command that no such thing will take place! K has got the Cabinet and War Council running scared with talk of pacifism rising among the French poilu. He's a devious cove!

The latest debate is conscription. Lloyd George is certain we need it. He's already got thousands of women into men's work, but he says we'll still need to conscript men soon. K is bitterly opposed. The word is that he is very disappointed about the calibre of the men in his New Army. He dare not go public about it, of course, but their physical condition, standard of education and discipline leave a lot to be desired – all very worrying, given that the outcome of the war is going to depend on them sooner or later.

I'm sorry you are witness to so much misery and inertia in the Dardanelles. K is sending Byng – very tough old bird. He should

make a difference. He is a soldier's soldier, very good horseman.
His nickname is 'Bungo' to distinguish him from his elder
brothers, 'Byngo' and 'Bango'. This story will give you a measure
of the man. Not an academic, while at Eton he once traded his
Latin grammar book and his brother's best trousers to a hawker
for a pair of ferrets and a pineapple. You'll like him.

I hope the nurses get their gongs — let me know if you need any
help. Thanks for taking the trouble to go and see them.

We see Goonie and the Jagoons during the week in London
and they come to us most weekends. They're on splendid form, but
we're all missing you.

Your devoted Winston

In St Omer, Cath Kenny and Mary Broxup have been invited to Sunday lunch with Katherine Furse and Kitty Stewart-Murray. The four women are sitting in the Café du Palais de Justice in Place Victor Hugo, the most fashionable restaurant in the city.

Katherine Furse smiles benignly. 'We thought we would have something very French, as it is Sunday and we're in one of St Omer's best places to eat. What about herb-marinated pork fillet, a sweet-onion potato gratin and some Provençal asparagus? Then a lovely maple syrup cream cheese *pot de crème*?'

Cath and Mary look at one another, mystified. As usual, Cath takes the bull by the horns. 'Sounds grand, Kath, but wot do'st "Provençal" mean?'

Katherine and Kitty smile sweetly. 'Oh, it's a cooking style from the south. It just means with garlic, onion, mushrooms, herbs.'

'Never 'ad garlic. 'Eard on it, but never tried it, but we'll gi' it a go, won't wi, Mary?'

'Aye, we'll try owt, us. We even 'ad 'orse meat t'other day. It wer alreet.'

'Very well. Shall we have some wine?'

'Beer fer us, please, Kath; one on them Belgian strong uns.'

This time, the two VAD leaders smile a little more thinly. The food is a great success. Cath and Mary devour everything in front of them, including all the bread on the table and the two refills of Belgian beer. Katherine Furse then takes a deep breath. 'Now, ladies, may I raise a delicate subject with you?'

'Aye, o' course.'

Cath and Mary eye one another knowingly.

'We have had a disturbing report from GHQ about an incident on Sunday 11 July.' She looks down at a document she has retrieved from her bag. 'At Vlamertinge.'

'Aye, the Welch Fusilier. Wot can we tell yer?'

'Well, it is a very distressing story. I suppose we just wanted to check that you are all right.'

'We're fine, but thanks fer askin'. So, this is wot 'appened: thi wer as drunk as lords. I provoked the big one bi tellin' 'im t'fuck off. They dragged us into a barn, med me strip off, then tried to rape me. Luckily – an' a can't tell yer 'ow lucky – there were a lad 'idin' in t'barn – he'd escaped fra t'Germans. He 'ad a shotgun; there wer a scuffle. I put a pitchfork in t'lad who wer attackin' me, an' then Mary shot t'bugger. Then CSM fra Somerset Light Infantry came in an' fettled it. That's it.'

Katherine and Kitty are wide-eyed and almost speechless. Kitty speaks eventually. 'You seem so calm about it.'

'Aye, well it's over now. No 'arm, except a losin' a bit o' dignity wi' me arse in t'air.'

'Well, we're so sorry it happened. It's a dreadful thing to happen to someone who's here to help.'

'Aye, well, 'e got 'is just desserts.'

'And the others?'

'In a military prison in Calais, for the duration.'

'And the lad with a shotgun?'

Cath smiles mischievously. 'He's rejoined his regiment, Welch Fusiliers. We were very grateful, o' course. Last we 'eard, 'e's gone into the line at Festubert with the Welch's 9th Battalion. They gave 'im a Military Medal for helping us at Vlamertinge.'

'Quite right, too.'

'Actually, Kath, there is somat' we could do fer 'im. He 'as a twin sister, Bronwyn Thomas. She's in t'QAIMNS. She wer at Pop-Hop wi' a Sister Margaret Killingbeck. Thi both went off to t'Dardanelles together. He's very keen to be in touch wi' 'er agin.'

'Oh, I'm sure we can trace her and get an address.' Furse shifts in her chair uneasily. 'Now, about this incident in the barn. As you might imagine, we'd like to keep it quiet. We don't want to upset the other girls and we don't want word to get back to the press. There would be an outcry that our soldiers could behave so badly.'

'Don't worry, Kath, we've said nowt to anyone except the MPs, and nowt to t'other girls either. But to absolutely guarantee our silence . . .' Cath pauses puckishly. Katherine and Kitty look concerned. '. . . You'll ata buy us another beer!'

While Kitty enjoys her lunch in St Omer and looks forward to her next tryst with her Grenadier Guards lover in London, her husband Bardie's long-held dream of getting involved in the fighting has become a reality. He and his Scottish Horse left Devonport aboard the *Transylvania*, bound for Mudros on 19 August. After a mid-Mediterranean scare involving a near-miss with a Spanish merchant-man, when it was discovered that the *Transylvania*'s captain was drunk on the bridge and had to be arrested, they are now disembarking at Mudros Bay on Lemnos. Bardie has just been informed that they are to sail to Suvla Bay on the Gallipoli Peninsula for a night-time landing in three days' time.

PART NINE: SEPTEMBER
The Battle of Loos

Wednesday 1 September

Suvla Bay, Gallipoli Peninsula, Turkey

Bardie Stewart-Murray is finally stepping into a battle zone, something he has been hoping for since the Great War began. As Britain's leading aristocrat, he knows that it is his duty to lead men in battle.

Even though he has already lost a brother and has another in a German prisoner-of-war camp, his fervour and patriotism are undiminished. Although he is a Scot and his first language is Scots Gaelic, his family has always supported the union with England, even against his own rebellious Scottish kinsmen, and even if it meant initiating and participating in the Highland Clearances.

It is ten o'clock and a dark night, but the sea is warm. Bardie is up to his waist in water and approaching C Beach in Suvla Bay. He and his men are unloading stores and equipment, a task made much easier in darkness, negating the threat of Turkish artillery, which still has the beach in its range.

Bardie looks around and calls to his adjutant. 'Captain, we need some sappers in the morning. Some rails along the beach would make getting all this material ashore a lot easier.'

'Yes, sir. I'll look into it.'

'Don't "look into it", Captain, make sure it's done.'

'Yes, sir, first thing.'

'No, not first thing; before dawn, Captain. Wake the buggers up.'

Bardie is in his element. One of the benefits of being a marquis from birth is that one gets used to telling people what to do. He told his servants what to do when he was a child at home, did the same at Eton and is now doing it with consummate ease in the army.

The Scottish Horse are at a loss without their horses, left behind in Britain, but Bardie had studied the situation in France carefully and, realizing that many of his men have been ghillies, deer-stalkers and gamekeepers, has obtained large numbers of telescopic sights for them. At dinner with Sir Ian Hamilton on Lemnos before they left for their landing, Bardie asked how they might be put to good use. At the dinner were Field Generals Peyton and Inglefield, who both suggested that Bardie should find one of Major Hesketh-Pritchard's top School of Sniping marksmen, Colour Serjeant Hywel Thomas, Welch Fusiliers.

'Captain, when we're settled tomorrow morning and the sappers are at work, I want you to go and find a sniper, Colour Serjeant Hywel Thomas. He's a Welch Fusilier, but currently attached to the Manchesters.'

'Very good, sir.'

The next morning, while his Scottish Horse moves into trenches vacated by the Scots Fusiliers, and the Royal Engineers begin to construct the rails across the beach he has requested, Bardie is eating breakfast on the move. With his regimental serjeant major, William McLaren, at his side, he is striding across the dry salt lake that lies to the north of Suvla Bay.

'Mr McLaren, it would be ideal if we could get three dozen of our best shots on that high ground to the north.'

'Aye, sir, but I think Johnnie Turk might have something to say about that.'

'It's hard to imagine that all these troops couldn't take these small hills.'

'Aye, Colonel, but 'ave yer seen how many have dysentery? How can a man run up a hill when he's shittin' himself twenty times a day?'

As the two men continue their conversation about the failures of the Gallipoli campaign, Bardie's adjutant, Captain Hugh Muir, appears, with Hywel Thomas a yard behind him. He is completely covered in summer camouflage, as are his rifle and sight.

'Colonel, this is Colour Serjeant Thomas, School of Sniping.'

'Thank you, Colour. Sorry to have dragged you away from your duties. Bagged much today?'

'Not many, sir. Mainly been keeping their heads down so that they don't get too many of our boys.'

'Are they any good?'

'Yes, very. German-trained; good snipers.'

'Now look, Thomas, Generals Inglefield and Peyton tell me you're one of the best, and General Hamilton says I can have you for a while.'

'Happy to help, sir.'

'We've got a lot of good shots in the regiment – ghillies, keepers and the like. Could you teach them your skills? There's a commission in it for you.'

'Sorry, sir. Did you say "commission"?'

'I did, into my regiment, assuming that a Welshman wouldn't mind joining a Scottish regiment.'

Hywel is beaming from ear to ear. 'I'd be delighted, sir. But what about Major Hesketh-Pritchard?'

'The general will write to him. I'm sure the major will be thrilled to hear that one of his men has been commissioned in the field. And when you've taught us what you know, he can have you back, Lieutenant Thomas.'

'Oh dear, sir, that sounds very odd.'

'Well, you'd better get used to it. So, where do we start?'

'Well, sir, I can't help men who can't shoot, but I can help good shots get better.'

'Well, we will only send you our best shots. See to it, Mr McLaren.'

'Aye, sir.'

The RSM then turns to Hywel. 'What else do you need, sir?'

Hywel takes a moment for the RSM's appellation of 'sir' to sink in before answering. 'We'll need to organize some kind of range, firing positions, targets and ammunition. Then we'll need materials for camouflage – hessian, vegetation and the like – and I'll need a shaded area so that I can show them how to calibrate their sights. I'll also need an observer for each sniper – they're vital – and each one will need a telescope or high-magnification field binoculars.'

Bardie is impressed. 'How long do you need?'

'Three to six weeks, depending on how good your men are.'

Bardie has been curious about Hywel's gloved hand since they met. 'So, why the glove?'

'It hides a gammy hand, sir. It's been shot through, repaired by a doc in Ypres. The glove is reinforced; it acts as a support.'

'Don't tell me you've only got one hand?'

'Well, I like to think I've got two and a half hands, because the gloved one is much better than a normal hand.'

'Fascinating, Lieutenant. So, let's summarize: when we make our next attack, assuming it's within the training time you need, I'd like to have an entire company of snipers ready who we can disperse throughout the regiment to support our advance, especially to take out their machine-gun nests. Agreed?'

'Understood and agreed, sir.'

Hywel walks away with a broad grin on his face. When the war began he was a broken man, alone on a dilapidated farm, his family scattered. Then good fortune intervened. A stranger in the form of Margaret Killingbeck made him reconsider his misfortune. Then he found a God-given gift, which took him to France and has now earned him a commission as an officer.

Wednesday 15 September

St John's Gate, Clerkenwell, London

Katherine Furse and Kitty Stewart-Murray are drinking tea in Katherine's office at St John Ambulance Headquarters in London. Kitty is pensive. She needs to confide in someone, and Katherine, despite her somewhat severe, matronly demeanour, is her only option.

'You know, Katherine, I often think of those two rough diamonds in Poperinghe, Kenny and Broxup. The war is a big adventure for them. Without it, their lives would be just like those of their mothers and grandmothers, and their daughters too, no doubt.'

'I know, but it's true for us as well. I am a widow with a decent pension. Before the war, my prospects were a quiet life here in London until my children leave me, then a retirement to the country or the south coast. Now I can't imagine anything more awful.'

'That's not quite the same for me. Life is changing – of that there's no doubt – but it is destroying my family. The duke is a broken man: one son killed, another a prisoner, and his heir clinging on to a strip of land under fire from 300,000 Turks.'

'It is so sad, and true of so many families. I don't have one friend who hasn't lost a relative. The other day I went to a memorial service for Henry Moseley, killed on

Gallipoli last month. I knew his father, Henry, an anatomy professor at Oxford, and his mother, Amabel, a championship chess player – a brilliant family. Young Henry was a King's Scholar at Eton, took an outstanding sciences degree at Trinity College, Oxford, before working with Ernest Rutherford at Manchester. They say he was going to win the Nobel Prize for Physics for something to do with atomic numbers, whatever they are. But he joined up as a signals officer and was shot through the head by a Turkish sniper. At the service Rutherford spoke, with tears rolling down his cheeks. He said a profoundly important thing: that Moseley was the brightest star of a glittering generation being extinguished by war, and he begged the government not to send any more of them to their deaths. There was not a dry eye in the house and many "hear, hear"s in support of his words.'

Kitty shakes her head. 'One hears so many similar stories of men of great promise – athletes, poets, scientists – being snuffed like candles in the wind. It's tragic. At Blair, our losses are not of great men, but they are good men, salts of the earth, the country's backbone. Of the staff and servants, almost all the men are fighting; the women are either tilling the land or working in Lloyd George's munitions factories. There's no one left, just the old people and the children.'

'What a topsy-turvy world – and the Kenny woman calls you Kitty!'

'Exactly, but perhaps she and her husband are earning the right to call me what they like.'

'And her husband will get the vote – as well she

might – after the war. Then we will be ruled by the social-ists and you aristocrats will go to the guillotine!'

'Don't, Katherine, not even in jest!'

'Sorry, Kitty.'

Kitty gets up and walks over to the window. She can see the medieval gate of St John's. 'Given our conversa-tion, it's amazing to think St John's goes all the way back to the Crusades.'

'Yes, our world has been nine hundred years in the making, and now it's changing overnight.'

Katherine watches Kitty staring across to the sunlit arch of St John's Gate and realizes that something is trou-bling her. 'What's bothering you, Kitty? Can I help?'

Kitty turns from the window and sits back down. There are tears in her eyes. 'Do you mind if I confide in you on a personal matter?'

'Of course not – although my life experiences are somewhat limited.'

'I'm afraid one doesn't need much of life's experience to help with my issue; it is not an unusual one.'

Katherine pours more tea as Kitty explains her dilemma. 'You see, Bardie and I have an "open" marriage; it is inscribed in a formal agreement between us. He has at least two illegitimate children, whom he supports. We don't have any children and, as I've now turned forty, there doesn't seem to be any prospect of us ever having any. I think Bardie still has lovers. He's like his father; he can't resist a pretty face.'

She hesitates and takes a gulp of tea. 'I've had a letter from him. He says that it's impossible for me to travel to the Dardanelles – which is a hellhole – or even to

Lemnos, the Greek island which is where they have their HQ. But he wants me to go to Alexandria, where he can see me when he's on leave and where he thinks his regiment will go after the Gallipoli campaign ends.'

'There are worse places, Kitty, and you can do vital things for us there: we have hundreds of girls in the hospitals in Egypt.'

'I know, and I would relish such a chance and, of course, I would be happy to spend time with Bardie; he's kind and can be very good company. But that's not the problem.'

'You have a lover, here in London?'

'How did you guess?'

'Come, come, Kitty. I said I had little experience of the world, not that I had none!'

'Do you remember that tall, fair Grenadier who came to a reception here last year: George Grey, invalided out, a patch over one eye?'

'Indeed I do. Lucky girl; he's a fine figure of a man.'

'Well, I've been seeing him ever since.'

'Do you want me to be blunt?'

'I wouldn't expect anything else.'

'Well, you'll have to tell him what's happened and then do as Bardie asks and go out to Alexandria. I can put you in charge of all our operations east of Gibraltar – keep you busy.'

'That's kind, Katherine, but I fear I'll lose George. He's only thirty, a major with a good pension after the war; handsome, a hero with an MC on his chest. Some pretty little twenty-year-old with a rich daddy will snap him up.'

'Do you want me to be blunt again?'

'Yes, please.'

'That's going to happen anyway, sooner or later. He knows there can never be anything permanent between you, and you're often not in London. Someone will tip their bustle in his direction and you will be in the way.'

'Hell, Katherine, that *is* blunt.'

'Sorry, but it is the way of things.'

The next day, Kitty writes to Bardie to tell him that she has been to the P&O office in London and booked a passage to Egypt for her and her maid, and will sail for Alexandria on SS *Mooltan* on 26 October. That evening she goes to see her lover in Pimlico. It is a passionate tryst, but one tinged with bitter regret, because both know it will be their last.

South Camp, Ripon, North Yorkshire

Tommy Broxup and John-Tommy Crabtree have been doing a lot of marching over the last two months. Eleventh Battalion East Lancs left Rugeley Camp on Cannock Chase on 31 July to begin a recruitment drive for yet more volunteers in their East Lancashire towns.

Its first visit was to Chorley, where the men paraded on Coronation Recreation Ground. Chorley's mayor, Alderman Ralph Hindle, was effusive in his praise, and so proud that the town was able to see the entire battalion parade through its streets. However, he was more than frank about how the people of Chorley should respond to the new recruitment drive. He addressed his words directly to the battalion's colonel, Arthur Rickman: 'There are a number of men without any ties who could and should enlist, and I should be glad if you would take those young shirkers with you. We don't want them. We can do without them.'

Hindle's caustic comments produce cries of derision from the crowd and a very polite decline from Colonel Rickman: 'Sir, Chorley has given us one company already, and we would happily take another, but perhaps as reservists, until they are rid of their "shirking"!'

The Accrington Pals then paraded through Blackburn and were inspected in the cattle market before appearing at the Lancashire Agricultural Show. There, a crowd of more than seven thousand applauded its energetic display of Swedish Drill.

The battalion was then given a couple of days' leave before it reassembled in Burnley for a civic reception, at which the Mayor of Burnley, Alderman James Sellers-Kay, presented Lance Corporal Harry Watson, a regular with 2nd Battalion East Lancs, with a gallantry medal. He was given a Distinguished Conduct Medal for his bravery at the Battle of Neuve Chapelle, where he rescued a man trapped in barbed wire while under heavy fire from the German trenches. Unfortunately, Watson was so badly wounded in the battle that he had to remain seated during the entire ceremony.

In Accrington preparations are underway to provide the War Office with the information it needs to proceed to national conscription. The work is undertaken by local teachers, who find 29,001 inhabitants eligible for National Registration. All men aged between eighteen and forty-one are listed on pink forms, while the forms of those involved in essential war industries are marked with a black star before being sent to London. Few realize what the outcome of the National Registration will be.

The Pals arrive at Ripon on the evening of the 15th. They are the last of 94th Brigade to reach Ripon to begin rifle training on the nearby Bishop Monkton Range. Ninety-fourth Brigade – Accrington, Sheffield and Barnsley Pals – joins 92nd Brigade (four battalions of Hull Pals: Commercials, Tradesmen, Sportsmen and T'Others) and 93rd Brigade (Leeds Pals, Bradford Pals, Durham Pals and 12th King's Own Yorkshire Light Infantry – Leeds Miners/Pioneers). Together, they form the army's new 31st Division, 12,000 men in all, northern volunteers to Kitchener's New Army. The vast majority are Yorkshiremen and Durhamites, but the numerical superiority does not inhibit the Accrington Pals from issuing challenges on the rifle range, and in every sport available.

Tommy and John-Tommy have decided to issue a challenge to the entire Yorkshire and Durham contingent to pick a 'select eleven' to face just one company of the Accrington Pals, Z Company, the Burnley lads. They will be an eleven from a pool of 2,250, to face a select team from over 10,000. The battalion's illicit bookmakers sense a killing and issue high odds against Burnley. Tommy and John-Tommy bet heavily on themselves. As far as he knows, John-Tommy is the only former professional in the whole of the 31st Division and is certain he can edge it for the Lancastrians.

As all the newly arrived battalions have been given the

day off, the game will be played the next morning, stumps at 11 a.m.

'So, Tommy, you open wi' Bert Clough; Harold Birkenshaw an' Cliff Wood three an' four, and I'll come in at five. Then Sutcliffe, Lieutenant Tough, Captain Ross, an' then Harry T., Bert Croft an' Billy Blenkinsop, nine, ten, jack. I'll open t'bowlin' wi' Billy B. Tommy, you're the only one who can keep wicket, so you're behind t'stumps. Any questions?'

There are none.

'Reet, let's show t'Tykes 'ow to laik at cricket.'

By lunch, the Lancastrians, who have won the toss and decided to bat, are 87 for 3. Tommy scores a hearty 28, including three 4s, before he is clean-bowled. Fellow-opener Bert Clough knocks 21. Harold Birkenshaw makes 19 in a partnership with Wood before he is caught behind, bringing John-Tommy to the crease for one nervy over before lunch.

In the impromptu pavilion, an army field tent, the Lancastrians guess at how many they need: 'A hundred and fifty, that should be enough t'bowl at.'

Tommy is concerned about the pace of one of their bowlers. 'That big bugger can bowl.'

John-Tommy scowls. 'Aye, he can play a bit. He's an officer in t'Hull pals, an', by his accent, a public schoolboy.'

'Tha's reet J-T, one o' theer lads said 'e's an Oxford Blue.'

'Bugger me! Let's hope the bugger can't bat as well as 'e can bowl.'

The afternoon session does not begin well for Z Company, which has adopted the name 'The King's Red Roses' for the match. John-Tommy scores 45 not out, but the rest of the batting collapses around him, leaving a total of 137 to defend.

The Yorkshiremen/Durhamites start well. The Hull Pals' officer, Cedric Willoughby, an alumnus of Hymers College in Hull, is unbeaten on 36 as the Yorkshiremen reach 52 for 1 at a canter. John-Tommy has decided not to open the bowling but has held himself back so that he can study Willoughby's batting. He calls Billy Blenkinsop over.

'Reet, our Billy, I'm puttin' thee at t'far end. Keep them leg breaks pitched up. I don't want 'im clippin' yer o'er top fer 4 every time. I'm gonna soften I'm up wi' a few rib ticklers. Let's see if wi can paint a bit o' Oxford Blue on to his ribcage. Don't reckon thi do too much o' that at Oxford – not cricket tha' knows!'

At the end of John-Tommy's first over, a maiden, he's managed to hit Willoughby on the shoulder, arm and thigh with successive deliveries. Although Willoughby is a well-educated and well-mannered young man, he is the son of a mining engineer and is not afraid of picking up John-Tommy's gauntlet.

'Why don't you try another of those, and I'll show you how far I can thump it?'

'An' how far will that be, young un?'

''Alfway to York if you can bowl it with enough pace.'

'Don't yer moither abaht t'pace on it, lad; just mek sure tha gets tha heed owt at t'road, or I might just part thi 'air on t'other side fer thi.'

Having made it is as obvious as he possibly can that his next ball will be a bouncer on middle and leg, John-Tommy thunders in and launches a toe-pinching yorker at the last second. Willoughby is already halfway into a hook shot before he reads it. He has no time to get his bat down again and is bowled at the bottom of the middle stump, sending it cartwheeling towards Burnley's wicketkeeper, Tommy Broxup.

As his victim trundles past him, John-Tommy cannot resist a final taunt. 'Not quite to York, then; although tha middle stump nearly med it.'

Willoughby gives John-Tommy a withering look as he passes. 'You're fortunate you're not in my platoon. I'd make your life a misery.'

'Aye, yer might at that, but am not, so yer can bugger off, can't yer?'

The East of the Pennines Select loses wickets quickly after Willoughby departs, and John-Tommy gets 7 for 33 as the King's Red Roses win by 29 runs.

The trophy, a cup donated by Colonel Rickman, is awarded to John-Tommy and his team by Major General Sir Archibald Murray, Deputy Chief of the Imperial General Staff, who is in Ripon to inspect the 31st Division.

'Fine batting and ferocious bowling, Crabtree. Do you play for Lancashire?'

'No, sir, I used to laik fer Burnley, Lancashire League, I were a pro at Oldham fer two yer, earned a bob or two, but not good enough fer Old Trafford.'

There's a shout from the men watching. 'Aye, an' he's earned a bob or two 'ere today!' Peals of laughter ring around the gathering.

'Anyway, Crabtree and the rest of your Red Roses, very well done.'

'Thank you, sir.'

John-Tommy raises the trophy aloft to loud cheers, before taking it over to Colonel Rickman. 'There you are, sir. Fo' t'trophy cabinet back 'ome.'

'Thank you, Crabtree.'

The colonel then leans forward to whisper in his cricket captain's ear. 'If I hear there's been a book running on the outcome of this game and that you're a recipient of the spoils, I'll have your guts for garters. Is that clear?'

'Oh yes, sir, absolutely clear. No book, sir, not that I'm aware of.'

'Good, then off with you to celebrate. You and the lads did the 11th proud today. There'll be money behind the bar of the Lamb and Flag at Bishop Monkton from me and the other officers.'

'Very kind, sir. Wilt tha join us fer one?'

'I'm afraid I can't. I have to entertain the general in Ripon tonight.'

Later that evening the Lamb and Flag is packed to the door, with many men standing outside. Although it is mid-September, the evening is warm; autumn is yet to bite. The Burnley boys, with the exception of their two officers, who have had to go to the general's dinner, are crowded around the bar, carousing to their hearts' content. The handsome silver cricket trophy sits on the bar in front of them and, although they have long since spent Colonel Rickman's tab, there is still plenty of money sitting in the trophy, which they are using as a drinks kitty.

'How much did we win today, J-T?'

'Not so loud, Billy. Mum's the word.'

Billy Blenkinsop is drunk, as are most of the Burnley boys. 'I'll share it out in t'mornin', but we're drinkin' most on it.'

There is a commotion by the door: 'Come on, out o' the way, where's them Burnley fuckers?'

About fifteen men – Barnsley, Leeds and Hull Pals – force their way to the bar and the knot of Burnley lads. None of them played during the day, but they clearly want to continue the War of the Roses from the afternoon. In their vanguard is a big man, a Barnsley miner, whose face looks like it has been hewn from the coalface itself.

John-Tommy straightens himself. 'T'Burnley fuckers are 'ere. Who wants to know?'

'I do. Jack Hobson, 2nd Battalion, Barnsley Pals.'

'Wilt tha 'ave a beer wi' us, Jack?'

It looks like Jack has had a skinful already.

'No, a fuckin' won't, not from winnin's from that book yer ran. Th's summat not right abaht it. You're a professional; that's not right.'

'I wer a pro seven year ago fer two seasons. Ave bin retired three year.'

'It's still not right, and you made a tit outta our Lieutenant Willoughby.'

'It's called tactics, Jack.'

'A don't care wot yer call it, we're callin' yer outside, to settle it.'

'Can't oblige yer, Jack, we're in uniform. Brawlin's a field punishment offence.'

'Well, tek that fuckin' jacket off.'

Somewhat reluctantly, a serjeant from Hobson's battalion

comes over. 'Come on, Jack, the Lanky lad's right, you'll be fer the high jump if you carry on.'

Hobson towers over the serjeant menacingly. 'Tell yer wot, Sarge, why don't you go an' sit down like a good boy?'

At that point, the Lamb and Flag's landlord sends one of his bar staff to get the Military Police, who have a van at the Mason's Arms nearby. John-Tommy, realizing that the Yorkshireman is not going to back off, looks at Tommy, who nods back.

John-Tommy turns his back on Hobson, puts his elbows on the bar and takes a drink from his pot of ale.

'Hey, Lanky, don't turn yer fuckin' back on me.'

John-Tommy doesn't move, so Hobson grabs his shoulder and pulls him around. As he does, John-Tommy hits him with a haymaker of a right-hand. The big Yorkshireman hardly flinches, so Tommy hits him as hard as he can. Again, there's little response – until, that is, the Yorkshireman's accomplices launch into anyone near them. All hell breaks out. Fists and boots fly; men careen over tables; pots, chairs and beer go in all directions. Hobson catches John-Tommy with a vicious jab to his left eye, splitting his eyebrow across its entire length. He sees another coming and has no choice but to smash his pot into the side of Hobson's head. Blood splatters everywhere and the burly miner falls over, holding the side of his face.

Before any more blows can be exchanged, shrill whistles mark the arrival of the MPs, who stream into the pub and grab the main protagonists in the brawl.

The next morning, at eight o'clock sharp, John-Tommy, Tommy and four members of Z Company's victorious team are lined up in front of Colonel Rickman, Battalion Adjutant Captain George Slinger and Battalion Serjeant Major Jimmy Shorrock.

Rickman is in a foul mood.

'In accordance with Military Regulations, 1914, I am issuing a Field Punishment Number 2 to all you brawlers. After three days of punishment at Catterick Camp, in shackles, you will return here for three weeks of hard labour, during which you will lose all pay and allowances. As for you, Crabtree, to hit a man with a beer pot is a cowardly disgrace. After yesterday's cricket, I had considered you for corporal's stripes, but I can tell you now that that will never happen while I command this battalion. You will receive a Number 1 Field Punishment. It will not be carried out at Catterick but here by the entrance to the camp, in full view of all in 31st Division and any locals who are passing. Reparations to the Lamb and Flag will come out of your pocket and so you will not receive any pay until the debt is paid.

'I had considered a court martial in your case, but Mr Shorrock pleaded your cause and said that you were provoked in the extreme. That has saved you, Crabtree. But your victim has had eleven stitches to his head and ear and is in a sorry state. Unforgivable, absolutely unforgivable.

'By the way, the trophy for the cricket has been sent to 3rd Battalion Hull Pals, the Sportsmen, Lieutenant Willoughby's battalion, with my compliments. Any questions?'

All the men shake their heads.

'Very well. Captain Slinger, make the arrangements at

Catterick. Mr Shorrock, take Crabtree to the Provost Marshal. I want him shackled to a gun wheel for eight hours a day for three of the next four days, and I want it done right outside the camp entrance at the side of the road.'

BSM Shorrock leans forward to whisper to his colonel. 'But the regulations say no more than two hours a day, sir.'

'I know what the regulations say, Mr Shorrock. But I want him punished. I hope passers-by throw eggs at him, and I hope his fellow soldiers spit on him!'

Saturday 25 September

Vermelles, Pas-de-Calais, France

Morgan Thomas has returned to his regiment, the Royal Welch Fusiliers. He has been given a hero's welcome and awarded the Distinguished Conduct Medal for escaping from captivity and for defending the honour of the QAIMNS nurses at Vlamertinge. He has gone back to his original unit, 1st Battalion, but is horrified to see that of the 109 reservists he left Wrexham with in October last year, only a handful are still with the battalion.

He is in a forward trench, primed to be part of a huge Anglo–French attack. First Battalion is part of 22nd Brigade, one of the three brigades of General Sir Thompson Capper's 7th Division. With the Welch is 2nd Queens to its left, and 2nd Warwicks and 1st South Staffs to its right.

Despite great reluctance to launch any more major offensives during 1915, significant Russian setbacks on the Eastern Front, including the fall of Russian Lithuania and the capture of 22,000 prisoners, bring a change of mind. Under pressure from the French, it is decided to support their attack in Champagne to the south with a major attack around the village of Loos. The ground is monotonously flat, except for the pitheads and slagheaps of the local mining industry. Six divisions will be committed: over 70,000 men, the biggest offensive of the year. Although heavy artillery shells and small-round ammunition are in short supply, the planners hope that 150 tons of chlorine gas in over 5,000 cylinders will tip the balance.

Morgan's trench is 750 yards east of the small village of Vermelles, now all but destroyed and abandoned after a year of war. He is nervous; his first experience of battle, at Zwarteleen in Flanders in November last, could not have been more traumatic. He lost his brother, his commanding officer and all his comrades and was almost killed himself.

He has prepared for what is to come, as most soldiers have. Last night he went into Béthune with half a dozen of his company. They had a few beers in a local café and then queued for an hour to visit the red-light girls. It was two francs well spent. The girl he bought was not much older than eighteen and nothing like as exciting as Cath Kenny, but Cath is back in Pop, and if the full-figured young French girl is to be his last sexual partner in this life, then he could have done a lot worse.

'Here, Taff, have a swig of this.'

Morgan's company serjeant major, John Hughes, an Englishman from Chester, offers him his canteen.

'No, ta, Sarge. I've got lots of water, thanks.'

'It's not water, it's rum. Have a good gulp.'

'How did you get that?'

'From battalion stores.'

'How?'

'The storeman was lying flat on his face, pissed, so I helped myself.'

'Thanks.' Morgan takes two big mouthfuls.

Two lance corporals appear, followed by half a dozen storemen.

'Private Thomas?'

'Yes, Corp, here.'

'These are yours. You're a signaller for the attack.'

Morgan was given a D3 telephone, one reel of wire, one large and one small signalling flag, some signalling blinds and a roll of rabbit-hutch wire.

John Hughes looks bemused. 'What the fuck is the rabbit-hutch stuff for?'

'Some bright spark at Division reckons that the netted wire will survive better than single cables, so if we run it between all the companies and back to HQ we can connect it up for the telephones.'

Incredulous, everyone looks at one another. CSM Hughes is apoplectic. 'You must be fucking joking. He's not carrying chicken wire, or whatever the fuck it is, along with all the other clobber.'

Morgan adds to the debate. 'And Corp, I'm not a signaller. I don't know what to do with it all.'

'I know, but the platoon's signaller has gone sick. Captain Thomas went down the list, saw that you've been with the battalion for nearly a year and that you've won a medal, so he said that you'd do.'

'But I was a POW for all of that time.'

'You mean you escaped to come back to this lot!'

Hughes interrupts. 'Never mind, Taff. You lot fuck off down the line.'

When they have gone out of earshot Hughes turns to Morgan. 'Lob it into the first shell-hole you come to. Fuck 'em.'

Like all his comrades, besides his Lee-Enfield, Morgan is carrying 200 rounds of ammunition, extra rations, a trenching shovel, four 'cricket ball' grenades, and a PH gas helmet under his service cap, both of which are fastened to his head by a piece of string under his chin.

After ten days of glorious weather, it is raining. It is 05:30 hours. Four huge underground explosions are detonated and create large holes in the German defences, but they also alert the enemy that an attack is imminent. Then the British artillery barrage begins, making the ground shake and confirming British intentions.

Morgan turns to CSM Hughes, who has a trench periscope. 'What's it looking like, Sarge?'

'Well, Fritz is getting a pasting, but they're only 18-pounders, not big enough to do much damage, and the wire is hardly touched.'

'Not great then?'

'No, but we're going to use gas. That'll put the wind up the buggers!'

'Hope so.'

'Aye, as long as the wind is blowin' in the right direction.'

'Which way is it moving now?'

'It's swirling around a bit, but mainly across no-man's-land from south-east to north-west.'

'That's the wrong way, isn't it?'

'Yes.'

'They wouldn't, would they?'

'Nah. Not even Haig is that stupid!'

A few moments later the artillery barrage stops, and

sappers with chlorine-gas cylinders move into the line and start to open the valves. John Hughes checks the wind direction. 'What the fuck are you buggers doing?' he shouts. 'The wind is against us!'

'Orders, mate. We've been told to release the gas as soon as the artillery stops.'

'But it's blowing back into the trenches!'

'So put your gas helmets on!'

Hughes bellows down the trench. 'Gas helmets! Get them on, boys.' He grabs Morgan by the arm. 'Get rid of that signalling kit and run to Captain Thomas. Tell him what's happening.'

He turns to the sappers' serjeant. 'Turn that fucking gas off. You're gassing our own men!'

'Can't. Orders. Put your helmet on.'

'Fuck me, I'll shoot you if you don't turn it off!'

'No, you won't. See that lance corporal behind you? He'll shoot you first.'

Hughes turns to see a Royal Engineer pointing a Lee-Enfield at him. He looks around. Men are already beginning to cough and splutter. He hears whistles and the sound of men going over the top, followed shortly afterwards by the whizz and zip of rifle and machine-gun fire. The attack has begun. Captain Thomas is nowhere to be seen. The gas is getting worse and filling the trench. His men look at him questioningly.

He takes command. 'Right, over we go, boys. Keep your helmets on.'

First Battalion Royal Welch Fusiliers makes its charge. They can hear the pipers of the Scottish regiments in the distance and the battle cries of men in every accent of the

British Isles echoing across no-man's-land. Hughes does not get very far; nor do most of his men. The hail of bullets is too severe and the shrapnel bursts from above wreak terrible damage. Limbs are severed, some men are decapitated, many are blown to pieces and, other than a few remnants of khaki, are unrecognizable, their body parts now no more than fertilizer. The first day of the Battle of Loos is going to be a long and painful one.

Thirty minutes later Morgan Thomas is still looking for Captain Thomas, but he is lost. He knows he is not far from Vermelles because, since dawn broke a few minutes ago, he has been able to see the ruins of the village church. However, no matter which way he turns in the labyrinth of trenches, he is unable to get closer to the village. Eventually, despite the shrapnel shells and the gunfire, he decides to clamber over the top of the parapet and make a dash for the village.

When he reaches open ground several shells burst above his head. He is knocked to the earth, the blast forcing his rifle out of his hands. His pack sticks in the heavy mud beneath him, so he pulls his arms free and leaves it on the ground. He sees a derelict barn 50 yards away with at least half its roof intact – a chance of cover. He makes a dash for it. He has crossed less than half the distance when he runs into a column of the Royal Sussex, a reserve company of men on their way to the battle. At their head is a company serjeant major, closely followed by a captain. The CSM holds his rifle across Morgan's path, and he shudders to a halt.

'So, where are you off to, laddie?'

'I'm looking for Captain Thomas. I've got orders from the Front.'

'You've overshot, lad. The Front is more than a quarter of a mile the other way.'

'I got lost back there, Serjeant.'

'Where's your rifle and pack?'

'Back there. There was a shell burst. The rifle got blown out of my hand and my pack got stuck in the mud.'

'Where?'

Morgan looks back. In the sea of mud and equipment that covers the ground he cannot recognize where he fell.

The Sussex's officer intervenes, a tall man no older than twenty-five who sounds as pompous as he looks. 'Your name and regiment, Fusilier?'

'Thomas, sir, Morgan, 1st Battalion, Royal Welch Fusiliers.'

'Well, Thomas. This doesn't look good. There is a big fight up there. Your battalion is in the middle of it, and you're here, hundreds of yards away, running in the wrong direction without your kit and rifle.'

'What do you mean, it doesn't look good, sir? CSM Hughes told me to go and report to our company CO, Captain Thomas, that the gas is being released with the wind in the wrong direction. It's our men who're being gassed.'

'And?'

'I got lost, sir.'

'Well then, I'm sure your CSM will vouch for you. In the meantime, we have to get forward, so I'm going to have to take you into temporary custody. Colour, have two men take this Fusilier back to the Provost Marshal's office.'

'But, sir, I just got lost. It was dark.'

'Then you've got nothing to worry about. Colour, see to it.'

'Yes, sir.'

As the Sussex men move off, Morgan looks around for an escape route. He is desperate to get his message about the gas to Captain Thomas or to Headquarters.

'Please, Colour, where is Divisional HQ?'

'Over there, in those railway buildings. But you're going with these two corporals for a little walk to the Provost Marshal's office in Béthune.'

'No, I'm not; I'm under orders. We're gassing our own men!' Morgan sets off at a sprint towards the railway buildings.

'Fusilier, halt! That's an order!'

The CSM bellows twice at Morgan to stop, but he carries on running. One of the corporals raises his rifle, but the CSM puts his hand on it.

'Let him go. We're not shooting one of our own, even if he is a deserter. He won't get far: the MPs will track him down. Take a note of his name and number.'

A single shot rings out.

The Sussex's captain, John James Rhodes, a twenty-eight-year-old solicitor's son from Chichester, a volunteer seeing his first action at the Front, has raised his Webley service revolver and shot Morgan in the back. The bullet has shattered his spine and he collapses to the ground in a heap.

'Fuck! Come on, boys.'

CSM Danny Capstick, a previously retired regular who has re-enlisted to serve his old regiment, runs to Morgan with his two corporals. 'Stretcher-bearers!'

When Capstick reaches Morgan, Captain Rhodes bellows at him. 'Leave him, Colour! Shot while running away from custody. Let the orderlies deal with him. I need you up here.'

Capstick mutters under his breath, 'Cunt!'

'Corporal, stay with the lad until the stretcher-bearers take him in. Join us when you can. Poor fucker. Is he breathing?'

The corporal puts his face to Morgan's mouth to check. 'Just, but it doesn't look good. He's shot through.'

Then the corporal notices something poking out of Morgan's pocket. 'Look, Sarge; sticking out of his top pocket. It's a ribbon.'

Capstick unbuttons Morgan's breast pocket and pulls out his medal. 'Fuck, it's a DCM. And we've shot the poor bugger.'

Captain Rhodes bellows at his colour-serjeant.

'Mr Capstick, I need you up here. Let's go.'

The CSM, livid at his CO's arrogance and ruthlessness, mutters under his breath.

'Bloody hell, I should put a bullet through him!'

He pushes the medal back into Morgan's pocket and fastens the button. 'Make sure the medics take care of him.'

The Battle of Loos continues for many days but, sadly, it is a repeat of so many previous catastrophes. Despite the pre-attack artillery bombardments being ineffective in many areas and much of the gas being blown back into British positions, the initial attacks gain much ground and many German trenches are overrun. But reserve battalions are not sent in support quickly enough to press home the advantage. Once again, communications break down and men from different battalions get mixed together, causing confusion in the chain of command – all of which gives the Germans time to consolidate new defensive positions and bring up reinforcements.

The French attack in Champagne is declared a success. Twenty-five thousand German prisoners are taken and 150 heavy guns captured. British losses, however, are severe. In one sector, after the seventh attempt to capture a copse called Bois Hugo ends in failure, with khaki-clad bodies thick on the ground, so appalled are the German officers in command at the carnage in front of them that they order a ceasefire for the rest of the day so that the British can bury their dead.

Fifty British battalions lose more than 300 men and more than three quarters of their officers from their strength of 650 to 700. First Cameron Highlanders lose 687 men and 19 officers; 9th Black Watch 680 men and 20 officers. Morgan Thomas's Battalion, 1st Royal Welch Fusiliers, loses 442 men and 16 officers.

The most well-known victim at Loos is Morgan's divisional commander, Major General Sir Thompson Capper, CO of 7th Division. During an advance on 26 September Capper visits the Front to view the enemy for himself from the captured trenches. Urging his men into a final assault, he stays behind to view the field and is struck by a sniper's bullet fired from houses along the line of advance which were thought to have been abandoned. The assault fails, and Capper is discovered by his retreating units and taken to Number 6 Casualty Clearing Station, to the rear of the British lines. The bullet has penetrated both lungs, doctors give him no chance of survival and he dies the following day, along with 5,200 of his men, in just three days of fighting.

'So be merry, so be dead'

Saturday 9 October

Marble Lodge, Blair Atholl Estate, Perthshire

'Good morning, Lady Helen. What a surprise.'

'Good morning, Maud. It's Helen, remember.'

'Sorry. Come on in, there's the chill of winter blowing down the glen today.'

Helen Stewart-Murray has ridden up Glen Tilt to see her father, who has not made an appearance at Blair Castle for months. Inglis, his factor, goes to see him at Marble Lodge to discuss finance; otherwise, Helen runs the house and the estate in his absence.

'How is he, Maud?'

'Oh, fine. A bit grumpy last night, but he's fine this morning. He had a good breakfast and is now reading the paper. That poor McFarlane boy cycles all the way up here every morning with the post and the newspapers.'

'I know; he's a sweet boy. Tragic about his father.'

'What do you mean?'

'Missing: they got a telegram last week.'

'Oh no. The poor little mite. He hasn't said anything.'

'He wouldn't. They're a stoical lot, the McFarlanes. He's got two younger brothers and an older sister.'

'How are they coping?'

'Very well under the circumstances. Jenny is doing some jobs for me, so they have a few shillings in the pot.'

Helen goes into the kitchen, where the duke has his head in *The Times*. 'Good morning, Papa.'

'Good morning, Helen. Another bloody shambles in France. A place called Loos; terrible losses. French is going to have to go. The man's incompetent; should have gone in the spring.'

'I have some letters from Hamish and Dertha. Shall I read them to you?'

'Yes, please. Maud, come and listen. Letters from the children.'

Maud comes in and sits with the duke. She places her hand on his. Helen smiles. It is a great comfort to her that Maud is so caring to her father.

My dear Father,

Here we already have signs of autumn – bright and sunny during the day, but frosty at night. Here is my daily routine: I get up between 7 and 8, breakfast (cocoa, roll, butter, jam). 9 a.m. Appel (roll call) outside our building. 9 a.m. to 10 a.m. tennis on the gravel court we have made. 10.30 to 11.25 English lessons to French pupil. 12, luncheon, usually fillet of beef and potatoes. 1.30 to 2.30 lesson in English to Russian pupil. 3.15 tea. 4 to 4.45 football on a somewhat sandy riding track, followed by a bath. 5.40 Appel. 6.30, supper, soup, oatcake and butter (could have more if I wished). Everyone has to be indoors at 6.30 and I usually read till 8, after which I receive lessons in German from a Russian. By 10 p.m. I am in bed. I have only just lately started to learn

*German and despair of ever being able to remember the genders
and declinations.*

Your affectionate son, Hamish

'Bloody hell, it sounds like a holiday camp. He'll be telling us next they bring in floozies from the local town!'

'Oh, Father, it sounds all very well for a single day, but seven days a week, week after week, cooped up like that!'

Helen produces another letter from her bag. 'So, this is from Dertha.' She reads again.

Dearest Father,

Harry has been passed fit again and given the 40th Division in the New Army. Of all queer things, it is the Bantam Div., that is, men under 5 foot 3. They are odd to look at, but mostly stocky little men. I saw a Welsh brigade of them, and they looked like they were meant to be that size. They will take some time to collect together, and Harry will be at Aldershot for the next month and then probably Bordon. Meanwhile, I am going to be living at Hythe, and he and I will meet at weekends, either here or there.

Of course, this makes Harry a Maj. Gen. for the present.

Your affectionate Dertha

'Bantams! I say, that's very appropriate. Although Harry's quite tall, he's a bantam in every other respect!'

'Father, don't be unkind! Harry's very nice, and Dertha thinks the world of him.'

The Duke ignores Helen's rebuke. He is still laughing at his derisory comment about his daughter's husband.

'Here's another from darling Dertha. It was posted just two days ago.'

Dearest Father,

I dare say you will be interested to hear that a Zeppelin came over us last night. It came from the north and had nothing to do with that dreadful attack on London, where I believe dozens have been killed. It dropped bombs over the artillery camp at Otterpool, 3 miles off. 14 men were killed, many more injured and lots of horses killed and maimed, which had to be put down. It then came back close to this house and over the main street and went back out to sea. All the little guns here lost their heads and went on popping for ages.

They say the camp brought it on themselves by having their lights blaring, even though they were warned.

Thought you'd like to know. Keep your eyes peeled up there.

Dertha

'War from the sky. What a terrible world we live in. We don't even fight wars like gentlemen any more!'

Maud gets up and heads towards the sink. 'I'll make a pot of tea, Helen. Iain, would you like some?'

'Yes, darling, I would, and a toasted teacake, perhaps?'

Helen's eyes light up. 'Me, too, please.' She moves closer to her father. 'Papa, I have a plan I'd like you to agree to.'

'Sounds ominous.'

'No, not at all. You know I've been organizing food parcels for the troops?'

'I do – been costing me a bally fortune!'

Maud taps the duke on his wrist. 'Don't be so mean, Iain. They deserve every little comfort we can send them.'

Helen smiles. 'I want to do more.'

'Sounds even more ominous.'

'Lots of people with room available are opening up their houses as hospitals for the wounded. I want to turn the ballroom into a ward.'

'Good God, woman! The place will be running alive with lice, diarrhoea and light-fingered soldiers!'

Maud scolds the duke. 'Don't be ridiculous, Iain. Helen, that's a wonderful idea. How thoughtful of you.'

The Duke looks at the two women, who are both beaming at him. He knows any more resistance is futile. 'Oh, very well, but tell Inglis to keep a strict eye on the costs and that I want a monthly report on expenditure.'

'Thank you, Papa, but you know the Red Cross will bear most of the costs.'

'I should think so. Where will you keep the staff?'

'The doctors in the main bedrooms, and the nurses in the servants' quarters.'

'Well, my room is out of bounds . . . and don't expect me to be changing bedpans!'

'Of course not. But I do expect you to play Father Christmas.'

On 13 October, in one of the continuing encounters in the Battle of Loos, a twenty-year-old captain in the Suffolk Regiment called Charles Hamilton Sorley takes part in an attack on the Hohenzollern Redoubt, just beyond Vermelles. A son of Aberdeen and, like Siegfried Sassoon, an alumnus of Marlborough College, he is shot in the head by a sniper and dies instantly. When his body is recovered, thirty-seven complete poems are found in his kitbag, including 'All the Hills and Vales Along'. It ends as follows:

> From the hills and valleys earth
> Shouts back the sound of mirth,
> Tramp of feet and lilt of song
> Ringing all the road along.
> All the music of their going,
> Ringing, swinging, glad song-throwing,
> Earth will echo still, when foot
> Lies numb and voice mute.
> On, marching men, on
> To the gates of death with song.
> Sow your gladness for earth's reaping,
> So you may be glad, though sleeping.
> Strew your gladness on earth's bed,
> So be merry, so be dead.

Saturday 16 October

'Where is he, Sister?'

'Over there, third bed beyond the stove.'

'How's he doin'?'

'Not good, I'm afraid. We can't get the bullet out. It's lodged in his vertebrae. We can't operate, and every time we move him the bleeding starts again.'

'What does that mean?'

'The doctors think he's got forty-eight hours at most. He shouldn't really be alive now, but he's a strong boy. He's survived for three weeks, which is remarkable. We have to treat him like a china doll.'

The sister leans forward towards Cath. 'He told me you were coming and how fond he is of you, but he is very ill. Try not to get him upset.'

Cath Kenny's eyes fill with tears. She and Mary Broxup have come to see Morgan. They have only just heard that he is wounded. When they reach his bedside his eyes are closed, his head wrapped in a bandaged splint to stop him moving. He has been sedated with morphine to help fight the considerable pain he is feeling.

Mary kisses him on the forehead; Cath does the same, but full on the lips.

'Eh up, 'ansome. Tha looks reet smart wi' that bonnet on tha heed.'

Morgan blinks so that he can focus properly. He speaks, but with difficulty. 'I asked for it specially to impress you.'

'Aye, well, it works a treat, dun't it, our Mary?'

'Aye, looks grand.'

Morgan's eyes swell with tears. He tries to move his head to look at his visitors.

'Tha marsn't move tha heed, Morgan.'

He swallows hard and draws a breath, which makes him wince with pain. 'He shot me in the back, Cath.'

'Who did?'

'An officer from the Sussex Regiment.'

'What fer?'

'He said I was running away, a deserter. I'd lost my pack and rifle – a shell burst. I was frightened. But I'd been told to report that we were gassing our own men. I had to try to tell someone.'

'Have you told the doctors what happened?'

'No, I don't trust anyone, because I know they'll cover it up.'

'What's his name?'

'Don't know. He was a captain in the Sussex Regiment – 2nd Battalion, I think. His CSM was called Capstick. I heard the officer call his name.'

'We'll find t'bugger, don't worry. Now you need to get some rest. We'll be back soon.'

Both women kiss Morgan goodbye and dash off in search of the men of the Sussex Regiment.

They drive south for over 30 miles, negotiating huge convoys of men and materials, and are at the HQ of 1st

Division at La Rutoire, a hamlet east of Vermelles, the base for 2nd Brigade, and for 2nd Sussex Battalion. The acting CO of the brigade is Brigadier Henry Fleetwood Thuillier, a Royal Engineer by background who has been in command for only two weeks. His two predecessors were both killed in September. He is a squat man with greying temples and a thin, neatly trimmed moustache. Were it not for his uniform, he could easily pass for a provincial bank manager.

'Ladies, if we could make this quick, I would appreciate it. There is to be another attack this evening.'

Before Cath and Mary can respond, a succession of shells lands in a line within yards of the *maison d'maître* which is acting as Thuillier's HQ. The shells explode like a series of rhythmical thumps on a big bass drum. The whole building shakes, and the glass in those windows that are still in their frames shatters into tiny fragments. Clouds of dust fill the air. When it clears, the brigadier and his two visitors find themselves on their backsides on the floor.

They all get up and dust themselves off. Thuillier bellows to his adjutant, 'Report, Captain?'

The adjutant shouts from the next room. 'One has hit the stables, sir. There were no men in there, but I'll check the horses.'

'Are you all right, ladies?'

'Yes, sir, thank you.'

'So, as you can see, things are a bit hairy here.'

'Yes, o' course, sir. We'll be reet sharp abaht it. We're lookin' fer a captain from 2nd Sussex. We don't know his name, but his colour serjeant is called Capstick, we think.'

'And what do you want to see him about?'

'He shot a Welch Fusilier lad. He's dyin'. The captain made a mistake. He needs to know that, and he needs to answer fer it.'

'I see. And what is your role in this?'

'Morgan Thomas is a friend o' mine.'

'Boyfriend?'

'Kind of.'

'I see – a wartime romance. And your name?'

'Cath Kenny. This is Mary Broxup.'

'I assume from the ring on your finger that it's Mrs Kenny?'

'It is. Me 'usband's a tunneller. Fer all I know, 'e could be 60 feet under us reet now.'

Thuillier sneers, making it obvious he disapproves of Cath's behaviour. 'I see: a brave man, your husband.'

Cath's ire rises. She looks at the brigadier's nameplate on his desk. 'Look, Henry, that's none o' yer business. But tha must remember, we lasses don't 'ave red or blue light houses to visit like you lads. An' Morgan's a lovely lad, and a long way fra 'ome, as we all are. Think on it, Henry, next time tha's wi' yer little mademoiselle from Armentières.'

The brigadier blushes noticeably and changes the subject.

'You are making a serious allegation, Mrs Kenny. You should go to the Provost Marshal's office in Béthune.'

'Aye, wi'v been there. They said they can't do owt wi'out a name, and they don't 'ave time to look 'im up, so we're doin' it.'

The brigadier looks at his watch impatiently. 'You are, to say the least, Mrs Kenny, a forthright woman.'

Mary interrupts. 'She is, but she's quite calm at t'moment. Don't get her moithered, though.'

'"Moithered"?'

'Annoyed.'

The brigadier relents. 'Captain, please bring in your reports for the past three weeks. When do you think this incident happened, Mrs Kenny?'

'Would have been 25 September, first day of the big push.'

The brigadier's adjutant runs his finger down his daily reports for the end of September. He pauses before looking at Cath and Mary. 'CSM Capstick, Colour Serjeant B Company, 2nd Battalion Sussex Regiment. Killed in action 25 September, body retrieved. The CO of B Company was Captain John James Rhodes. Killed by shell burst, 26 September, body not found.'

The adjutant pauses. He looks at Cath closely. 'He was a friend of mine, and a good man.'

Cath begins to speak, but Mary digs her in the ribs. She goes up to the brigadier and captain and shakes their hands. 'Thank you. We'll be on our way now. You lads are busy. Come on, Cath.'

Cath trudges towards the door. When she gets there, she stops and turns. Her eyes are full of tears. 'They're all dyin' fer nowt, aren't they, Henry?'

'I hope not, Mrs Kenny. I hope not.'

'Please call me Cath; I 'ate formality.'

'Very well, Cath. I think our cause is just, despite the dreadful losses. By the way, you were right; your relationship with your Fusilier is none of my business. I hope he recovers.'

'Thanks, Henry. 'E won't, but it's nice of yer all t'same.'

Cath and Mary say very little to one another on the way north to Poperinghe. By the time they reach the town, it is late. They go straight to Pop-Hop. There is a different sister on duty.

'Hello, Sister,' says Cath. 'We're 'ere t'see Fusilier Morgan Thomas? He's on t'reet beyond t'stove.' The sister looks at them both with a pained expression.

Cath peers into the darkness of the ward. Morgan's bed is empty. 'No!' She rushes into Mary's arms, convulsing with anguish.

The ward sister ushers them into her office. 'He died this afternoon. Must have been the onset of pneumonia, which I'm afraid was always inevitable. He started coughing, which set him off bleeding again. We gave him some morphine, so he wasn't in much pain at the end.'

Mary sits Cath down. 'Nurse, bring some tea.'

'Bugger that!' Cath gets up and wipes her eyes. 'Sorry, Sister, didn't mean to be rude, but I need more 'n tea. Come on, Mary, beer an' chasers is called fer.'

The sister reaches into her apron pocket. 'I take it you're Cath.'

'Aye.'

'He scribbled a name for you.' She hands Cath a small folded piece of paper. It has a name on it, written in bold capital letters – BRONWYN. 'She's his twin sister. He asked if you would tell her he loves her and always did, and that he was sorry that he didn't come after her when she left home. We're very fond of Bronwyn here. A wonderful girl. She went to the Dardanelles at the beginning of May with Sister Margaret Killingbeck. QAIMNS in

442

St Omer will be able to contact her for you. Their older brother, Hywel, was also here. He's a sniper. He went to the Dardanelles but will be harder to find. But there's a School of Sniping run by a chap called Hesketh-Pritchard, a major, I think. He might know where he is.'

'Thanks, Sister.'

The sister puts her hand on Cath's arm. 'He also asked me to tell you that he loved you very much and that you had made the last few weeks of his life the most wonderful time he'd ever had.'

Cath turns to leave, her chest heaving with spasms of grief. 'Thanks, Sister. I've got t'go. Come on, Mary.'

'One last thing. He said please don't forget him.'

Cath starts to run. 'I won't! I promise, Morgan, I won't forget you.'

An hour later Cath and Mary are watching the staff of the Maison de Ville in Pop's Grande Place as they begin to stack the chairs and clear the tables at the end of another long day. For the staff, the war is a bizarre experience. Soldiers come and go; they get to know some of them quite well, then they disappear and never return. Some of the girls have brief affairs with these transient figures in khaki so, for them, the turnover of smiling, innocent young men is particularly painful.

Cath and Mary look at the empty bottles of beer in front of them and the half-empty bottle of marc d'Alsace, a pomace brandy made from leftover skins and stalks from the vineyards. It is not cognac, and is barely drinkable, but Cath in particular has made a significant dent in the bottle's crystal-clear but potent liquid.

'I've been a reet tart, 'aven't a, Mary?'

'You are who you are, Cath. Tha's not gonna change now. But Mick loves yer, and so do I . . . and so did Morgan. I'm reet sorry abaht wot happened t' 'im.'

'Thu's no point tekin' it any further wi' Provost Marshal's office, is there?'

'No. Let it rest, Cath.'

'Aye. But that's not t'end on it.'

''Ow d'yer mean?'

Cath takes another mouthful of her beer and pours another glass of marc.

'Tha's 'ad enough, Cath,' says Mary. 'Let's away.'

'Aye, but tha's summat I 'ave to tell yer. I'm in a reet pickle.'

'No, Cath!'

'Aye, I'm pregnant; three month.'

'Bloody 'ell! Are you sure?'

'Aye.'

'It's Morgan's?'

''Course. Unless I'm the bloody Virgin Mary!'

'I think we should 'ave that drink after all.'

Sunday 31 October

Hoe Farm, Hascombe, Surrey

F. E. Smith is spending the day with Winston at Hoe Farm. While Winston's political star has been waning, FE's has been waxing. In May he was made Solicitor General in Asquith's government and given a knighthood, and he has just heard that he is to be made Attorney General, with a seat in the Cabinet, in succession to Sir Edward Carson, who has resigned from Asquith's coalition government over its policy in the Balkans.

Winston, no longer privy to confidential documents, is keen to know of Carson's motives. 'Why is Carson so exercised about the Balkans?' he asks.

'Well, in particular, he is adamant that we should support Serbia after the German/Austrian invasion. But, in general, it is more to do with his lack of faith in Kitchener, who he thinks is dragging us further and further into a deeper and deeper hole, and his antagonism towards Asquith, who he thinks is interested only in his own political survival.'

'Well, as you know, I concur about both things. But Kitchener must go first. Only the Old Block can do that, so he must have a stay of execution until we have a new war leader. Then we can get behind LG, who is the only possible successor to Asquith.'

'A word of caution, Winston. You know, you seem to have lost LG's support. He feels he can't trust you any more.'

'I know. He thinks I'm just another opportunist.'

'Like him!'

'Quite. The truth is, this dreadful war has turned friend against friend, ally against ally. We are all afraid of failure and run away from responsibility for fear of blame. It is impossible to be decisive and take risks. And, as you know, you can't fight a war without taking risks; some of them huge.'

'Good grief, Winston, we miss you so much at the heart of things.'

'You are so kind, FE, but I'm afraid I'm going to go altogether. I wrote to OB yesterday, offering my resignation from the government. But I did ask, once and for all, for him to let the country know the full facts about the Dardanelles.'

'Will he allow that?'

'Probably not.'

'What will you do?'

'Paint a bit more. I'm thoroughly enjoying it.'

'Don't be ridiculous. You can't sit and paint pretty pictures of an English garden while the world is consumed by the flames of war.'

'Actually, they're not at all pretty. They have a drama of their own: vibrant colours; battles between light and shade; vital tensions between backdrop and detail.'

'Stuff and nonsense, Winston. As I've often said about you, you are the consummate master of the impromptu remark. So what will you really do?'

'There's talk of me taking command in East Africa.'

446

'Malaria, poor food – and good wine's almost impossible to get.'

'Quite. I'd like a brigade in France, but K won't hear of it, only a battalion.'

'Beneath you.'

'Possibly, but I've not commanded before.'

'Except the entire British political scene for the past dozen years.'

'Not quite, FE. Then there's new technology. I've asked for command of a new air ministry more than once. These latest Zeppelin raids convince me of its future. But not those fat cigars full of hot air.'

'You mean Asquith's Cabinet, of course.'

'Very droll. No, the Zeppelins are quite effective. I mean aeroplanes – the bombing of trenches and, particularly, supplies and communications. Can you imagine the impact of the destruction of German munitions factories and cutting their rail links to the Front?'

'What are the chances?'

'Minimal, as long as K is in harness. He won't even consider it. But I've been promoting another idea: armoured vehicles.'

'Not more of Winston's Rolls-Royces? The press will have a field day.'

'No, much better than that. I've got Hankey's ear, and he's dripping the idea into Cabinet when he can. It started with a dinner with Bendor Grosvenor at the beginning of the year. As you probably know, he developed some armoured Rolls-Royces like mine, but they're not much good in the mud of Flanders, so they went off to Egypt and the Middle East, where they've been quite effective.

There were a couple of good sorts at the dinner – Tom Hetherington, an RNAS flyer and an engineer, and Stace Tennyson-d'Eyncourt, a naval architect and brilliant designer. We talked tracked vehicles with armoured compartments for the men, and of how a vehicle could span trenches.

'We recruited Ernie Swinton, a colonel at the War Office, who also believes that machines could break the deadlock in the trenches. We kept the designs secret, under the title "Water Carriers for Russia", which became "WCs for Russia". Now, Swinton has christened them "tanks", and we've formed a "Landships Committee".

'Unfortunately, when Balfour took over from me, he called in d'Eyncourt and asked him if he had nothing better to do at the navy than bugger about with these "confounded landships". So the whole thing's ground to a halt.'

'Typical. What will you do?'

'Bide my time. Believe me: the day of the "tank" will come.' Winston gets up from his chair and goes to the window. 'What is the latest from Downing Street?'

'Another storm is brewing. Hamilton has been brought home from the Dardanelles as a failure. Birdwood is in charge until Charles Monro arrives to take command. There is a growing feeling that Kitchener has to go, and that he is loathed by more than a few, but Asquith knows of his popularity in the country so won't do it. To appease the anti-K lobby, he has sent him to Gallipoli to assess the situation. The majority view is that we should pull out of the Dardanelles altogether, but nobody dares grasp the nettle, least of all the Prime Minister.'

448

'Bloody hell — eleven thirty, soon be lunch. We must have a snort or two before Clemmie calls us in. What will you have?'

'G and T, please. What shall we do this afternoon?'

'I'm going to paint, and you can watch and keep me amused.'

While he paints after lunch Winston outlines to FE what will be in his resignation speech to the House of Commons.

'I'm going to begin with the line, "At the outbreak of this war, megalomania was the only form of sanity, but now it is a different war."'

'Good start.'

'Then I want to talk about adversity: "We are passing through a bad time now, and it will probably be worse before it is better, but that it will be better, if we only endure and persevere, I have no doubt whatever."'

'Good, are you going to try to score a few political points?'

'Obliquely. I'd thought of this: "What those neutral peoples not yet committed to the cause do not realize is the immense capacity of the ancient and mighty nations against whom Germany is warring to endure adversity, to put up with disappointment, to tolerate the mismanagement of their leaders, to renew their strength, to toil with boundless obstinacy through endless suffering, to the achievement of the greatest cause for which men have ever fought."'

'Bravo, Winston. You would have made a formidable advocate.'

'God forbid, you know very well what I think of the odious profession of lawyers.'

'You are very unkind about my colleagues, Winston, although I do recall one judge with whom I wrestled whose intellect was hardly on a par with that of a Cockney chambermaid. I had been trying for some time to outline a very subtle legal point, after which he said to me, "I've listened to you for an hour and I'm none the wiser." I replied, "None the wiser, perhaps, my lord, but certainly better informed."'

Winter Returns

Tuesday 16 November

Larkhill Camp, Durrington, Wiltshire

It has been a busy month for 11th Battalion East Lancs. It has completed its rifle-range training in Ripon, been to Hurdcott Camp on Salisbury Plain, where, in atrocious weather not unlike that on the Front itself, it has been engaged in defence-and-attack trench-warfare exercises, and it is now at Larkhill Camp for more rifle training.

The weather is still appalling and the camp facilities are far from finished. Fortunately for all concerned, the redoubtable Colonel Arthur Rickman is in his element. It is 7 p.m. and he still has his pack on his back, following an early-morning fifteen-mile route march from Hurdcott, a slog enlivened only by the close proximity of the beguiling sight of Stonehenge. None of the men had ever seen it before, and few had heard of it, so the ancient temple has occupied the conversation for the rest of the day.

Rickman's considerable energy and organizational skills have produced dinner for the men, coal for the stoves, beer for evening relaxation and beds for the night. He is a very popular colonel. Except, that is, with John-Tommy Crabtree and Tommy Broxup, who are still smarting from the field punishments they endured in September and the humiliating loss of their cricket trophy.

John-Tommy and Tommy have kept their heads down

since the incident, especially when any of the officers have been in the vicinity. They are carrying sacks of potatoes, bought by Rickman from a local farmer, from the lorries to the kitchen. Tommy sees Rickman coming and switches the sack he is carrying from one shoulder to the other, hoping that the colonel will not recognize him. But he is not quick enough.

'Broxup, isn't it?'

'Aye, sir.'

'Please say "yes", Broxup, not "aye".'

'Will do, sir. Sorry, sir.'

'Where's Crabtree?'

'Over theer, sir, carryin' a bag o' spuds.'

The colonel calls John-Tommy over. 'Crabtree, Captain Ross has been pleading your case to me. He tells me that you are quite a leader among the men and that, if I understood the viciousness of a northern pub brawl, I would not have been so harsh with you. What do you have to say?'

'Well, sir, it's very good o' Captain Ross, but we did wrong and wi got punished fer it. That's it, o'er an' done wi'.'

'Do you have nothing to say in your defence?'

'Well, sir, if I may?'

'Of course.'

'T'lad wot caused all t'bother would a done me a serious damage if ad let 'im. He were a big ugly bugger, an' intent on fettlin' us reet good an' proper. I 'ad t' 'it 'im wi' summat. But a took care to avoid his face an' neck, so caught him above t'ear, wheer I could only damage his thick skull. Tha knows wot thi say, sir: "Wheer th's no sense, th's no feelin'."'

'Yes, point taken. Captain Ross and Lieutenant Tough

tell me your behaviour is exemplary and your scores in all aspects of training are among the highest in the battalion, as are yours, Broxup.'

'Thank you, sir.'

'Are you going for supper and a beer when you've finished unloading?'

'Yes, sir, after a bit. Wi'v got carrots an' cabbages after this lot.'

'Good. Captain Ross made a very good point, which I've been thinking about. I was born in the Home Counties and went to school at a place called Winchester College, a school known more for its Latin grammar than for its brawling, so I know little of pub brawls. But I did see two farmers in a knife fight over a sheep in the Transvaal during the Boer War, so perhaps I get the gist of it. Captain Ross reminded me of the viciousness of trench warfare, which we've been in training for, and how your reaction in the bar is the kind of response we would expect of you in hand-to-hand fighting in battle. Very shrewd of him, and I don't want to send the wrong message to the rest of the battalion. So, I have a suggestion to make. Why don't we wipe the slate clean? I've contacted Brigade and had your field punishments removed from the records. We have a war to win, so let's close the book on the past.'

Rickman offers his hand to Tommy and John-Tommy.

'Very good of yer, sir. A clean slate is fine by us, innit, Tommy?'

'Aye, grand. Thank yer, sir.'

'Oh, and I've contacted the Hull Sportsmen's CO. They've agreed to share the trophy until a rematch can be arranged. It will be back with us for when we're posted overseas.'

Tommy and John-Tommy smile broadly. John-Tommy grabs Rickman's hand again. 'Thank you, sir. 'Ope thi keep t'bugger well polished.'

'By the way, I'll be telling the battalion in the morning. I've heard today that we're going overseas next month.'

'France, sir?'

'No, Egypt, so it might be Gallipoli.'

'That's grand, sir, a bit o' sunshine'll do us a power o' good.'

Rickman smiles wryly but decides not to shatter John-Tommy's naïve illusion.

When the two Pals finally complete the unloading of the vegetables it is dark, but there is still time for a well-earned beer. As they are about to enter the battalion canteen, they bump into Captain Ross and Lieutenant Tough.

'How are you, J-T, Tommy?' says Captain Ross.

'Very good, sir. Just off fer an ale.'

'So are we. Shame we can't do it together.'

'Aye, sir, but regs are regs. By the way, the colonel told us wot yer said to 'im abaht us. Very kind o' yer.'

'Not at all. He was perhaps a little harsh.'

'Anyway, 'e's wiped slate clean. It's off our record, an' t'trophy's comin' back t'battalion.'

'Excellent news.'

'He's a good lad, the old colonel, a reet good lad.'

'He is indeed.'

'He told us 'e went to a school wheer thi did Latin or summat; didn't do much feighten'.'

'No, he wouldn't, not at Winchester, it's one of England's best schools.'

'He also said he were in't Boer War.'

'He was, and highly decorated. He has six battle clasps to his South Africa medals. We're lucky to have him.'

'Aye, we are. He's definitely gone up in our estimation, in't that reet, Tommy?'

'Aye, a good man, that's fer sure.'

'Oh, an' he told us that we're off t'Egypt next month.'

'Yes, we heard today; exciting news.'

'It'll b' Gallipoli then?'

'Not necessarily. Johnny Turk is kicking up all over the Middle East. It could be Mesopotamia.'

'Wheer the hell is that?'

'A long way the other side of Egypt.'

'That's almost in India!'

'Almost. Enjoy your beer, lads.'

'Ta, an' you.'

Wednesday 17 November

Kephalo Bay, Imbros, Greece

Along with nine other sister ships, HMS *Grafton* is an Edgar Class cruiser. Built in 1890, she has a complement of 570 men and has been on bombardment duties in the Dardanelles since July. In August she was struck by a Turkish shell during the operations at Suvla Bay, when nine of her crew were killed. She is at anchor in Kephalo Bay, off the remote Greek island of Imbros, undergoing final snagging on her repairs before resuming duties off the Gallipoli coast.

Tom Crisp is *Grafton*'s new ship's carpenter, his predecessor having been invalided home to Wales. When it was discovered in early April that the damage to Tom's previous ship, HMS *Inflexible*, which she suffered off Cape Helles, would take several months to repair, he asked his skipper, Captain Richard Phillimore, for a transfer. His request was granted in August, and he joined *Grafton* in early October.

There is a collier tied up to the *Grafton*, loading coal into her bunkers, and Tom is organizing the dunnage to keep the coal from spilling all over the deck. Unlike the *Inflexible*, a much larger battlecruiser, on *Grafton* Tom has only one carpenter and one apprentice boy to work with. The small team makes for long days and hard work.

The coal will soon be stored away, so Tom knows it will not be long before they sail for the Dardanelles. Only too readily, he remembers witnessing the tragedy of the marine landings in February and the loss of his mentor Billy Cawson in March and has heard repeatedly the stories of the hell the troops have been going through since.

Understandably, like everyone else onboard, he is anxious. He looks up at the November sky. To the north, the horizon is pitch black, and there is already a sharp chill on the breeze. There have not yet been any winter storms, but the old salts onboard have told him what happens when the Turkish mainland gets cold: all hell breaks loose in the seas around its coast. All the talk below deck is about what will become of the troops in their narrow trenches and deep gullies when the weather breaks on Gallipoli. There is also a consensus about what should happen: everyone should go home before it gets any worse.

Thinking that *Grafton* may well sail the next day, Tom decides to take a boat to the Taverna Esperides in the harbour, a small, white-painted building hard against the harbour wall. Before the Allied ships arrived, the small bar and café served the tiny community of local fishermen. Now, it tries to cope with hundreds of British service personnel. Its turnover has increased twenty-fold, and its once-monthly shipment of food and drink from Salonika has become once daily.

To the east of the harbour are rows of wooden huts, almost all of them rapidly constructed hospital buildings which are acting as overflow accommodation to the larger facility in Mudros Bay on nearby Lemnos.

As he passes the window of the Esperides, he sees his

reflection in the glass and notices his beard, a growth that has been almost eight months in the making. He runs his fingers through it, thinking that perhaps he should shave it off: is it getting too long? He is, after all, about to depart on a new voyage and a new adventure.

He sits down and pours a bottle of Fix, Greece's staple beer, of which he has become quite fond. Sitting opposite him in the far corner is a group of Queen Alexandra's nurses, looking immaculate in their red-and-grey uniforms. They are making quite a lot of noise, celebrating the return to duty of the most senior among them. She has been ill with dysentery since August. After initial treatment on Lemnos, she has spent the last month getting her strength up on Imbros. Her ship, the *Essequibo*, now making its deliveries of cargoes of stricken men to Imbros, because all the field hospitals on Lemnos are full, is waiting in the harbour ready to return to Gallipoli for yet another consignment of pitiful men.

One of the nurses, another sister but younger than the others, is not joining in with the banter. She is leafing through a bloodstained notebook, something that has preoccupied her more and more since a dying officer gave it to her at the beginning of June. Lieutenant Allan Hudson, a young man from the Manchester Regiment, wanted her to write a final entry for him to his fiancée but died before he could utter the words. She has decided not to hand it to his battalion's adjutant but to deliver it to Hudson's fiancée in person after the war. It was, of course, a similar gesture that changed her own life over a year ago, when the woman who is now her mentor and lover pulled her out of the gutter in Tiger Bay.

460

She turns and looks out through the window of the Esperides, out across the picturesque Greek bay, which is glowing blood red in the setting sun. How different it is from the grey waters of Cardiff Docks and the industrial squalor of its grime-covered buildings. And how different is her life since those harrowing weeks spent alone in a nasty world of cheap drugs, squalid sex and pervasive menace.

She reads from the notebook every day. It is full of messages of love and longing from a lonely soldier. There are poetic passages, some humour, some sadness and not a little description of the horrors he saw and faced. There are amusing little sketches and drawings and sometimes sexual innuendos that arouse her and make her think of erotic episodes with the two men and one woman in her life.

She looks across at the woman, her saviour. She wants to kiss her and caress her, but she cannot. It would cause an outcry, not only among their highly conservative Greek hosts but also among her fellow nurses, for whom love between two women is taboo.

When the bearded man walks up to her she does not recognize him. He looks like most other bearded sailors in uniform. Then he speaks.

'Bron?'

His Shropshire Borders accent is unmistakable. Then she sees the bright-blue eyes and realizes who is standing before her. It is a ghost from the past she does not want to see. She is so mortified she cannot speak. Margaret Killingbeck, her friend and lover, who is sitting next to her, realizes something is wrong; so do the others at the table. The conversation stops.

461

'Bron, it's me, Tom.'

Bronwyn jumps up and pushes past the man who was once her fiancé, lover and childhood sweetheart. She bolts for the door, her starched uniform crackling as she runs. Margaret chases after her. She finally catches her but only after more than 50 yards. Bronwyn would have carried on running, but she has reached the end of the harbour wall; there is no dry land left. She tries to pull herself up the high wall, as if to throw herself over it and into the water.

'Bron! Stop! Please!'

'No, Margaret! Let me go! I can't face it.'

Margaret has worked out who Tom is. 'It's Tom from Presteigne, isn't it?'

'Yes, yes! The one I cheated on. We were happy; then . . . well, you know what happened.'

Bronwyn is hysterical, screaming. 'Oh God! Why has this happened now? You're better; we were about to go back to work. Now this! Why?'

Margaret puts her arms around her and tries to stop her frenzied shaking. 'Bron, so much has changed. Tom will understand, I'm sure.'

Bronwyn begins to take deep breaths and calms down a little. 'If you mean we're going to talk to him, then forget it. I can't!' She begins to look around for an escape route. 'I need to get away from here, Mags.'

'You can't run away. He's here. He must be on one of the Royal Navy ships. This is a tiny island.'

'I know, but we sail for the beaches tomorrow, and they're a long way away.'

'But is it fair to Tom?'

'I don't care. I can't hurt him any more than I already have. Come on, Mags; please get me on board the *Essequibo*. I'll feel better there.'

Tom Crisp stares out of the window of the Esperides as Margaret shepherds Bronwyn on to a small rowing boat and watches as one of the *Essequibo*'s crew rows them into the bay to where the ship is at anchor.

His head swirls with so many questions about what has happened to Bronwyn since that fateful day in August last year. He comes up with so many possible answers. He begins to cry.

One of the nurses who had been with Margaret and Bronwyn taps him on the shoulder. 'You obviously know Bronwyn.'

Tom wipes his eyes on his sleeves. 'Yes, Bronwyn Thomas. We're from the same village. Presteigne in Radnorshire.'

The nurse knows there is some tittle-tattle to be had, so probes further. 'She seemed shocked to see you.'

Tom realizes what the nurse's motives are, so is evasive. 'Well, it's been a while. What's the name of her ship?'

'The *Essequibo*.'

'Thanks.'

Friday 19 November

Convalescent Hospital No. 6, Alexandria, Egypt

The plan by Margherita, Lady Howard de Walden, for a convalescent hospital in Alexandria did not start well. When her husband, Tommy Scott-Ellis, 8th Lord Howard de Walden, Second-in-Command, Westminster Dragoons, was posted to Alexandria, she decided to respond to the desperate shortage of hospitals and nurses. Thanks to Tommy, one of Britain's richest men, she was able to rent Maison Karam, a very large and luxurious house outside the city owned by a Syrian merchant. She then sailed to London to hire a matron and eleven nurses and to buy all the supplies and resources they would need.

However, before she returned to Egypt she was summoned to see General Sir Alfred Keogh, Director General of Army Medical Services at the War Office. With Keogh was the formidable matron-in-chief of Queen Alexandra's Imperial Military Nursing Service, Emma McCarthy. Keogh refused Margherita permission to start a hospital, telling her that all necessary medical services were in hand and that he did not 'require or wish for any private enterprise in Egypt'.

Margherita ignored Keogh and set sail the next day.

Keogh then cabled ahead to General Sir John Maxwell, Commander of British forces in Egypt, insisting that

Margherita and her nurses be denied access to the country, which Maxwell duly did.

However, Sir Ronald Graham, a British diplomat in Cairo, sent a launch to take off Margherita and her nurses. He had arranged for Maison Karam not to be a hospital, for this was what Keogh had prescribed, but a convalescent home for those who had been operated on or were recovering from wounds.

When Kitty Stewart-Murray arrived in Alexandria at the beginning of November, she heard about Lady de Walden's venture and sought her out.

Now she is trying to make her contribution and being given her tasks for the coming weekend by Margherita at her daily staff briefing.

'Kitty, I'm afraid I have a rather unpleasant job for you. The dysentery lavatories and washrooms need disinfecting. There is a hose in there, and overalls and gumboots in the laundry. Good luck.'

'Thank you, Margherita. I've mucked out many a stable. I don't suppose it's all that different.'

Margherita then talks to the group. 'We've worked out the procedure for uniforms and pyjamas. We've got new blue-striped pyjamas, so when the men arrive their previous hospital clothes or uniforms will be removed, labelled and stored in the cellars. Then they put on our bright blue stripes, which everyone locally will recognize. This will stop them going off into the village for a drink, or for girls. If anyone serves or services them, the police have promised to fine them heavily.

'Last week, we had a big Irishman fall down the grand staircase. He was dead drunk, but we couldn't understand where he got the alcohol from. Then we found some red ink in a ginger-beer bottle that he'd been drinking. God only knows how, but it seemed to have worked – not that I would recommend it! So, be vigilant, ladies. And I want to hear immediately of any lurid advances, gestures or comments. This is a hospital, not a brothel!

'Our list at the moment includes New Zealand Maoris, white New Zealanders, Australians, all four British races, men from the Zionist Mule Corps and several sailors, and, as I'm sure you know, some of the Antipodeans and our own provincials can be a little too explicit with their vocabulary and a little too amorous with their intentions. Which reminds me: Nurse Phipps, a little less lipstick and cologne might help stop that brute of a Maori from putting his hand up your dress.

'The Mayor of Alexandria is coming this afternoon to talk about our absentee servants, so let's make a good impression.'

When the mayor arrives later that day, a huge man well over 30 stone in weight, he brings two dozen servants with him to add to the Maison's staff who have not run away. He then climbs halfway up Karam's grand staircase and proceeds to lecture them in Arabic for fifteen minutes. When he finishes he joins Margherita and Kitty for tea. Margherita fusses around him like a mother hen. 'Lemon in your tea, Mr Mayor?'

'Yes, please. But please call me Mustafa, Lady de Walden.'

'Only if you call me Margherita.'

A handsome woman of central European descent,

small, dainty, with long auburn locks tied neatly in a bun, Margherita charms her Egyptian host, who revels in being waited on by a western aristocrat.

'What did you say to the servants?' she asks.

'I told them that if any more of them went absent they would be given a severe beating, man, woman or child.'

The women are shocked. The mayor looks surprised. 'Surely you beat your servants if they are disobedient?'

'Not any more, Mustafa.'

He smiles. 'Don't worry. I won't need to do it, but they are like children: the warning will suffice.'

'Thank you, Mustafa. But if you do have to do any beatings, please do it elsewhere.'

'Of course. I would do it in the village square, so that everyone can see.'

Kitty and Margherita look at one another, not altogether certain how serious the mayor is being.

'By the way, I trained as a doctor as a young man,' he goes on, 'so I will come two afternoons a week to help. Which two would you like?'

'Oh, that's very kind. Monday and Thursday, please.'

'Very well. I shall be here at 2 p.m. every Monday and Thursday.'

Two days later Jack Churchill arrives at Maison Karam when the Royal Naval Division comes through Alexandria. He invites all of the nurses not on duty to join him in Cairo for a huge banquet given by Prince Hussein, Sultan of Egypt. Plucked by the British from the quiet life of an intellectual in Paris, the sultan has replaced the Ottoman sympathizer Khedive Abbas Hilmi, who has been banished to Constantinople.

With the sultana looking on, hidden from view but able to see the guests, the Egyptians, in evening dress, with a fez and tassel, mingle with the British elite, military and civilian. Four different European wines are served, with over a dozen food courses.

After the dinner, which, to the Europeans' dismay, includes smoked salmon, certain to induce the Cairo Quick-step, Kitty and Margherita are standing together when Professor Marc Ruffer, who is in charge of the Red Cross in Egypt, comes over to them.

'Lady de Walden, Lady Stewart-Murray, lovely to see you. May I congratulate you on the wonderful work you're doing.'

Margherita beams. 'Thank you, Professor Ruffer.'

'This is a bit overindulgent, is it not? Who are we trying to impress? Aren't we all on the same side?'

Kitty rushes to the defence of the extravagance. 'I rather think it's a show of unity.'

'Perhaps, but I'd prefer to pack up whatever's in the kitchens and on the tables – except the smoked fish, of course – and distribute it around the military hospitals in Egypt.'

Margherita is more sympathetic to the professor's point. 'What a good idea. Kitty, when we leave, let's get the nurses together and, like locusts, we'll strip the place bare.'

Margherita, a trained opera singer, is then asked to sing by the sultan. Taken by surprise, she is not sure what to sing, so chooses '*Un bel di vedremo*' from Puccini's *Madame*

Butterfly. She sings it so beautifully, producing so much power from her small frame, that when she is finished there are several people in the room in tears.

Later, Margherita, Kitty and the nurses enlist Jack Churchill to help them collect food. They travel back to their hotel, Shepheard's, the most famous and luxurious in Egypt and British Headquarters Near East, by donkey, and have several nightcaps. It is a beautiful night and, from the hotel's top-floor terrace, they can see in the distance the desert glowing in the moonlight like a becalmed sea.

As they relax, Kitty cannot resist quizzing Jack about his brother. 'How is Winston taking his fall from grace?'

'With typical stoicism and optimism.' Jack knows that his answer is a little economical with the truth but does not want to feed any gossip.

'What will he do?'

'Go to the Front and fight; that's what he's good at. What about Bardie? Have you heard anything?'

'He says it's very testing. He wasn't allowed to take his horses, so it's an infantry war for him. You haven't bumped into him?'

'No, Kitty, sorry. But I will try to.'

'Oh, please do, Jack. He'll be so delighted to see you.'

'I'll make it a priority when I go back.'

'Which is when?'

'Tomorrow evening.'

'What's going to happen? I'm worried for Bardie.'

'I think the game's up. Everyone knows it. The Turks have us in a bind: there's no way forward, and we can't hold our ground over a Gallipoli winter. Believe it or not, it snows and the temperature plummets. It will be unbearable . . . Well, what I mean is it's unbearable now, but it will get worse.'

'How long?'

'Kitchener is there now, which is why I'm here, to look at where we might put 100,000 men. The old warrior could not believe what he saw when he arrived. He said the ground was far more difficult than he imagined, and that the taking of it, and particularly holding it, was remarkable. He got an amazing reception from the men, like Achilles, the bravest of the brave. If only they knew.'

'I thought he was a hero?'

'He was, but not a general and certainly not from a desk at the War Office.'

'It sounds like we should never have gone in the first place.'

'Correct, which is why Winston was right. We should have forced the Straits first then sent in the army, but more of them. We underestimated the Turks – perhaps our biggest mistake – and we had not the admirals nor the generals to grasp a victory when it was there before us, within touching distance.'

'Will we lose many men if we evacuate?'

'I pray not, Kitty. But we will have to do it by stealth, like a fox slinking away in the night.'

'What an embarrassment, running away with our tail between our legs.'

'Indeed, Kitty. I doubt we British will ever be the same again.'

'I think that's true. Perhaps Winston can give us back our pride?'

'I think he can, but not yet. Not until this war is over.'

Jack stares across at Margherita, who is drinking with the nurses. 'Didn't she sing beautifully tonight?'

'She did, she's a wonderful person.'

'Talking of wonders, that Nurse Phipps is a pretty little creature.'

'She is. On that note, off to your bed, Jack Churchill. You've got to get back to Gallipoli and get my Bardie off safely. Give him my love when you see him.'

'I will. I don't suppose Phipps is available to tuck me in?'

'Go on, off with you! You've been away from Goonie for too long.'

Kitty watches Jack go up to his room before turning to stare at Nurse Phipps, the raven-haired beauty who is the talk of every officers' mess in Alexandria. What will become of the young woman, who only three months ago was sitting in a vicarage in Worcestershire thinking of marriage to a local farmer, with its attendant children, cakes, tea and the Women's Institute. Now she can pick from any man in England – or a Middle Eastern potentate. Kitty's mind drifts off to thoughts of George Grey, the lover she may never see again. This war is changing everything and everyone.

Jack leaves for Gallipoli the next day. The following week a committee is formed in Alexandria to discuss what to do about nurses' recreation time. It has been noticed that the several dozen nurses in the area have nothing to do when they are off duty and have been seen in bars which are 'less than salubrious', and even on street corners, talking to their soldier friends.

471

Margherita has asked Kitty to come up with a solution. She is in the midst of presenting her idea to the impromptu gathering of generals, diplomats and female British residents. 'Ladies and gentlemen,' she says, 'a nurses' club is the answer. We have found premises. It is an old bank with a very nice balcony for the evenings. There is room for both a cafeteria and a bar, and even a place for a small band and a little dancing.'

A rather portly figure, Miss Daphne Hope-Cullingham, QAIMNS Matron-in-Chief for Egypt, whose rounded form sits rather tightly in her gull-grey uniform, makes a comment, with no small amount of displeasure. 'Are you suggesting, Lady Stewart-Murray, that these "activities" – drinking, dancing and tête-à-têtes with young officers – take place in the evenings? Surely, like young ladies' institutions in England, it should not be open after 6 p.m. and not at all on Sundays.'

Kitty rises to the challenge. 'Well, Matron, as most of the girls are working during the day, it is the evenings when they need to relax. But is it your experience that the male of the species is at its most predatory after dark, and particularly on the Sabbath?'

The matron, very indignant and a little embarrassed, responds immediately. 'Of course. Is it not your experience?'

'Yes, it is. Nevertheless, I do think it best for our girls to meet the beasts on their own ground as equals. After all, the female of the species can be quite ferocious, either in the glare of daylight or in the shadows of the night.'

All the men in the room smile knowingly, as do several

472

of the women. Ten minutes later Kitty's proposal for the Alexandria Nurses' Club is agreed, and Mayor Mustafa offers to pay for the building's refurbishment and its fitting out. In the months that follow it becomes the city's most popular watering hole.

Sunday 21 November

Guards Division HQ, La Gorgue,
Nord-Pas-de-Calais, France

It was a tearful departure for Winston Churchill at his brother's home on the Cromwell Road in London on Tuesday last when he gave a farewell lunch for his family and friends. It was a bitter-sweet occasion. Some were happy that he would at last have the chance to be the warrior he so craves to be. Others were sad that it might have marked the passing of a dazzling political career, uncannily like the end of his father's glittering career in 1886.

Besides Winston's and Goonie's families, Margot Asquith was there, as were Clemmie's sister, Nellie Hozier, and good friend Violet Bonham Carter. Lady Randolph, Winston's mother, was also there but spent most of the time upstairs in paroxysms of tears. Eddie Marsh was also in tears, inconsolable at the loss of his mentor.

Violet Bonham Carter recalled the gathering later: 'Winston alone was at his gayest and his best, and he and Margot held the table between them.'

The next day Clemmie got a letter from James Masterton-Smith, Winston's naval secretary at the Admiralty for his entire time in office.

It is half past ten and the shutters of the old familiar private office are going up . . . To those of us who know and understand, Winston is the greatest First Lord this old Admiralty has ever had – or is likely to have. With those of us who shared his life here, he has left an inspiring memory of high courage and tireless industry, and he carries with him to Flanders all that we have to give him – our good wishes.

Winston crossed to France the following day. When he arrived in Boulogne he was met by a car, sent for him by the commander-in-chief himself, Sir John French. He used it to travel to see his friends at the regimental head-quarters of his old regiment, the Oxfordshire Hussars at Bléquin. That night he had dinner with French, who was very kind to him and offered him either a role on his staff as an ADC, or the command of a brigade. Winston chose a brigade but asked if he could first gain experience of the trenches with the Guards Division.

On the 18th he heard that Lord Cavan, Commander of the Guards Division, has agreed to take him on.

Winston wrote to Clemmie immediately. He was in his element.

18 November, St Omer

Hot baths, decent beds, champagne and all the conveniences. I am sure I am going to be entirely happy out here and at peace. I must try to win my way as a good and sincere soldier.

He also wrote to his brother, Jack, in the Dardanelles: 'I am extremely happy and have regained a peace of mind to which I have long been a stranger.'

He is now at the HQ of the Guards Division at La Gorgue, 12 miles east of St Omer. He writes to Clemmie at midnight after an evening with the elite regiments of the British infantry.

I went this afternoon to see my regiment. They were very caressing and highly approved of my course of action and thought it very right and proper. Altogether, I see that the army is willing to receive me back as 'the prodigal son'. I am very happy here. I did not know what release from care meant. It is a blessed peace. How I ever wasted so many months in impotent misery, which might have been spent in war, I cannot tell.

Winston is attached to 2nd Battalion Grenadier Guards, a battalion with a pedigree that includes service to his ancestor the Duke of Marlborough, who was an ensign in the Guards and later its Colonel. It has fought in all the Great War battles since August last year but has suffered appalling losses. In the 1st Battle of Ypres it lost all but four officers and 140 men from a strength of over 600.

Second Battalion is due to go into the line at Neuve Chapelle that afternoon, and Winston goes with them. As he strides across the desolate landscape, with the constant rumble of artillery in the distance, his host, Lieutenant Colonel George Jeffreys, says nothing for over an hour. Eventually, he reveals the reason for his silence.

'I think I ought to tell you that we were not at all consulted in the matter of you coming to join us.'

Winston, embarrassed, responds sheepishly. 'I'm afraid I wasn't told which battalion I would be joining either, but I'm sure we can make the best of it.'

Another silence ensues until the battalion adjutant, Lieutenant Wilfrid Bailey, clearly annoyed at how many personal items Winston has brought to the Front, speaks.

'I'm afraid we've had to cut down your kit rather. There are no communications trenches here, so everything has to be carried over open ground. The men have little more than they stand up in. We have found a servant for you, a good man, who is carrying a spare pair of socks and your shaving gear. We have had to leave the rest behind, which includes the four cases of alcohol.'

There is an exchange of glances between the six staff officers who are escorting Winston, who now realizes that his arrival has not been greeted with much enthusiasm.

'I quite understand, Lieutenant,' he says. 'I'm sure I'll be very comfortable, and there is always the rum ration to keep away the chill. Please send the cases back to Division HQ and ask that they be put behind the mess bar for the convenience of the members.'

Winston's sleeping quarters is a derelict farm, christened Ebenezer Farm, 800 yards from the front line, just north of the ruined village of Neuve Chapelle. He chooses to sleep in the signals office, an eight-foot-square room that is occupied all night by a signaller sending Morse messages and the body of a Grenadier shot by a sniper earlier in the day.

The next day he is in a front-line trench for the first time. He writes to Clemmie once more.

My Darling Cat,

Everyone is continuing to be kind, and I think I'm overcoming the 'bloody politician' tag. Our trenches have been left in a mess by the previous occupants, but the Grenadiers, with their usual efficiency and discipline, are making progress in rendering them both habitable and defendable. Colonel Jeffreys is very severe with me and clearly thinks I'm a burden, but I'm sticking with him because there's no doubt he's a fine soldier, one of the army's best, and his knowledge of trench warfare is profound.

> *Please send the following with all speed to GHQ in St Omer:*
> *2 bottles Hine (My original shipment has been thought too bulky!)*
> *Sardines*
> *Chocolate*
> *Potted meats*
> *Three small face towels*
> *1 pr brown leather boots (Fortnum and Mason) – laces to the top*
> *2 pr khaki trousers*
> *Kisses to you and the Kittens,*

W
PS Your little pillow is a boon and a pet.

Winston's next letter paints a vivid picture of life in the trenches, even in a relatively quiet sector.

Darling,

I am with Eddie Grigg (you know, writer for The Times*). He is CO No. 1 Company 2nd Battalion, and I am in his dugout.*

Fritz is snoring 130 yards away (we measured it fairly accurately this afternoon). We have whisky, which is allowed against the cold. The night is clear and sharp, but we are still fighting the squalor left by lazy soldiers and their officers, who should be demoted to the ranks for their indolence. Filth and rubbish everywhere. Graves built into the defences, and bodies scattered about, feet and clothing breaking through the soil. Troops of enormous bats creep and glide about the scene to the unceasing accompaniment of rifle and machine-gun fire and the venomous whining and whirring of the bullets which pass overhead.

But amid this scene, and despite the cold and wet, I have found happiness and contentment such as I have not known for months. No newspapers, no political backbiting, no envy; just honest men defending their country and their loved ones.

I love you,
Pug

His life at a crossroads, on 30 November Winston spends his forty-first birthday in the trenches, sleeping in a dug-out only two feet six inches high. But he is happy. Colonel Jeffreys, who he seems to have won over, advises him to take a battalion rather than a brigade.

'If you take a brigade, you'll be out of touch with the fighting and, having watched you this week, I know you'll prefer to be in the thick of it. Take a battalion, where you can lead from the front.'

That evening news arrives that the decision has been taken to withdraw from the Dardanelles. Winston feels that the news might bring the opportunity for revenge. He writes to Clemmie:

My conviction that the greatest of my work is yet to come is still within me. I expect it will be my duty in the early months of next year – if I am all right – to stand up in my place in Parliament and endeavour to procure the dismissal of Asquith and Kitchener. I feel a great assurance of my powers . . . nothing can assail me.

But politics is still cruel to Winston. Asquith, aware that he will be asked a question in the Commons about Winston's credentials to take a command, writes to Sir John French, vetoing a brigade for him and suggesting only a battalion. But Winston is not too disappointed. He knows Colonel Jeffreys is right: he will relish the challenge of being an active soldier as a colonel much more than becoming a sedentary tactician as a brigadier.

PART TWELVE: DECEMBER

Evacuation

Wednesday 8 December

Dickebusch, West Flanders, Belgium

Fourth Battalion Royal Fusiliers has had a quiet winter and is now supporting the Royal Engineers in digging and repairing trenches near Ypres. It is backbreaking work, especially in the heavy rain that seems to fall every day.

The entire Front in the sector around the Ypres Salient has become a warren of interconnected trenches and saps. From the air, in the cockpits of the new reconnaissance aircraft now being used by both Allied and German strategists, the ground looks like a jigsaw puzzle but pock-marked with bomb craters like the surface of the moon.

The second winter of the Great War has taken a firm hold. Little vegetation survived the first year, but now a huge meandering snake of barren ground from the Belgian coast, across Flanders, into France and all the way to Switzerland is a desert of mud, mottled by a detritus of machines, refuse and bodies. It is a pitiless void infested by men in their setts and burrows, but also by ravenous rats, creeping bats, feral cats and wild dogs. The only remedy for the human scavengers is to eat the pests, not only because it reduces competition in the food chain but also because, with nourishment scarce, vermin are a vital source of protein.

No one who sees it for the first time can believe that

civilized men can live and die in such an abhorrent mess. Surely warring droves of swine would find a more wholesome place in which to slaughter one another?

All the ills of winter are returning: trench foot, trench fever, typhoid, pneumonia, influenza, as well as the ever-present venereal disease and shell shock. Perversely, perhaps the most soul-destroying phenomenon of the onset of winter in 1915 is the lethargy of boredom. After the intensity of the last few months of 1914, when men had little time to reflect on anything other than staying alive, 1915 has been a year of tedious static warfare, when men have had too much time to contemplate the awfulness of their predicament. Levels of morale have been plummeting, made worse because decades of regimental tradition and discipline have been difficult to maintain when most of the veterans who embody them have been killed.

Wednesday 8 December is a day of triple celebration for the 4th Fusiliers. After much toil as temporary sappers, it is their first day of rest in billets at Dickebusch, three miles south-west of Ypres. Secondly, at roll call, they are addressed by their new commanding officer, Major George Ottley, formerly of the King's Own Yorkshire Light Infantry. Ottley, who gives a rousing speech, has risen from being a lieutenant at the beginning of the war to be a major and brevet colonel, the commanding officer of a battalion. It is a record that appeals to battle-hardened soldiers.

The men take to him straight away, especially when he tells them that he will be sleeping in the forward trenches whenever the battalion is in the line. At the end of his speech he introduces the third reason for celebration: the return from a long recuperation in hospital in Boulogne of two of the battalion's most famous sons.

'Gentlemen, please join me in welcoming two men who epitomize what the Fusiliers are all about. They are both highly decorated; they are both veterans of the Boer War and India; and both are survivors since the first landings of the BEF last year – and there are not many of those around.'

There is a huge round of applause and loud cheers.

'I believe one of them is nicknamed the Leyton Lash, the other Modest Mo. The second name I understand; the first one I need to do some research on.'

There is a voice from the back of the ranks. 'Ol' 'Arry likes his beer cold an' his women warm, sir!'

'Don't we all!' is Ottley's quick riposte, which only adds to the men's liking of him. 'Now, I have to tell you that both had tickets home, having received severe wounds, one at Hooge in July, the other at Bellewarde Ridge in June, but they declined the chance to return to Blighty, preferring to stay with us. That speaks volumes for them, and also for the battalion and the regiment.'

'More fools them!' is the light-hearted cry from several men.

'Needless to say, they have both spent the last five months chasing the nurses, drinking the beer and enjoying the sea air in Boulogne.'

More cheers, and various bawdy comments follow, including one that suggests that half the nurses in Boulogne are pregnant and another that half the French women of Boulogne are also pregnant.

'Gentlemen, I give you Company Serjeant Majors Harry Woodruff and Maurice Tait.'

Harry and Maurice march in smartly, although Maurice has a noticeable limp, and salute Major Ottley before they are swamped by the men. They look immaculate in their clean and pressed uniforms, their polished boots and chestful of medals gleaming brightly.

That night they are the centre of attention at the Maison de Ville in Poperinghe. There is no shortage of beer bought for them to drink and no shortage of well-wishers. One of them, a young serjeant who has just arrived from London with a reserve battalion of the Middlesex, is curious about their decision to stay.

'So, you two boys got some sort o' scam goin' or wot? Fags, booze, girls?'

Harry takes an instant dislike to him. 'Where are you from?'

'Fulham.'

'Some kinda Fulham wide-boy, are yer?'

'Might be. Aren't we all? Reckon you've got something goin' or you'd be in Blighty by now.'

'What's yer name, son?'

'Dave. Dave Woods. I know a few fellas in West London who might be interested in gettin' involved as suppliers if yer interested.'

'Listen, Dave. I do 'ave a proposition for yer.'

'I'm all ears.'

'Fuck off and leave us alone. We've got beer to drink.'

Young Dave, not used to being insulted, is livid, but scrutinizes Harry carefully. He then looks at those around them, who are now watching the exchange in silence.

Harry's eyes are unblinking but carry a menace Dave has seen before in men who do not have to prove their worth. He decides that discretion is the better part of valour, pushes through the throng and walks off, muttering to himself. Maurice smiles at Harry, who is shaking his head.

'Bloody cheek, Mo. Do we look like dodgy types?'

'Must do . . . Well, you do.'

Later that evening, when most of the men welcoming them back have gone, Harry and Maurice, now made sombre by a bucketful of Belgian beer, reflect on their decision to return to their battalion.

'S'pose what we did was a bit doolally, Mo?'

'Yeh, but what would we do in Blighty?'

'Open those pubs we always talked about.'

'But we'd 'ave to find a missus fer that, and I'm not ready to settle down yet. Mebbe after the war.'

'Fuck me; we'll be dead by then.'

'Then it won't make any odds, will it?'

'S'pose not. D'ya reckon there'll be a truce an' a kick-around wiv Fritz again this Christmas?'

'Dunno. If there is, we need to beat 'em this time.'

'Well, we can't beat 'em wiv a rifle an' bayonet – perhaps football's our best chance.'

'Perhaps we could settle the whole ruck wiv a game of football. Then we could all fuck off home.'

'That'd be too easy. We wouldn't need generals fer that, an' they'd all be out of a job.'

'That's why it won't 'appen.'

'You heard those rumours that 60,000 Frenchies 'ave broken through in the south?'

'Oh yer, like the one that the Ruskies 'ave surrounded Berlin and are holdin' the Kaiser hostage!'

'It's all bollocks. An' what about Gallipoli? The word is that we're pullin' out.'

'I 'ope that one's kosher. We could do wiv those boys over 'ere.'

'So, three days in billets, then back to diggin' for the bloody sappers.'

'That's all right – better than bein' picked off by Fritz like sitting ducks!'

Friday 10 December

St Eloi, West Flanders, Belgium

Jack Norton-Griffiths' latest tunnelling innovation involves the power of huge machines rather than the human toil of his clay-kickers. He is at St Eloi, the base for the major tunnelling operations south of Ypres, with Lieutenant Horace Hickling and several of the COs from the army's tunnelling companies.

'The big blow of Messines Ridge is on. Horace and I met with Haig and his staff at the beginning of the week and presented our "4-Bomb Big Bang" plan. They said no; but yesterday I got a call saying yes. The word is that the really big push that everyone is waiting for is on for June or July, and they've finally worked out that the big concrete emplacements the Germans have built on the Ridge are an obstacle that neither the infantry nor the artillery can handle. So we dig.'

One of the engineers puts up his hand. 'How far?'

'Sixteen hundred yards.'

'Bloody hell.'

'Exactly. That's why we need these.'

Norton-Griffiths gets out an engineering drawing and spreads it across the table.

'It's a Stanley Heading Machine, made in Nuneaton. They use them for cutting the Underground in London.

One is on its way as I speak. Captain Cropper, I want you to try it. Your objective is Wytschaete village. The shaft and tunnels, SP13 at Petit Bois, that Horace's men, Serjeant Kenny and his crew, have been working on will be ideal.'

Cecil Cropper, a dour Northumberland mining engineer, does not like taking orders, or working in a team. 'If it's Hickling's hole, then he can look after the machine.'

'Cecil, Horace is a brilliant tunneller; you're a mechanical engineer. I want you to work together.'

'Will the beast cope with the thick blue clay here?'

'The manufacturers are modifying the cutters, but they say yes, and it will cut a tunnel six feet in diameter at a pace of two feet per hour.'

'But the Germans will hear the bugger.'

'Well, let's wait and see.'

Norton-Griffiths then leads the way to the top of the shaft, where the Burnley moles are working. There are half a dozen men at the top, waiting to relieve Mick Kenny and his crew. 'When is Serjeant Kenny due up?' he asks.

'Sixteen hundred hours, sir.'

He looks at his watch. 'Five minutes ago. Typical. Mick always wants to do an extra yard.'

There is a moment's silence as the gathering listens for the sound of the winding gear coming to life. However, instead of a mechanical clank and grinding, there comes the sound of a small explosion followed by an ominous rumble. 'It's a camouflet! Get them out now!'

Norton-Griffiths turns to Hickling. 'They're new. The Germans have been using them for a couple of weeks. If they hear us, they bore towards the sound with an auger, six to eight inches or so, put a pipe bomb down the hole and *bang*!'

Everyone looks towards the shaft. The relief moles have gone down to see what has happened. All goes quiet for a while, so Norton-Griffiths scampers down on the ladders. When he reaches the bottom, he witnesses a terrible scene.

Amidst the stench of the explosive charge and pools of runny clay made liquid by the explosion, the relief crew has leaned two crumpled bodies against the shaft wall. One is just about recognizable, his features visible beneath a covering of thick clay. The other has no face. Where it was, a craterous lump of bloodied clay sits in his skull.

'He took the brunt of it, sir. They're both dead.'

'The others?'

'Sagar's back there. He's breathing, but he's got a lungful of mud and I think he may have lost an eye.'

'Serjeant Kenny and Sapper Haythornthwaite?'

'Don't know, sir. They must have been on the other side of the blast. They're digging now.'

'I'm going up.'

'Don't, sir. Wait here – you'll be in the way up there.'

Norton-Griffiths knows he is right, so sits and waits. Despite his passion for clay-kicking, he is not a clay-kicker himself and not enamoured of confined spaces. His fascination is geology and the engineering and skills to conquer its challenges. He looks at his claustrophobic, cold and wet surroundings and quakes. For his men, where he now sits is only the beginning of a subterranean world that stretches for hundreds of yards into even smaller nooks and crannies. His tremors turn to real anxiety, and he glances upwards to see the light 60 feet above. But it is no longer there; darkness has fallen. The serjeant of the relief crew notices his all-too-obvious unease.

'You alreet, sir?'

'I will be when we're out of this little hole. What's your name, Serjeant?'

'Postlethwaite, sir.'

'Do you have a brother?'

'Did, sir. He were a tunneller, copped it back in June.'

'I'm sorry to hear that. There's a Haythornthwaite down there.'

'I know. Nearly as daft a name as Postlethwaite.'

The two men stare at one another for what seems like an eternity.

'If you don't mind me askin', sir; you're CO Tunnelling, but you don't reckon t'bein' in one?'

'I used to dig tunnels for a living. I'm an engineer. Now I build them to help us win this war.'

'I don't like 'em either; never have. But wheer I come frae, tha goes down t'pit whether tha likes it or not.'

'How do you cope?'

'When I'm down an' a get a bit freet, I ollus imagine am crawling around in t'long grass in t'hay meadows, like when I wer a little lad. Sky's blue an' sun's shinin'. That sorts me.'

'Your accent sounds like you're from the same part of the world as Mick and his men.'

'Nay, sir! Miles away; they're Lankies. I'm frae Barnsley; different world. Sun ollus shines i'Barnsley; it's ollus rainin' i'Burnley.'

Norton-Griffiths smiles to himself as he tries to decipher

the difference between two northern accents, which, to him, sound identical. Another long silence follows.

It is finally broken by the sound of men dragging themselves along the tunnel.

After a few minutes their exhausted, mud-splattered faces appear. One man has a rope in his hands, and pulls on it with all his might. Another shouts out as he approaches: 'Got 'em both on this dolly!'

Norton-Griffiths questions the man with the rope anxiously. 'Do you need the Novita?'

'Yes, oxygen for one of them. He's breathing, just, but he needs help. They survived the blast, but the roof buried them.'

'Serjeant Kenny and Sapper Haythornthwaite?'

'Yes, sir. Kenny's dead.'

'Dreadful way to go.'

'Nothing worse. Married man, sir?'

'Yes. Serjeant Kenny told me his wife's out here driving an ambulance.'

'Better make sure we don't put him in hers then.'

'Good point. Let's get them up top.'

'He was a brave man, sir, and very strong. When we found them, Kenny was on his hands and knees, with Haythornthwaite underneath him. He must have been trying to protect him. I don't know how he held all that weight. Anyway, there was clear air between him and the man under him. Then he must have run out of air, but he still held his position. He saved Haythornthwaite's life – bloody amazing.'

Twaites is concussed by the blast but is alive. He is taken away to a waiting ambulance.

Vinny Sagar has lost an eye and his lungs are damaged by the blast. He is taken to a dressing station, where a surgeon operates on his broken eye socket. But it is his breathing that is causing the greatest concern. He is not getting enough oxygen and is unable to gather enough breath to speak. He begins to panic. 'Nurse! Morphine, please.'

The morphine has the desired effect and Vinny begins to relax.

Norton-Griffiths appears and asks the doctor on duty how he is doing.

'Fifty-fifty, Major; no better than that. The biggest issue is infection in the lungs before they can get rid of all that blast material.'

'We had a couple of fatalities today in the same incident. One of them has a wife out here, driving an ambulance – FANY or VAD.'

'Name?'

'Cath Kenny.'

'Bloody hell! Feisty sort, she is. Lancastrian. Calls a spade a fucking shovel!'

'That'll be her. Mick was a hard-case; ex-miner, tough as old boots.'

'Not any more. Now he's just fertilizer for the farmers of Flanders.'

'He was a good man, Doc. Show some respect.'

'Sorry, Major, but we don't see them as men, can't afford to; we'd go doolally.'

'How do I find Mrs Kenny?'

'She does the Ypres–Pop route. Mainly to Pop-Hop. The big military hospital in the old lace mill. Ask for Noel Chavasse; he'll know where to find her.'

'Thanks, Doc. Do what you can for Haythornthwaite; he's another good lad.'

'They're all good lads, Major. That's the tragedy of it all.'

Vincent Anthony Sagar, fine amateur cricketer and foot-baller, who once came close to playing for his beloved Burnley Football Club, dies in the middle of the night. His lungs cannot cope with the damage caused by the blast. The morphine he has been given means that he is not too conscious of his predicament but, just before he dies, he wakes up. He looks around; all he can see with his one functioning eye is the light of sporadic oil lamps and row upon row of stretchers, each with a man lying on it covered by a blanket and a sheet. There is a nurse in the distance with a torch, checking the patients one by one, but she is too far away for him to attract her attention.

He hopes to see Mick and Twaites; he does not know that Mick is dead. He wonders how Tommy and John-Tommy are and what has become of Cath and Mary. Then his chest tightens and he finds it harder and harder to get his breath. He raises his hand as high as he can, appealing for help, but none comes. His hand falls back to the stretcher and his life slips away. Today is his nineteenth birthday. He had planned to celebrate it with Mick and Twaites after their shift. Twaites had asked their favourite café in nearby Vormezele to bake Vinny a cake. It sits on the bar waiting for them.

Sunday 12 December

Cath Kenny and Mary Broxup are drinking in Poperinghe. It is their day off. They have had lunch, during which they consumed a carafe of wine. They have now returned to the beer they were drinking before their food arrived. Cath is now five months pregnant and is beginning to show.

Cath's tears usually accompany their discussions about Morgan Thomas's baby. Today is no different.

'Sometimes, our Mary, I feel like drinkin' a bottle of gin an' gettin' shut of this little lad, but a lost one afore, an' am not losin' another.'

'Then tha' marsant, Cath.'

'But what abaht Mick? He puts up wi' me, but it's a lot to ask on 'im to accept another lad's babby.'

'Tha'll 'ave to tell 'im sooner o' later. Perhaps wi should see if we can find 'im?'

'Aye, perhaps we should – next week? When's our day off?'

'Friday.'

'Reet, Friday it is.'

The two women have not noticed Major Jack Norton-Griffiths stride into the Maison de Ville. He speaks to the barman, who points him towards Cath and Mary.

'Good afternoon, ladies. Jack Norton-Griffiths, Royal Engineers.'

Cath stiffens. She remembers the name of the man Mick told her was called Hell-fire Jack. She also remembers Mick's description of a tall, imposing man with a full moustache and a deep, gravelly voice.

'I'm looking for Cath Kenny, the wife of Serjeant Mick Kenny.'

Mary looks on anxiously. Cath tries to stay strong.

'That's me, lad. Sit tha'sen down. So Mick made Serjeant – don't know 'ow t'big lummox managed that.'

'By being a fine soldier.'

Norton-Griffiths sits down. As he does so, three large brandies, which he ordered when he spoke to the barman, are brought to the table. Cath stares at the amber liquid as it laps gently in her glass. Her eyes fill with tears. Mary grabs her shoulders as they start to heave.

'S'pose you've come t' tell 'e's now a dead soldier?'

'I'm afraid so, Mrs Kenny.'

'How?'

'In a tunnelling incident at St Eloi, south of Ypres.'

'What sort of incident?'

'He was underground, digging a tunnel towards the Messines Ridge. The Germans must have heard them. They fired a camouflet – a pipe bomb. It killed some of Mick's team outright, but he was buried. Unfortunately, when we got to him, he had died.'

'Jesus Christ, that's what he always feared most, being buried alive.'

Mary interrupts. 'What about Vinny Sagar an' Nat Haythornthwaite – we call him Twaites?'

'Twaites survived, thanks to Mick, who shielded him with his body in an extraordinary act of strength and courage. We got Vinny out, but he died that night in a field hospital. You should be very proud of them.'

Cath is trying to compose herself. 'Aye, wi are. Wheer are they?'

'In a new military cemetery just behind St Eloi.'

'Reet, Mary, we'll go in t'mornin'.'

'But we're on duty, Cath.'

'Not any more. I'm goin' to see me 'usband's grave.' Anger begins to rise in her voice. 'Then I'm goin' back to St Omer to hand in t'keys o' t'ambulance. Then am goin' home.'

'T'Burnley?'

'No, t'London. I'm goin' t'see Henry Hyndman.'

'Whatever fer?'

Cath begins to shout at the top of her voice. 'Ave 'ad enough! Should never o' come in t'first place. Drivin' ambulances fer them toff lasses who look down their noses at us – we must be bloody barmy. Now Mick's dead, buried alive in a fuckin' tunnel! I almost got raped by a drunken soldier, an' they shot Morgan in the back cos he was tryin' to deliver a message! I'm joinin' t'anti-war lot. Henry will know how to find 'em. I'm gonna speak up abaht wot's goin' on out 'ere!'

Cath turns to Jack, who looks shocked by Cath's outburst and, for a change, is lost for words. 'I hear thi call thi Hell-fire Jack?'

'Apparently so.'

'Well, it's *apparent* to me that thi should be buyin' us another brandy – an' mek it a double.'

*

Two hours later Norton-Griffiths helps Mary put a very drunk Cath to bed in their one-room apartment in Poperinghe.

'Cath is a formidable woman,' he says.

'She is that.'

'Do you know how to get to St Eloi?'

'No, but we'll find it. Thank you fer comin' in person to tell us abaht Mick and t'lads.'

'Not at all, the least I could do. Mick, Vinny and Twaites are a credit to you and Burnley, the kind of men who are going to win this war.'

'Do you think it can still be won?'

'Yes, don't you?'

'I'm not sure — Cath may be reet. Is it reet that we should be feighten' in t'first place?'

'I leave that to the politicians, Mary.'

'Aye, trouble is, Cath's a politician. I don't think she's sure yet, but I think she's beginning to realize it.'

'Well, I wish you and her all the best. If you or Cath ever need anything, you can contact me via Royal Engineers HQ in St Omer, or at the tunnelling companies recruitment office, Central Buildings, Westminster.'

The next day Mary and a very hungover Cath drive to St Eloi to visit Twaites and see the graves of their menfolk. Twaites is sedated but recovering well from his ordeal. Mercifully, he has no recollection of the explosion and has not been told of the deaths of his friends. Mary and Cath decide not to wake him and add more woe to his predicament. St Eloi's cemetery is a small patch of levelled, open ground in a desolate landscape ravaged by war. The nearby hamlet of St Eloi is just a pile of ruined cottages. The graveyard is no more than three lines of small mounds of earth, perhaps three dozen graves in all, each topped by a simple wooden cross.

The two Burnley names are not difficult to find. The black paint forming the lettering on their whitewashed crosses is the most recent. The paint is still tacky as Cath touches her husband's name: 'Serjeant Michael Kenny, 172nd Tunnelling Company'. She is sitting on the ground, talking quietly to Mick, as if he were sitting next to her in the pub. She is explaining to him in a very measured and earnest way why she got involved with Morgan and why she is sorry to have let him down. She does not spare him anything and explains that she is pregnant. Then she stops, her anguish preventing her from saying any more.

Mary, trying not to listen, is laying flowers on the mound belonging to Vinny. It is raining hard and the air is cold, so the rain begins to turn to a harsh sleet, but Cath is so distressed she does not feel anything.

Eventually, Mary lifts Cath up and guides her back to the ambulance. Cath rests her head on Mary's shoulder. 'Yer know wot, Mary,' she says, 'Mick ne'er stopped me bein' who I wanted to be.'

The drive back to Pop is a harrowing one for Cath. She knows it will be a long time, if ever, before she can visit his grave again. After a while Mary breaks the silence. 'Were yer serious last neet abaht goin' t'London?'

'Aye. Wil't tha come wi' me?'

''Course a will, if that's wot yer want. But 'ow will wi live?'

'Henry'll tek care on us.'

'I'm sure he will! But tha knows what 'e'll want in return.'

'I know, but am a single woman wi' a child on t'way. There's nowt fer us i' Burnley, so I 'aven't got much choice, 'ave I?'

'But 'e's an old man, Cath.'

'Aye, but a very clever an' attractive one.'

'Do'st really think so?'

'Oh, I don't know, Mary, but he's very likeable an' very kind. That's not a bad start.'

'Well, I'm not gettin' involved in any o' that three in a bed malarkey.'

'Neither am I. That wer just drink talkin'.'

'An' wot abaht this pacifism? Is'ta serious abaht it?'

'Aye.'

'But Henry reckons it's a just war, an' that everythin' will change when it's over.'

'Well, Henry's wrong. Nothin's worth wot's 'appenin' out 'ere. An' things aren't changin' quickly enough. Our Mick and Vinny are cold in t'ground, killed feightin' fer Britain. But they weren't allowed to vote fer the politicians wot sent 'em 'ere. An' when they got 'ere, wot did they find? They 'ad to doff their caps to toff officers who still had bum fluff on their chins, who parade around wi' their own horses, grooms an' personal servants. They can't eat wi' 'em, drink wi' 'em, or even shag the same tarts! And think abaht 'ow many poor buggers wiv 'ad in t'back o' this ambulance – blown to bits, blinded, gassed, maimed fer life. Even t'ones in t'trenches who aren't injured 'ave diarrhoea an' t'pox!'

Mary looks thoughtful; she stares straight ahead, not taking care to avoid the many bumps and hollows in the road.

'Careful, Mary!' shouts Kath. 'Do yer want me t'drive?'

'No, I wer just thinkin' abaht summat. Reach in me pocket. There's a letter there fra Tommy.'

Cath takes the letter from Mary's greatcoat and begins to read it. 'Bloody hell, Mary! John-Tommy tied to a gun wheel out in t'open fer eight hours a day fer defendin' 'imself! I thought they'd stopped all that years ago.'

'Aye, well, apparently not. To be fair, Tommy sez that Ross an' Tough spoke up fer 'im an' Tommy, an' Rickman changed 'is mind an' cleared their names.'

'Even so, Mary, it's barbaric, an' shows everythin' wot's wrong wi' Britain. We're still livin' in t'Middle Ages!'

Mary smiles at Cath's belligerence.

'So, Cath, London, 'ere wi come, to start a revolution!'

'Aye, lass – workers of the world unite!'

Saturday 18 December

Hostellerie St Louis, Clairmarais, St Omer, Pas-de-Calais, France

It is Sir John French's last day as Commander-in-Chief of the British Expeditionary Force, a role he has fulfilled since the BEF landed in August 1914. He is regarded as an outstanding cavalry soldier, some saying the best since Cromwell, but the static warfare of the Western Front, what he calls 'a siege on a gigantic scale', has become an insoluble mystery to him, as it has to military leaders everywhere.

Perhaps coming as a blessed relief, political machinations in London have finally put an end to his tenure. Criticisms about the delay in committing the reserves at the Battle of Loos, and whether he or Douglas Haig was to blame, have begun to threaten both Kitchener's and Asquith's positions. It thus becomes obvious that someone of seniority has to be blamed. The King has been brought into the intrigue and the outcome is that French has been told to resign, a request to which he has, with great reluctance, agreed.

Hostellerie St Louis is a small country hotel a few miles north-east of St Omer. Its surroundings are green and tranquil, not unlike the Home Counties, and the food excellent. Sir John and Winston have been driven out for a quiet lunch together.

'I know Haig is going to replace me. So does he, but yesterday morning I sent a telegram to the War Office and one to Downing Street, asking if I might be given formal confirmation of who my successor will be. I got a reply only an hour ago. It read, "Lord Kitchener and the Prime Minister have both gone to the country this weekend. Expect a reply on Monday." Bugger me, Winston, there's a war on!'

'I know, John. Let's hope that they've all gone to the country in Berlin.'

'I recommended that Robertson take over from me, but that's been ignored. Haig's not the man for the job; he can't even speak in public without his knees knocking.'

When the pair return to GHQ at St Omer, Douglas Haig agrees that he has no objection to Winston being given a battalion. That night Winston, still livid that Asquith bent to political pressure to deny him a brigade, writes to Clemmie, begging her not to discuss anything of importance about him with Asquith or his wife, Margot: 'Asquith will throw anyone to the wolves to keep himself in office. He presides over a weak, irresolute and incompetent government, but I worry not, I let it all slide away without a wrench. I have priorities that are more important. I shall give my battalion my very best.'

He then writes to F. E. Smith: 'I find myself treated with goodwill, tho' I'm often urged to go home and "smash the bloody government".'

While waiting to hear from Haig which battalion he will be given, Winston returns to London for Christmas with his family. While there, he has dinner at the Reform Club with Lloyd George and is delighted to hear that the

Welsh Wizard is determined to bring Asquith down and that, should that come to pass, Lloyd George would have him back in the government. Winston scribbles a note to Lloyd George after their dinner: 'Don't miss your opportunity, the time has come.'

Back in France for the end of the year, he travels to the very north of the Western Front, to Nieuwpoort on the Belgian Coast, where the trenches stop on the sand dunes and barbed wire runs into the sea. He then travels to Vimy Ridge, where the British sector ends and the French trenches begin, and where he finds a much more benign atmosphere than in some of the British lines: 'I think I am the only Englishman to have ventured this far. The lines are only a few yards apart and here the sentries don't skulk under cover, but stare at one another only a few yards apart. While I was there, the Germans passed the word to the French that their officer was about to start shelling, which he duly did. How very civilized!'

When he returns to GHQ, he learns that he is to command 6th Royal Scots Fusiliers, a battalion of the 9th Division. Raised in Ayr at the beginning of the war as part of Kitchener's New Army, they arrived in France in May. But it is now a battalion in mourning. It lost so heavily at the Battle of Loos that only one of its officers is a regular soldier, an eighteen-year-old, who joined them only a few months earlier. The rest of the officers are volunteers: Scottish solicitors, chemists, engineers and civil servants. Fortunately, Winston has managed to secure as his second-in-command an old friend from the Liberal Party, Archibald Sinclair.

He writes to Clemmie, asking for a copy of Burns:

'I will soothe and cheer their spirits by quotations from it. But I shall have to be careful not to drop into mimicry of their accent! You know I am a great admirer of that race: a wife, a constituency and now a battalion! You see, I love the Scots!'

He then reaffirms his antipathy towards Asquith: 'I have found him a weak and disloyal chief. I hope I shall not have to serve under him again after his "perhaps he might have a battalion" letter. I cannot feel the slightest regard for him. He was a co-adventurer, approving and agreeing at every stage. And he had the power to put things right. But his slothfulness and procrastination ruined the policy and his political nippiness squandered the credit.

'I have examined the entire Front as far as I can. We must expect another year of war. I do not see how any end will be reached in 1916, and the probability is that 1917 will dawn next year in worldwide bloodshed and devastation. We must be unyielding and unflinching. We must do more than we have ever done before. We must find a way to win.'

Winston ends the year receiving the news that his plans for a trench-crossing caterpillar vehicle are not being pursued and that Asquith, fearing the political consequences, is still resisting the idea of national conscription. When he hears, he opens his latest letter to Clemmie and adds a postscript: 'God, for a month of power and a good short-hand writer!'

Sunday 19 December

Nibrunesi Point, Suvla Bay,
Gallipoli Peninsula, Turkey

'All snipers ready and in position, sir.'

'Very good, Lieutenant. Excellent work.'

Bardie Stewart-Murray and his Scottish Horse are among the last to leave Suvla Bay and Anzac Cove in the great evacuation of the Gallipoli Peninsula. He has asked his newly commissioned lieutenant, Hywel Thomas, to get the company of snipers he has been training to dig themselves into various camouflaged positions above the beach to cover the final withdrawals.

Kitchener's visit in the middle of November, to see for himself what Gallipoli is like, heralded the decision to abandon the campaign, and set off a polemic of blame and recrimination that will last for decades. However, where the landings and subsequent attacks were gross examples of ineptitude and mismanagement, the evacuation is a military master class. The arrival of General Charles Monro has made a difference.

Forty thousand men have already left during the day on the 18th, and another 20,000 the previous night. So far, the Turks are not aware that anything untoward is happening. The artillery bombardments continue as normal and all the campfires are lit, despite most of the camps being abandoned. Blankets are laid to deaden the footsteps of retreating men, trails of salt and flour to guide men in the darkness. Barbed wire and booby traps are set to hinder pursuit.

When the evacuation ships come in close to the beaches, empty boxes of supplies are unloaded, which convinces the Turks that they are just routine shipments. Then the ships are loaded with men under cover of darkness. They are old soldier's tricks, the sort of thing at which they are very good. Unfortunately, it is the new 'tricks' of warfare in which they have been found wanting.

'Now, what have you devised for disguised covering fire?' asks Bardie.

Hywel leads Bardie away to show him what he has prepared in the forward trenches.

'Two things, sir. We've rigged three dozen rifles on timber supports, each with its trigger attached to water-powered weights so that when the water trickles away the trigger is released. We've put varying amounts of water in the containers so that the rifles will fire at random intervals.'

'Ingenious, Lieutenant.'

'We've also done several of these. As it's a calm day, we've got these candles under taut strings to the triggers. When we leave, we'll light the candles, which will slowly burn through the strings, then, bingo: the Turks will think we're still here.'

'Bloody marvellous. Where did you learn all this?'

'I didn't, sir, but being a hill farmer in the Welsh hills

teaches you to be resourceful. Again, we've varied the number of pieces of string, so that they burn through at different rates and the rifles fire at different times.'

'Excellent. Lieutenant, I intend to be the last British soldier to leave Suvla Bay. Would you like to accompany me?'

'It would be an honour, sir, but only after I fire the last shot in anger from the top of Lala Baba.'

'Agreed.'

As evening turns to night, Hywel's sharpshooters cover the withdrawal of the last few thousand men at Suvla and Anzac as they troop in single file along the prepared footpaths to the beach. Occasionally, a shot rings out as another Turk has carelessly put his head above the parapet. It is a long night, but eventually all the British, Indian and Anzac men are taken off. Bardie waits by his small boat as Hywel and his men set the automatic rifles they have rigged. When they are ready, Hywel calmly walks to the top of Lala Baba to seek his prey and settles into position. He is the last Allied soldier in the north of the peninsula.

The weather has been kind to the evacuation. In the area's worst autumn in 40 years, after weeks of rain, some of it turning to snow, the night is clear, the air still. There is a waxing half-moon, giving Hywel enough light to see into the Turkish trenches. He soon sees his target, a Turkish kabalak poking above the parapet, a lighted cigarette in the hand of its wearer.

Some of his auto-firing rifles begin to fire. The kabalak and the cigarette disappear. But moments later they come into view once more. Hywel squeezes the trigger, then pauses. Over a million men have been committed to the fighting on Gallipoli. The Turks have suffered a quarter of a million casualties, over 80,000 dead. The British dead number more than 21,000; Australian fatalities almost 9,000; New Zealanders' almost 3,000, from a contingent of 8,500.

Hywel decides on an act to defy the odds. He pulls the trigger and watches as the bullet strikes the anonymous Turk's head. But it strikes the red-crescent cap badge of his kabalak, sending it reeling into the air. In a last act of compassion on a peninsula that has become a mass grave-yard for over 100,000 men, Hywel spares one life. The now bareheaded Turk ducks down below the parapet, offers a quick prayer of thanks to the Prophet and lives to fight another day.

Hywel then runs down to the beach where, waist deep in water, Bardie is waiting for him.

'Did you bag one?' he asks.

'No, sir. It didn't seem right. Just put the wind up him a bit.'

Bardie smiles and offers Hywel his hand to help him aboard. 'Perhaps you're right. I suppose there's been enough killing for a few yards of worthless sand and rock.'

Both men clamber aboard, Bardie being the last to lift his foot from Turkish sand. As they make for the lighter which will carry them to Imbros, both men look back to the empty beaches and barren hinterland of Gallipoli. Abandoned supply dumps are blazing, sending sparks and embers high into the dawn sky. Artillery shells are blowing ammunition dumps, as are carefully laid explosives, timed by the sappers to go off thirty minutes after the last men depart.

The fires create an eerie orange-red glow across the desolate landscape.

'A foreign shore if ever there was one, Lieutenant.'

'Indeed, sir. Was it ever worth the effort?'

'I suppose not, but hindsight's a wonderful thing.'

'So, Egypt for us.'

'Yes. Kitty, my wife, is there. So it will be a happy Christmas and Hogmanay for us. What about you?'

'I don't have a sweetheart, sir, and my two brothers died in Flanders last year. I have a sister out here somewhere on a hospital ship. Hopefully, she'll end up in Egypt eventually, and I'll find her there.'

'Well, let's make sure you do. I'll speak to someone on Lemnos with RAMC and track her down. What's her name?'

'Bronwyn Thomas, QAIMNS.'

'Regard it as done, Lieutenant, and my grateful thanks for all you have done for the Scottish. You've produced a fine company of sharpshooters. What will you do after Egypt?'

'Well, if your regiment is posted to France, I'd like to go with you. If not, I'll ask to be transferred back to the School of Sniping.'

'Good, then let's hope we both go to the Western Front.'

The faultless withdrawal from Anzac and Suvla Bay will be repeated with the same flawless precision at the tip of the peninsula, at Cape Helles, a few days later.

Remarkably, after all the death and destruction of the previous months, all three Allied bridgeheads are evacuated without a single casualty. Jack Churchill writes to his brother:

> *Monro and Birdwood carried out the whole operation, and I think the government and Lord K owe them a great deal. A disaster would have sealed it for the government, I should imagine, but this will give them a new lease of life – more's the pity! It was a great feat – but we're all very depressed at having to come away. The Anzacs feel it very much. One of them said to me, 'We have lots of friends sleeping in those valleys. We should never have been told to leave them.'*

Several years later, the new leader of his nation, Mustafa Kemal – Atatürk – will gladden the hearts of the loved ones of all those Allied dead left behind on Gallipoli with the words:

> *Those heroes that shed their blood*
> *And lost their lives.*
> *You are now lying in the soil of a friendly country.*
> *Therefore, rest in peace.*
> *There is no difference between the Johnnies*
> *And the Mehmets to us, where they lie side by side*
> *Here in this country of ours,*
> *You, the mothers,*
> *Who sent their sons from far-away countries*
> *Wipe away your tears,*
> *Your sons are now lying in our bosom*
> *And are in peace*

After having lost their lives on this land they have
Become our sons as well.

Atatürk's immortal words will later be carved on a memorial stone above Anzac Cove on Turkey's Gallipoli Peninsula for future generations to read.

Friday 31 December

Myrina, Mudros Bay, Lemnos, Greece

The second year of the Great War closes quietly. It is as if the world is taking a breath before another year of anxiety and suffering begins. The conundrum of the Western Front continues to muddle the minds of the generals, so they have hibernated for a while, hoping that a magical solution will occur to them in their slumber. The anguish of Gallipoli has passed, leaving the combatants to lick their wounds. The Eastern Front is locked in the icy grip of winter, allowing, at least, time to count the dead.

There has been no Christmas truce to offer a spark of hope on Christmas Day. One British divisional order declared bluntly, 'Nothing of the kind is to be allowed on the Front this year. The artillery will maintain a slow barrage throughout the day and all men will be instructed to shoot on sight any of the enemy exposing themselves.'

At one point on Christmas Eve, near Plugstreet Wood, a fine German tenor began to sing arias from *La Traviata*, but stopped suddenly and was not heard again. Near Wulvergem, in a repeat of the previous year, a Christmas tree, complete with lighted candles, appeared at the top of a German parapet. The British officer opposite ordered that it be shot down. A few moments later the candles were extinguished and the tree cut to pieces in a hail of bullets.

There was just one exception, an incident that will be covered up until after the war, when the story will finally emerge. Encouraged by their German enemies opposite, a few foot guards from 1st and 2nd Scots Guards and 1st Coldstream wander into no-man's-land in sight of a junior officer. Only when a senior officer bellows at them do they return. GHQ in St Omer is so outraged by the incident that Lord Cavan, Commander-in-Chief, Guards Division, is asked to account for himself. The junior officer concerned is sent home in disgrace and Cavan has to issue a grovelling apology on behalf of his entire division.

At Blair Atholl, Helen Stewart-Murray's Red Cross Hospital is up and running, and the Ballroom Ward is full of Scottish NCOs and rankers from various Scottish regiments. Helen's fiancé, David Tod, has taken over the administration of the hospital and is acting as its supplies officer and book-keeper. The 7th Duke is in better spirits over the holiday period and Maud Grant even persuades him to travel to Blair Castle for Christmas lunch, although he declines the invitation to play Father Christmas and deliver Red Cross parcels to the patients.

Harry Woodruff and Maurice Tait are still digging and repairing trenches for the Royal Engineers near Dickebusch in Flanders. But they were in billets for Christmas Day, when the cooks managed to serve roast pork, courtesy of the local Belgian farmers, and a surfeit of Christmas puddings, some of which the men will still be eating well into 1915, courtesy of the Red Cross and hundreds of well-wishers at home.

Having resigned from the VAD earlier in the month and handed in the keys to their ambulance, Cath Kenny and Mary Broxup are in digs in London, waiting for Henry Hyndman to return from a speaking tour of Wales and the West Country. Cath has been examined at the London Hospital and been told that her baby seems to be developing well and is strong and healthy.

After going to an inspiring speech by pacifist Chrystal Macmillan, they have already made contact with several peace and women's groups in London, and Cath in particular is determined to campaign to bring Britain's soldiers home and to win the vote for women and working-class men.

Their rifle training at Larkhill Camp on Salisbury Plain finished, the Accrington Pals left Devonport on 18 December and are now aboard SS *Ionic*, a steam-powered ocean liner. The battalion's thirty-one officers are enjoying the luxury of *Ionic*'s first- and second-class passenger accommodation, including private cabins, a tea lounge, a well-stocked library and a smoking room furnished with burgundy leather sofas. They also are relishing the ship's bar, which they have commandeered as their mess. The NCOs have claimed the ship's dining room as their mess, while the men have had to make do with the stark, empty space of the ballroom. The men, all 1,003 of them, sleep in hammocks below decks, but soon move on to the open decks when *Ionic* sails beyond Malta towards the warm waters of the North African coast.

Ionic is due to dock at Alexandria tomorrow morning, New Year's Day, 1916. It is a relief to all concerned. Many of the men, including Tommy and John-Tommy, have never been at sea before, and almost everyone has been seasick. The constant threat of submarine attack and a near-run thing off the coast of Crete, when a torpedo missed by a hundred feet, has spoiled a pleasant 'cruise in the sun', as the Accrington newspapers report the journey. There has also been one tragedy. James Wixted, an iron-moulder from Accrington, got sunstroke on the 29th and died from dehydration that night. He was buried at sea the next day.

The Pals have just been told by Colonel Rickman that when they reach Alexandria they will have three days' leave before embarking for Port Said to guard the Suez Canal against a Turkish attack.

None of the Pals has any idea where Port Said is or what it is like, until some of *Ionic*'s crew, two West Ham boys who work in the kitchens, inform them that, 'It's a right fuckin' khazi, full of thievin' gypos who'd sell their grannies for a bob an' slit yer throat for two!'

In Alexandria, Kitty and Bardie Stewart-Murray are getting dressed to go to a ball at the British Consulate. Bardie, who has been personally commended by General Birdwood for his actions on Gallipoli, feels he is entitled to some rest and relaxation and, as it is New Year's Eve, intends to make the most of it. It also gives them the opportunity to see if they can restore some warmth to their marriage.

*

Now that the trauma of the Mediterranean Expeditionary Force is over, Christmas and New Year are being celebrated in a mood of immense relief on the Greek island of Lemnos. In vast numbers, wounded men are being transferred to Egypt, Malta and Gibraltar and fit men are being loaded on to troop ships bound for Alexandria, Marseilles and Southampton.

Bronwyn and Margaret have said goodbye to *Essequibo*. She is taking her wounded to Alexandria and the two QAIMNS sisters are waiting to be transferred to Marseilles for a train north to the Western Front. Fortunately for Bronwyn's peace of mind, there has been no sign of Tom Crisp since their fateful encounter on Imbros a month ago. It took Bronwyn almost a week to recover from seeing him. She spent many hours crying in Margaret's arms. All her worst nightmares from the previous year came flooding back. She has had enough problems coming to terms with what happened between her and Philip Davies, but seeing Tom has reminded her that there was another victim of her torrid affair, a childhood sweetheart she has rarely thought about since. That thoughtlessness has only made her guilt worse.

Margaret and Bronwyn are strolling along the harbour of the small town of Myrina on Mudros Bay. It is late and there is a fierce north-westerly wind blowing, making both women shiver. They have been drinking to celebrate being awarded the Red Cross Medal, which was given to them in a ceremony presided over by *Essequibo*'s captain. Bronwyn needs some air.

'What am I going to do about Tom, Mags?' she asks.

'Well, if you don't see him, nothing. If you do, you'll

have to talk to him and explain to him that the past is the past. You were a country girl; he was a country boy; now it's very different. The world has changed; we've all changed.'

'It's easy for you to say that, Mags, but you don't have to look him in the eye. We were so much in love until . . . well, you know.'

'I know, but that's what happens sometimes. I'm sure Tom has met other girls. He will have grown up as well. He'll understand.'

A voice suddenly calls to them. 'Bron?'

For a moment Bronwyn thinks the Shropshire Borders accent belongs to Tom but, mercifully, it is not Tom, it is her brother, Hywel. Margaret shrieks. 'Hywel, look at you – all those shiny buttons! You're an officer!'

Bronwyn rushes to embrace her brother.

'Lieutenant Hywel Thomas, Scottish Horse, at your service.'

'How did you find us?'

'My colonel is very well connected. He said he would find out where I could find you, and he did.'

'So how did you get those pips, big brother?'

'I got them from him, Colonel Stewart-Murray, CO of the Scottish Horse. He asked me to train a company of snipers for him.'

Margaret begins to blush. 'Bardie Stewart-Murray, son of the Duke of Atholl?'

'Yes, a nice man and a good soldier. He was the last man off Suvla Bay.'

Margaret smiles meekly. Bronwyn supplies an explanation. 'Margaret had a little fling with his brother, Hamish, didn't you, Mags?'

Margaret nods sheepishly.

'The colonel told me that his brother is a prisoner of war in Germany,' says Hywel.

Margaret is pleased to hear that he is safe.

'Strange coincidence: Philip used to sell his saucy prints to Hamish and Bardie's father. Small world,' says Bronwyn.

Margaret and Bronwyn tell Hywel about the encounter with Tom on Imbros. Hywel has not seen his boyhood friend since he walked out of their village eighteen months ago.

'So, he's a sailor?' he asks.

Bronwyn looks sombre. 'Looks like it. He's got the bell-bottom pants and the full beard. I didn't recognize him at first.'

'How did he get from Presteigne to the Royal Navy?'

'Don't know, but you could ask the same of all of us. How did we all get where we are?'

'Fate, Bron.'

Bronwyn looks bereft. 'Fate is a terrible thing. I hate it! I wish it would leave me alone.'

Hywel grasps both women by the hand. 'Come on, I know a little bar round the back of the town where the ouzo is cheap.'

'Bron and I have had some beer and wine already.'

'Good, then you need an ouzo to finish off the evening. Come on, it's New Year's Eve. Only an hour to go.'

'We were thinking of going to bed; we were told we might sail tomorrow.'

'Then all the more reason to have a last drink in Greece and see in 1916 properly.'

Bronwyn, thinking that she may as well drown her sorrows, persuades Margaret to see in the New Year, but when the trio reach the Astron Taverna it is so crowded Margaret and Bronwyn have to wait outside while Hywel goes to get the drinks. It is a full ten minutes before he returns, with a tray loaded with three large bottles of beer, a jug of ouzo, one of water and three small glasses. Margaret finds some chairs and a table.

'Here we are – enough to keep us warm and see us through till midnight. I don't fancy facing that crush again. The place is full of sailors from the *Lord Nelson*, de Robeck's flagship. Most of them are three sheets to the wind!'

When midnight strikes there are kisses and embraces between everyone, friend and stranger alike. 'Auld Lang Syne' breaks out and the sailors from the *Lord Nelson* pour out of the Astron and start singing and dancing in the narrow streets.

Tom Crisp is among them. He is as drunk as the other tars he is with. Without seeing who they are, but because they are female and everyone else is kissing them, he turns to kiss Margaret and Bronwyn. When they recognize one another, they freeze, as if time has suddenly stopped. Hywel breaks the silence.

'Good God, Tom! I heard you were a sailor. Look at you – a full set of whiskers.'

'Yes, I'm ship's carpenter on the *Grafton*. I'm a sailor boy now. And you're a bloody officer?'

'I am. You're supposed to salute!'

'Bollocks!'

'Agreed. Come on, let's have a drink.'

Hywel looks at Bronwyn and realizes that a drink might not be what she has in mind. She turns to leave, but Margaret grabs her arm and sits her down.

'Bron, Hywel and I are going for a walk to the harbour. We'll be back in twenty minutes. You and Tom can have a chat.'

'No, Mags, please. I want to go.'

'Bron, remember what I said. Now's the time. You owe it to Tom.'

Bron looks as white as a ghost and is visibly shaking but does not move as Margaret and Hywel walk away.

'Was that a good idea?'

'I hope so, Hywel. How amazing that they should bump into one another in the middle of nowhere, but it's for the best. Bron will have to deal with it sooner or later.'

'I suppose you're right. I hope they sort it out, for both their sakes.'

When the two of them reach the water's edge Margaret sits against an upturned fishing boat and looks out to the armada of Allied ships, their lights glinting and bobbing in the bay.

'Hywel, there is something I need to tell you, but I'm scared. But, like Bron and Tom, it will have to be said sooner or later.'

Hywel sits down close to her and speaks gently. 'When we first met, you said some things to me that helped me turn my life around. I'll always remember that. So you can say whatever you want.'

'That's nice of you, but I don't think you want to hear what I have to say.'

'You mean that you and Bron are lovers?'

Margaret stands up in shock. 'My God, Hywel, how do you know?'

'I've got a good pair of eyes, but you don't have to be a sniper to see how the two of you are together. You both seem very happy, so that makes me happy.'

'Aren't you shocked that two women can love one another?'

'I might have been once, but I've learned a lot since I left home. I know that there are men who like men – I've met some of them, and they seem normal enough to me – so why can't women like women?'

'Hywel, that's such a relief. There aren't many people, men or women, who would react like that. I'm so glad you understand. Bron will be thrilled.' She plants a big kiss on Hywel's cheek and throws her arms around him.

'Come on, let's get back and see how Bron's got on with Tom.'

With the gaiety of the New Year celebration swirling around her table, Bronwyn is sitting staring into a void when Margaret and Hywel return. They sit down next to her. There is silence for a while, until Bronwyn, her eyes bloodshot, turns to Margaret, who stretches out her hand to comfort her.

'How did it go?' she asks.

'All right, I think. It felt very odd. I don't know him any more. He was like a stranger. I know this sounds callous, but I felt nothing for him.'

'That's not surprising, Bron. A lot's happened.'

'I told him what you said to say, and he said he

understood. Then I told him about . . .' She stops herself and looks at Hywel.

'It's all right: he knows. I was going to tell him, but he'd already guessed. He's shrewd, your brother . . . and he doesn't think we're wicked or obscene.'

Bronwyn reaches out to Hywel. He takes her hand and caresses it. 'Hywel, thanks for being such a great big brother to me. I'm so happy with Margaret.'

'That's what big brothers are for. So how did you leave it with Tom?'

'He asked me if there was any chance we could start again. So I told him about me and Mags.' Bronwyn pauses and takes a swig of her ouzo, which makes her grimace and shake her head.

'What did he say?'

'He didn't, he just stared at me for a while. He had a strange look on his face, as if he was wondering what sort of hideous creature he'd got himself mixed up with.' She takes another swig of the ouzo. 'Then he got up, pushed back his chair and walked off . . . He just looked sad. As he left, he said to tell you that he hoped to see you one day back in Presteigne.'

There is a pause as everyone thinks about Tom and how he must feel. Then Margaret gets to her feet. 'Come on, Hywel, let's get Bron to bed. We're staying in camp at the far end of the harbour. Will you walk us back?'

''Course I will.'

The next morning at 11:00 hours, Margaret, Bronwyn and Hywel are aboard SS *Huanchaco*, bound for Marseilles. There are several troopships leaving at the same time, packed to the gunwales with men in khaki. They sail past HMS *Grafton*, which is about to raise anchor. As they pass her bows they see Tom Crisp leaning against the ship's rail. Even though he is over a hundred yards away, they can see the sagging shoulders and tilted head of a broken man. Bronwyn walks away; she cannot bear to look.

From the thousands of men returning home there are cheers of delight, and loud singing rings around the bay. This time last year the men were singing cheerful songs like 'A Long Way to Tipperary'. Now the mood is much more sombre and across the calm blue waters of the Aegean Sea drift the lyrics of the latest soldiers' favourite:

> *Overseas there came a pleading,*
> *'Help a nation in distress.'*
> *And we gave our glorious laddies*
> *Honour bade us do no less,*
> *For no gallant son of freedom*
> *To a tyrant's yoke should bend,*
> *And a noble heart must answer*
> *To the sacred call of 'Friend.'*
> *Keep the Home Fires Burning,*
> *While your hearts are yearning,*
> *Though your lads are far away . . .*

Epilogue

At the end of 1915 the strategic situation in the Great War for Civilization does not seem to be all that different than it was at the end of 1914. Many more are dead, of course; morale is even lower than it was at the end of the trauma of the first year of the war; and what glimmer of hope that still existed at the beginning of the year is now only a memory. Other than a couple of forlorn gestures between a handful of peacemongers, there has been no Christmas truce.

However, although it has been a static year on the Western Front, elsewhere it has been a year of change. Kitchener's New Army is nearly ready, women are pouring into the factories to work, a new coalition government has been formed and a new front has been tried – and failed – in the Eastern Mediterranean.

The war has spread to the Balkans, and Italy has joined the Allies. There are hints of new military technologies that may offer solutions to the appalling stalemate of trench warfare. War from the skies – aeroplanes and Zeppelins; war from the bowels of the earth – high explosives underground; war by new devices – gas and flamethrowers; war from beneath the sea – mines and submarines; and talk of war by armoured vehicles – machines capable of withstanding gunfire and able to breach obstacles. Perhaps victory will come to whomever first grasps the potential of technology.

However, at the end of the year, the truth is that no one has any idea how to end the military impasse, other than by yet more slaughter, on a scale even more horrific than before.

The year 1916 will be one of utter wretchedness, one that will make the previous two pale by comparison. The battle that history will record as one of the deadliest, the bravest and most futile ever fought will begin at the citadel of Verdun. The Easter Rising in Dublin will throw Anglo–Irish politics into bitter turmoil once more. The German High Seas Fleet will eventually challenge the dominance of the Royal Navy off the Danish coast of Jutland. The war in the Middle East will take a dramatic turn as a young archaeologist and soldier, Thomas Edward Lawrence, leads an Arab Revolt against Ottoman rule.

The high summer will bring the great proving ground for Kitchener's New Army, the Battle of the Somme. It will be a massacre of the innocents on an unparalleled scale, but the great field marshal will not see it, having died when a ship he was travelling on is sunk by a German submarine.

The war on the Eastern Front will continue in its unrelenting barbarity. Conscription to the British Army will become a reality and, finally, after two years of grim survival, the Asquith government will fall in December, leaving a small chink of light that might illuminate Winston Churchill's return to national politics.

Acknowledgements

I am indebted to the following primary sources for the factual background to this fictionalized account of the Great War during 1915. Each represents astonishing dedication to the cause of presenting accurate historical detail. Such diligent endeavours are often much more valuable than textbook histories, which usually give only a partial view and are invariably heavily laden with opinion and interpretation. Needless to say, I have used many of them, but they are too numerous to list here. Nevertheless, I am grateful for their insight.

The Community: Presteigne

Glover, Michael & Riley, Jonathon. 2007. 'That Astonishing Infantry': The History of the Royal Welch Fusiliers 1689–2006. Pen and Sword Books.

Howse, W. H. 1945. Presteigne Past and Present. Jakemans.

Laws, Sarah & Purcell, Clare. 1998. Impressions of Presteigne: An Oral History. Menter Powys.

Leversedge, Cherry. 1988. Pictorial Presteigne of Bygone Days. Leominster Print.

Parker, Keith. 2008. A History of Presteigne. Logaston Press.

Royal Welch Fusiliers Museum, Caernarfon Castle, North Wales.

Ward, Dudley H. 2005. Regimental Records of the Royal Welch Fusiliers. Naval and Military Press.

The Regiment: Royal Fusiliers

Fusilier Museum, Royal Regiment of Fusiliers, Tower of London.

O'Neill, Herbert Charles. 2002 (new edition of the 1922 edition). *The Royal Fusiliers in the Great War*. Naval and Military Press.

The Politician: Winston Churchill

Gilbert, Martin. 1971. *Winston S. Churchill (Volume III: The Challenge of War: 1914–1916)*. Hillsdale College Press.
Soames, Mary. 1998. *Speaking for Themselves: The Personal Letters of Winston and Clementine Churchill*. Doubleday.

The Estate: The Stewart-Murrays, Dukes of Atholl

Anderson, Jane. 1991. *Chronicles of the Atholl and Tullibardine Families*. Atholl Estates.
Hetherington, S. J. 1989. *Katharine Atholl, 1874–1960, Against the Tide*. Aberdeen University Press.
Katharine, Duchess of Atholl. 1958. *Working Partnership*. Barker.

The Pals: D Company (Burnley Company), 11th Battalion, East Lancashire Regiment, 'Accrington Pals'

Chapman, Tom. 2006. *Old King Coal*. Tom Chapman.
Duke of Lancaster's Regiment, Lancashire Infantry Museum, Fulwood Barracks, Preston.
Howarth, John. 2000. *Another Time, Another World*. Burnley and District Historical Society.
Jackson, Andrew. 2013. *Accrington Pals: The Full Story*. Pen and Sword Books.
Turner, William. 1992. *The Accrington Pals*. Pen and Sword Books.
Whelan, Peter. 1982. *The Accrington Pals*. Methuen.

I am also more grateful than words can adequately express to all those at Michael Joseph/Penguin Books for their faith in me and their outstanding professionalism. I should highlight its outstanding sales team, without whom no amount of angst and endeavour from an author would produce the revenue that warms his or her hearth. I am particularly grateful to Francesca Russell, whose charm and perseverance wins over the critics and the reviewers, and Nick Lowndes, who sweats blood to make sure the book is presented as pristinely and accurately as possible. Also, a very special thank-you to Sarah Day, an editor who not only has an astonishing eye for detail and an amazing grasp of our wonderful language, but is also my invaluable guide to the subtleties of complex characters and their interactions and helps me make them work much better for the reader. And to publisher Alex Clarke, who is, quite simply, a legend. Self-effacing, kindly, charming, but very shrewd; he is the kind of guardian angel about whom every author dreams.

Finally, to my family and friends – thanks for being so supportive, generous and absolutely wonderful!

Dramatis Personae

(In approximate order of first appearance in the novel.)

The Community: Presteigne

Philip Davies, 41, born in Hereford: auctioneer, Urban District Councillor for Presteigne and Captain, 1st Battalion Royal Welch Fusiliers.

Hywel Thomas, 20, born in Presteigne: farmer, eldest son of the Thomas family of Pentry Farm.

Morgan Thomas, 19, born in Presteigne: farmer, second eldest son of the Thomas family of Pentry Farm.

Bronwyn Thomas, 19, born in Presteigne: farmer and domestic, only daughter of the Thomas family of Pentry Farm; twin sister of Morgan.

Geraint Thomas, 18, born in Presteigne: farmer, third son of the Thomas family of Pentry Farm.

Tom Crisp, 20, born in Presteigne: local carpenter.

Noel Chavasse, 30, from Oxford: Surgeon Captain, 10th Battalion King's (Liverpool Regiment, Liverpool Scottish). He graduated with a First Class degree from Oxford in 1907 and ran in the 400 metres for Great Britain in the 1908 Olympic Games in London.

Dame Emma McCarthy, 56, born in Paddington, New South Wales, Australia: highly decorated war-time nurse. She left Australia in 1891 to study nursing in England. After qualifying, she was appointed as a sister at the London Hospital and served as

Sister-in-Charge at the Sophia Women's Ward during the South African War. This was followed by seven years' service with the Army Nursing Service Reserve. When the Great War broke out McCarthy was posted to the British Expeditionary Force and served in France and Flanders. As Matron-in-Chief, she was in charge of all British and Allied nurses working in the extended region (around 6,000 nurses at its peak).

Major Vernon Hesketh-Pritchard, 38, from Hertfordshire: explorer, adventurer, big-game hunter and marksman who made a significant contribution to sniping practice within the British Army during the Great War. He was concerned not only with improving the quality of marksmanship; the measures he introduced to counter the threat of German snipers were credited by a contemporary with saving the lives of over 3,500 Allied soldiers.

William Arthur Cawson, 45, from Stratton, Cornwall: Chief Ship's Carpenter, HMS *Inflexible*.

Richard Fortescue Phillimore, 51, from Shedfield, Hampshire: Royal Navy officer who went on to be Commander-in-Chief, Plymouth, promoted to Admiral and knighted. He took part in the response to the Boxer Rebellion in 1900. He was given command of HMS *Mohawk* in 1903 and then led the Naval Brigade Machine Guns in Somaliland the next year. He was then given command of HMS *Juno* in 1907 and the battlecruiser HMS *Inflexible* in 1911.

General Sir Ian Standish Monteith Hamilton, 63: senior officer in the British Army, most notable for commanding the Mediterranean Expeditionary Force during the Gallipoli campaign. Politically a Liberal, he spoke English, German, French and Hindi, and was considered charming and thoughtful. He appeared frail, yet was full of energy. He was twice recommended for the Victoria Cross. On the first occasion he was considered too young, and on the second too senior.

He was wounded in the wrist in the First Boer War at the Battle of Majuba, leaving his left hand almost useless. His left leg was shorter than his right, as a result of a serious injury caused by falling from a horse. People came to hold differing opinions of him. Prime Minister H. H. Asquith remarked that he had 'too much feather in his brain', whereas Charles Bean, war correspondent covering the Gallipoli campaign, considered he had 'a breadth of mind which the army in general does not possess'. He opposed conscription and was considered less ruthless than other successful generals.

Rupert Chawner Brooke, 28: English poet known for his idealistic war sonnets written during the Great War, especially 'The Soldier'. He was also known for his boyish good looks, which were said to have prompted the Irish poet W. B. Yeats to describe him as 'the handsomest young man in England', and for his infectious charm and warmth.

Richard Raymond Willis, 39: English recipient of the Victoria Cross and a captain in the 1st Battalion, Lancashire Fusiliers, when the following deed took place:

> *On 25 April 1915 west of Cape Helles, Gallipoli, Turkey, three companies and the Headquarters of the 1st Battalion, Lancashire Fusiliers, when landing on W Beach, were met by a very deadly fire from hidden machine guns which caused a large number of casualties. The survivors, however, rushed up and cut the wire entanglements, notwithstanding the terrific fire from the enemy, and after overcoming supreme difficulties the cliffs were gained and the position maintained.*

Captain Willis was one of the six members of the regiment elected for the award (immortalized as the 'Six VCs before Breakfast'), the others being Cuthbert Bromley, John Elisha Grimshaw, William Keneally, Alfred Joseph Richards and Frank Edward Stubbs. Willis later achieved the rank of Major. He died in Cheltenham on 9 February 1966 at the age of ninety.

Kemal Mustafa, 35: Turkish army officer, reformist statesman and the first President of Turkey. He is credited with being the founder of the Republic of Turkey. His additional surname, Atatürk (meaning 'Father of the Turks'), was granted to him in 1934 and forbidden to any other person by the Turkish parliament. Atatürk was a military officer during the Great War, during which he distinguished himself on several occasions, showing great resolve and leadership. Following the defeat of the Ottoman empire in the war, he led the Turkish National Movement in the Turkish War of Independence. Having established a provisional government in Ankara, he defeated the forces sent by the Allies. His military campaigns led to victory in the Turkish War of Independence. Atatürk then embarked upon a programme of political, economic and cultural reforms, seeking to transform the former Ottoman empire into a modern and secular nation-state. Under his leadership, thousands of new schools were built, primary education was made free and compulsory, and women were given equal civil and political rights, while the burden of taxation on peasants was reduced. His government also carried out an extensive policy of Turkification. The principles of Atatürk's reforms, upon which modern Turkey was established, are referred to as Kemalism.

Edward Unwin, 52: in 1915, when planning began for the amphibious landing on the Gallipoli Peninsula, Unwin proposed beaching the 4,000-ton collier SS *River Clyde* on the narrow beach beneath Sedd-el-Bahr at Cape Helles, V Beach, thereby allowing 2,000 troops to be landed together. Unwin was promoted to acting Captain and given command of the *River Clyde* for the operation. The plan called for a steam hopper to form a bridge from the ship to the shore. However, the Dardanelles current swept the hopper away, so Unwin, accompanied by Able Seaman William Charles Williams, who had been ordered to stay by his side, dived overboard and manhandled two lighters into position, lashing them together to form the bridge. All the while, Unwin was under fire from the Turkish defenders. When Williams was mortally wounded, Unwin went to his aid, and the lighter he was holding was swept away. Unwin collapsed from cold and exhaustion, his place being taken by other men. After an hour of rest, he returned to the lighters, until he was wounded and collapsed again. Once the attempts to land had ceased, Unwin went out a third time to attempt to recover wounded from the beach; according to one account, he retrieved seven men. For his actions, he was awarded the Victoria Cross. When British forces evacuated the peninsula in December, Unwin was aboard the last boat to leave the beach. When a soldier fell overboard, Unwin dived in to rescue him. Observing this act, General Julian Byng, the new IX Corps commander, remarked to Commodore Roger Keyes, 'You really must do something about Unwin. You should send him home; we want several more little Unwins.'

Lieutenant General Sir Aylmer Gould Hunter-Weston, 51: British Army general who served in the Great War at Gallipoli and in the very early stages of the Somme offensive. He was also a Member of Parliament. Nicknamed 'Hunter-Bunter', Hunter-Weston has been seen as a classic example of an incompetent Great War general. He was described by his superior Sir Douglas Haig as a 'rank amateur' and has been referred to as 'one of the Great War's spectacular incompetents'.

Lieutenant Colonel Godfrey Estcourt Matthews, 50: his pre-Great War career was dominated by service as a marine with the Egyptian Army, to which he was seconded in January 1897. With the exception of a few months, he served in Egypt for sixteen years. When the European War broke out he was commanding the Royal Marine Depot at Deal. He commanded the Plymouth Battalion, Royal Naval Division, in the Gallipoli campaign. He was wounded in December 1915 and made CMG. Matthews was promoted to brigade command in June 1916 as GOC, 198th Brigade, 66th (2nd East Lancashire) Division TF. 198th Brigade did not go abroad until February 1917. Brigadier General Matthews was wounded by a shell explosion at Cambrin on 12 April and died the following day. He was the thirty-second British general to be killed in action or to die of wounds on the Western Front.

Mary Fitzgibbon, 36, from Cork, Ireland: nursing sister, QAIMNS.

General Sir Frederick Stopford, 62: British Army officer commanding the Suvla Bay Landing in August 1915 during the Battle of Gallipoli. The younger son of James Stopford, 4th Earl of Courtown, and his second wife, Dora Pennefather, Stopford was commissioned into the Grenadier Guards in 1871. He was blamed for the failure to attack following the Suvla Bay landing. However, responsibility ultimately lay with Secretary of State for War, Lord Kitchener, who had appointed the elderly and inexperienced general to an active corps command, and with Sir Ian Hamilton, who had accepted Stopford's appointment. Stopford had chosen to command the landing from the sloop HMS *Jonquil*, which was anchored offshore, but slept as the landing was in progress. He was quickly replaced by General Byng. He retired in 1920.

The Regiment: Royal Fusiliers

Maurice Tait, 35, from Leyton, London: career soldier, Serjeant, C Company, 4th Battalion, Royal Fusiliers (designated 'Z' Company during the Great War).

Harry Woodruff, 35, from Leyton, London: career soldier, Serjeant, C Company, 4th Battalion, Royal Fusiliers.

Billy Carstairs, 43, from Plaistow, London: career soldier, Company Serjeant Major, C Company, 4th Battalion, Royal Fusiliers.

George O'Donel, 31, from County Mayo, Ireland: Captain and Adjutant, 4th Battalion Royal Fusiliers. He died on 16 June 1915 at Bellewarde Ridge. He has no known grave and is commemorated on the Menin Gate at Ypres.

Winston Leonard Spencer-Churchill, 40: son of Lord Randolph Churchill (Chancellor of the Exchequer in the 1890s under Lord Salisbury) and Lady Randolph Churchill, the American heiress Jennie Jerome. Veteran of several conflicts around the world, including the Boer War and the Battle of Omdurman. He was Liberal MP for Dundee and First Lord of the Admiralty. He is known as Pig, Pug and Amber Dog to his wife, Clementine.

Clementine (Clemmie) Churchill, née Hozier, 29: wife of Winston Churchill and daughter of Sir Henry Hozier and his wife, Lady Blanche. Known to Winston as Cat, Kat and Puss.

F. E. (Frederick Edwin) Smith, 33: lawyer, Conservative MP for Walton, life-long friend of Winston.

Diana Spencer-Churchill, 6: Winston's first-born child, known to the family as Puppy.

Randolph Spencer-Churchill, 4: Winston's second born, and eldest son, known to the family as Chumbolly.

Sarah Spencer-Churchill, born 7 October 1914: the third of Winston's children (who were often referred to by their father as 'kittens').

John Strange ('Jack') Spencer-Churchill, 35: younger brother of Winston. Veteran of the Boer War, in which he was badly wounded, he was very close to his brother.

Lady Gwendoline ('Goonie') Theresa Mary Churchill (née Bertie), 29: Jack Churchill's wife.

John George Spencer-Churchill, 6: Jack Churchill's first-born child.

Peregrine Spencer-Churchill, 2: Jack Churchill's infant son, known to the family as Pebbin. (Winston nicknamed Jack's family the 'Jagoons'.)

William Lygon, 7th Earl Beauchamp, 43: Liberal politician and Governor of New South Wales between 1899 and 1901. He was a member of the Liberal administrations of Sir Henry Campbell-Bannerman and H. H. Asquith between 1905 and 1915 and leader of the Liberal Party in the House of Lords between 1924 and 1931.

Harold Herbert Asquith, 62: British Liberal Prime Minister. Nicknamed 'Old Block' or 'OB' by Winston.

Margot Asquith (née Emma Alice Margaret Tennant), Countess of Oxford and Asquith, 54: married Herbert Asquith, Prime Minister from 1894 until his death in 1928. She was Asquith's second wife. (He had five children with his first wife, Helen, who died in 1891, and five with Margot, but only two of them survived infancy.)

Anthony Asquith, 13: son of H. H. Asquith, Prime Minister, and Margot Asquith.

Beatrice Venetia Stanley, 28: British aristocrat and socialite. The youngest daughter of Edward Lyulph Stanley, 4th Baron Sheffield. Venetia met Asquith through her close friendship with his daughter, Violet. Asquith, who was an avid letter writer, especially to attractive society women, began his correspondence with Venetia in 1910. During the next three years, Asquith wrote voluminously to her, even during Cabinet meetings, while Venetia responded almost as often. However, Asquith destroyed Venetia's letters on a regular basis to maintain confidentiality. The letters Asquith wrote during Cabinet meetings are often the only record of those meetings and a crucial source of historical information on British strategy during the war.

Sir Edward ('Eddie') Grey, 53: British Foreign Secretary from 1905 to 1916. It was Grey who remarked on 3 August 1914 as he stood at his window in the Foreign Office watching the gas lamps being lit: 'The lamps are going out all over Europe. We shall not see them lit again in our time.'

Admiral Sir Herbert William Richmond, 45: officer of the Royal Navy during the Great War. Having specialized as a torpedo officer, he was employed intermittently at the Admiralty between periods of sea-duty.

Admiral Sir Sackville Hamilton Carden, 58: British admiral who, in cooperation with the French Navy, commanded British naval forces in the Mediterranean Sea during the Great War. In September 1914 he was appointed Commander of the British Squadron operating in the Mediterranean under the leadership of a French admiral. In November 1914 Carden was asked by the British Admiralty to develop a strategy to force open the Dardanelles Straits in January of the following year.

Commander-in-chief of British naval forces during the Dardanelles campaign, Carden was successful in early offensives against Turkish defences from 19 February until early March, when he was relieved of command due to his failing health and replaced by Admiral John de Robeck.

Admiral of the Fleet John Arbuthnot 'Jacky' Fisher, 1st Baron Fisher, 76: known for his efforts at naval reform, and often considered the second most important figure in British naval history, after Lord Nelson. He first officially retired from the Admiralty in 1911 on his 70th birthday, but became First Sea Lord again in November 1914. He resigned seven months later in frustration over Winston Churchill's Gallipoli campaign.

Admiral of the Fleet Sir John de Robeck, 53, born in Ireland: commanded the Allied naval force in the Dardanelles during the Great War. He was second-in-command, to Admiral Sir Sackville Carden, of the Allied naval forces at the Dardanelles from February to March 1915, when he succeeded Carden in command.

Admiral of the Fleet Sir Arthur Knyvet 'Tug' Wilson, 75: served in the Anglo-Egyptian War and then the Mahdist War, being awarded the

Victoria Cross during the Battle of El Teb in February 1884. Appointed by Winston Churchill as an adviser at the start of the Great War, he was an early supporter of the use of submarines.

Herbert Horatio Kitchener, 65: victor of the Battle of Omdurman and hero of the Boer War; Secretary of State for War. 'K' is Winston's nickname for him.

David Lloyd George, 42: Liberal politician, and Chancellor of the Exchequer from 1908 to 1914.

General Sir William Birdwood, 55, born in Kirkee, India: saw active service in the 2nd Boer War on the staff of Lord Kitchener. He saw action again in the Great War as Commander of the Australian and New Zealand Army Corps during the Gallipoli Campaign in 1915, leading the landings on the peninsula and then the evacuation later in the year.

Sir Charles Hobhouse, 43: Liberal politician, and Post-Master General between 1914 and 1915.

Henry Charles Keith Petty-Fitzmaurice, 5th Marquess of Lansdowne, 70: British politician and Irish peer. In 1915 he was leader of the Conservative Party in the House of Lords.

Andrew Bonar Law, 57: born in the colony of New Brunswick (now in Canada), he was the only British Prime Minister to have been born outside the British Isles. In 1915, he was leader of the Conservative opposition.

Reginald McKenna, 42: Liberal politician, and Home Secretary from 1911 to 1915.

Sir John French, 62: renowned cavalry officer, Boer War veteran, Commander-in-Chief of the British Expeditionary Force.

Douglas Haig, 54: veteran of the Sudan and Boer wars, General and Commander 1st Corps, British Expeditionary Force.

Horace Smith-Dorrien, 62: veteran of Egypt, Sudan, the Zulu and Boer wars; General and Commander 2nd Corps, British Expeditionary Force.

Lady Randolph Churchill (née Jennie Jerome), 61: mother of Winston and Jack Churchill and wife of Lord Randolph Churchill, who died in 1895. Lady Randolph married George Cornwallis-West in 1900.

John Gough, 36: Serjeant, Special Branch, Metropolitan Police; Winston Churchill's protection officer.

Admiral of the Fleet John Rushworth Jellicoe, 55: fought in the Egyptian war and the Boxer Rebellion; commanded the Grand Fleet at the Battle of Jutland in May 1916.

Valentine Fleming, 35: son of wealthy Scottish banker Robert Fleming. He joined the Queen's Own Oxfordshire Hussars (Winston's and Jack's regiment), rising to the rank of Major.

Sir Edward Marsh, 42: British polymath, translator, arts patron and civil servant. He was the sponsor of the Georgian school of poets and a friend to many poets, including Rupert Brooke and Siegfried Sassoon. In his career as a civil servant he worked as private secretary to a succession of Britain's most powerful ministers, particularly Winston Churchill. Marsh was a discreet but influential figure within Britain's homosexual community.

Charles ('Sunny') Spencer-Churchill, 9th Duke of Marlborough, 43: British soldier and Conservative politician, and Winton's cousin. He was an officer in the Queen's Own Oxfordshire Hussars, fought in the Boer War and was subsequently appointed Assistant Military Secretary to Lord Roberts, Commander-in-Chief of the British forces in South Africa. He returned to active service in the Great War, when he served as a Lieutenant Colonel on the General Staff.

Consuelo Vanderbilt, 37: member of the prominent American Vanderbilt family. Her marriage to Charles Spencer-Churchill, 9th Duke of

Marlborough, became an international emblem of the socially advantageous but loveless marriages between American heiresses and European aristocrats common during America's so-called Gilded Age.

Major General Sir Alfred William Fortescue Knox, 45: career British military officer and later a Conservative Party politician. Born in Ulster, he joined the British Army and was posted to India. In 1911 he was appointed the British Military Attaché in Russia, where he served as a spy. A fluent speaker of Russian, he became a liaison officer to the Imperial Russian Army during the Great War.

Sir Stanley Brenton von Donop, 56: commissioned into the Royal Artillery, he played a key role in the Great War, having been appointed Master General of the Ordnance in 1913. He became the target for much of Lloyd George's criticism during the Shell Crisis of 1915. He stood down in 1916, when he was given the minor role of General Officer Commanding Humber Garrison.

Maurice Hankey, 39: British civil servant who became the first Cabinet Secretary as Secretary to the War Council under H. H. Asquith from November 1914.

James Louis Garvin, 48: from humble origins in Birkenhead, J. L. Garvin became an influential British journalist. In 1908 he became editor of the *Observer*.

Sir John Lavery, 60: society painter. Lavery was appointed an official artist in the Great War and was a close friend of the Asquith family.

Lady Hazel Lavery, 30: painter, and John Lavery's second wife. Her likeness appeared on banknotes of Ireland for much of the twentieth century.

Eustace Henry William, Tennyson-d'Eyncourt 48: British naval architect and engineer.

Thomas Gerald Hetherington, 48: joined the Royal Flying Corps on its formation in May 1912 and was then attached to the Royal Naval Air Service for experimental work.

Sir Charles Carmichael Monro, 56: British Army general during the Great War. He went to France at the start of the war and played a vital role in the 1st Battle of Ypres. After the failures of the Gallipoli campaign, General Ian Hamilton was dismissed as Commander-in-Chief of the Mediterranean Expeditionary Force and replaced by Charles Monro in October 1915. Monro oversaw the evacuation of the forces from Gallipoli.

Sir Edward Carson, 62: Irish unionist politician, barrister and judge. He was leader of the Irish Unionist Alliance and the Ulster Unionist Party between 1910 and 1921. In May 1915 Asquith appointed Carson Attorney-General when the coalition government was formed after the Liberal government was brought down by the Shell Crisis.

Major General Sir Ernest Swinton, 46: British Army officer who was a leading figure in the development of the tank during the Great War. He is said to have coined the word 'tank' as a code name for the first tracked, armoured fighting vehicles.

Nellie Hozier, 28: daughter of Colonel Sir Henry Montague Hozier and Lady Henrietta Blanche Hozier and sister of Clementine Hozier, Winston Churchill's wife.

Violet Bonham-Carter, 29: daughter of H. H. Asquith, and Winston Churchill's closest female friend.

Field Marshal Frederick Rudolph Lambart Cavan, 10th Earl of Cavan, 56: British Army officer and Chief of the Imperial General Staff. He had retired from the army in 1913 but was recalled at the start of the war and was appointed commanding officer of the 4th Guards Brigade.

General George Jeffreys, 1st Baron Jeffreys (second creation), 38: British military commander and Conservative member of parliament. He saw action in Africa and in the Boer War as a young officer, and went to France with his battalion at the start of the Great War.

Edward Grigg, 1st Baron Altrincham, 37: British colonial administrator and politician. At the start of the Great War, Grigg enlisted in the Grenadier Guards. Serving in France, he distinguished himself in combat before his transfer to the staff in 1916.

Field Marshal Sir William Robertson, 56: British Army general who served as Chief of the Imperial General Staff (CIGS) – the professional head of the British Army – from 1916 to 1918.

Archibald Sinclair, 26: soldier, politician and later leader of the Liberal Party. He served on the Western Front during the Great War and rose to the rank of Major in the Guards Machine Gun Regiment. He served as second-in-command to Winston Churchill, when, after he had resigned as First Lord of the Admiralty, he commanded the 6th Battalion of the Royal Scots Fusiliers on the Western Front.

Private Isaac Reid: in his book published in 1919, *A Private in the Guards*, Stephen Graham gives his account of what happened to Private Reid: During the battle of Neuve Chapelle, 'Private X' was dazed by shellfire, and 'straggled in later, unable to give an account of himself'. 'Serjeant Major Y', a dour martinet who 'through army training, had become the sort of man who presented every fault in the worst possible light', reported him as a deserter; a court martial took the serjeant major's testimony against the confused account of the private, and he was sentenced to death. His fellow soldiers know the sentence is unjustified, but some of them are commanded to form the firing squad. And not a man has mutinied. Such is the force of the discipline. The mutiny has only been in the heart. 'Serjeant Major Y' became a marked man, sent to Coventry and forced to drink alone. When he was mortally wounded at Festubert, no one would give him a drink of water, though he kept asking for it. He is buried apart from the other eighty soldiers who fell in the battle.

Graham's account of 'Private X' has been verified as Reid's story and that the CSM concerned, 'Serjeant Major Y', was Shropshire soldier James Lawton, an acting CSM, who gave evidence against Reid. Lawton was badly wounded by shell splinters at Festubert on 16 May 1915 and died the following day, aged thirty-five. However, the story of him being shunned by his peers has not, so far, been verified.

The Estate: The Stewart-Murrays, Dukes of Atholl

John ('Iain') James Hugh Henry Stewart-Murray, 7th Duke of Atholl, 74: Chief of the Clan Murray and Commander-in-Chief of the Atholl Highlanders, Europe's only private army.

John ('Bardie') George Stewart-Murray, Marquess of Tullibardine, 44: eldest son of the 7th Duke; veteran of the Boer War and Conservative MP for West Perthshire and Commander of the Scottish Horse.

Lord James ('Hamish') Stewart-Murray, 36: veteran of the Boer War and a major in the Cameron Highlanders.

Lord George ('Geordie') Stewart-Murray, 42: veteran of the Boer War; a former ADC to Lord Elgin, Viceroy of India, and a major in the Black Watch.

John William Dunne, 40: son of Irish aristocrat General Sir John Dunne; powered-flight pioneer.

Lady Katharine ('Kitty') Stewart-Murray (née Ramsay), 40: wife of 'Bardie'; accomplished musician and social activist.

Lady Dorothea ('Dertha') Stewart-Murray, 50: the 7th Duke's eldest child, married to Harold Ruggles-Brise, a career soldier.

Lady Helen Stewart-Murray, 48: the 7th Duke's second child, she lives at Blair Atholl and acts in the place of her deceased mother, Louisa, the Duchess of Atholl, who died in 1902 in Italy.

Lady Evelyn Stewart-Murray, 47: the 7th Duke's third child, and youngest daughter. Emotional problems in her childhood led her parents to send her away to be cared for by a governess; she now lives in Malines, in Belgium, in the company of a companion.

Jamie Forsyth, 59: butler, Blair Atholl Castle.

John Jarvis, 56: butler, Eaton Place, London.

Eileen Macallum, 9: illegitimate daughter of Bardie Stewart-Murray, the Marquess of Tullibardine. Eileen's mother is thought to be a 'Lady Macallum'.

David Tod, 59, born in Edinburgh: businessman and sculptor and friend of Lady Helen Stewart-Murray.

Mrs Maud Grant, 54: widow and resident of Glen Tilt on the Blair Atholl Estate.

Dougie Cameron, 23: first footman, Blair Castle household.

John Inglis, 41: factor, Blair Atholl Estate.

Matthew White Ridley, 2nd Viscount Ridley, 40: British Conservative politician and owner of Blagdon Hall, Northumberland.

Charles Sorley, 21: British poet of the Great War. Sorley spent six months in Germany from January to July in 1914, having enrolled at the University of Jena. He returned to England and volunteered for military service, and was killed in action near Hulluch, where he was shot in the head by a sniper at the Battle of Loos.

Thomas Scott-Ellis, 8th Baron Howard de Walden, 4th Baron Seaford, 36: a British peer, landowner, writer and patron of the arts. He was also a motorboat racer who competed in the 1908 Summer Olympics. He was second-in-command of the Westminster Dragoons, and a veteran of the Boer War.

Marc Armand Ruffer, 56: At the outbreak of the Great War, he was head of the Red Cross in Egypt.

Hussein Kamel (Prince Hussein): Sultan of Egypt from December 1914 to October 1917, during the British protectorate over Egypt.

The Pals: D Company (Burnley Company), 11th Battalion, East Lancs, 'Accrington Pals'

John-Tommy Crabtree, 43, born in Harle Syke: steward, Keighley Green Working Men's Club. Formerly a weaver; retired cricketer and renowned fast bowler for Burnley Cricket Club.

Tommy Broxup, 24, born in Burnley: weaver.

Vincent ('Vinny') Sagar, 18, born in Padiham: weaver.

Nathaniel ('Twaites') Haythornthwaite, 18, born in Sabden: weaver.

Michael ('Mad Mick') Kenny, 26, born in Colne: collier.

Catherine ('Cath') Kenny, 23, born in Nelson: weaver.

Mary Broxup, 23, born in Burnley: weaver.

Dame Katherine Furse (née Symonds): Founder of the English Voluntary Aid Detachment (VAD) force, in 1909 Furse joined the Red Cross Voluntary Aid Detachment, attached to the Territorial Army. On the outbreak of the Great War she was chosen to head the first Voluntary Aid Detachment unit to be sent to France, and was later in charge of the VAD Department in London.

Henry Hyndman, 73, born in London: radical activist and leader of the British Socialist Party.

John Harwood, 68, born in Darwen: cotton entrepreneur, President of Accrington Stanley Football Club, Mayor of Accrington, founder of 11th Battalion (Service) East Lancashire Regiment (Accrington Pals).

John Howarth, 39, born in Accrington: manager, Burnley Football Club.

Jimmy Dowd, 23: born in Armagh, Ireland: weaver.

James 'Jimmy' Severn, 56, born in Bow, London: retired soldier, training NCO, 11th Battalion, East Lancashire Regiment.

Frederick Arnold Heys, 27, born in Oswaldtwistle: solicitor, Lieutenant, D Company, 11th Battalion East Lancashire Regiment.

Raymond St George Ross, 32, born in Lancaster: analytical chemist, Captain, D Company, 11th Battalion East Lancashire Regiment.

Arnold Bannatyne Tough, 25, born in Accrington: dentist, Lieutenant, D Company, 11th Battalion, East Lancashire Regiment.

Andrew Muir, 56, born in Maryhill, Scotland: retired soldier, training NCO, 11th Battalion, East Lancashire Regiment.

George Lee, 53: born in Widecombe, Devon: retired soldier, training NCO, 11th Battalion, East Lancashire Regiment.

Richard Sharples, 65, born in Haslingden: solicitor and territorial soldier, Colonel and CO, 11th Battalion, East Lancashire Regiment.

George Nicholas Slinger, 49, born in Bacup: solicitor and territorial soldier, Captain and Adjutant, 11th Battalion, East Lancashire Regiment.

John Norton-Griffiths, 45, born in Somerset: known as Empire Jack or Hell-fire Jack. He was the son of John Griffiths, a clerk of works at St Audries Manor Estate, West Quantoxhead. He was elected to Parliament in 1910 and was until 1918 the Conservative Party's MP for Wednesbury, Staffordshire. Using his experience as a successful engineer, Norton-Griffiths formed the first units of the Royal Engineers Tunnelling Companies in early 1915. By incorporating his second given name, 'Norton', he changed his name to Norton-Griffiths by deed-poll in 1917.

George Henry Fowke, 52: joined the Royal Engineers in 1884, and saw service in the South African War at the Defence of Ladysmith, where he was mentioned in despatches. At the outbreak of the Great War, he was appointed to the post of Brigadier General Royal Engineers in the BEF, the senior engineering advisor. In 1915 he was made Engineer-in-Chief and oversaw the formation of the Royal Engineers Tunnelling Companies, after a proposal from John Norton-Griffiths.

Robert ('Ducky') Napier Harvey, 48: with 'Hell-fire Jack' Norton-Griffiths, he is regarded as the father of Great War mining operations and was appointed Inspector of Mines in January 1916.

Arthur Wilmot Rickman, 41: Lieutenant Colonel, CO, 11th Battalion, East Lancashire Regiment.

Chrystal Macmillan, 44: Scottish Liberal politician, barrister, feminist and pacifist. She was an activist for women's right to vote and for other women's causes.

Sydney (S. F.) Barnes: English professional cricketer who is generally regarded as one of the greatest ever bowlers. Barnes was unusual in that, despite a very long career as a top-class player, he spent little more than two seasons in first-class cricket, representing Warwickshire and Lancashire. He preferred to play for league clubs in the Lancashire, North Staffordshire, Bradford and Central Lancashire leagues, where he could earn a living as a professional. Barnes played for England from 1901 to 1914, taking 189 wickets with one of the lowest Test bowling averages. In 1911–12 he helped England win the Ashes when he took thirty-four wickets in the series against Australia. In 1963, Barnes was named by *Wisden Cricketers' Almanack* in its hundredth edition as one of its 'Six Giants of the Wisden Century'.

Casualty Figures of the Great War

Estimates of casualty numbers for the Great War vary greatly: from 9 million to over 15 million. Military casualty statistics listed here include 6.8 million combat-related deaths as well as 3 million military deaths caused by accidents and disease and deaths of men while prisoners of war. The figures listed below include about 6 million excess civilian deaths due to war-related malnutrition and disease, which are often omitted from other compilations. The civilian deaths also include the Armenian Genocide (1915), but civilian deaths due to the Spanish flu (1918–20) have been excluded. Also, the figures do not include deaths during the Turkish War of Independence (1919–22) and the Russian Civil War (1917–22).

Allied Powers

Country	Population (millions)	Military deaths	Direct civilian deaths (military action)	Excess civilian deaths (famine, disease & accidents)	Total deaths	Deaths as % of population	Military wounded
Australia	4.5	61,966	–	–	61,966	1.38%	152,171
Canada	7.2	64,976	–	2,000	66,976	0.92%	149,732
India	315.1	74,187	–	–	74,187	0.02%	69,214
New Zealand	1.1	18,052	–	–	18,052	1.64%	41,317
Newfoundland	0.2	1,570	–	–	1,570	0.65%	2,314
United Kingdom	45.4	886,939	2,000	107,000	995,939	2.19%	1,663,435
Belgium	7.4	58,637	7,000	55,000	120,637	1.63%	44,686
France	39.6	1,397,800	40,000	260,000	1,697,800	4.29%	4,266,000
Greece	4.8	26,000	–	150,000	176,000	3.67%	21,000
Italy	35.6	651,000	4,000	585,000	1,240,000	3.48%	953,886
Empire of Japan	53.6	415	–	–	415	0%	907
Montenegro	0.5	3,000	–	–	3,000	0.6%	10,000
Portugal	6.0	7,222	–	82,000	89,222	1.49%	13,751
Romania	7.5	250,000	120,000	330,000	700,000	9.33%	120,000
Russian Empire	175.1	1,811,000 to 2,254,369	500,000 (1914 borders)	1,000,000 (1914 borders)	3,311,000 to 3,754,369	1.89% to 2.14%	3,749,000 to 4,950,000
Serbia	4.5	275,000	150,000	300,000	725,000	16.11%	133,148
USA	92.0	116,708	757	–	117,465	0.13%	205,690
Total	800.4	5,712,379	823,757	2,871,000	9,407,136	1.19%	12,809,280

Central Powers

Country	Population (millions)	Military deaths	Direct civilian deaths (military action)	Excess civilian deaths (famine, disease & accidents)	Total deaths	Deaths as % of population	Military wounded
Austria-Hungary	51.4	1,100,000	120,000	347,000	1,567,000	3.05%	3,620,000
Bulgaria	5.5	87,500	–	100,000	187,500	3.41%	152,390
German Empire	64.9	2,050,897	1,000	425,000	2,476,897	3.82%	4,247,143
Ottoman Empire	21.3	771,844	–	2,150,000	2,921,000	13.72%	400,000
Total	143.1	4,010,241	121,000	3,022,000	7,153,241	5%	8,419,533

Neutral nations

Country	Population (millions)	Military deaths	Direct civilian deaths (military action)	Excess civilian deaths (famine, disease & accidents)	Total deaths	Deaths as % of population	Military wounded
Denmark	2.7	—	722	—	722	0.03%	—
Norway	2.4	—	1,892	—	1,892	0.08%	—
Sweden	5.6	—	877	—	877	0.02%	—
Total	10.7	—	3,491	—	3,491	0.03	—

Combined casualty figures

All nations: Allied Powers, Central Powers & neutral nations	Population (millions)	Military deaths	Direct civilian deaths (military action)	Excess civilian deaths (famine, disease & accidents)	Total deaths	Deaths as % of population	Military wounded
Grand total	954.2	9,722,620	948,248	5,893,000	16,563,868	1.74%	21,228,813

In addition to New Commonwealth troops listed below, Britain recruited Indian, Chinese, Native South African, Egyptian and other overseas labour to provide logistical support in the combat theatres. Included with British casualties in East Africa are the deaths of 44,911 recruited labourers. The Commonwealth War Graves Commission reports that nearly 2,000 workers from the Chinese Labour Corps are buried with British war dead in France.

Colony	Military deaths
Ghana (1914 known as the Gold Coast)	1,200
Kenya (1914 known as British East Africa)	2,000
Malawi (1914 known as Nyasaland)	3,000
Nigeria (1914 part of British West Africa)	5,000
Sierra Leone (1914 part of British West Africa)	1,000
Uganda (1914 known as the Uganda Protectorate)	1,500
Zambia (1914 known as Northern Rhodesia)	3,000
Zimbabwe (1914 known as Southern Rhodesia)	>700

Ireland

In 1914, the whole of Ireland was part of the United Kingdom, and 206,000 Irishmen fought for Britain during the Great War.

Location of War Graves

In March 2009, the Commonwealth War Graves Commission produced the following statistics for the resting places of the British dead in the Great War. The figures include all three services:

Buried in named graves: 587,989; no known graves, but listed on a memorial to the missing: 526,816, of which buried but not identifiable by name: 187,861; remains not recovered, therefore not buried at all: 338,955.

The last figure includes those lost at sea. Thus, about half are buried as known soldiers, with the rest either buried but unidentifiable, or lost.

Glossary

Adrian helmet

The M15 Adrian was a helmet issued to the French Army during the Great War. It was designed to offer protection from shrapnel. Steel blue in colour, it was introduced in 1915 and served as the basic headgear well into the 1930s. The design was created by French General August-Louis Adrian.

Ammonal

Ammonal is an explosive compound of ammonium nitrate and aluminium powder. The composition of ammonal used in the Great War was two-thirds ammonium nitrate, one fifth aluminium and the rest trinitrotoluene (TNT), with a trace of charcoal. Ammonal is still used as an explosive in quarrying and mining.

Artois, 2nd Battle of Artois

The 2nd Battle of Artois began on 9 May 1915 and lasted until 18 June. Under the command of French general Philippe Petain, the French 33rd Corps attacked the German lines and forced the defenders back towards Vimy Ridge. But the attack was not supported quickly enough, nor was their adequate artillery support and the Germans regained their ground. The British attacked towards Aubers Ridge, but the assault ended in failure.

AWOL

Being AWOL (Absent Without Official Leave) is deemed to be an act of desertion where a duty is deliberately not carried out or a post is abandoned.

Back-to-back houses

Back-to-back houses were (although a few still exist) rows of terraced house where the parallel houses shared a rear wall (or in which the rear wall of the house directly backed on to a factory or other building). They were built for factory and mill workers and were dark and lacked ventilation and internal sanitation. Most of these were pulled down during the twentieth century, but some have survived, notably in Leeds and Birmingham.

Band of Hope

The Band of Hope was founded in 1847 by Reverend Jabez Tunnicliff, a Baptist minister in Leeds. It was a temperance movement dedicated to warning children about the dangers of alcohol. Famously, adherents 'signed the pledge', promising to refrain from drinking alcohol.

Bantam battalions

In 1914 Alfred Bigland, MP for Birkenhead, incensed that men below regulation army height (5 foot 3 inches) were being refused as volunteers, pressed the War Office for permission to form a 'bantam' battalion of men who failed to reach this requirement but were otherwise perfectly capable of serving. About three thousand men – many of whom had previously been rejected – rushed to volunteer. These first bantams were formed into the 1st and 2nd Birkenhead Battalions of the Cheshire Regiment (later redesignated the 15th and 16th Battalions). The height requirement was lowered, but there was still a minimum height, of five foot.

Others followed Bigland's lead, for example, the 20th Battalion of the Lancashire Fusiliers, raised at Salford in March 1915, through recruiting efforts by local MP Montague Barlow and the Salford Brigade Committee. The West Yorkshire Regiment, the Royal Scots and the Highland Light Infantry all had bantam battalions. Many of the recruits were miners, and some of the units were formed into the British 35th Infantry Division. The 40th Division had a mixture of bantam and regulation units, although it is generally considered to have been a bantam division. The bantams were very popular at home and were often featured in the press.

Bar and clasp

In the rubric of military decorations, a 'bar' to an award for gallantry is given if the recipient receives the same award more than once: rather than receiving a second medal, a bar is attached to the ribbon of the original one. For a Military Cross the bar is decorated with a crown; for the Victoria Cross, with a laurel wreath. A clasp is awarded as an addition to a campaign medal and marks the recipient's participation in a specified battle within a campaign. The name of the battle is inscribed on the clasp, which is attached to the ribbon of the medal. Confusingly, clasps are often also called bars, but bars bear only a design, whereas clasps bear the name of the battle.

Belle Époque

Belle Époque (meaning 'beautiful era') is a period in European history dating from 1871 up to the start of the Great War in 1914. It was a time of optimism, peace at home and in Europe, advances in new technology and scientific discoveries. Peace and prosperity in Paris allowed the arts to flourish, and many masterpieces of literature, music, theatre and the visual arts were produced in this era.

Bénédictine

Bénédictine is a herbal liqueur produced in Fécamp, Normandy. The secret recipe, an aromatic mix of herbs and spices, was invented by local wine merchant Alexandre Le Grand, in 1863. The members of Burnley Miners' Club in Lancashire are the world's greatest consumers of Bénédictine. Its local popularity began when men of 11th Battalion, East Lancashire Regiment, were billeted at Fécamp during the Great War, where they acquired a taste for it.

Big Bertha

Big Bertha is the name given to a type of large mortar developed by Krupp, the German armaments manufacturer. Big Berthas weighed almost 100,000lbs (43 tons) and had a 16.5-inch barrel. They could hurl a 1,800-lb shell almost seven miles.

Billets

Billets are soldiers' living quarters. The term derives from *billet*, French for a 'ticket', which was issued to a soldier entitling him to a room or place to stay.

Billy-do

'Billy-do' is a colloquial translation of the French *billet-doux* (literally, 'soft note'), a love letter. It is thought that the term 'billy-do' came into use in soldiers' parlance because of the soft paper on which messages were sent during and before the Great War.

Binns of Edinburgh

Binns was a chain of department stores that traded in northern and eastern England, with one branch in Edinburgh. It has now been incorporated into the House of Fraser, although one store in Darlington continues to trade under the Binns name.

Black Hole of Calcutta

The Black Hole of Calcutta refers to an incident that took place in Fort William, Calcutta on 20 June 1756. Troops of the Nawab of Bengal, Siraj ud-Daulah, captured Calcutta and the East India Company's British garrison surrendered. The British prisoners-of-war were held for the night in a small jail, known as the 'Black Hole'. It was a room only 18 feet long and 14 feet wide, with only two small windows. The conditions were so cramped that the majority of the prisoners died. The precise number of those incarcerated and those who died are the subject of much debate. Original reports claimed 23 survivors from a total of 146 prisoners, but later studies suggested 21 survivors from 64 prisoners.

Bob Fitzsimmons

Robert 'Bob' Fitzsimmons was a British boxer who became Middleweight, Light Heavyweight and Heavyweight World Champion – the first man to win world titles at three different weights. He weighed only 170lbs, but had a powerful upper body and an exceptional punch and is regarded as one of the greatest boxers in history. He retired from the ring in 1914.

Brevet

A brevet was a military commission where an officer was granted a higher rank as a reward for outstanding service, but often without the authority or pay. A full promotion usually followed quite quickly.

British Army School of Musketry

The British Army School of Musketry was founded in 1853 at Hythe, Kent. In September 1855 a corps of instructors was added to the establishment, consisting of 100 first-class and 100 second-class instructors, who, as soon as they were sufficiently experienced, were distributed to depot battalions and regiments as required. The use of the term 'musketry' in their name was, in fact, a misnomer, as, by then, muskets (smooth-bore weapons) were being withdrawn from service to be replaced by weapons with rifled bores (rifles).

British Expeditionary Force

Britain's army in 1914 was a volunteer professional army of great tradition. Although there had been significant reforms in the nineteenth century, it was still based on centuries-old practices and prejudices. Most officers needed a private income of at least £250 per year, or £400 for cavalry regiments, which required a man to keep a charger, two hunters and three polo ponies. Some men of the ranks came from long-standing military families, but most enlisted as unskilled labourers. These were largely from urban slums, men who were uneducated and often undernourished.

The army required that men be 5 foot 3 inches in height and 133lbs in weight, with a 33-inch chest. Despite these minimal standards, many applicants failed. Although their living standard was hardly luxurious, soldiers got regular pay, had clean living conditions, adequate food and were given a rudimentary education. Camaraderie was generally good and professionalism high, especially in basic combat skills and musketry. There was mutual respect between officers and men, and non-commissioned officers were drawn from highly disciplined veterans and of the highest calibre.

In May 1914 British military prowess rested on its immense Royal Navy, which was the envy of the world. The regular army was small compared to its European counterparts and was 11,000 short of its establishment of 260,000. The number of men under arms on UK soil was 137,000, including recruits undergoing training. The rest were in numerous garrisons throughout the empire. The BEF sent to France in August 1914 was designated at 48 infantry battalions and 16 cavalry regiments, plus heavy and light artillery and support services. This was many more than the army could muster, so over 70,000 reservists were called to the colours. Although these men had been regular soldiers, most had grown accustomed to civilian life, lacked training and had lost their battle-hardened readiness. Many battalions had to include several hundred reservists to bring them up to a strength of around 1,000 men.

Approximately 100,000-strong, the BEF's mandate was challenging: to help throw back a German force of 1 million in cooperation with a French Army that was equally huge. Its commander, Sir John French, was required to support the French generals but not to take orders from them. However, he had to rely on their goodwill for railway transportation, accommodation and lines of supply. John French was a better fighting soldier than he was a strategic general. He was liked by his subordinates and had a good reputation within the army, but he was short-tempered and argumentative and suffered from violent mood swings, which veered from overt optimism to deep pessimism. His subordinates Sir Douglas Haig, who commanded I Corps, and Sir Horace Smith-Dorrien, who commanded II Corps, were also highly respected, experienced soldiers, but neither had a good relationship with French, especially Smith-Dorrien, who was appointed against his wishes. Haig was extremely efficient and hard-working, much liked by all around him, but was intensely shy and awkward. Smith-Dorrien was brave and aggressive but prone to extreme outbursts of temper.

The BEF was to take up position to the east of Cambrai, between Maubeuge and Hirson, on the left flank of General Lanrezac's 5th French Army of 250,000 men. Here it would meet the thrust of the German advance through southern Belgium, led by General Alexander von Kluck's 1st Army, which was 300,000 strong.

Burnley Lads' Club

The Burnley Lads' Club was formed in 1899 to cater for boys from disadvantaged backgrounds. Many of the original members of the club fell in the Great War, serving with the famous D Company, Accrington Pals, along with the club's first leader, Captain Henry Davison Riley. The club still flourishes. In 1968 the Lads' Club merged with the Police Youth Club to create Burnley Boys' Club. The merger enabled the two groups to pool their resources and membership, which included girls, and the club is now called Burnley Boys' and Girls' Club. It is a youth and community centre for all young people between the ages of six and twenty-one, irrespective of gender, race and ability. Young people with disabilities are welcome up to the age of twenty-five.

Camouflage

In 1914 British scientist John Graham Kerr persuaded First Lord of the Admiralty Winston Churchill to adopt a form of disruptive camouflage which he called 'parti-colouring', or 'dazzle' camouflage. A general order to the British fleet, issued on 10 November 1914, advocated the adoption of Kerr's method, which used masses of strongly contrasted colour, making it difficult for a submarine to decide on the exact course of the vessel to be attacked. Artists known as 'camoufleurs' were employed to design the camouflage of the ships, some of which were so eye-catching that people would come and gawp at them in dock. It was applied in various ways to

British warships such as HMS *Implacable*, where officers noted that the pattern 'increased difficulty of accurate range finding'. However, following Churchill's departure from the Admiralty, the Royal Navy reverted to plain-grey paint schemes.

Carbolic acid

Carbolic acid is an antiseptic substance, also known as phenol, developed by Sir Joseph Lister, a British surgeon and pioneer of antiseptic surgery. By applying Louis Pasteur's advances in microbiology, he promoted the idea of sterile surgery while working at the Glasgow Royal Infirmary. Lister successfully introduced carbolic acid to sterilize surgical instruments and to clean wounds, which led to a reduction in post-operative infections and made surgery safer for patients.

Le Cateau

The Battle of Le Cateau took place on 26 August 1914. British General Horace Smith-Dorrien took a calculated gamble during the retreat from Mons, which was against direct orders. Feeling his men were in disarray in a retreat hindered by thousands of French civilians, he decided to fight: 40,000 British troops formed a defensive line just south of the Cambrai–Le Cateau road and just west of Le Cateau itself. Britain suffered many more casualties than at Mons – 7,812 – in a hard-fought encounter. German losses were much higher, perhaps as many as 20,000. However, Smith-Dorrien's decision meant that the rest of the retreat from Mons could be undertaken with much less arduous harassment and it could well have saved a greater part of the BEF from destruction.

Central Powers/Allied Powers

The Central Powers were one of the two warring factions in the Great War, composed of Germany, Austria-Hungary, the Ottoman (Turkish) empire and Bulgaria (also known as the Quadruple Alliance). This alignment originated in the alliance of Germany and Austria-Hungary, and fought against the Allied Powers that had formed around the Triple Entente. The members of the Triple Entente were the French Republic, the British empire and the Russian empire. Italy ended its alliance with the Central Powers and entered the war on the side of the entente in 1915. Japan, Belgium, Serbia, Greece, Montenegro, Romania and the Czechoslovak legions (a volunteer army) were secondary members of the entente.

Chatelaine

A woman who owns or controls a large house (a feminine form of chatelain, the commander of a castle).

Chechia fez

Chechia fez is the North African name for the conical fez, also called a taqiyah, or kufi, worn by many Muslims out of respect for the prophet Mohammed, who was thought to have covered his head. In military or ceremonial use, it is often red with a contrasting tassel; in the case of the Senegalese Tirailleurs, the tassel was of gold braid.

Cherry bums

'Cherry bums' was a term used by Lord Cardigan for his regiment, the 11th Prince Albert's Own Hussars, which, notoriously, he led in the Charge of the Light Brigade in 1854 in the Crimean War. The 11th Hussars wore bright red cavalry trousers in honour of the livery of Prince Albert's House of Saxe-Coburg-Gotha. The term came to be used by infantrymen in sections of the army as a derogatory expression for cavalrymen in general.

Chlorine gas and other chemical weapons

The first use of chlorine gas in the Great War was by the German Army on 22 April 1915, at the beginning of the 2nd Battle of Ypres. Chlorine gas reacts with water in the mucus of the lungs to form hydrochloric acid, to lethal effect. It was pioneered by Fritz Haber, a German scientist, in collaboration with the chemical company IG Farben.

The first use of gas by the British was at the Battle of Loos on 25 September 1915, but it was a disaster. The wind proved to be a problem and the gas either settled in no-man's-land or blew back on the British trenches. Phosgene was introduced to overcome the deficiencies of chlorine. Colourless, and having a less distinctive smell than chlorine, phosgene was difficult to detect. Phosgene was deadlier than chlorine, but took longer to take effect.

The most widely used gas of the Great War was mustard gas. It was introduced by Germany in July 1917, prior to the 3rd Battle of Ypres. Mustard gas was not particularly effective as a killing agent but disorientated the enemy and caused chaos on the battlefield. The gas remained active for several days, weeks, or even months, depending on the weather conditions. The skin of the victims blistered, they began to vomit and suffer from internal and external bleeding. It sometimes took victims four or five weeks to die.

Chitty

An Anglo-Indian word for 'note', derived from the Hindi *cittha*, meaning 'note'.

Chloroform

Chloroform is a heavy, transparent, colourless liquid compound composed of carbon, hydrogen and chlorine which vaporizes easily and has a strong, sweet odour. It is a potent general anaesthetic which was first used in 1847 by Sir James Y. Simpson, a Scottish physician. However, chloroform can cause severe damage to internal organs, especially the heart, liver and kidneys, so is no longer used medically and has been replaced by anaesthetics with less dangerous side effects.

Clay-kicking

Clay-kicking is a British method of digging tunnels in clay-based soils. The clay-kicker rests on a board at a 45-degree angle from the face and inserts with his feet a tool with a rounded end. By turning the tool manually, a section of soil, can be released and placed to the side to be extracted. During the Great War, the system was used by the Royal Engineers Tunnelling Companies. Unlike German digging, which adopted pick-axes and shovels, it was virtually silent, and significantly quicker.

Clogs

There are two explanations of the development of the English-style clog. They may have evolved from foot pattens (soles), which were slats of wood held in place by thongs or similar strapping. These were usually worn under leather or fabric shoes to raise the wearer's foot above the mud of the unmade road (not to mention commonly dumped human effluent and animal dung). Those too poor to afford shoes wore wood directly against the skin or hosiery, and thus the clog was developed, made partly of leather and partly of wood. The other explanation has clogs dating back to Roman times, and possibly earlier. The wearing of clogs in Britain became more visible with the Industrial Revolution, when workers needed strong, cheap footwear. The heyday of the clog in Britain was between the 1840s and 1920s and, although traditionally associated with Lancashire, they were worn all over the country (for example, in the London fish docks, fruit markets and in the mines of Kent).

Cockney rhyming and other London slang

Arris – bottle and glass – arse

Barney moke – poke (sexual intercourse)

Birch an' broom – room

Bull an' cow – row

Butcher's (hook) – look

Cocoa/ I should Cocoa – I should say so

Crimea – beer. Also Christmas cheer, Charlie Freer, Pig's ear; and *Daily Mail* – ale

Crown an' Anchor – wanker

Crust (crust of bread) – head

Currant bun – sun

Feather-plucker – fucker

Fife an' drum – bum

Gaff – although often thought to be a Cockney expression, 'gaff', meaning 'house' or 'place of work', is a slang term of Irish origin.

Gates of Rome – home

Goose and Duck – fuck

Granny Grunt – cunt

Hampton (Wick) – dick

His Majesty's Pleasure – treasure

Fourpenny one – fourpenny bit – hit. A fourpenny bit was an old British silver coin, also called a groat, worth four old pennies. It ceased to be minted in 1856.

Iron hoof – poof – homosexual

Khazi – toilet – latrine. Although not strictly rhyming slang, the word is thought to have Cockney origins and derive from the Italian *casa* ('house'), via the 1870s Cockney word 'carsey', or to be a contraction of 'gazebo', or from African sources. In Zulu or Swahili the word *m'khazi* means a latrine.

Little Red Riding Hoods – goods

Mazawattee – potty – crazy. Mazawattee was one of the most popular brands of tea from mid-Victorian times onwards. Owned by the Densham family and using tea from the newly established tea plantations of Ceylon, its name is Sinhalese in origin and means 'pleasure garden'. The popularity of the tea was boosted by the Temperance Movement and the company's clever slogan 'The cup that cheers but does not inebriate'. The brand was distributed from the company's warehouse on Tower Hill in London and became a Cockney favourite. The brand declined after the Great War, and its Tower Hill warehouse was destroyed during the Blitz in the Second World War. By the 1960s Mazawattee tea was no longer being produced.

Miss Fitch – bitch

Old nag – fag – cigarette. This term was common in the trenches of the Great War but does not seem to have survived beyond the 1920s.

Plates o' meat – feet

Pony (and trap) – crap (useless/poor quality)

Ribbons and curls – girls

Robin Hood – good

Ruby red – head

Rum – odd (probably not Cockney; could be from Romany 'rom', 'man')

Safe an' sound – ground

Silver spoon – moon

Tiddly (wink) – drink

Tommy rollocks – bollocks – testicles

Two an' eight – state (as in a state of agitation)

Willies – to feel fear or apprehension; in use since the nineteenth century. Its origins are obscure and do not lie in Cockney rhyming slang. Two possible explanations have been suggested:

i) That it comes from the slang expression 'willie-boy', meaning 'sissy', presuming that these would be the sort to be prone to the 'willies'.

ii) The romantic ballet *Giselle*, written in 1841 by French composer Adolphe Adam. The 'wilis' (or 'willis') in the ballet take their name from the Slavic word *vila*, a wood-nymph or fairy, usually the spirit of a betrothed girl who has died after being jilted by her lover. Thus 'willi', the spirit or ghost, became the 'willies'.

Copperplate

Copperplate is a style of calligraphy that uses a sharp, pointed nib instead of the flat nib used in most calligraphy. The name derives from the copybooks students learned, which were printed from etched copper plates. Today, the term 'copperplate' is usually used to refer to traditional and very precise handwriting.

Creeping barrage

During the Great War, before an infantry advance it was a common strategy to bombard enemy defences with all available heavy artillery. It was believed that preliminary bombardment would weaken the enemy's position and enable attackers to capture enemy trenches. This strategy was largely unsuccessful so, in 1916, both sides began to use what became known as a creeping barrage. It was first used in a small section of the line at the Battle of Loos in 1915, but the infantry did not advance behind it, and its first significant use was at the Battle of the Somme in 1916, when artillery fire moved forward in stages just ahead of the advancing infantry. By the autumn the Allied forces had developed a system where the barrage moved forward at 50 yards per minute. To work, the strategy required precise timing by both the heavy artillery and the infantry. Failure in this would result in the artillery killing its own soldiers.

Cricket-ball grenade

A cricket-ball grenade was a weapon used by the British Army during the Great War. It was a time-fused grenade, in a cast-iron body. To arm the grenade, the user had to remove a cover on the fuse, then strike it with an igniter. There were two types of fuses, five-seconds for throwing and nine-seconds for use in a catapult.

Croix de Guerre

The Croix de Guerre is a French military honour that was first created in 1915. It can be, and often is, awarded to soldiers of France's allies.

Crystal Palace

Between 1895 and 1914 the FA Cup Final was played at Crystal Palace. On 25 April 1914, in front of over 72,000 people, Burnley beat Liverpool 1–0, thanks to a goal by Bert Freeman in the fifty-eighth minute. The trophy was presented by King George V, the first time a reigning monarch had done so.

D3, or Fullerphone

The D3, or Fullerphone, was invented by Captain Algernon Fuller of the Signals Service of the Royal Corps of Engineers, the forerunner of the Royal Corps of Signals. It could not pass voice messages, only Morse, but the Germans could not detect the signals, which could be sent by one wire and an earth. The signal could even 'jump' breaks in the ground if the broken ends were earthed and not too far apart.

Defence of the Realm Act

The Defence of the Realm Act (DORA) of 1914 governed all lives in Britain during the Great War. The Act was added to as the war progressed and listed everything that people were not allowed to do in time of war. The first version of the Defence of the Realm Act was introduced on 8 August 1914. It stated that:

- No one was allowed to talk about naval or military matters in public places
- No one was allowed to spread rumours about military matters
- No one was allowed to buy binoculars
- No one was allowed to trespass on railway lines or bridges
- No one was allowed to melt down gold or silver
- No one was allowed to light bonfires or fireworks
- No one was allowed to give bread to horses or chickens
- No one was allowed to use invisible ink when writing abroad
- No one was allowed to buy brandy or whisky in a railway refreshment room
- No one was allowed to ring church bells
- The government could take over any factory or workshop
- The government could try any civilian breaking these laws
- The government could take over any land it wanted to
- The government could censor newspapers

As the war evolved, so DORA evolved. The new rules introduced by the government included:

- The introduction of British Summer Time to give more day-light for extra work
- The cutting of pub opening hours
- The watering down of beer
- A ban on customers in pubs buying a round of drinks

Perhaps predictably, several of these 'temporary' wartime measures became permanent.

Depth bombs (depth charges)

The first attempt at developing an anti-submarine weapon was to attach aircraft bombs to lanyards which would trigger their charges. A similar idea was a 16-lb guncotton charge in a lanyarded can; two of these lashed together became known as the Depth Charge Type A. Problems with the lanyards tangling and failing to function led to the development of a chemical-pellet trigger: the Type B. These were effective at a distance of around 20 feet. The best concept arose in a 1913 Royal Navy Torpedo School (at HMS *Vernon*, Portsmouth) report describing a device intended for a 'dropping mine'. At Admiral John Jellicoe's request, the mine was fitted with a hydrostatic firing mechanism developed in 1914 by Thomas Firth and Sons of Sheffield. Pre-set to fire at 45 feet, it was launched from a ship's stern platform. The first depth charges were not, however, effective weapons during the Great War. Between 1915 and the end of 1917, the charges destroyed only nine U-boats. They were improved in 1918, and that year were responsible for destroying twenty-two U-boats.

Desoutter Brothers

Marcel Desoutter was one of six children of an immigrant French watchmaker. With his four brothers, he trained as a watchmaker. He learned to fly, and at an Aviation Meeting held at Hendon Aerodrome in 1913 his plane crashed. Desoutter's leg was badly broken, and had to be amputated above the knee. He was fitted with a wooden leg, but his younger brother, Charles, created a jointed Duralumin alloy leg only half the weight, allowing Marcel to return to flying. In 1914 the pair formed Desoutter Brothers Limited to manufacture artificial limbs. The firm expanded greatly during and after the Great War.

Digger

'Digger' is a slang term for soldiers from Australia and New Zealand which has become part of the Anzac legend. Before the War, the term was widely used in Australasia to mean a miner, and also referred to a kauri gum-digger (diggers of resin from the kauri tree) in New Zealand, and was closely associated with the principles of 'mateship'.

Distinguished Conduct Medal

The Distinguished Conduct Medal (DCM) was, until 1993, a very high (second-level, second only to a Victoria Cross) award for bravery. The medal was instituted in 1854, during the Crimean War, to recognize gallantry within the ranks, and was equivalent to the Distinguished Service Order (DSO) awarded for bravery to commissioned officers.

Doolally tap

Deolali, India, was the site of a British Army transit camp notorious for the psychological problems of soldiers who passed through it. Its name is the origin of the phrase 'go doolally' or 'go doolally tap'. 'Tap' may derive from the Urdu word *tap*, meaning a malarial fever.

Draught Bass

Bass Brewery was founded in 1777 in Burton-upon-Trent by William Bass. A hundred years later it had become the largest brewery in the world, producing 1 million barrels a year. It took control of a number of other large breweries in the early twentieth century, and Draught Bass became its signature beer.

Droste

Founded by Gerardus Johannes Droste in 1863, Droste Chocolate was based in Haarlem and started as a confectionary business, selling various types of chocolate products. The famous image of the woman in nurse's clothes, holding a plate with a cup of milk and a box of Droste cocoa, first appeared on Droste products around 1900. This illustration was probably inspired by a pastel known as *La Belle Chocolatière* ('The Pretty Chocolate Girl').

Dunnage

Dunnage is timber or other material (often discarded or surplus) used to store or secure equipment. The term is used in naval and construction terminology.

East Lancashire, Pennine Dialect

Agate – say/said; 'Be agate' – to say
Alreet – all right
Any road – anyway

Barm cake – barm is the foam, or scum, formed on the top of liquor (fermented alcoholic beverages such as beer or wine, or feedstock for hard liquor) when fermenting. It was used to leaven bread, or set up fermentation in a new batch of liquor. In parts of the north-west of England and throughout Yorkshire, a 'barm' or 'barm cake' is a common term for a soft, floury bread roll; on menus in chip shops there is often an option of a chip barm. The term 'barmy' may derive from a sense of frothy excitement.

Barmskin – leather apron

Blather (or *blether*) – from Old Norse *blathra*, to talk nonsense.

Bee-ast – Old English form of 'beast'

Best slack – slack are very small pieces of coal, almost coal-dust. Best slack would be less dust, more small pieces. (Nutty slack would be bigger, more expensive pieces.)

Brass – money

Cald – cold

Champion – good, great, excellent

Childer – children

Cock o' t'midden – King of the Castle; a midden is, specifically, a waste dump, but also a 'patch', as in territory.

Dacent – decent

Daft appeth – silly person. 'Appeth' is derived from 'halfpennyworth'.

Feight – fight

Fettle – sort out

For-ard – forward

Fra – from

Frossen – frozen

Heed – head

Laik – play

Lanky – Lancastrian

Like talking to a wood stoop – talking to someone who doesn't listen or can't hear. A stoop is a raised flat area in front of a door, usually with one or more steps leading up to it.

Lummox – big lump

Moither – worry

Neet – night

Noss – nose

Nowt – nothing

Owd – old

Oyel – hole, as in 'Put t'wood in th'oyel': 'Shut the door.'

Marsant – must not

Mebbe – maybe

Me'sen – myself

Na'er – never

O'er – over

Ollus – always

Once every Preston Guild – very rarely

Owt – anything

Peg/pegging – sexual intercourse

Pie-eyed – drunk (strictly speaking, a term not confined to the East Lancashire dialect)

Pop your clogs – die (in this context, 'pop' is to pawn. A living person would never pawn his clogs; they would be pawned only when a person died.)

Rec – recreation ground

Reet – right

Road, as in 'any road' – anyway

Sen – self

Sithee – see you

Sken – look

Slark – pour in large amounts. More West Riding than Lancashire, but heard in the Burnley area.

Summat – something

Sum'un's – someone's

Toaty soup – potato soup

Tek – take

Th'sels – themselves

Tha'sen – (thou) yourself

Tha'sens – (thou) yourselves

Th'eed – the head

T'morn – tomorrow (or tomorrow morning)

T'neet – tonight

Tyke – Yorkshire person

Wheer – where

Wick – infested, crawling with. Usually applied to lice or vermin, but sometimes to people and places. Can also mean 'alive' or 'thriving'.

Winda – window

Yonder – over there, or beyond

Eleven-a-side moustache

Of the dozen or so common styles of moustache, the thin, close-cropped 'eleven-a-side' is better known as the 'pencil' moustache. It is thought to be distinctly English in origin and probably Victorian, reflecting the period when the eleven-man sports of cricket and football were growing in popularity.

Emily (Emmeline) Pankhurst

Emmeline Pankhurst was a leader of the British suffragette movement, which helped women win the right to vote. At the beginning of the Great War, Emmeline and her eldest daughter, Christabel, called a halt to the suffragette's militancy and supported the British government's fight against Germany. They urged women to work industrial production and encouraged young men to fight. In 1918, the Representation of the People Act granted votes to all men over the age of twenty-one and women over the age of thirty. Women gained full adult suffrage in 1928.

Enfilade / defilade

Enfilade and defilade are terms that describe exposure to or protection from hostile fire. You are in an enfilade position if the enemy can fire along your axis – for example, at 90 degrees to a trench, or down a column of men. You are in a defilade position if you use your surroundings or artificial obstacles to shield or conceal yourself from fire.

Enteric fever

Enteric fever is another name for typhoid, a common worldwide bacterial disease transmitted by the ingestion of food or water contaminated with the faeces of an infected person containing the bacterium *Salmonella*.

Enverieh (Enver Pasha helmet)

An enverieh is a Turkish officer's kabalak (military headdress), named after Turkish leader Enver Pasha.

Enver Pasha

Enver Pasha was a leader of the 1908 Young Turk Revolution. He was the main leader of the Ottoman Empire in both Balkan Wars and in the Great War and took the decision to enter the Empire into the Great War, on the side of Germany. He was also one of the principal participants in the Massacre of the Armenians, which began in April 1915 and cost 1.5 million lives.

Estaminet

'Estaminet' is a word taken from Walloon to mean a modest café, bar or bistro in French-speaking Belgium and north-eastern France.

Executions

Three hundred and forty-six British and Commonwealth soldiers were executed during the Great War. Such executions, for crimes such as desertion and cowardice, remain a source of controversy, with some believing that many of those executed were suffering from what is now called shell shock. Between 1914 and 1918 the British Army identified 80,000 men with what would now be defined as the symptoms. However, senior commanders believed that if such behaviour was not harshly punished, others might be encouraged to behave in the same way and the whole discipline of the British Army would collapse. Some men faced a court martial for other offences, but the majority stood trial for desertion from their post: 'fleeing in the face of the enemy'. A court martial was usually carried out with some speed, and the execution followed shortly after. In his testimony to the post-war Royal Commission examining shell shock, Lord Gort said that it was a weakness and was not found in 'good' units. The continued pressure to avoid the medicalization of shell shock meant that it was not, in itself, an admissible defence.

Executions of soldiers in the British Army were not commonplace. While there were 240,000 courts martial and 3,080 death sentences handed down, of the 346 cases where the sentence was carried out, 266 British were executed for desertion, 18 for cowardice, 7 for quitting a post without authority, 5 for disobedience to a lawful command and 2 for casting away arms. In some cases, for instance that of Private Harry Farr, men were executed who had previously suffered from shell shock and would very likely today have been diagnosed with post-traumatic stress disorder or another psychiatric syndrome and so would not be executed. Immediately after the Great War there were claims that the execution of soldiers was determined by social class. During the war fifteen officers were sentenced to death, but all received a royal pardon. In August 2006 the British Defence Secretary Des Browne announced that, with Parliament's support, there would be a general pardon for all 306 men executed in the Great War. A new law passed on 8 November 2006, and included as part of the Armed Forces Act, pardoned men in the British and Commonwealth armies who were executed. The law removes the stain of dishonour with regard to executions on war records, but it does not cancel out sentences. Des Browne said, 'I believe it is better to acknowledge that injustices were clearly done in some cases – even if we cannot say which – and to acknowledge that all these men were victims of war. I hope that pardoning these men will finally remove the stigma with which their families have lived for years.'

Fag

Fagging was an archaic tradition in British public schools, where younger pupils (fags) acted as servants to senior boys. Fagging involved harsh discipline, constant humiliation and, invariably, various forms of corporal punishment. The system often led to sexual abuse by the older boys. The tradition slowly disappeared during the 1970s and 1980s.

Falkland Islands, Battle of

After defeat at the Battle of Coronel on 1 November, the Royal Navy sent a large force to destroy the victorious German squadron under the command of Admiral Maximilian von Spee. His squadron consisted of two armoured cruisers, *Scharnhorst* and *Gneisenau*, the light cruisers *Nürnberg*, *Dresden* and *Leipzig* and three auxiliaries.

The British squadron was much larger: the battlecruisers *Invincible* and *Inflexible*, the armoured cruisers *Caernarvon*, *Cornwall* and *Kent*, the armed merchant cruiser *Macedonia* and the light cruisers *Bristol* and *Glasgow*. On December 8 1914, von Spee attacked the British supply base at Port Stanley in the Falklands, but the British ships were lying in wait and when von Spee realized he was out-gunned, he made a dash for it. All except *Dresden* and the auxiliary *Seydlitz* were hunted down and sunk. Von Spee went down with his ship, the *Scharnhorst*.

Fenian

Is shorthand for the Fenian Brotherhood and the Irish Republican Brotherhood, which were committed to freedom from British rule and the establishment of an independent Irish Republic. The term originated in 1848 and was coined by Gaelic scholar John Francis O'Mahoney. The word derives from Fene, an Old Irish name for a tribe of ancient Irish people.

Field Punishment

Field Punishment was introduced in 1881 following the abolition of flogging and was a common punishment during the Great War. Field Punishment Number One consisted of the convicted man being placed in fetters and handcuffs and attached to a fixed object, such as a gun wheel, for up to two hours per day and was issued by the British Army on over 60,000 occasions during the Great War. In Field Punishment Number Two, the prisoner was again placed in fetters and handcuffs but was not attached to a fixed object and was therefore still able to march with his unit.

Fix is a make of Greek beer. The Fix brewery in Athens was founded in 1864 by the Fuchs family, who had moved to Greece from Bavaria.

Flammenwerfer

The *Flammenwerfer* was developed by German scientist Richard Fiedler. A portable version, the *kleine Flammenwerfer*, or Kleif, could be operated by two men. The German army adopted the Kleif in 1906, and by 1912 the Guard Reserve Pioneer Regiment boasted its own regiment of *Flammenwerfer* troops. The weapon was first used at Verdun on 26 February 1915. The French managed to capture a Kleif, which their weapons researchers promptly disassembled. At the Battle of Hooge, six Kleif operators attacked British forces on the night of 29/30 July 1915. The Germans were able to capture several trenches, but the effectiveness of the *Flammenwerfer* was more psychological than tangible. The Allies soon developed their own versions of the weapon.

HMS *Formidable*

HMS *Formidable* was a pre-Dreadnought battleship sunk by two torpedoes from a German submarine 20 miles off Start Point at 2.20 a.m. on 1 January 1915. The first torpedo hit the number-one boiler port side; a second explosion caused the ship to list heavily to starboard. Huge waves 30 feet high lashed the stricken ship with strong winds, rain and hail, sinking it in less than two hours. Captain Loxley, his second-in-command, Commander Ballard, and the signaller stayed at their posts throughout, sending flares and rockets off at regular intervals. When the ship gave a tremendous lurch, the captain shouted, 'Lads, this is the last, all hands for themselves, and may God bless you and guide you to safety.' He then walked to the forebridge, lit a cigarette and, with his terrier, Bruce, on duty at his side, waited for the end, in true Royal Navy tradition.

In a storm that followed the sinking of HMS *Formidable*, a life raft containing bodies was blown along the coast to Lyme Regis. The cellar of the Pilot Boat, a pub in the port, was used as a mortuary. When the bodies had been laid out on the stone floor, the landlord's dog, a half-collie called Lassie went down to the cellar and began to lick the face of one of the victims, Able Seaman John Cowan, who eventually moved. He was taken to hospital and made a full recovery. The story was told far and wide and in 1938 Eric Knight wrote 'Lassie Come Home', the inspiration for the Hollywood 'Lassie' movies.

Frostbite

Frostbite is a medical condition in which damage is caused to skin and other tissues due to freezing. At or below $0°C$ ($32°F$), blood vessels close to the skin start to constrict, and blood cannot reach the extremities. It can also be caused by exposure to high winds. The lack of blood eventually leads to the freezing and death of skin tissue in the affected areas.

Gangrene

This is a life-threatening condition that arises when body tissue dies. It may be caused by injury or infection, or occur in people suffering from poor blood circulation.

Geophone

The geophone was invented by Professor Jean Perrin of the Sorbonne in 1915 and was a device used to detect enemy tunnelling. It consisted of two discs with mica membranes holding mercury and attached to a stethoscope. By placing the discs on the floor or walls of a tunnel, sounds were magnified two and a half times; a skilled listener could estimate how far away and how deep the German tunnels were, giving warning of the enemy's activity, or enabling counter-mines to be dug.

Gewehr 98 Mauser rifle

The Mauser G98 was a bolt-action rifle which fired cartridges from a five-round magazine and was German standard issue from 1898 to 1935.

Golok

'Golok' ('gulok' in the Philippines) is a term applied to a variety of machetes found throughout the Malay archipelago, used both as an agricultural tool and a weapon. The word is of Indonesian origin but is also used in Malaysia where the word is also often used for the longer and broader parang.

W. G. Grace

William Gilbert 'W. G.' Grace was an English amateur cricketer who is recognized as the most significant pioneer of the game and one of its greatest players. He played for forty-four seasons from 1865 to 1908.

Green spot ammunition

Snipers rely on their skill, the quality of their rifle and its sight, but also on their ammunition. The first 5,000 rounds out of a new mould are packaged with a green spot so that they can be used by snipers, as the balls of later rounds suffer from minor deteriorations in the ball-mould through wear.

Hackles

The hackles are the long, fine feathers which are found on the backs of certain types of domestic chicken. They are often brightly coloured, especially on roosters, and are often used as fly lures. In military parlance, the hackle is a clipped feather plume that is attached to a military headdress. In the British Army the hackle is worn by some infantry regiments, especially those designated as fusilier regiments and those with Scottish and Northern Irish origins. The colour of the hackle varies from regiment to regiment. The Lancashire Fusiliers wear primrose yellow; the Royal Fusiliers, white; the Royal Northumberlands, red over white; and the Royal Welch, white.

Hansom cab

A hansom cab is a kind of horse-drawn carriage designed in 1834 by Joseph Hansom, an architect from York. 'Cab' is an abbreviation of 'cabriolet' (carriage). Hansom cabs were light enough to be pulled by a single horse and agile enough to be steered through the crowded streets of nineteenth-century London.

Havercakes

A havercake is an oatcake, a type of flatbread, made from oatmeal, and sometimes flour, cooked on a griddle or baked in an oven. In Lancashire and Yorkshire, oatcake was a staple of the diet up to the Great War, and the regional name comes from *hafr*, the Old Germanic word for 'oats'. The word is perpetuated in the nickname 'Havercake Lads' for the 33rd Regiment of Foot (the Duke of Wellington's Regiment, West Riding) and also in the term 'haversack'.

Howitzers

A howitzer is an artillery weapon. Typically, they have relatively short barrels, fire relatively small missiles and at relatively high trajectories. Howitzers sit between 'guns' – longer barrel, larger missiles and flatter trajectories, and 'mortars' – even higher angles of ascent and descent.

HMS *Inflexible*

Built in 1907, HMS *Inflexible* was an *Invincible*-class battlecruiser of the Royal Navy. She and her sister ship, HMS *Invincible*, sank the German armoured cruisers SMS *Scharnhorst* and SMS *Gneisenau* during the Battle of the Falkland Islands.

Jack Johnson

'Jack Johnson' was Great War slang for the large shells used by the German artillery (also called black boxes). They emitted thick black smoke and punched a big hole wherever they landed, or in whatever they hit, thus the use of the name of America's famous black heavyweight boxer Jack Johnson, who was world champion from 1908 to 1915.

Jack Tar

'Jack Tar' is a traditional term for seamen of the Merchant or Royal Navy. Its origin is not certain, but there are several suggestions:

i. Before the invention of waterproof fabrics, seamen were known to 'tar' their clothes before departing on voyages in order to make them waterproof.
ii. Seamen would often plait their long hair into a ponytail and smear it with high-grade tar to prevent it getting snared in the ship's rigging.

iii. In the age of wooden ships, hemp ropes were soaked in tar to prevent them rotting.

Jaeger

'Jaeger' means 'hunter' in German and was used by the Landgrave of Hesse when he formed an elite infantry unit in the Hessian Army. The word is used to describe elite light infantry, especially skirmishers, scouts, sharpshooters and couriers.

Junkers

Meaning 'Young Lord', Junkers is a term to describe the members of the landed nobility of Prussia. After 1871 they were the most powerful part of the German military, political and diplomatic establishment. They controlled the Prussian Army and their influence was widespread in the north-eastern half of Germany: Brandenburg, Pomerania, Silesia, West Prussia, East Prussia and Posen.

Kabalak

The kabalak was the headgear worn by Turkish soldiers in the Great War. It came in various forms, sometimes with an internal frame with khaki-coloured cloth material wound around it and sometimes made from heavy canvas. They were conical in shape, like a pith helmet. Officers' kabalaks often had a spike on top like a German pickelhaube, and an Ottoman crescent cap badge at the front.

Kepi

The kepi was, and still is, the most common cap of the French Army. In 1914 they were worn in battle, but were replaced by the Adrian helmet in 1915. However, they were still worn away from the battle-field and on ceremonial occasions.

King's shilling

The 'King's shilling' refers to the shilling given in the eighteenth and nineteenth centuries to men who agreed to serve in the army or navy. To 'take the King's shilling' is still in use informally (to take the Queen's shilling).

Knur and Spell

Knur and Spell is an ancient Pennine folk game, akin to the southern English games of trap-ball and probably an ancestor of golf. Often associated with gambling, it was very popular in the nineteenth and early twentieth centuries, especially in the fields around moorland pubs. The object is to hit a 'potty' (knur), sometimes a small piece of heartwood or a small pottery ball, as far as possible with a long, flexible club. The longest hit takes the prize. Distances of several hundred yards could be achieved. The game and its name are thought to be Norse in origin.

Kukri

The kukri is a Nepalese knife similar to a machete, a weapon used by Gurkha regiments throughout the world.

Lant trough

A lant trough is a receptacle for collecting human urine. Fermented human urine (lant) was used for various purposes from as early as Roman times. The Romans used it as a cleaning agent for stained clothes and even as a whitener for teeth. The emperor Nero imposed a highly lucrative tax on the urine industry. In nineteenth-century Lancashire, lant was used in the tanning and woollen industries as a cleanser for the removal of natural oils in the production of leather and wool.

Laverbread

Laverbread is made from laver (seaweed), which is boiled then minced or pureed. It can then be eaten as it is or rolled in oatmeal for frying. Laverbread is traditionally eaten fried with bacon and cockles as part of a Welsh breakfast.

Lee-Enfield rifle

The Lee-Enfield rifle was the main infantry weapon used by the military forces of the British Army from the early twentieth century until 1957.

Lee-Metford rifle

The British Army's Lee-Metford service rifle replaced the Martini-Henry rifle in 1888. It had a bolt-action and a ten-round magazine with a seven-groove rifled barrel designed by William Ellis Metford. It was replaced by the Lee-Enfield in 1913.

Lewis gun

The Lewis gun, a light machine gun, was developed in the United States in 1911. It was far lighter than the Vickers machine gun and in 1915 the British Army ordered it for use on the Western Front. The Lewis could be made much more quickly than the Vickers and, although too heavy for efficient portable use, it became the standard support weapon for the British infantry.

Long johns

Long johns are thermal underwear (long legged and long armed), usually made of cotton. There are various explanations about the name and their origin, but they can be traced back to as early as the seventeenth century.

Lyddite shell

Shells filled with Lyddite (solidified picric acid named after Lydd in Kent where it was first tested) were the first British generation of modern 'high explosive' shells.

Maconochie's and Moir Wilson British Army rations

These were just two of the many manufacturers of Great War army rations. Maconochie's, an Irish stew produced in Fraserburgh and Stornoway in Scotland, was the most popular. Soldiers got a weekly ration of 12oz dried 'bully' beef, 1lb 4ozs bread or flour, 4oz bacon, 3oz cheese, plus sugar, tea, jam, salt, pepper and mustard when available. As in the navy, a 'tot' (half-a-gill/70 mls) of rum was issued daily; double before a battle. Ten thousand copies of the *Daily Mail* were also sent to the Front every day.

Mad minute

This was a pre-Great War term used by British Army riflemen during training at the Hythe School of Musketry to describe scoring a minimum of fifteen hits on a 12-inch round target at 300 yards within one minute using a bolt-action rifle (usually a Lee-Enfield or Lee-Metford). It was not uncommon during the Great War for riflemen to exceed this score. Many could average more than thirty shots. The record, set in 1914 by Serjeant Instructor Alfred Snoxhall, was thirty-eight hits. During the Battle of Mons, there were numerous German accounts of coming up against what they believed was machine-gun fire when in fact it was squads of riflemen firing at this rate.

Mackeson

First brewed in 1907, Mackeson is a milk stout containing lactose, a sugar derived from milk. Thought to be highly nutritious, milk stout was recommended to nursing mothers and distributed to geriatric patients in many British hospitals until the 1970s.

Marne, 1st Battle of

The 1st Battle of the Marne was fought between 5 and 12 September 1914 and resulted in an Allied victory against the German Army. The battle effectively ended the month-long German offensive that opened the war and had reached the outskirts of Paris. The counter-attack of six French field armies and one British army along the Marne River forced the German Imperial Army to abandon its push on Paris and retreat north-east, setting the stage for four years of trench warfare on the Western Front. The 1st Battle of the Marne was an immense strategic victory for the Allies, wrecking Germany's bid for a swift victory over France and forcing it into a protracted two-front war. The Allied armies were over a million-strong and faced a German force of over a million and a half.

Allied casualties were over 263,000, of whom over 81,000 died. German losses were at least 220,000 dead or missing.

Marquis of Queensberry rules

The code of traditional rules in the sport of boxing is named after John Sholto Douglas, 9th Marquis of Queensberry, who publicly endorsed the code. The Queensberry rules were the first to require the use of gloves in boxing. In popular culture the term is some-times used to refer to a sense of sportsmanship and fair play. The rules were written by John Graham Chambers, a Welshman, and drafted in London in 1865, before being published. The Marquis of Queensberry's third son was Lord Alfred 'Bosie' Douglas, the close friend and lover of Oscar Wilde.

Maschinengewehr 08, or MG 08

A hybrid of Hiram S. Maxim's 1884 Maxim gun, the MG 08 was the German Army's service machine gun in the Great War. With a lethal firing rate of up to 400 rounds per minute, it devastated Brit-ish infantrymen throughout the war.

Massey's Brewery

The Massey family dabbled in the cotton trade but were better known for being the owners of the Bridge End Brewery, founded around 1750. The company once owned over 150 pubs and off-licences in Burnley, and its owner, Edward Stocks Massey, was generous with his wealth. Its beers included Massey's Special Mild Ale, Prize Stout, King's Ale, Golden Bitter Beer and Pale Ale. In 1996 Massey's was taken over by Charrington United Breweries, which ultimately became Bass Charrington. The Bridge End Brew-ery ceased brewing in 1974 and the building was demolished shortly afterwards.

Mauser C96

The Mauser C96 is a semi-automatic pistol that was originally pro-duced by German arms manufacturer Mauser. Winston Churchill used one at the 1898 Battle of Omdurman and during the Second Boer War, as did Lawrence of Arabia during his time in the Middle East.

Maxim machine gun

The Maxim machine gun was adopted by the British Army in 1889. In 1912 the army turned to the Vickers Gun and the lighter Lewis Gun.

Melton blue

Melton blue is a blue-dyed version of Melton cloth, a heavy, smooth woollen fabric with a short nap, particularly used for army uniforms and overcoats. Its name comes from Melton Mowbray, in Leicestershire, the traditional centre for its production.

Mee-maw

Mee-maw was a form of speech with exaggerated movements of the mouth to allow lip reading. It was used by weavers in the mills in Lancashire in the nineteenth and twentieth centuries because the noise in the weaving shed rendered normal hearing impossible. Each mill had its own dialect.

Mills grenade

The 'Mills bomb' became the British Army's service grenade in 1915. Designed by William Mills, they were developed at the Mills Munition Factory in Birmingham. It was a grooved, cast-iron weapon which resembled a pineapple, with a central striker held by a closed hand lever secured by a pin. A man with a good arm could hurl it more than 50 feet.

Minenwerfer

Minenwerfer are a class of short-range mortars used extensively during the Great War by the German Army. They were used to clear obstacles like barbed wire, and the British soldiers called them 'Moaning Minnies' because of the distinctive sound they made.

Mons, Battle of

The Battle of Mons began on the morning of 23 August 1914 with a heavy German artillery barrage. The men of the British Expeditionary Force, many of whom had only just arrived at the battlefield, were exhausted. They were carrying 80lb packs; many had new boots and were walking on cobbled roads. Nevertheless, they formed up along the Canal du Centre, west and north of Mons, in defensive position nine miles long, and nine and a half British battalions (10,000 men) held four German divisions (70,000 men) for most of the day.

The Germans attacked in large numbers, but in close formation, suffering significant casualties from extremely accurate British infantry marksmen. However, by midday large numbers of Germans had crossed the canal and some British units began to fall back. The tactical withdrawal lasted until dusk, but the Germans did not follow in hot pursuit; they had suffered unexpectedly high casualty figures and called a ceasefire to lick their wounds.

British losses on the day were 1,642 killed, wounded and missing. They included 400 from 4th Battalion Middlesex Regiment and 300 from 1st Battalion Royal Irish Regiment. German losses were at least 6,000, but could have been as many as 10,000.

Morse Code & SOS

In Morse code, SOS is the internationally recognized distress signal (· · · — — — · · ·). It was first introduced by the German government in radio regulations in 1905 and later became recognized worldwide by the 2nd International Radiotelegraphic Convention, in 1906. SOS has become associated with such phrases as 'Save Our Ship' or 'Save

Our Souls' or 'Send Out Succour', but SOS does not actually stand for anything and is not an abbreviation.

North British Rubber Company

The production of wellington boots was dramatically increased at the outbreak of the Great War, when the North British Rubber Company was asked by the War Office to make a boot suitable for the conditions in flooded trenches. Over a million pairs were made. The company is now known as Hunter Boots Ltd.

Novita

Novita was a piece of oxygen resuscitation equipment used by both sides during the Great War. They were manufactured in Italy for use in the Italian mining industry.

Old Contemptibles

Kaiser Wilhelm II of Germany reportedly issued an order on 19 August 1914 to 'exterminate . . . the treacherous English and walk over General French's contemptible little army'. Thus, the regular soldiers of Britain's standing army of 1914, who went to France as the British Expeditionary Force, became known as 'The Old Contemptibles'. However, no concrete evidence has ever been found to suggest that such an order was ever issued by the Kaiser. It was likely to have been a British propaganda invention, one that has since become accepted as fact and made legend.

Omdurman, Battle of

Taking place four miles outside Omdurman, just north of Khartoum in the Sudan, the Battle of Omdurman was fought on

2 September 1898. It was a decisive military engagement in which Anglo-Egyptian forces, under Major General Sir Herbert Kitchener (later Lord Kitchener), defeated the forces of the Mahdist leader Abdullah al-Taashi and thereby won Sudanese territory that the Mahdists had dominated since 1881.

The most famous incident in the battle was the charge of the 21st Lancers, one of the last full-scale cavalry charges of the British Army. The 350 men of the 21st Lancers attacked what they believed to be a body of about 700 dervishes. However, as one participant in the charge, the young Lieutenant Winston Churchill, later wrote, the situation soon changed: 'A deep crease in the ground appeared where all had seemed smooth, level plain; and from it there sprang, with the suddenness of a pantomime effect and a high-pitched yell, a dense white mass of men nearly as long as our front and about twelve deep. A score of horsemen and a dozen bright flags rose as if by magic from the earth.' In fact, 2,000 tribesmen who had remained concealed in a deep gulley engaged the lancers in desperate hand-to-hand combat. Although the 21st Lancers had not seen battle before, they managed to cut their way out of the ambush. The regiment suffered 70 men killed or wounded and the loss of 119 horses, the highest casualty figures of any British regiment engaged at Omdurman. Three Victoria Crosses were later awarded to members of the 21st Lancers who had helped to rescue wounded comrades during the action.

PH gas helmet

The PH gas helmet was an early type of gas mask issued by the British Army in the Great War, to protect troops from gas attacks. It first appeared in July 1915 and around 9 million were made.

Packet steamers

Packet steamers were steam ships that carried mail and packages across the globe. They also carried passengers in the days before passenger liners.

Petrograd

During the Great War the Imperial government renamed St Petersburg Petrograd, meaning 'Peter's City', to remove the German words *Sankt* and *Burg*. (In 1924, after the Bolshevik Revolution of 1917, the city was renamed Leningrad; the city became St Petersburg again in 1991 following the end of communist rule.)

Pickelhaube

From the German *Pickel*, 'point' or 'pickaxe', and *Haube*, 'bonnet', *Pickelhaube* is a generic word for 'headgear'. Strictly speaking, the German Army headgear in the Great War was called a *Pickelhelm*, a spiked helmet also worn by firemen and police. Although typically associated with the Prussian Army, the helmet was widely imitated by other armies during this period.

Pips

Badged insignia for officers in the British Army were introduced in 1810. They consisted of (and still do) crowns, swords and stars. The stars became known as 'pips': three for a captain, two for a lieutenant, one for a second lieutenant.

Poilu

'Poilu' is a term for a French Great War infantryman, meaning, literally, 'hairy one', and reflects the typically rustic background of the French infantryman.

Pol Roger

The favourite champagne of Winston Churchill, Pol Roger is still owned and run by the descendants of Pol Roger, who produced his first vintage in 1853. Pol Roger is located in Épernay in France's Champagne region.

Pom-poms

Pom-poms were small auto-cannon artillery pieces firing 1lb or 2lb shells. The first gun to be called a pom-pom was the 37mm Nordenfelt-Maxim, or QF 1-pounder, introduced during the 2nd Boer War, the smallest artillery piece of that war. Their name came from the distinctive sound of the rapid-fire mechanism.

Poteen

Poteen is a traditional Irish drink distilled in a small still. The term is a diminutive of the Irish word *pota*, meaning 'pot'. It is traditionally distilled from malted barley, grain, treacle, sugar beet, potatoes or whey.

Puttees

A puttee (or 'puttie') is the name, adapted from the Hindi *patti*, for a bandage covering the lower part of the leg from the ankle to the knee. Consisting of a long, narrow piece of cloth wound tightly and spirally round the leg, it served to provide both support and protection. It was worn by both mounted and dismounted soldiers, generally taking the place of the leather or cloth gaiter. The puttee was first adopted as part of the service uniform of foot and mounted soldiers serving in British India during the second half of the nineteenth century. The puttee originally comprised long strips of cloth worn as a tribal legging in the Himalayas. Puttees were in general use by the British Army as part of the khaki service uniform worn during the Great War.

Queen Alexandra's Imperial Military Nursing Service

In March 1902 Queen Alexandra's Imperial Military Nursing Service (QAIMNS) was established by Royal Warrant, and named after Queen Alexandra, who became its president. It replaced the Army Nursing Service, which had been established in 1881.

Quim

The noun 'quim' in Victorian times was used specifically to refer to the fluids produced by the vagina, specifically during orgasm. In modern usage it is primarily heard in British slang and is a derogatory or vulgar term for the vagina itself. The word is rarely used today in English but is still heard in Wales. The word may be related to Welsh *cwm*, meaning 'hollow' or 'valley'.

Race to the Sea

The race began in late September 1914, after the end of the Battle of the Aisne, the unsuccessful Allied counter-offensive against the German forces halted during the preceding 1st Battle of the Marne. The route of the race was largely governed by the north–south railways available to each side: the French through Amiens and the Germans through Lille.

In a series of attempts to outflank one another, the race involved a number of battles, from the 1st Battle of the Aisne (13–28 September) to the end of November.

Rhadamanthus

In Greek mythology, Rhadamanthus, Minos and Aiakos were the three judges of the dead in the Underworld. They were originally mortal men, sons of the god Zeus, who were granted their position after death as a reward for the establishment of law on earth.

Raspberry cranachan

Raspberry cranachan is a dessert made from whipped cream, whisky, honey and fresh raspberries. It is topped with toasted oatmeal which has been soaked overnight in whisky. Not unlike Eton Mess, it is Scottish in origin and 'cranachan' is a Scots Gaelic word.

Rittmeister

Rittmeister is German for 'riding master' or 'cavalry master', the military rank of a commissioned cavalry officer in the armies of Germany, Austria-Hungary and Scandinavia, among others. The equivalent of a captain, he was typically in charge of a squadron or troop.

Royal Army Medical Corps

The Royal Army Medical Corps (RAMC) is a specialist corps in the British Army which provides medical services to all British Army personnel and their families in war and in peace. Because it is not a fighting arm (non-combatant), under the Geneva Convention members of the RAMC may only use their weapons in self-defence. For this reason, there are two traditions that the RAMC perform when on parade: officers do not draw their swords (instead, they hold their scabbard with their left hand while saluting with their right); other ranks do not fix bayonets. During the Great War, the RAMC lost 743 officers and 6,130 soldiers were killed.

Royal Flying Corps

The Royal Flying Corps (RFC) was the air arm of the British Army during the Great War. In 1918 it merged with the Royal Naval Air Service to form the Royal Air Force. Its main role was photographic reconnaissance. This led its pilots into aerial battles with their German counterparts. Later in the war its role expanded to include the strafing of enemy infantry and artillery, the bombing of German airfields and later the bombing of German industrial and transportation facilities.

Royal Navy

In 1914 the Royal Navy was the most powerful navy in the world and had been central to the establishment of the British Empire and its security. At the outbreak of war, the navy had 18 modern dreadnoughts (6 more under construction), 10 battlecruisers, 35 cruisers, 200 destroyers, 29 battleships (pre-dreadnought design) and 150 cruisers. Its total manpower was over 250,000 men.

Royal Naval Air Service

The Royal Naval Air Service was formed in July 1914. It was the flying wing of the Royal Navy and administered by the Admiralty, but in 1918 it merged with the British Army's Royal Flying Corps to form the Royal Air Force, the world's first military air force.

Royal Red Cross

The Royal Red Cross was created by Queen Victoria in 1883. It is a decoration awarded for services in military nursing, either to reflect exceptional devotion and competence over time, or for a specific act of bravery.

Royal Small Arms Factory

The Royal Small Arms Factory was a weapons factory in the Lea Valley, Enfield. It began production in 1816 and produced swords, muskets and rifles, including the Martini-Enfield and the Lee-Enfield rifles. The RSAF closed in 1988 and the site is now a major housing development.

Sandhurst

Known simply as 'Sandhurst', The Royal Military Academy Sandhurst, is the British Army officer training centre, close to the village of Sandhurst, in Berkshire.

Saps

Saps were short trenches dug out into no-man's-land at 90 degrees to forward trench, and served two purposes: they were often joined together to form a more forward trench, by digging rather than fighting; and they were also used as listening posts, to eavesdrop on German conversations and planning.

Serjeant

'Serjeant' with a 'j' was the official spelling of 'sergeant' before and during the Great War and appeared in King's Regulations and the Pay Warrant, which defined the various ranks. Even today, Serjeant-at-Arms is a title still held by members of the security staff in the Houses of Parliament. Also, in the newly amalgamated infantry regiment the Rifles (as successor to the Light Infantry, which also used it), the 'j' in the spelling of 'serjeant' is retained.

Scharfschütze

Scharfschütze is the German term for a sniper.

Shell Crisis

A significant shortage of artillery shells was a problem that had hindered the British Army on the Western Front from the earliest days of the war. The situation became acute in May 1915 and led to a political crisis in Britain. The crisis weakened the power of the Prime

Minister, Herbert Asquith, and led to the formation of a coalition government with Lloyd George as Minister of Munitions.

Shell shock

See 'Executions' above.

Shillelagh

A shillelagh (Irish: *sail éille*) is a wooden walking stick or cudgel, made from a large knotty stick with a large knob at the top.

Slit trench

A slit trench is a shallow trench, usually dug as a temporary defensive position or in an emergency.

Slitting mill

A slitting mill was a mill designed to transform bars of iron into rods, for the manufacture of nails. The bars were heated then rolled between water-powered rollers.

Slouch hat

A slouch hat was first introduced by the Australian Army in 1885. A wide-brimmed khaki hat, it is worn with a chinstrap and with one brim turned up. A similar hat is also worn by Ghurkha regiments and by the US military.

Snotties

'Snotties' is British naval slang for the most junior officers (midshipmen).

Sobranie

The Sobranie cigarette was created in London in 1879. It was a luxury brand developed by the Redstone family. Known as 'Black Russians' they became very fashionable.

'Sosban Fach'

Written in the Welsh language, *Sosban fach*, which means 'little saucepan', is an old Welsh folk song. It has become closely associated with Llanelli's tin-plating industry, the town's famous rugby team, Welsh rugby as a whole and Welsh national identity.

Standard Dress army caps

British Soldiers wore a British Army SD (Service Dress) woollen serge cap (the same material as their SD uniforms) at the outbreak of the Great War. Soon after they started digging trenches it was found to be impractical because of its stiff peak and wired top, so a 'soft' trench cap was issued early in 1915 that could be stuffed in the pocket when not in use.

Stanley heading machine

The Stanley heading machine was a tunnel-boring rig with two cutting blades that was used in tunnelling work in the UK, particularly in the construction of the London Underground system, powered by generators on the surface and built by Stanley Brothers Engineering in Nuneaton.

Stew an' 'ard

Stew an' 'ard is a traditional dish of North-east Lancashire, especially in Burnley, Nelson, Colne and Barnoldswick ('Barlick').

'Hard', the staple of the dish, are oatcakes made from oatmeal, yeast, sugar, salt and water, made into a pancake batter, then cooked each side on a 'girdle' (griddle) pan, cooled and either used, soft, immediately, or dried to preserve them, leading them to be called 'hard'. The 'stew' would usually be mutton, occasionally chicken, rarely, beef. The stew would either be poured on to the 'hard' cakes, or they would be used to dunk into it.

Stop-tap

'Stop-tap' is an archaic expression for pub closing-time.

Subaltern

A subaltern is a junior officer in the British Army. It referred to the rank of Second Lieutenant, the most junior officer rank.

Submarine

Numerous experimental military submarines had been developed over many years, but they first made a significant impact in the Great War. At the outbreak of the war, Germany had twenty submarines available whereas the Royal Navy had seventy-four, although of varied quality. Submarines increased in number and quality during the war and German boats were particularly effective against North Atlantic shipping, sinking more than 5,000 Allied ships.

Suffragettes

Suffragette is the term used to describe members of the late nineteenth and early twentieth century's political movements that campaigned for the right of women to vote – the female suffrage movement. Emmeline and Christabel Pankhurst were prominent

British suffragettes. Suffragettes engaged in a range of protest activities, some passive, some more violent. They chained themselves to railings, poured chemicals into letter boxes and broke windows of prominent buildings. Many were imprisoned and force-fed after going on hunger strike.

Swedish Drill

Swedish Drill was a series of callisthenic exercises for military training, usually undertaken with a rifle, designed to increase strength, suppleness and stamina. The exercises were based on the pioneering work of Swedish physical educationalist Pehr Henrik Ling.

Sweet Caporals

Although British soldiers in the Great War thought that Sweet Caporals were French cigarettes, they were in fact produced by the American Tobacco Company, which also produced the Pall Mall and Mecca brands. Caporals were issued to French soldiers, were made from dark tobacco and had a particularly pungent flavour and smell.

Tackler

A 'Tackler' was the name given to a supervisor in a Lancashire textile factory. He was responsible for the good working order of a number of power looms and the weavers who worked them. The name derived from the essential part of his job, which was to 'tackle' – repair – any mechanical problems.

Telescopic sight

Experiments to provide rifle-shooters with optically enhanced aiming began in the early seventeenth century. In the nineteenth century, sights were developed in New York by Morgan James, based on designs by John R. Chapman (the Chapman–James sight). In 1880, August Fiedler, forestry commissioner of Austrian Prince Heinrich Reuss developed a refracting sight and versions were soon in use in the German and Austrian armies.

The Aldis Telescopic Sight was developed by Arthur Cyril Webb Aldis. He and his brother, Hugh Lancelot, owned Aldis Brothers Ltd, which was located in Sparkbrook, Birmingham, and was a maker of lenses and other photographic equipment. The company was bought by the Rank organization after the Second World War, and concentrated then on making slide projectors and episcopes.

Tilley lamp

The Tilley lamp is named after John Tilley, a manufacturer of kerosene pressure lamps. The lamp became so popular during the Great War that its name became synonymous with all kerosene lamps.

Tommy Atkins

'Tommy Atkins', often just 'Tommy', is a generic term for a common soldier in the British Army. It is particularly associated with the Great War. One of the many theories about its origin is that the name was chosen by the Duke of Wellington because he was moved by the bravery of a soldier at the Battle of Boxtel during the Flanders campaign in 1794. After a fierce engagement, the duke saw the best man-at-arms in the regiment, Private Thomas Atkins, terribly wounded. The private said, 'It's all right, sir. It's all in a day's work,' and died shortly after.

Trench fever

Trench fever is a debilitating disease transmitted by body lice. It infected all armies in the Great War; from 1915 to 1918 between a fifth and a third of all British troops reported had the disease at some stage.

Trepanning

This is a surgical operation in which a hole is drilled or scraped into the human skull, exposing brain matter, often used to relieve pressure beneath the surface. A circular section of the skull would be removed using an instrument called a trephine.

Typhoid

Typhoid is a common worldwide bacterial disease transmitted by the ingestion of food or water contaminated with the faeces of an infected person which contain the bacterium *Salmonella enterica*. The disease has been given various names, such as gastric fever and enteric fever.

Uhlans

Uhlans were originally Polish light cavalry who carried lances, sabres and pistols, but lancer regiments in the Russian, Prussian and Austrian armies. also later adopted the title. There were twenty-six Uhlan regiments in the German Army in 1914. German hussar, dragoon and cuirassier regiments also carried lances in 1914, so there was a tendency among their French and British opponents to describe all German cavalry as Uhlans. After seeing mounted action at the beginning of the Great War, the Uhlan regiments were then either dismounted to serve as 'cavalry rifles' in the trenches of the Western Front or transferred to the Eastern Front, where more primitive conditions meant that the horse cavalry still had a useful role to play. All the German Uhlan regiments were eventually disbanded in 1918–19.

Under-fettler

An under-fettler is a junior 'fettler' or cleaner. It is a Lancashire name used in a number of contexts and trades. The verb to 'fettle' variously means to fix, sort or clean; it is also used in the sense of 'sorting someone out'.

Vickers gun

In 1912 the British Army adopted the Vickers as its standard machine gun. Produced by the Vickers Company, it was a modified version of the Maxim machine gun. The Vickers used a 250-round fabric-belt magazine and was regarded as a highly reliable weapon. It could fire over 600 rounds per minute and had a range of 4,500 yards. Being water-cooled, it could fire continuously for long periods.

Voluntary Aid Detachment

This organization was founded in 1909 with the help of the Red Cross and the Order of St John. By the summer of 1914, there were over 2,500 Voluntary Aid Detachments in Britain. Each individual volunteer was called a detachment, or simply a VAD. Of the 74,000 VADs in 1914, two thirds were made up of women and girls.

At the outbreak of the Great War, VADs offered to help the war effort, but the British Red Cross was reluctant to allow civilian women a role in overseas hospitals and the military authorities would not accept VADs at the front line. However, they gradually earned the right to play a direct role through their enthusiasm and courage and as a result of the shortage of trained nurses.

During the four years of war, 38,000 VADs served in hospitals and as ambulance drivers and cooks. Many were decorated for distinguished service, and famous VADs included Enid Bagnold, Mary Borden, Vera Britten, Agatha Christie and Violet Jessop.

Wachtmeister

A *Wachtmeister* is a non-commissioned officer, originally assigned to guard duties.

Webley revolver

The Webley Mk V was standard issue at the start of the Great War but there were many more Mk IV revolvers in service in 1914, as the initial order for 20,000 Mk V revolvers had not been completed by the time the war began.

From May 1915 to the end of the war, the Webley Mk VI was the standard sidearm for British and Commonwealth troops, being issued to officers, airmen, naval crews, boarding parties, machine-gun teams and tank crews. The Mk VI was a very reliable and hardy weapon and well suited to the mud and adverse conditions of trench warfare. Several accessories were developed for it, such as a bayonet, and a stock which allowed the revolver to be converted into a carbine (short-barrelled rifle).

'Welch' (spelling)

The spelling of 'Welsh' as 'Welch' is a much-cherished historical peculiarity in the Royal Welch Fusiliers. When the Regiment was given its Welsh designation in 1702, the spelling 'Welch' was in common use and it became a regimental tradition. That is, until 2006, when the Royal Welch Fusiliers merged with other Welsh regiments to form the 'Welsh Regiment'.

Whizz-bang

A 'whizz-bang' was the name given to the noise made by shells from German 3-inch field guns. The shells fired from light artillery travelled faster than the speed of sound, so the 'whizz' of the shell was heard before the 'bang' made by the gun itself. Thus, there was almost no warning of an incoming attack.

'Willie' Woodbines

Woodbine is a brand of English cigarette first made in England in 1888 by W. D. & H. O. Wills. Strong and unfiltered, Woodbines were very popular with soldiers during the Great War.

'Wipers'

The name of the Belgian town of Ypres was difficult to pronounce for the many thousands of British soldiers who were billeted there or passed through, so it very soon became universally known as Wipers.

Wonk

'Wonk' has several meanings, including referring to an expert, or someone who has an excessive interest in detail or trivia. However, in British naval slang, a wonk is either an incompetent sailor, or, more usually, a junior cadet, who, in the past, performed menial duties for more senior officers, usually midshipmen.

Ypres, 2nd Battle of

The 2nd Battle of Ypres was the only major attack launched by the German forces on the Western Front in 1915, their High Command preferring to concentrate on the Eastern Front. Begun in April, the battle concluded in failure for the Germans in May. As a consequence, the Germans gave up their attempts to take the town, choosing instead to demolish it through constant bombardment, reducing it to rubble.

The 2nd Battle of Ypres is generally remembered as marking the first use of gas on the Western Front. Over 5,000 canisters of chlorine gas were released at sunrise on 22 April against French Algerian and territorial division troops. A pall of greenish-yellow gas rolled across from the German front lines to the French positions. The impact was devastating. The terrified Allied troops fled towards Ypres. Ten thousand men, half of whom died of asphyxiation within ten minutes of the attack, were affected. Those who survived were temporarily blinded and suffered awful bouts of coughing. Two thousand were captured as prisoners of war. The two advancing Germans corps, wearing primitive respirators, paced warily through a clear 7-kilometre gap in the Allied lines. After advancing two miles, they were stopped by General Horace Smith-Dorrien's counter-offensive.

The Germans released a second batch of chlorine gas on 24 April, this time directed against Canadian troops situated north-east of Ypres. Once more, the Germans gained ground against the unprotected Canadian troops. The advancing German infantry sustained heavy losses from the defending Canadians, who were relieved by British reinforcements on 3 May. During this time the Canadians had suffered 5,975 casualties, including 1,000 fatalities. Fighting renewed around Ypres on 8 May and continued until the 13th, and then again on 24–5 May, with repeated use of gas attacks. However, the Allied lines held and a shortage of supplies and manpower led the Germans to call off the offensive.

Losses during the 2nd Battle of Ypres are estimated at 69,000 Allied troops (59,000 British and empire; 10,000 French and empire), against 35,000 German; the difference was caused by the German's use of chlorine gas. Although this was condemned by the Allies as barbaric, they soon developed their own form of gas warfare, with the British using gas at Loos at the end of September 1915, where, tragically, the prevailing wind changed and blew the gas back into the British trenches.

Zeppelin

A Zeppelin is a type of rigid airship named after the German Count Ferdinand von Zeppelin, who pioneered rigid airship development at the beginning of the twentieth century. On 19 January 1915 two German Imperial Navy Zeppelin airships, the L3 and L4, took off from Fuhlsbüttel in Germany. Both airships carried 30 hours' worth of fuel, 8 bombs and 25 incendiary devices. They crossed the coast north of Great Yarmouth, Zeppelin L3 curving south-east towards Great Yarmouth and Zeppelin L4 north-west towards Kings Lynn. Zeppelin L3 found Great Yarmouth and dropped its bombs, killing Samuel Alfred Smith, the first British civilian to be killed by aerial bombardment. L4 followed a route over the coastal villages until it finally came to Kings Lynn, bombing as it went. Fourteen-year-old Percy Goate and twenty-six-year-old Alice Gazely were killed.

Zouave

Zouave is a term of Arabic/Berber origin and was given to the infantry regiments of the French Army serving in North Africa. Zouave's wore distinctive uniforms, which included short, open-fronted jackets, baggy trousers (serouel) and often sashes and oriental headgear.

Genealogies

The Family of Winston Spencer-Churchill

Grandparents

Paternal

John Winston Spencer-Churchill (7th Duke of Marlborough)	1822–1883
Lady Frances Vane	1822–1899

Maternal

Leonard Jerome	1817–1891
Clarissa Hall	1825–1895

Parents

Lord Randolph Churchill	1849–1895
Lady Randolph Churchill (*née* Jennie Jerome)	1854–1921

Brother

John Strange ('Jack') Spencer-Churchill	1880–1947

Children

Diana	1909–1963
Randolph	1911–1968
Sarah	1914–1982
Marigold	1918–1921
Mary	1922–2014

The family of the Dukes of Atholl

5th Duke

John Murray	1778–1846
(second son of the 4th Duke; never married)	
Siblings	
Lady Amelia Sophia Murray	1780–1849
James Murray, 1st Baron Glenlyon	1782–1837

6th Duke

George Augustus Frederick John Murray	1814–1897
(eldest son of James Murray, 1st Baron	
Glenlyon)	
Spouse	
Anne Home-Drummond	1814–1864

7th Duke

John James Hugh Henry Stewart-Murray	1840–1917
(only son of 6th Duke)	
Spouse	
Louisa Moncrieffe	1844–1902
Children	
Dorothea ('Dertha')	Born 1866
(married Harold Ruggles-Brise, 1895)	
Helen	Born 1867
Evelyn	Born 1868
John ('Bardie')	Born 1871
(married Katharine ('Kitty') Ramsay, 1899)	
George ('Geordie')	Born 1873
James ('Hamish')	Born 1879

Maps

Britain in 1915

Europe in 1915

Central Powers
Allied Powers
neutral countries
front lines

Helsingfors
St Petersburg

R U S S I A

Moscow

Warsaw

Kiev

Caspian Sea

UNGARY

ROMANIA
Bucharest
Black Sea

rade

BULGARIA
Sofia

Constantinople

O T T O M A N   E M P I R E

GREECE
Athens

Crete
Cyprus

British Sector Positions and
Local Towns and Villages, January 1915

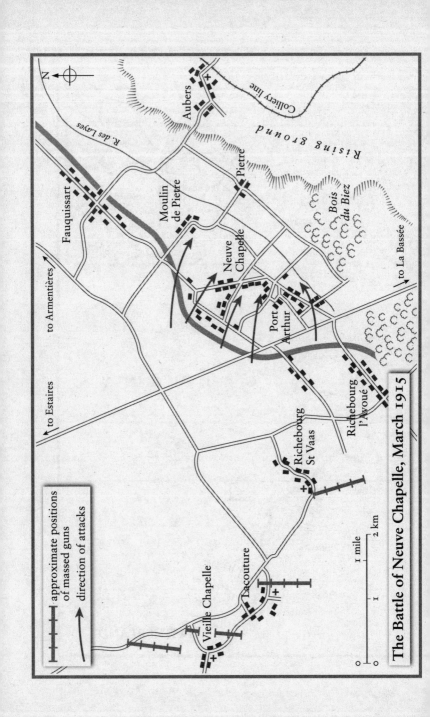

The Battle of Neuve Chapelle, March 1915

approximate positions of massed guns
direction of attacks

N

to Armentières
to Estaires

R. des Layes

Fauquissart

Aubers

Colliery line

Rising ground

Moulin de Pietre

Pietre

Bois du Biez

Neuve Chapelle

Port Arthur

to La Bassée

Richebourg St Vaas

Richebourg l'Avoué

Vieille Chapelle

Lacouture

1 mile

2 km

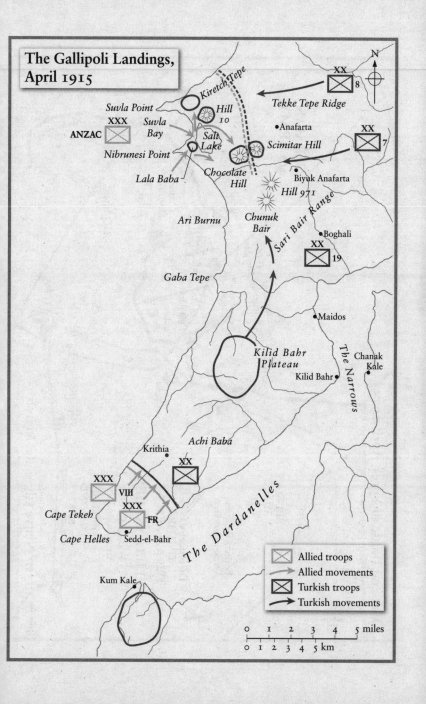

The Gallipoli Landings, April 1915

Kiretch Tepe

Tekke Tepe Ridge

XX 8

Suvla Point

Hill 10

Suvla Bay

ANZAC **XXX**

Salt Lake

Nibrunesi Point

Lala Baba

• Anafarta

Scimitar Hill

XX 7

Chocolate Hill

• Biyuk Anafarta

Ari Burnu

Hill 971

Chunuk Bair

Sari Bair Range

• Boghali

XX 19

Gaba Tepe

• Maidos

Kilid Bahr Plateau

The Narrows

Chanak Kale

Kilid Bahr •

Achi Baba

Krithia •

XX

XXX VIII

Cape Tekeh

XXX FR

Cape Helles

Sedd-el-Bahr

The Dardanelles

Kum Kale

	Allied troops
	Allied movements
	Turkish troops
	Turkish movements

0 1 2 3 4 5 miles
0 1 2 3 4 5 km

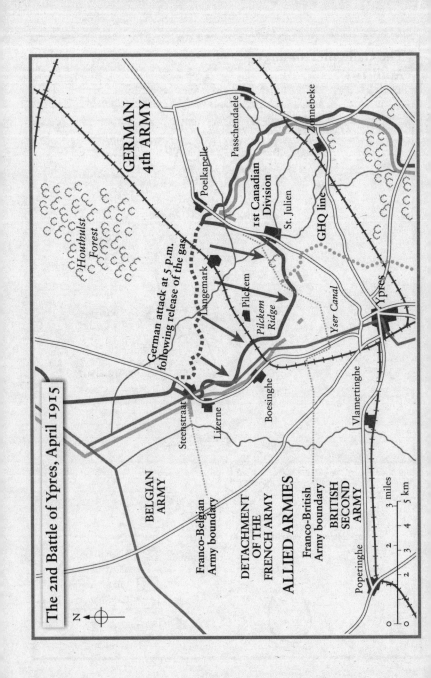

The 2nd Battle of Ypres, April 1915

GERMAN 4th ARMY

Houthulst Forest

Passchendaele

Zonnebeke

Poelkapelle

1st Canadian Division

St. Julien

GHQ line

German attack at 5 p.m. following release of the gas

Langemark

Pilckem

Pilckem Ridge

Yser Canal

Steenstraat

Lizerne

Boesinghe

Ypres

Vlamertinghe

Franco-Belgian Army boundary

BELGIAN ARMY

DETACHMENT OF THE FRENCH ARMY

ALLIED ARMIES

Franco-British Army boundary

BRITISH SECOND ARMY

Poperinghe

N

0   1   2   3 miles
0 1 2 3 4 5 km

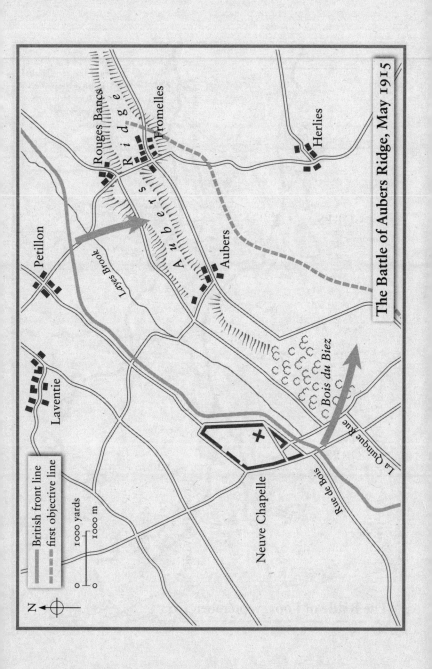

The Battle of Aubers Ridge, May 1915

N

British front line
first objective line

1000 yards
1000 m

Rouges Bancs
Fromelles
Herlies
R i d g e
A u b e r s
Petillon
Laies Brook
Aubers
Laventie
Bois du Biez
Neuve Chapelle
Rue de Bois
La Quinque Rue

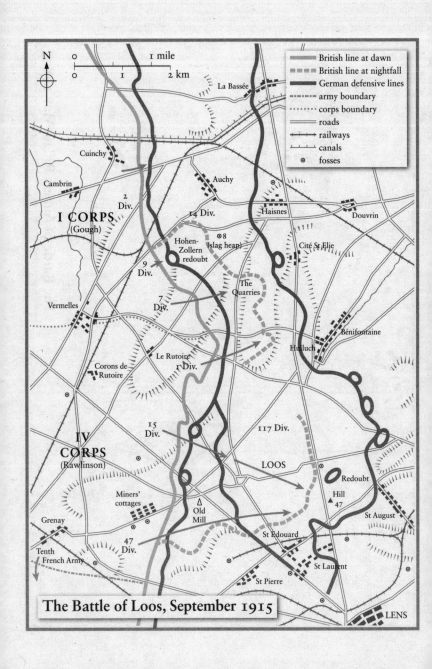

The Battle of Loos, September 1915

STEWART BINNS

CONQUEST

1066 – Senlac Ridge, England. William the Bastard, Duke of Normandy, defeats Harold Godwinson, King Harold II of England in what will become known as the Battle of Hastings.

The battle is hard fought and bloody; thousands of lives are spent, including that of King Harold. But England will not be conquered easily – the Anglo-Saxons will not submit meekly to Norman rule.

Although his heroic deeds will nearly be lost to legend, one man unites the resistance. His name is Hereward of Bourne, the champion of the English. His honour, bravery and skill at arms will change the future of England. His is the legacy of the noble outlaw.

This is his story.

'Stewart Binns has produced a real page-turner, a truly stunning adventure story'
Alastair Campbell

Stewart Binns

CRUSADE

1072 – England is firmly under the heel of its new Norman rulers. The few survivors of the English resistance look to Edgar the Atheling, the rightful heir to the English throne, to overthrow William the Conqueror. Years of intrigue and vicious civil war follow: brother against brother, family against family, friend against friend.

In the face of chaos and death, Edgar and his allies form a secret brotherhood, pledging to fight for justice and freedom wherever they are denied. But soon they are called to fight for an even greater cause: the plight of the Holy Land.

Embarking on the epic First Crusade to recapture Jerusalem, together they will participate in some of the cruellest battles the world has ever known, the savage siege of Antioch and the brutal Fall of Jerusalem, and together they will fight to the death.

'A fascinating mix of fact, legend and fiction ... this is storytelling at its best' *Daily Mail*

STEWART BINNS

ANARCHY

1186 – England. Gilbert Foliot, The Bishop of London, has witnessed first-hand the terrifying and bloody civil wars that have ripped the country apart under the reign of King Henry II – a time in history so traumatic it became known as The Anarchy.

The greatest letter writer of the 12th Century, Foilot writes of a man who has impacted history. Harold of Hereford, one of the nine founders of the Knights Templar, is a heroic survivor of the fearsome battles of the Crusader States and a loyal warrior in the cause of Empress Matilda.

During a time of ruthless brutality, greed and ambition, Harold carries the legacy of England's past, and its hope for the future.

'Stewart Binns has not only produced a thrilling adventure story and a remarkable tale . . . he has also painted an amazingly vivid picture of 11th century England and Europe' **Lord Sebastian Coe**

'Stewart Binns has produced a real page-turner, a truly stunning adventure story' **Alastair Campbell**

STEWART BINNS

LIONHEART

1176 – England

King Henry II reigns over a vast empire that stretches the length of Britain and reaches the foothills of the Pyrenees. But he is aging, and his powerful and ambitious sons are restless.

Henry's third son, Richard of Aquitaine, is developing a fearsome reputation for being a ruthless warrior. Arrogant and conceited he earns the name Richard Lionheart for his bravery and brutality on the battlefield.

After the death of his brothers, Richard's impatience to take the throne, and gain the immense power that being King over a vast empire would bring him, leads him to form an alliance with France.

And so, Richard begins his bloody quest to return the Holy Land to Christian rule.

STEWART BINNS

THE SHADOW OF WAR

June 1914.

The beginning of another long, prosperous summer for Britain. But beneath the clear skies, all is not as it seem - as the chill wind of social discontent swirls around this sceptred isle.

Shots ring out in a distant European land - the assassination of a foreign aristocrat. From that moment the entire world is propelled into a conflict unlike any seen before.

This is the story of five British communities, their circumstances very different, but who will all share in the tragedy that is to come. All that they have known will be changed for ever by the catastrophic events of the Great War.

This is a story of love and comradeship, of hatred and tragedy - this is the story of the Great War.

He just wanted a decent book to read ...

Not too much to ask, is it? It was in 1935 when Allen Lane, Managing Director of Bodley Head Publishers, stood on a platform at Exeter railway station looking for something good to read on his journey back to London. His choice was limited to popular magazines and poor-quality paperbacks – the same choice faced every day by the vast majority of readers, few of whom could afford hardbacks. Lane's disappointment and subsequent anger at the range of books generally available led him to found a company – and change the world.

'We believed in the existence in this country of a vast reading public for intelligent books at a low price, and staked everything on it'
Sir Allen Lane, 1902–1970, founder of Penguin Books

The quality paperback had arrived – and not just in bookshops. Lane was adamant that his Penguins should appear in chain stores and tobacconists, and should cost no more than a packet of cigarettes.

Reading habits (and cigarette prices) have changed since 1935, but Penguin still believes in publishing the best books for everybody to enjoy. We still believe that good design costs no more than bad design, and we still believe that quality books published passionately and responsibly make the world a better place.

So wherever you see the little bird – whether it's on a piece of prize-winning literary fiction or a celebrity autobiography, political tour de force or historical masterpiece, a serial-killer thriller, reference book, world classic or a piece of pure escapism – you can bet that it represents the very best that the genre has to offer.

Whatever you like to read – trust Penguin.